I0580092

KNIGHT ERRANT

KNIGHT ERRANT

KNIGHTS OF THE FLAMING STAR BOOK ONE

PAUL BARRETT

STEVE MURPHY

Copyright © 2019 by Paul Barrett & Steve Murphy

Cover Design by Robyne Renee Pomroy

All rights reserved.

No part of this book may be reproduced in any form or by any electronic or mechanical means, including information storage and retrieval systems, without written permission from the author, except for the use of brief quotations in a book review.

Steve: To my high school English teacher Mrs. Graham, who encouraged me on a better path by letting my creativity fly and sparing me from the mundane.

Paul: To Richard Crawford, who told his daughter a long time before it ever happened that I would be the one in the group who would really make something of myself.

A DAMSEL IN DISTRESS

Trouble walked into the bar and Hawk took notice.

Patrons threw irritated glances toward the door as unwanted light streamed into the murky tavern and a breeze stirred the alcohol-tinged air. Protests in several languages demanded a return to darkness. As soon as the door closed, and shadow reclaimed the room, the dissent settled. Hands, tentacles, and pseudopods continued lifting glasses.

No one else paid attention to the man who entered. Hawk, seated at a side table, saw the warning signs. Tense shoulders, clenching hands, darting eyes; all symptoms of a person on the edge of doing something stupid, dangerous, or both.

Hawk scanned the room. His gaze wandered over a multitude of species. He saw one other person observing the twitching newcomer: a slender human female with olive skin and black hair. Her eyes reflected a light of pure gold, marred only by the thin black dots of her pupils. She wore a deep blue executive unisuit and an expression of dread as she stared across the room. A corp-rat of some sort, she appeared completely out of place in a dive like the *Ripspace Grotto.*

Guess she's slumming, Hawk thought as he poured a shot of Trill's Gutter Run—his fifth in the past half-hour—and slammed it down his throat. He knew he shouldn't be drinking so much, but that didn't stop him. It hadn't stopped him in five years, ever since...

He squashed the thought. He didn't mind getting tipsy on self-pity, but he refused to wallow in it.

To distract himself, Hawk returned his attention to Twitch. He had begun stalking through the bar, head jerking back and forth as he searched the gloom, most likely seeking the corp-rat.

I won't get involved, Hawk told himself as he poured another shot. *I'm here to meet a contact about a job, and that's it. I won't get involved.* He suddenly wished he had brought along Wolf or Ashron for back-up, but the client had requested discretion. Wolf, a Uraxian who stood two-and-a-quarter meters tall and had muscles stacked on top of sinews, didn't fit the bill. Ashron, a lizard-like Lorothian, would have blended well with the *Grotto's* clientele.

Golden Eyes slid through the crowd, trying to keep bodies between herself and Twitch. Her movement had the opposite effect. Like a laser, the man's eyes honed in. He carved a direct path toward her, heedless of who or what he shoved aside.

The commotion caught the woman's attention. She froze as the man bore down on her.

Hawk studied him: just shy of two meters, a solid hundred and twenty kilos, sallow skin, and no hair. *A little taller than me, maybe twenty kilos heavier,* Hawk observed. *It would be an ugly fight, so it's a good thing I'm not going to get involved.*

He downed the shot and licked his lips to catch stray drops. His thick mustache prickled his tongue.

The man's twitching had ceased after he spotted his quarry, but his fists and jaw remained clenched. He stopped in front of the woman and glowered down at her. She stared back, terror on her face. Neither moved as the patrons, unaware or choosing to ignore the situation, carried on around them.

I won't get involved, Hawk reminded himself as he reached up, pulled his coffee-colored hair off his shoulders, and stuffed it into his shirt collar.

"Let's go, Anne," the man rumbled.

"I'm not going anywhere with you, you bastard," the woman said, her defiant words betrayed by a trembling voice.

"Don't make this difficult. Mr. Daratar said to bring you back, and that's what I'm going to do. Legs whole or broken, he doesn't really care."

Anne looked around, the panic of a trapped animal rolling off her.

Adrenaline surged through Hawk. He grabbed the bottle of Trill's by the neck and lowered it to his side. *I won't get involved…but I can take him if I have to.*

The man continued in a near whisper Hawk barely heard. "No one in this hole gives a damn about a little corporate tramp, so just follow me nice or things will get ugly."

Her golden eyes fell on Hawk, a plea for help burning into him.

Hawk sighed. *I guess I'm going to get involved.*

He covered the distance in two steps and stood beside the terrified woman. "Anne?"

"Yes?"

"It is you!" Hawk said in a boisterous voice. He grabbed her in a hug. "How in the galaxy have you been?"

"Just fine," she said, hesitating before returning the hug.

"You're interrupting," Twitch said.

Hawk let go of Anne and turned to face the man. "Oh, I'm sorry." He shifted the bottle to his left hand and held out his right. "Sean Grey. Anne and I are old friends."

Twitch didn't offer his hand. "I don't believe you. I think you're some punk with Good Samaritan Fever, a disease which has been known to inflict great pain."

Hawk lowered his hand and transferred the bottle. "I'm forty-two, much too old to be a punk. You did get the Good Samaritan part right, and I have to admit that's an apt description." Hawk smiled. "'A disease which has been known to cause great pain.' I would never have expected a low-credit goon like you to come up with something that good. Used it before?"

Anger flashed across the man's face. "I don't have time to stomp your ass right now. We have to go." He reached out to grab Anne. Hawk intercepted him, seizing his wrist. Twitch stared at Hawk, eyes wide with shock, as if he couldn't believe someone would have the audacity to touch him. "Oh, buddy, you just—"

Hawk didn't let him get any further. His hand came up and the bottle smashed atop Twitch's skull. It shattered, glass and brown liquid sliding across the man's bald head. The immediate area filled with acrid fumes. Blood formed where the glass cut Twitch's hairless skull. Hawk pushed Anne behind him, waiting for the man to fall.

Twitch grinned as he shook his head, flinging liquor and blood through the air.

Uh oh, Hawk thought.

Hawk blocked the first punch, a bruising jolt echoing through his forearm. The second swing aimed for his head and he ducked, hearing the *whoosh* of the meaty fist as it flew by. Twitch had power, but no training. He was a brawler, used to winning by strength, toughness and his intimidating size. Hawk had to act fast. If one of the big man's punches landed, it would be all over. His thoughts zeroed in on his target; he barely heard the rumble of the crowd placing bets.

He stepped in and delivered a jab to Twitch's stomach, followed by a power punch to the kidney. Twitch stumbled back. Hawk pressed the advantage. Three rapid hits to the abdomen preceded a knee to the groin. As Twitch doubled over, Hawk stepped back and delivered an elbow to the back of the big man's skull, followed by a leg sweep. Twitch crashed to the alcohol-stained floor. His head made a loud thud as it hit the wood. Hawk moved in for some follow-up work, but Twitch remained motionless.

"Now, why couldn't you have done that when I hit you with the bottle?" Hawk said as he rubbed his bruised left forearm with his throbbing right hand. He heard groans of disappointment and saw credit chips changing hands. "What were the odds?" he asked the nearest patron, a short female alien with more hair than skin.

"Three to two against," she chittered gratefully, holding up a stack of plastic.

Hawk nodded and turned to look at Anne. "Tell me I saved you from a fate worse than death."

"Not quite," she said. "However, you did save me from a lot of trouble."

Hawk studied the woman. Everything about her spoke of class, from her form-fitting clothing to her upright posture. She practically swam in corporation, so why was she here? He found himself intrigued; he also sensed a job opportunity. "Would you like to have dinner with me?"

Anne's eyebrows rose. "You don't waste any time, do you?"

"It's not every day I get to save a damsel in distress."

Anne glanced at the prone assailant. "Really? Seems to me like you might have done that a time or two."

Hawk shrugged. "My line of work occasionally requires it."

Her golden eyes flashed with interest. "Tell me which pit your ship is in, and I'll pick you up in an hour."

"How do you know I have a ship?"

It was Anne's turn to shrug. "We're in a spaceport tavern, you handle yourself like ex-military, and you talk about a job where you have to fight. It seemed a reasonable assumption."

Hawk smiled. "Beautiful *and* smart. My ship is in pit 39. Will an hour be enough time for you?"

"Plenty," Anne said. "I just wanted to give *you* time." She held out her petite hand. "Anne Siliar, Damsel in Distress."

Hawk shook her hand. "Sean Grey, Knight Errant."

"I'll see you in an hour, Sir Knight."

Hawk looked at Twitch, who groaned and shifted, coming out of unconsciousness. "Will you be safe until then?" he asked Anne.

Anne nodded. "I can disappear for an hour."

"I'd better escort you out of here. I need to get to my ship and get properly dressed since we're going to Fitzcarlo's."

"Fitzcarlo's? Very nice. Escort away."

Hawk sidled through the bar, gently pushing aside patrons to make space for the lady, who followed close behind. Squinting his eyes in preparation, he pushed open the door and stepped into the harsh glare of Pa'tris Prime's large sun settling to the horizon. The roar of approaching and departing spacecraft filled the air from the port two miles away. His multivis contacts adjusted to the glare, shielding his eyes. Anne closed her eyes tight and placed her hand against her temple.

"Are you okay?" Hawk asked.

"Yes," Anne said, eyes still closed. She reached into her purse and pulled out an oversized pair of dark glasses. She opened her eyes as she put them on. Before they disappeared beneath the tinted glass, Hawk saw that her pupils had almost disappeared into her golden irises.

"I forgot it was so bright today," she said. "I'm not used to being outside so much. There's my car." She pointed to a gleaming Lexsun Hovsport that felt as out of place on the grime-coated streets as she did. "One hour."

"One hour," Hawk agreed, watching her as she slipped into the car and drove off; the sound of starcraft drowned out the engine's soft hum.

Hawk decided against returning to the *Grotto* to leave a message for Basikel. The contact was already an hour late, so he wouldn't be showing. Twitch might be revived by now, in a lousy mood and spoiling for a rematch. Hawk had no interest in a second brawl.

He walked to his vehicle; a silver, seven-passenger van, and slipped behind the wheel. He paused to make sure he felt okay to drive. Five years ago, six shots of Trill's would have put him on his ass; now he barely felt the effects. It still helped to block the pain, so he would continue to drink it. When it stopped working, he had no idea what he would do.

He started up the machine and pulled into the flow of traffic, mostly freight trucks and cabs bringing ships' crews to the hive of bars and brothels surrounding the port.

As he drove, Hawk pondered what had just happened. With the rush of chivalric adrenaline worn off, leaving a vague lassitude, the whole encounter struck him as wrong. Why, out of all the bruisers in the *Grotto*, would her eyes settle on him as a potential savior? For that matter, what had made her consider the *Grotto* as a sanctuary? The Port District was a long way from the Pa'trais City Center, with its corporate spires and business megaplexes. There were far safer places for a corp-rat to run if she was getting unwanted attention. She could have found people in the hierarchy with more power and better connections than anybody she would spot in a portside dive. Anne had come to that specific tavern, with the express intent of finding him.

Now you're just being paranoid, Hawk thought. But he had learned long ago—in an all too brutal way—the price of not being paranoid enough.

Still, coming to the *Grotto* solely to find him seemed a stretch. She may have come there seeking aid because no one in her corporation would help her. She had settled on Hawk because he had been the only one brave or stupid enough to make eye contact.

Guess I'll find out soon enough, he thought as he reached the outer perimeter of the port and guided the van onto the down ramp that led to the ship pits.

He drove another kilometer through the two-lane concrete tunnel until he reached his pit, number thirty-nine. The doorway stood open, so he pulled in and stopped.

"I'm back, Ship," Hawk said.

"I see you," the contralto voice answered through the van's speakers.

Hawk didn't move for a moment, taking time, as he always did, to admire the dark blue shimmer of the craft's crystallized hull. A seven-pointed star, wreathed in flames of red and orange, covered the thirty-five-meter height of the rear port side, while white letters proclaimed her *The Flaming Star* to the universe.

At one-hundred and ninety meters and twelve-thousand tons, she wasn't the biggest ship on the block, but her twin flex-mounted front lasers and turret-mounted side lasers gave her teeth. Her two missile launchers and the turreted light plasma cannon gave her punch too, but she wasn't the toughest fighter in the cage. She boasted average speed, standard armor, and an adequate rip engine for FTL travel. There was nothing terribly special about her. Except she belonged to him and he belonged to her, a bond forged in blood and sacrifice. Hawk felt a twinge of the old pain as the liquor's medicine wore away.

He shook off his mood and dragged himself back to the light. He had forty-five minutes to get ready for a date with a mystery woman; he knew his other lady would forgive him for being rushed. He drove the van onto the cargo lift, wincing as the wheels jolted over the metal divots that would hold the machine in place.

"Take me up, Ship," he said. Her name might be *The Flaming Star* to the rest of the galaxy, but everyone on board just called her Ship.

"Welcome back, Captain," Ship said as the hoist activated with a rumble of gears and hiss of hydraulics.

"Glad to be back," he said, his spirits rising as the lift drew him closer to Ship's interior. He enjoyed the multitude of planets his work with Force 13 allowed him to visit, but Ship had been home for twelve years. He always felt most comfortable aboard her. "Any messages?" he asked as the lift clanked into its up position with a final hiss and the hull slid closed.

"Your stockbroker sent a relay," Ship answered. "Universal Data closed up thirty-five points. She wants to know how much to sell."

Hawk opened the door and slid out of the van. "Which Universal Data?"

"The Kalosian Conglomerate. The Terran Fed portfolio is taking a painful dive."

"How much Kalosian do I have?"

"Eight thousand."

"What do you think?" Hawk asked as he walked past *Little Star*, the ship's shuttle, and headed for the elevator that would take him two decks up to the living quarters.

"The two analysis computers disagree. One predicts an extreme dip and the other looks for a sharp increase and a possible split. I think you should sell half and see what happens."

"Tell her to sell half and hold the rest to see what happens."

"I love your decisiveness."

Smiling, Hawk reached the elevator. He jumped back when he found Ashron, Ship's weapons master, standing there with the door open. His eyes, colorless except for a jet-black vertical slit, appraised Hawk as his elongated jaw spread into a grin, revealing two rows of sharp mushroom-colored teeth. "So, what's the job?"

"There is no job." Hawk shoved Ashron's large, scaled tail aside with a foot and stepped into the elevator. "The contact never showed."

"Never showed? You've been gone for almost two hours."

"I wanted to give him time in case he got delayed."

As the door closed and the elevator began its ascent, Ashron's round nostrils flared and his forked tongue flickered from his mouth. Hawk suppressed a shudder. Despite knowing the Lorothian for almost five years, Ashron's reptilian features still gave Hawk an occasional case of the creeps, even though Ashron often reminded the crew his ancestors were lizards, not snakes.

"You were drinking, weren't you?" Ashron said.

"Yeah. That's not what you smell, though. There was a fight at the bar." The door opened, and Hawk started down the hall.

Ashron followed. "A fight? There was a fight and you didn't invite me?"

"I didn't plan for there to be a fight; it just happened."

"Nothing ever 'just happens' with you. What was it?"

"There was a woman who needed some help."

"A woman? A fight, a woman, and drinking. How come you get to have all the fun?"

Hawk stopped at the hatch to his quarters and turned to Ashron. He frowned for a moment and then grinned. "Because. I'm the captain. Ship, open please."

"Aye, aye, Captain," Ship piped from the speakers as the cabin hatch slid open.

"Now go away." Hawk gave Ashron a shooing gesture. "I have to take a shower and get ready for my dinner date with her."

Ashron's nictitating membranes flicked three times in rapid succession. "Dinner? Oh, you're killing me."

"I might," Hawk said, slipping into his room. "Bye."

Hawk turned as the hatch closed and stripped off his alcohol-soaked clothing. "If he weren't such a good demolitions expert I would have spaced him a long time ago."

"Of course," Ship said.

Hawk stepped into the shower. The door slid closed and water sprayed forth, frothing as the soap mixture blended in. He relaxed as the hot liquid washed over him, chasing away alcohol and soreness. "Ship, send a message to Grendarin. Tell him Basikel never showed, so I have no lead on the job. Then see if you can re-establish contact and find out why Basikel stood me up. The only excuse I'll accept is dead or in prison."

"Aye, Captain."

"Then make reservations for two at Fitzcarlo's, seven-thirty."

"This must be some girl," Ship said.

"Strictly business," Hawk said. "She was a corp. exec hanging out in at the *Grotto*. Some goon came after her. There's got to be a story there that might get us some work. She even hinted as much."

"Uh-huh," Ship said, voice modulation doing an excellent imitation of being unconvinced.

"Well, it doesn't hurt that she's nice-looking, but that's not the main reason."

"Uh-huh."

"Cut it out. Speaking of goons, see if you can find any information on a Mr. Daratar, no first name. I assume he's local. See if there's anything on Anne Siliar, too."

"Will do."

"Shower off. Dry." The water flow ceased; a soft hum filled the stall as water repellers clicked on. The water leaped off Hawk's body, creating a fine mist. Collectors whirred, sucking the water into the wall. In seconds, Hawk's body and the stall were bone dry.

"I have information on Mr. Barto Daratar. He's one of the vice-presidents of Positron Medical and manager of the local office. Anne Siliar is his assistant."

Hawk frowned as he began to dress. "Interesting. She struck me as more the executive type."

"Why do you say that?"

Hawk shrugged. "Don't know. Something about her manner. She seemed like the type who would have assistants, not be one. She certainly didn't drive an assistant's car. Anyway, it seems Mr. Daratar may want her to assist in things that weren't in her job description."

"I guess you'll know soon enough. She's here."

"What? She's early. Have Trey stall her while I get ready."

"Aye, Captain."

———

Anne studied the ship's sleek lines as she walked up the stairs, set at a steep angle to reach the vessel's entry hatch ten meters above the steelcrete floor. Glowing an iridescent cerulean under the pit's wall lights, the ship looked like a strange flying wedge, the bottom portion twice as the length of the upper decks. The hull's atmospheric streamlining gave it an elegant, swept-back flair. Anne could see why some people appreciated such machines. She reached into her purse as she arrived at the entry hatch. A female voice spoke to her from a speaker set in the hull. "Welcome to the *Flaming Star*. Someone will be with you shortly."

Anne nodded, searching for the video hole that allowed the people inside to see her. She didn't find it before the hatch hissed opened. A boy, eleven or twelve she guessed, stood in the hatchway, pushing a hank of long brown hair away from his thin, pale face. When he saw her, his hazel eyes grew wide, and red crept into his cheeks.

"H..hi," he stammered. "Are you Ms. Siliar?"

"Call me Anne, cutie," she said, putting honey into her voice. His blush grew deeper. Anne smiled. Whatever his age, he was old enough to appreciate seductively attired women. She had dressed in a tight red outfit belted at the waist and cut low in the front, revealing ample olive skin. Her black hair she draped around her shoulders, using it to accent her round face and gold eyes.

"I'm Trey, Ship's cabin boy." He stared at the floor and kicked it with one foot while his hands nervously picked at the front of his cream-colored shirt. "The captain isn't quite ready yet. Please come in."

"Thank you, Trey," Anne said as she stepped inside, still smiling. If her appearance affected Sean half as much as it seemed to be affecting Trey, her plans for tonight would go well.

"Please follow me." Trey still wouldn't meet her eyes. They walked about thirty meters down the corridor, its blue coloring a few shades lighter than the hull, and stepped into an elevator.

As the door closed, Trey finally looked at her again. He frowned for a moment and then his face brightened. "You have very pretty eyes."

She stared deep into the boy's glittering blue-green eyes and turned on all her charm. "Thank you. So do you."

She thought he might drop dead of embarrassment right there. He returned to staring at the floor, saying nothing else until they had left the elevator, walked another twenty meters, and stopped at an oval metal hatch.

As the hatch opened, Trey, still not meeting her eyes, said, "This is the wardroom, which is the place where everybody gathers when we're not doing much of anything else." Trey stepped inside. Anne followed him. She saw four other people and immediately stopped.

"This is the rest of the crew," Trey said.

A one-and-a-half-meter tall lizard leaped up from his chair. Anne first thought he was naked, then realized his green vest and pants almost blended in with his emerald scales. He held out a taloned hand as his long jaw split into a terrifying, tooth-filled grin. "I'm Ashron, weapons master."

"Anne," she said, tentatively offering her own petite hand.

"Ashron, you're scaring our guest," a woman said as she walked across the room. She stood a little taller than the lizard. Even though her loose-fitting grey jumpsuit hid her body, her movement told Anne the fabric concealed a lithe figure. She had exceptional features, with bronze skin and short chestnut hair.

"He didn't scare me." Anne stared into the other woman's eyes, the color of wet sand. "It's just that a Lorothian's natural exuberance can be startling."

"Especially Ashron, who has the energy of three Lorothians. I'm Laura Benzing, ship's doctor and co-captain."

Anne coolly shook the proffered hand.

"That's Gerard and Wolf." Trey pointed at the other two crew members. "Wolf's the engineer and Gerard's...well, Gerard does a lot of things."

Anne studied the two men, who couldn't have been more different. Wolf caught her attention first by virtue of size. He sat in a huge chair obviously designed specifically for his bulk. She guessed him at just shy of two-and-a-half meters tall, almost one-and-a-half wide, and massing at least two-hundred and a quarter kilos. His skin resembled gray leather and overflowed with muscles. Even his face appeared oversized, with a thick, square jaw and angular cheeks. Dense black hair covered his head. Strangest of all were his sparkling blue eyes, entirely inappropriate for his cement face.

On the other end, Gerard's pale skin appeared almost translucent, which enhanced his bright green eyes. Thin hair, also white, stuck out in unkempt tufts from beneath a tattered blue, billed cap. He wore a brown jumpsuit that seemed overlarge on his lanky, frail-looking body.

His most notable feature was his right arm, a cybernetic appendage like none she had ever seen. Twenty-four-carat gold, she guessed. It cast a brilliant shine across Gerard's face as he moved it, giving a yellow glow to his ivory skin. Thin, purple-colored wires ran embedded over the entire arm in an intricate knot-work design. They diverged into seven separate filaments at the wrist and terminated at one of the seven fingers on the hand. Each finger had a series of intricate violet tracery, and these ended in a circular pattern at the tips.

She looked at Wolf. "Since you're Uraxian," Anne said to the large man, "I assume Wolf is not your real name."

Wolf nodded. "It is Wofanienlapabeko."

Ashron smiled at her again. "Hawk has a standing thousand unit offer to anyone other than Wolf who can pronounce it."

"I don't think I'll try." Her attention went to Gerard. "And you're Berolian. Are you a Preternatural Scientist?"

Gerard winced. "I've always hated that name. Not only is it pretentious, it's also essentially incorrect."

"How so?" Anne asked.

"Because what we study is no more preternatural than astrophysics. It's just a different set of rules and mathematics."

"Rules and mathematics to perform magic?"

"An acceptable term, though still not quite correct." Gerard shrugged. "It makes people feel better to label it such."

"So, if you don't like to be called a Preternatural Scientist, what do you prefer?"

"Gerard."

"We just call him a spellburner," Trey said with a smile.

Gerard frowned. Anne, sensing this wasn't the right tact, spoke before Gerard could reprimand Trey.

"Your arm is exquisite. I've never seen anything like it."

"Thank you," Gerard said, smiling.

"Do you use it in your…magic?"

"It helps with that, yes."

"I didn't think magic and technology could work together."

"They usually can't."

Frustrated by the pale man's reticence, Anne cast around for something else to say when Sean saved her by speaking up behind her. "I'm sorry you were forced to meet this rag-tag bunch, but you caught me by surprise."

"That's quite all right." Anne turned to find a groomed and finely dressed Sean, his mustache trimmed and his long hair pulled back and hidden beneath the collar of his stylish blue suit. "They've been very nice and I've learned a lot. You look great."

"I think that's the first time I've ever seen him in a suit," Ashron said.

"Suits aren't exactly my style," Sean admitted. "Tonight, I'll make an exception. Are you ready to go?"

"I haven't met the rest of your command staff."

"Command staff? You've met my entire crew."

"Five people for a Light Support Cruiser?" Anne said. "You're joking."

"We hire extra crew for refit and on-shore duties, but the ship is easily run with five people," Hawk said.

"Believe me," a female voice piped from nearby speakers. "Five is more than enough for me to worry about."

"Who is that?"

Anne caught momentary discomfort in Sean's eyes before he could hide it. "That's the ship. Well, the ship's computer. The previous owner programmed it for sarcasm. Sometimes I think they did too good a job."

"I'll remember that next time you want me to go into emergency overdrive," Ship told him.

"See what I mean?"

"Amazing what they can do these days," Anne smiled. She hadn't wasted her trip here.

"Aren't you going to introduce me?" Ship asked.

Sean sighed. "Ship, this is Anne. Anne, this is Ship."

"Ship? Is that her official name?"

"Well, no. The Starship Registry wouldn't allow me to register with that, so her registered designation is *The Flaming Star*.

"I'm pleased to meet you, Ship," Anne said to the air.

"Pleased to meet you. Make sure you keep Hawk in line."

"Hawk?"

"Nickname. We have a Hawk, a Wolf, and a snake." He pointed at Ashron with a grin. "Get some cages and we'd have a zoo."

"I'm a distant cousin of lizards, thank you," Ashron said.

Anne offered another smile. "Hungry?" she asked Hawk.

"Ravenous. Shall we? The ground-car is back here in the shuttle bay. Follow me."

"Let's take my car," Anne said. "It's right outside, and it'll be more convenient than yours."

Surprise lit Hawk's face. "Okay."

Anne looked at the others. "It was a pleasure meeting all of you. I hope to see you again soon."

The others offered their goodbyes and Hawk led the way back through Ship.

"Is that really all of your crew?" Anne asked as they moved down the cerulean hallway.

"Yes," Hawk said. "The ship is extremely self-sufficient."

"I'm sure," Anne murmured.

As they reached the elevator, Hawk turned back toward the ward-room. "Ashron," he shouted.

Green head and snout appeared in the doorway.

"Record the game for me, will you?"

Ashron's tongued flickered from his mouth twice. "You sure?"

"Positive. I really want to see how it comes out."

"Okay," Ashron disappeared back into the room.

"Sorry about that," Hawk said to Anne. As the elevator door opened, he added, "After you, ma'am."

2

GOOD NIGHT GONE BAD

Hawk slid into the Hovsport as Anne took her seat on the driver's side. The doors shut and a waft of hyacinth perfume drifted to him, momentarily overpowering the car's scent of newness. The vehicle couldn't be more than a few weeks old. "Nice car," Hawk said, watching Anne for her reaction.

She nodded as she pulled away from Ship and headed for the pit tunnel. "It was a gift from Mr. Daratar."

"Your boss?"

"Among other things," she answered, slipping into the tunnel and heading for the surface. "How did you know that?"

Hawk shrugged. "Deduction. You're obviously corporate, and Twitch at the bar mentioned his name."

Anne gave Hawk a confused glance. "Twitch? Oh, you mean Malix. He's Daratar's hired thug. A kilo of muscle and a gram of brain. He wouldn't have hurt me...I don't think."

"You have a higher opinion of his restraint than I do," Hawk said. "Is that why you showed up at the *Grotto*? To find someone to end your problems with your boss?"

Anne left the tunnel and merged into the main road. "Fitzcarlo's," she said as she released the wheel. With a soft click, the car accelerated as the navigation computer linked to the road network. The steering wheel receded to the dashboard, giving Anne more leg room. She crossed those legs as she turned to Hawk, and he appreciated the view she offered. "We can talk about why I showed up at the *Grotto* later. Right now, I want to know more about you."

"Me?" Hawk pulled his eyes back up to her face. "What do you want to know?"

"Everything," she said with a smile. "I don't make a habit of going out with men I meet at bars after they pummel someone in front of me. But *if* I were there looking for assistance, then I would certainly perform due diligence."

"*Everything* would take a long time. Can you narrow it down?"

"We'll start with something simple. How did you get Hawk as a nickname?"

Frowning, Hawk turned away and stared out the windshield. They had left the Port District and now traveled on a bridge over the Middle Sector. The car sped along thirty meters above the houses, apartments, and shops that surrounded the heart of the Pa'trais Corporate Center, with its towering glasstic and pseudochrome buildings. Something simple, she said. But something personal, shared with few people. "You know, as many times as I've been to this planet, this is the first time I've ever seen both moons full."

"It's a rare occurrence," Anne agreed.

Hawk turned away from the window and studied Anne. Her golden eyes reflected the passing highway lights. Her face showed patient curiosity. Hawk shrugged. The pain attached to the story had disappeared years ago, so what did it matter if she knew? His cynical side spoke up. *Some sympathy might even help get the job, if there's a job to get.*

"My father gave me the nickname," he said. "He said to me, 'As far as I'm concerned, you might as well be a hawk. They're extinct, and I wish you were too.' That was about a year before he lost me to another man in a poker game."

"He lost you?"

"Gave away is probably more accurate. I'm sure he lost the game on purpose."

"Why would you keep such a horrible name?"

"I didn't for a long time. Then, about fifteen years ago, geneticists on Earth managed to recreate a pair of red-shouldered hawks, and they began to reproduce. My father's dead and the hawks came back. It seemed appropriate."

"Didn't your mother have any say?"

"She had already been dead for three years."

"How old were you?" Anne asked.

"Seven when she died, ten when I went to live with Tahorton, the man who won me."

"It must have been horrible."

"It was the best thing that ever happened to me," Hawk said. "Tahorton raised me far better than my father would have."

Before Anne could speak, the car's computer interrupted her. "Approaching city surface streets. Grid disengaging in thirty seconds." She straightened and took a driving position as the wheel extended from the dashboard.

"Where did you get your ship?" Anne asked as she put her hands on the wheel.

"Tahorton willed her to me and…another person, to help us start our own business."

"What other person?"

Hawk returned to looking out the window. "His name was Moran."

"Was?"

"Off limits," Hawk said, his tone clipped.

"Sorry."

Hawk stared out the window, and Anne said nothing more until they reached Fitzcarlo's a few minutes later.

Anne's questions about Moran threatened to throw Hawk into another fit of gloom, but he shook it off, determined to enjoy the evening. As they stepped from the car and it drove away to auto park, Hawk regretted his abrupt manner and offered his arm in a conciliatory gesture. Anne took it, and they walked into the restaurant.

Fitzcarlo's was as swanky as Hawk expected. A live maitre d' dressed in a vibrant blue and white uniform greeted them and guided them through the restaurant, resplendent with dark wood walls and tastefully expensive statues dotting the floor. A six-meter high, three-tiered fountain, sculpted from an ochre-colored stone, occupied the center of the dining room. Water flowed from the top, making a soothing, almost musical sound as it sluiced from bowl to bowl. They walked past it. Hawk saw several small fish darting about the bottom container.

The maitre d' sat them in a booth that provided a clear view of the fountain while somehow cutting the water's noise level to little more than a melodic whisper.

They studied the menu while a server android, gleaming of silver and blue plating, appeared with a loaf of hot bread and ramekin of fresh butter, and then waited with mechanical patience.

"After you, Anne," Hawk said.

"I'll have the vern-ka in feyd sauce and a pillara salad," Anne said.

"Are the escargot really from Earth?" Hawk asked.

"Yes, sir. Flown here on the fastest rip engine freighter available to assure maximum freshness."

Hawk doubted the truth of the android's last statement. "Are they breaded?"

"No, sir, they are sautéed in butter and garlic and served with a light *baolin* sauce."

"We'll have the escargot as an appetizer, no sauce. I'll take the fasil steak and a pillara salad." He looked at Anne. "A bottle of wine?"

"Certainly."

"A bottle of the Kalos Seven Pinar," Hawk told the android.

"Excellent, sir," the server said, taking their menus.

"I understand this place employs live chefs," Hawk said as the android wheeled away.

"I would hope so, considering those prices."

Even though he agreed, Hawk waved a hand, dismissing her concerns. "It's not that bad. I've invested well."

"So, how does Hawk and his crew make a living?"

"We're corporate mercenaries."

"Corp Mercs? I knew it had to be something exciting." Her face lit up. "Of course, I should have made the connection when I saw your ship's name. So, you're the captain of the Knights of The Flaming Star."

"You've heard of us?" Hawk asked, surprised.

"A friend of mine works for Computronic Gridlinx. She told me about your recovery of their CEO. A great job, from what she said."

"Thank you. We try."

Their wine arrived, and the conversation paused. When the android waiter had served them and moved away, Anne said, "Have you ever done any work with the Planetary Council?"

"No," Hawk lied.

"That's a shame. I hear government contracts can be very lucrative."

"They can be. So are corporation deals, and they let us do things our way. I've heard from others there's way too much bureaucracy with the Council."

It was time to steer the conversation in another direction. More questions about work would lead to 'I could tell you, but I'd have to kill you' type answers.

"Enough about me," Hawk said. "Tell me about what you do, who Mr. Daratar is, and what we might be able to do to help you."

"As you guessed, Mr. Daratar is my boss. I've worked for him for about four years. We've been having an affair. I told him I wanted to end it. He doesn't want it to end, and he's been pressuring me to continue. I decided it was time to put some pressure back on him. A friend of mine told me I could find some muscle at the *Grotto*. Obviously, Barto had me followed, and that's why Malix showed up."

"That's it?" Hawk said.

Anne didn't speak for a moment, her eyes shifting down to the table. "Well, yes."

"I don't mean to make light of it," Hawk said, "I just expected there to be more. Exactly how much 'pressure' do you want applied?"

"Just enough to get him to leave me alone and convince him it's over."

"Wouldn't it be easier to find another job?"

"I'm already checking into that. I still need him to know I'm serious when I say no."

The waiter rolled up with the escargot and the pillara salads and laid everything on the table.

"I think we can help you," Hawk said, picking up his silverware and taking a deep whiff of the pungent gray pillara leaves. Though they weren't the most appetizing-looking vegetables, Hawk couldn't resist their flavor, a mélange of roasted walnut, garlic, and onion. "What's more, we won't even charge you."

Anne picked up her cutlery. "I thought mercenaries charged for everything."

"We're corporate Mercs," Hawk said. "You're not a corporation. I don't like women being mistreated, especially by people they think they can trust." Hawk gave a wide grin. "Besides, I can't see it taking more than a half-hour, so it's not worth the time it would take to bill you."

"You think you can get him to leave me alone that quickly."

"I can almost guarantee it. I'll come by with Wolf tomorrow, and we'll chat with him. Wolf can be persuasive with few words."

"I believe it," Anne speared her salad with a fork.

"I would still consider looking for different work, though." Hawk picked up his wine glass. "Here's to you, and a life where you get what you desire."

"Sounds good to me," Anne said, raising her glass.

***

With business settled, they finished their meal discussing the non-topics that occupy casual conversation. A few times Anne tried to ask questions about Ship and her crew. Hawk gently steered the discussion into safer areas, claiming he preferred to talk about anything but work. Hawk found the meal pleasant, despite the occasional awkward silence of two people who don't know each other and his near certainty that Anne wasn't talking to him so much as probing for information.

"Would you care for dessert?" the robot asked as it cleared away their plates.

Anne looked at Hawk. "I know this wonderful ice cream parlor a few streets over. Let's get dessert there."

"Perfect. Dessert, and then perhaps dancing afterward at this little club I know," Hawk said.

"You dance?" Anne asked with upraised brows.

"I do. And I would appreciate your discretion in not mentioning it to my crew."

"Sounds fantastic. Your secret is safe with me."

"No dessert," Hawk told the robot.

"Very good, sir. The check has been handled by your vessel. Thank you for dining at Fitzcarlo's. Have a wonderful evening."

As they stepped out of the restaurant, a brisk wind blew down the street. Dressed in a suit coat, Hawk didn't really feel the air's chill bite. When Anne drew up her arms, Hawk wrapped his arm around her, trying to offer some warmth.

"That was a wonderful dinner." Anne moved closer. "And good company."

"On both sides," Hawk said.

Anne pointed down a small side street. "Let's cut through here. It leads straight to the shop."

Here's the moment of truth, Hawk thought. They stepped onto the side street and left the bright lights of the main way at their backs. While Hawk scanned the alley, he made two sharp clicks with his tongue, the signal for a status report.

"Game on," Ashron's voice spoke in Hawk's head, courtesy of the receiver implanted against his jawbone Though Hawk couldn't see them, he knew Ashron had a bird's eye view of the alley through three impeller drones, watching for signs of anything suspicious.

Where the alley was at its darkest, Hawk caught surreptitious movement in the shadows ahead.

"You've got three in front and three in back, sticking to the shadows," Ashron said. "Big guys with really nice particle weapons. Not your standard street thugs. And your girlfriend has a Pin laser in her purse, so don't put your back to her."

What a shame, Hawk thought. "Anne," he said softly.

"Hmmmm?" Her gold eyes regarded him.

"Keep walking and don't be alarmed; I think we're about to be attacked."

"Really?" She asked, glancing around.

"Yes," Hawk told her, trying to keep his gaze in all directions.

"I've got a small Pin laser in my purse if you think it will help."

"Thanks for telling me. Do you know how to use it?"

"I've practiced, but I've never had to use it for real."

"Keep it hidden for now, until I know what we're up against. I've got a plan." He turned to her and held her close. "You'll have to play along."

He leaned over to kiss her. She returned his embrace with equal enthusiasm. Either she was good at her job, or she wasn't in on the ambush. He broke off the kiss and spotted a small recess between two buildings. "Follow me," he said.

They jogged about five meters into the alley and slipped into an alcove. It gave him ample cover and kept Anne close. As he kept a watchful eye on the narrow lane, he pulled out a snub nose automatic and a double-edged knife. "Now they have to come to us," he said, holding the gun hidden in shadow.

"So, what did the kiss have to do with your plan?" Anne asked, her voice light.

"Nothing," Hawk said with a smile. "I just wanted a kiss from a beautiful woman."

Anne's return smile didn't reach her eyes.

He put his attention on the alley, watching for the assailants. A pair of red brick, three-story buildings designed in an old architectural style formed the alleyway. Hawk touched the wall; real brick, not a molded plastic façade. Flying debris could be a problem. He spotted low brick holding pens at six-meter intervals, no doubt filled with trash cans. It would do for protection, as long as no one had a grenade and good aim. The windowless buildings decreased the chances of random witnesses. It was a prime spot for an ambush. One he would have chosen himself. Hawk clicked his tongue twice again.

"They're getting close," Ashron said, "walking like they own the place. I can take them out right now. Just give the word"

"I wonder what they want?" Hawk asked.

"Who cares?" Ashron returned.

"Probably our money," Anne said at the same time as Ashron, unable to hear his response.

"I think it's more than that," Hawk said, answering them both. "I'm sure they'll let us know."

"Fine," Ashron said. "But don't yell at me if they shoot first and ask questions later."

Six men approached, three from either side. The dim light from the main road silhouetted the ones in front, and darkness hid the ones behind. Hawk couldn't discern facial features, yet he easily spotted the H&K TL7 particle pistol each man held.

"Hold steady," Hawk said in a low voice, meant more for Ashron than Anne.

"Okay," Ashron said. "If they gun you down in cold blood, can I have your cabin?"

The mystery men stopped approximately six meters away. This close, light filtered down from the twin full moons above and revealed the men's grim faces.

The largest man stepped forward, gun held in front, his hairless head gleaming under the moonlight.

"Twitch?" Hawk asked. "Look, that thing back at the bar was nothing personal. I was defending the lady's honor. Let's discuss this like rational men."

Malix placed his oversized hand against his dark and swollen face. "Are you Sean Grey, also known as Hawk, member of Force 13 and leader of the C5 team known as the Knights of The Flaming Star?"

"You already know the answer. Who's asking?"

The bald man offered a shark's grin. "One-Eye sends his regards and says he'll see you in hell."

That surprised him. "One-Eye? Who the hell is One-Eye?"

Before Malix could answer, Hawk heard the whine of a Pin laser powering up behind him. He turned and found Anne aiming the small weapon at his head.

"I told you not to put your back to her," Ashron said.

"I hate it when I'm right," Hawk said. "I'm guessing everything you've told me since we met is bullshit."

"I did enjoy dinner, but I've had better kisses," Anne told him, her voice ice.

Hawk shrugged. "I figured I should get at least one kiss before I got screwed."

Anne's gold eyes narrowed. "Out of professional curiosity, how did you know?"

"Call it intuition. A lot of things didn't add up. For what it's worth, I was really hoping I was wrong."

"Sorry to disappoint you. Like you told Malix, it's nothing personal."

"If it's not personal, the least you could have done was pay for your half of the meal. Game's over."

Anne gave him a puzzled cock of her head. A sudden whining buzz overhead drew her attention upward. A flare exploded two meters above them with a burst of white light. Anne cried out, shielding her sensitive eyes from the brightness.

Hawk lashed out, swinging the knife toward Anne while lifting his pistol and shooting at Malix.

The knife caught Anne in the forearm. She shrieked in pain and dropped the laser as the blade sliced deep.

Malix's expression disappeared as a crimson fountain replaced his nose. He collapsed to the ground. Hawk fired at the man standing to the dead man's right. The second man fell, a slug through his chest. A third assailant, to Malix's left, lurched forward with a surprised look on his face and several needler rounds protruding from his back.

"Got him," Ashron said.

The other three scattered for cover, firing wildly.

"Help!" Anne screamed as she ran toward a crowd gathering at the end of the alley.

As he dove over the nearest brick partition, Hawk fired his gun in the general direction of the attackers. He slammed into several metal containers. Pungent refuse poured from the upset cans as their lids popped off with dull clangs. More dust and brick chips poured on him from the wall behind as it took a pounding from the attacker's wild fire.

He wiped the grime from his face and glanced around. As he

suspected, it was a garbage pen. Above the odor of rotted food, Hawk smelled burning fabric. He looked down to find his suit coat on fire. A particle beam had passed close enough to ignite the cloth. He patted the flames out. "Can you take them out?" he asked Ashron.

"They've settled, so yes."

"Do it."

Ashron giggled like a kid. "Death from above."

A laser beam lanced down from the sky six meters above Hawk and struck three meters away. It surprised him one of the assailants had gotten that close.

A second later the beam disappeared, then reappeared. Reaching out at an angle, it hit seven meters away.

The third assailant realized what was happening. He jumped up from hiding and ran down the alley. The laser caught him at the base of the neck and severed his spine. He flopped like a boneless doll and slammed into the ground.

"And that's what you get for messing with the best," Ashron said as he strolled into the alleyway, a monitoring remote in his hand. The light from the screen gleamed off his scales.

"Or at least the cockiest."

"You're one to talk," Ashron said. "'Let's see what they want.' I could have killed all six, no mess. But you had to get them stirred up. The drones don't do well with moving targets."

"Then perhaps you and Gerard should invent better drones." Hawk turned toward the end of the alley.

"I'm going to tell Gerard you said that," Ashron said. Hawk didn't pay attention. He spotted Anne's lithe form as she stood in the crowd, a hand over her bleeding arm. Hawk didn't dare risk a shot with her so close to civilians. She caught his eye, waved, and then walked away. Sirens wailed, drawing close

"Shit." Hawk hated letting her escape. Though not as much as he hated the thought of sitting in a jail cell trying to explain the six dead bodies. "Where's the transport?"

"Right there." Ashron pointed toward the end of the alley away from the crowd, at an economy model white vehicle.

"What is that?"

"Hopefully something the police won't notice," Ashron said. "Ship hacked into the grid and borrowed it. She'll return it when we're done. With a bit of luck, she'll have it there before the owner even leaves the restaurant and finds it gone."

They ran the fifteen meters, Hawk fearing any moment to see police cars barreling toward them. None showed up as they slipped in and pulled away, Ashron at the wheel.

"We're on our way back, Ship," Hawk said. "Take care of the cameras, lose any evidence of us, this van, and the fight."

"Taking care of the recording; if they had any live personnel monitoring at the central hub, not much I can do about that."

"Have to take our chances they were asleep or inattentive."

"Everyone wants to know: what happened?"

"Assassination attempt. As I feared, Anne—or whatever her name is—was in on it. Ever heard of someone named One-Eye?"

"No. Is it important?"

"One of her hired goons mentioned One-Eye wanting to see me in hell."

"Oh, an enemy! That will stretch my database limits, but let me check."

"Funny. Speaking of that: did you record Anne when she was on board?"

"Of course."

"Take it and start a search. I need a full profile on her."

"Already on it. It might take a while."

"I know," Hawk said. "She said she was originally from Paraquan. It's as good a place to start as any, even though I'm sure she lied. Check the database here on Pa'trais Prime also, in case she left tracks."

"Aye, Captain. Anything else?"

"That's it. We'll be back soon." As Ashron drove, Hawk sat back, keyed up, and trying to let the adrenaline-induced jitters seep out of him. As he waited to reach the spaceport, one question echoed through his mind: *Who the hell is One-Eye, and what does he have against me?*

3

THE PLAN IN MOTION

Alexic Salakon, owner and CEO of Unicybertronic Technologies, watched as Moran, his business associate, stared at the viewscreen set in the wall. An urgent signal had just come through, and they waited while the relays connected with another view screen light years away. Though they had been expecting the call, Alexic saw the tension in Moran's body, his firm jaw clenched, his muscles pushing against the snug silver shirt and black pants.

Moran's hired assassin appeared on the screen. Her golden eyes shone with defiance. One look at her bandaged arm and bedraggled appearance took Alexic to the same conclusion Moran voiced a second later.

"You failed." His voice remained neutral even as his eyes narrowed in annoyance.

"I've had a temporary setback," the assassin said, scratching absently at the bandage. "He had backup, he got in a lucky shot, and I had to evacuate before the authorities arrived."

"The way I see it, you underestimated him and then ran when the situation got out of control," Moran's voice edged toward anger.

"You can see it however you want," the woman said with her own snap. "If you had let me go with my plan instead of forcing me to grandstand in the alleyway, he would have been dead as soon as I boarded his ship." She seemed unconcerned by Moran's agitation. Alexic found himself both impressed by her bravery and annoyed by her insubordination. If any of his employees spoke that way to him, they found themselves seeking new employment; he suspected Moran was even less forgiving.

His associate surprised him. Instead of rebuking the woman for her defiance, he tilted his head thoughtfully, his loose-curled black hair shaking at the motion. After a moment, he said, "I'm certain your reputation is well-earned, but any one of the crew could have killed you before you blinked. It doesn't matter for now. What's done is done. Did you find out what I wanted to know about the ship?"

"Yes. I confirmed everything you suspected." She held up a peach-colored purse, scuffed black in several spots, and pointed to the side. "I got holo."

Alexic saw nothing on the purse but assumed she had a camera concealed in the side

"Excellent," Moran's voice swung from chill to something that made him almost sound pleased. "I will send full payment for the information. Your bonus will have to wait since Hawk is still breathing."

"I can remedy that."

"Not yet. I have another plan for now. I'll be in touch."

The woman started to speak; Moran hit the disconnect button. Her image faded off the screen.

Alexic waited patiently for Moran to return his attention to their interrupted discussion. Alexic was a patient man, a trait that had served him well in his eighty-eight years. It had taken twenty-five years to build his company to its present position of power and respect in the cybernetics industry. Others had laughed at his cautiousness, his unwillingness to swiftly grow in a rapidly expanding industry. Those others no longer laughed. They had blossomed like supernovas and collapsed just as violently, victims of their accelerated expansion.

Which left slow, patient Unicybertronic sitting on their smoking ruins.

As he waited, Alexic studied Moran, trying to guess the thought behind those inhuman black eyes. While the left eye simply appeared soulless, the right was, in truth, an unfeeling cybernetic implant. The only flesh involved with that orb was the muscles that moved it and the nerve that transmitted the information. Alexic tugged at the wrinkled flesh on his neck, idly wondering if he should get surgery to remove the sags and folds age had brought to his papery peach skin.

Moran walked over and sat in the plush leather chair in front of Alexic's desk. Alexic could hear the faint clicking and hissing of the man's other cybernetic enhancements. He wondered, as he had many times before, how much of the real Moran remained. Alexic had no upgrades; he felt them a violation of the natural order. However, his morals didn't prevent him from making a profit from other people's dependence on the technology.

"What do you think?" Moran asked.

Alexic ran his finger along the edge of his *kroa* desk, enjoying the smooth feel of the dark alien wood. He decided he would get the surgery if Moran achieved his goals. It would be a reward to himself for his faith in his strange compatriot. "Assuming the holo proves what you believe about the ship, this could be a lucrative venture."

"It will," Moran assured him. "I have suspected it for too long to be wrong about it. We need to institute phase two."

"Why go that route? Why not move in and take the vessel by force?"

Moran's dark eyes stared at Alexic. Their expressionless glaze made him squirm. "Two reasons. First: Hawk has enough pull with the Planetary Council that we would have a hundred capital ships breathing down on us wherever we moved, whether Hawk was alive or otherwise. Second: I want Hawk to know who destroyed him and took his ship. I want him to pay."

Moran spoke with such vehemence that a shudder ran down Alexic's spine. He said nothing for a moment, reflecting on the depth of his associate's hatred.

They had met five years ago, Moran presenting himself as an

entrepreneur and inventor. Alexic found the dark-haired man's ideas radical to the point of lunacy, but Moran's fervor won Alexic's respect. Alexic saw in this younger man the person he often wished he had been, or perhaps the son he would have raised had he been capable. Although Alexic would never admit it, he had begun to feel old. Despite his success and wealth, life had somehow passed him by. With no time for a wife and no ability to produce an heir, he had turned into another soul dead corporate master: a slave to the very creation he was supposed to control.

Moran woke up Alexic's dormant sense of adventure. Rich beyond common sense and bored with anything life had to offer, Alexic decided to take a chance and invest in Moran's lunatic plans. If nothing else, it would occupy his time.

The gamble paid off almost immediately. Moran's strange ideas turned out to have merit, and he proved to be a shrewd businessman.

Not long after their partnership formed, Moran began exhibiting disturbing behaviors. Alexic often caught him muttering to himself, long dialogues in his native speech that had the tone of argument beneath them. He often screamed at his subordinates and threatened them with physical violence. Alexic had been forced to replace several staff members who quit.

After years of such behavior, Alexic came to believe Moran was not entirely rational and, considering his high number of implants, undoubtedly suffered from low-level cyberpsychosis. By the time Alexic realized it, Moran had entrenched himself firmly in the company and knew too many of Alexic's personal and professional secrets to be easily disposed. As long as he continued to make a profit for the company, the board members choose to ignore what they saw as nothing more than idiosyncrasies.

Recently, Moran had begun discussing his vendetta against someone named Hawk. He spoke little about his past, only letting Alexic know Hawk and others in his employ had betrayed him. Alexic had tried to learn something about Moran's history. The best efforts of his people had revealed nothing. Any probing questions to Moran met with silence and a cold stare. After a while, Alexic gave up. Moran's private feud, like his mental tics, did not affect his profitability, so Alexic held his peace and offered what little aid the man requested. It seemed Moran's vendetta would still make money for the company.

He seemed to have the Midas touch.

"As you wish," Alexic said, rubbing his hand across the thinning strands of his ash colored hair. "Implement phase two. You have *carte blanche*." He paused a moment, and then, to reassure himself as much as Moran, added, "I trust you."

Moran gave him a curious stare, his mouth twisting into an enigmatic half-smile. "Thank you," he said as he stood. "I'm waiting for a progress report on our experiments. I'll let you know when it arrives."

Alexic nodded. He didn't like to think about the experiments, which were a necessary part of the plan. His hand still rubbing his head, he decided he would add a full head of hair to his surgery order.

Moran turned to leave and then turned back. "You should call a board meeting tomorrow. That way we can make sure they agree with our plan and get rid of any who don't."

Alexic suppressed a shiver at his associate's choice of words. Even though he had no proof Moran had ever killed anyone, the large man appeared fully capable of such an act. "They'll all agree," Alexic assured them both. "When they find out how much money they stand to make, you won't have any dissension."

"The illegality of it won't bother them?"

It was Alexic's turn to offer a crooked smile. "Has it ever?"

Moran nodded. "Call the meeting anyway. It will also allow us to ferret out the Council spy."

"Spy? There's no spy on our board."

"Of course there is. I spotted him when he joined your little company a year ago. He's almost as clumsy as the man you have spying on me."

Alexic didn't waste time denying Moran's accusation. His mind rolled back a year, trying to remember who had joined the organization then. A face formed in his mind, a thin face of pale skin and gleaming red hair. "Yonath Maratai is a Council spy?"

Moran nodded.

"I'll get rid of him immediately."

"Don't bother. I have other plans for him, and they'll work in perfectly with what we need to do. I'll take care of it." Moran turned and left.

Alexic stared at the door for a few seconds after it closed. News that a spy had slipped in under his nose and remained for a year disturbed him. Still, if Moran said he would deal with it, then Alexic would let him. Obviously Yonath had discovered nothing actionable yet, so one more day wouldn't matter.

He pushed a button under his *kroa* desk and heard the click of the main door locking. Business with Moran always set him on edge, and he felt a need to relieve his tense muscles. Time to indulge in one of the few secrets his associate didn't know about. "Come here now," he said, turning his wrinkled head to the right.

A concealed panel slid open in the plum-colored wall. A slender boy, wearing only a pair of sheer blue pajamas, emerged from the secret room where he had hidden while Moran and Alexic talked. Alexic's eyes followed the youth like a cat; he licked his lips as he relished in the boy's cream-colored skin and hair so golden it almost glowed.

As the boy, his eyes downcast, moved towards him, Alexic's smile grew broader. Just because he couldn't have a son didn't mean he couldn't care for them in the same way his father had cared for him.

4

TAKEN

Yonath Maratai left the Unicybertronic Technologies building and strolled across the parking lot. He put on a cheerful face for any who saw him, so they would have no idea his life had been yanked from under his feet.

His engineered grin projected calm even as his mind raced. *Everything by the book, no time for mistakes,* he thought as he reached his hovercar. He made a show of brushing back his hair, using it to wipe the sweat from his forehead. He could smell his fear.

He pulled his magkey, attached to a thin, rectangular fob, from his coat pocket. Fob held against the bronze vehicle, he pressed the top of the device. A small whine emitted as it scanned the car for any unusual electronic or chemical traces that might indicate explosives or surveillance equipment. Negative. Yonath opened the door and slipped in.

After powering up, he sat for a moment and observed the parking lot. His smile slid away as the shock of what he had learned overtook his need for deception. Since managing to infiltrate Unicybertronic as an employee and board member a year ago, Yonath had found precious little to report to the Criminal Surveillance unit of the Planetary Council. Though several of the company's practices skirted legality, they had done nothing that required direct Council involvement.

Until today.

When Moran walked into the board meeting that morning, Yonath thought he stared at a ghost. Only his extensive training kept the astonishment from showing on his face. He had thought Moran dead five years ago, but there the man stood, the only notable changes a new cybernetic arm and eye. Yonath, through surgery, had been altered considerably in the intervening time since they last saw each other. The Planetary Council surgeons had thinned his face almost to gauntness. His whole body had the lean appearance of a marathon runner. His ordinarily blond hair they micro tinted to a nearly unnatural copper color.

"I'm sure he didn't recognize me," Yonath said. He hoped hearing it aloud would make it sound more convincing. It didn't.

Moran's appearance had been only the first shock of the morning. When Moran explained his reasons for being there, horror hit Yonath like a blow to his gut. He struggled to keep his face impassive. Even worse, when the other board members applauded Moran's genius, reveling in the riches and power they would soon possess, Yonath had smiled and clapped, all the while tasting the sour bile of revulsion in the back of his throat.

One positive thing had come from the board meeting: Yonath had information that would force the CS branch to act. All he had to do was tell them about Moran's "experiments," and they would descend on Unicybertronic like a force of nature. Remembering Moran's descriptions of his experiments made Yonath gag. He pushed the disgust aside and focused. Whether his cover was blown or not was now irrelevant. He couldn't return knowing what he knew. He had to report his findings to his superior and then warn Hawk about Moran's plans so the Knights could take appropriate defensive measures.

First, he had to get home and get his family to safety before things got ugly.

"Tasha, would you call the children in for lunch, please," Dona Maratai yelled from the kitchen.

"Okay," Tasha replied from the living room. As she strolled toward the back patio, her willowy tail swished back and forth in a playful manner in anticipation of the children. Tasha wasn't her real name, only a close approximation of the sounds her name made when spoken in her language. Tasha was easier for her employers—indeed, most others not her race—to say. "Lunch!" She yelled when she reached the porch.

"Watch this, Tasha," Yoseph stood at the end of the diving board. The thin ten-year-old bounced twice and attempted a forward flip. He failed miserably, landing in a tremendous belly flop which sent a spray of water through the air. Several droplets fell on Tasha's loose green unisuit.

Tasha made a move for the pool. When Yoseph surfaced with a pained expression and a shaky, "How was that?" she had to grin. Children, no matter the race, were made of eighty percent rubber.

"That was great, Yoseph," she said as she dried him off on the way to the house.

"I'm going to do it backwards tomorrow," he declared.

"If you say so dear, but I'd wait till I got the forward part down first."

"Whisker rub," eight-year-old Patishi yelled as she jumped out of her deck chair and ran to Tasha.

The children loved to play 'whisker rub' whenever they could. Soft fur, chocolate brown with tawny and russet streaks throughout, covered Tasha's body. The area around her whiskers and along her cheeks was exceptionally silky. The two children enjoyed rubbing their faces against her's and cooing like kittens. Patishi referred to it as "cat kissing" even though Tasha sternly reminded her that Pralins were in no way related to cats.

After a short "whisker rub," Tasha tickled Patishi, who screamed in delight and ran to the house, followed closely by Yoseph. Tasha walked into the house and found the two children seating themselves at the table as Dona placed bowls of soup in front of them.

"I'm going to finish cleaning the living room," Tasha told her. "Give me a call if these two monsters get to be too much for you."

"Thanks, Tasha. I made cookies, so I imagine I'm safe until after dessert."

Tasha walked into the living room as Dona sat down at the table with her soup bowl. "Pass me the crackers," she said to Yoseph.

A van advertising "Carpet Installation and Repair" sat across the street from Yonath and Dona Maratai's house. Five men waited inside. One listened to a receiver in his ear as it delivered instructions.

"Okay," the man said, his assignment received. Looking at the others, he said, "Maratai's left and should be here in fifteen. Let's get into position. We move when he arrives."

Lunch was almost over. Bored that she hadn't argued with her brother for the past five minutes, Patishi said, "I can do a flip better than you."

"Cannot," Yoseph retorted. "I do great flips."

"You do great belly busters," Patishi snapped back, giggling. Dona smiled. *Score a point for the ladies,* she thought.

"Well, I still do jackknifes better than you."

"Yeah, but you're ten. When I'm ten, I'll be able to do every dive there is, and even invent some."

"You'll invent the dummy dive, 'cause that's what you are," Yoseph said, grabbing some more crackers.

Patishi stuck out her tongue. "Takes one to know one."

"That's enough," Dona said. The tongue was a sure sign things were approaching the out-of-control point. "Finish up and I'll bring out the cookies."

"Okay," they said simultaneously, and then giggled. They began eating in silence, and Dona started for the kitchen to get the plate of cookies.

"Hello, Mister Maratai," she heard Tasha say from the living room. "You're home early."

"We have to leave," Yonath said, his voice tense.

So, it's finally happened, Dona thought as she walked toward the living room.

No sooner had Yonath entered his house than four of the five men, clad in workman's overalls, stepped out of the van and crossed the street. Two walked to the front door, and two strolled toward the backyard. In the back, they found a large, open sliding glass door. The men could hear the children's voices as they discussed their day's exploits. The leader signaled to his partner, who quickly took a small silver colored cylinder out of his pocket.

"What's going on?" Dona asked when she saw Yonath.

"We need to leave. I saw Moran at work, and he may have recognized me."

"Moran? I thought he was dead."

"So did I. Tasha, get some clothes packed for all of us and get my go-bag."

"Yes, Sir." Tasha bounded up the stairs.

"Dona, get the kids ready. I have to make a call."

Dona headed for the kitchen as Yonath went to the house phone. His mobile had been unable to call out, which told him all he needed to know. He could only hope they hadn't compromised his house line.

"Come on, kids." Dona stopped when a small metal object arced into the kitchen and landed at her feet with a hollow metallic thud. She bent to pick it up when it split open with a sharp *pop*. The gas hit her, and she collapsed to the floor. The children got out a startled cry before they were overcome and slumped in their chairs.

At the same time, the front door burst open and two men moved in. Before Yonath could react, one of them fired a needle pistol. The dart hit Yonath in the neck. The bioengineered neurotoxin rendered him unconscious. He fell, the phone dropping from his hand. The attackers grabbed his inert body and dragged it into the kitchen.

Dona lay on the floor next to the expended gas grenade. The children sat back in their chairs; Yoseph's half-eaten sandwich lay on the floor where he had dropped it.

"Gather them up. You, go find the maid and take her out."

They moved to their tasks. The man sent to neutralize Tasha got no further than the doorway when she appeared in front of him with a furious snarl.

He hardly had time to register what was happening. With a feral yowl and a quick thrust, her three-inch claws sank into the man's torso. She raked through his stomach. Entrails spilled to the carpet. She withdrew her hand and slashed across his throat and jaw. Blood sprayed. He released a wet gurgling sound as he fell to the floor.

"Holy shit!" The second man yelled as he backed up, slamming into the glass door. Tasha raised the pistol in her left hand and fired. The beam pierced his right eye through the iris and punctured its way through the back of his skull, stopping as it melted a dimple in the glass.

One of the men had been picking up Yoseph when Tasha burst into the room. He quickly stood up, holding the limp boy like a shield. Tasha leaped next to the man. Before he could react, she pressed the pistol between his eyes and fired. The man dropped, Yoseph on top of him.

The leader pulled his needle pistol and flipped the selector switch, arming the barrel with lethal barbs. As Tasha turned on him, he fired. The needle plunged through her fur and sank into her neck. The force pushed her back against the doorframe, throwing off her shot; the laser burned wood six inches above the leader's head.

Tasha leaped, releasing a yowl of fury. Startled, the man fired twice. Both hit home, striking her below the chest. She landed squarely on top of the kidnapper. With a savage hiss, she raked three deep furrows across his chest before collapsing from the needles' poison.

A primal scream of fury and agony escaped from the man as he pushed her limp form off his pain-racked body. Blood coursed from the foot-long gashes, and fire burned in the cuts. He pulled himself upright, every movement torture, forcing himself to remain conscious. The fifth man, who had been sitting in the carpet van when he heard the commotion, appeared at the glass door.

"What the hell?" he said after a quick survey of the scene.

"Shut up," the leader snapped, gasping at the pain. "Grab those kids."

The driver sidestepped the corpse at his feet, picked up the kids, and slung one over each shoulder. The leader grabbed a towel from the counter and stuck it underneath his gore-drenched coveralls. The pain was lessening. He was thankful for that, even though it could be a bad sign. Grabbing Dona by the neck, he pulled with all his strength and moved for the doorway. He had to stop as the effort made his head spin.

"Put the kids in the van and then come back and get Maratai," he said weakly.

"What about her?" the driver asked, indicating Tasha.

"Leave that bitch to rot," he said through clenched teeth. "Let's get out of here and get me to our medic."

They crept to the front and loaded the bodies into the van. They no longer looked like simple carpet cleaners. If someone had seen them, they would doubtless have called the authorities. But it was 1:25 p.m. local time in the middle of the week. Everybody was at work earning their keep, or enjoying their own lives indoors. The two men pulled onto a quiet, deserted street and drove away; their mission accomplished despite the efforts of one young nanny.

5

CALL TO ARMS

"Checkmate." Trey stood up and walked over to the cooling unit.

"What?" Hawk said as he studied the pieces, carved of jet and ivory. They could have easily played with holographic representations, but Hawk enjoyed the tactile sensation of actual stone. He felt it improved his game. Obviously not enough, because Trey had beaten him. Again. "Well, I'll be damned. What does that make it now?"

Trey pulled a Planetbuster Fizz drink from the cooler and wiped the top with his shirt sleeve. "Six to two, my favor."

Gerard, who sat at a nearby table working on a disassembled cleaning robot, chuckled.

"You got something to say?" Hawk mock snarled at him. "Why don't you play him?"

"Yeah, please play me, Gerard. I need a challenge."

"Ship, dock this boy's pay," Hawk said.

"We don't pay him, Captain," her contralto voice informed him.

"Well, make it proactive. That way, when we do start paying him, he'll owe it all back to us for a few years."

Trey ignored Hawk's threats and walked over to Gerard. "How about it?"

Gerard considered the robot, which lay in pieces scattered about the table. He turned to Trey. "Why not?"

"Filamentous," Trey said. He popped open his drink, walked over to the board, and started to set up the pieces.

"Don't bother," Gerard said, standing. "We're not going to play chess. We're going to play something a little different."

"Different?"

"Yes." Gerard walked over to the wardroom closet and opened it. Bypassing the shelves of games and physical books, he reached to the top shelf and pulled down a dark wooden box carved with intricate designs of serpents and birds.

"Uh-oh, you're in for it now," Hawk said.

Gerard returned to the table. "It's obvious your tactics are sound since Hawk is no slouch as a chess player. Let's see how you do on a larger dimension." He pushed the chessboard aside and sat the box in the center of the table. Lifting the lid, he pulled out a table-sized mat and two bags of stones.

Trey stared at the new board a few seconds. "What is it?"

"It's called Go, which is Ancient Earth Japanese for five." Handing one of the stone-filled bags to Trey, he opened his own and laid several small white disks on the board. "This is the setup."

As Gerard explained the rules, Hawk walked over to the counter that separated the wardroom from the kitchen. He grabbed a loaf of bread, some sliced *balin,* and a jar of soynaisse. "Sandwich?" he asked the other two.

They both declined, so Hawk prepared one for himself.

Since leaving Pa'tris Prime two days ago, they had been adrift, waiting to see if their errant contact would try to re-establish a meeting. Hawk itched to do something. Ship's search had so far turned up several people named "Anne Siliar," none of which matched his attacker. The only Anne on Pa'tris Prime worked at the local office of Positron Medical, which Ship had learned earlier. A quick call revealed she had no problems with her boss and knew of no one matching the false Anne's description.

Hawk knew Ship's search, akin to seeking a grain of sand on a beach, would most likely end without a match. Physical features were too easy to change if you had the right connections. This meant losing the only lead on the identity of the mysterious One-Eye. The Knights had built a substantial list of enemies in their career, and Hawk didn't relish the idea of tracking each of them down separately until he found the culprit.

On the other hand, if he waited long enough, another attempt would be made, thus giving them a chance to catch a lead.

He had been lucky in the alleyway and didn't care to make himself a target again.

The sandwich finished, he grabbed a Talosian Dark, his favorite beer, out of the cooler and a bag of rye chips from the counter. He returned to the wardroom to find Trey and Gerard had already started their game. He sat down to watch.

Twenty minutes later, with Trey losing and Gerard explaining why, Ship said, "Captain, I have a message coming in from Force 13. It's coded *Firefall.*"

"I'm on my way." Hawk spilled his drink in his haste to stand. "Dammit. Clean that up, Trey."

"Please," Ship reprimanded Hawk.

"No time for please," Hawk said, leaving the room.

"There's no contact video, Captain, only a recorded message."

Hawk stopped. "What? That's not S.O.P."

"Be that as it may, it came in as a recording, no video."

Warning flags went off in Hawk's head. He walked back over to his chair while Trey grabbed a cloth. "Play it."

After a second, a voice Hawk didn't recognize piped through the bridge's speakers. "To Hawk, Commander Force 13 C5 unit Knights of The Flaming Star, from Hostada Sivali, Planetary Council Agent. A friend of yours has gone missing. Meet us at the Seldon Excelsior in Ivaros as soon as possible. Message ends."

"That's it?" Hawk asked.

"What was your first clue?" Ship said with asperity. "The 'message ends' announcement or that I didn't play anything else?"

"Get the cr-" He stopped as the other three crew members walked into the wardroom.

"Already done," Ship said.

"I can see that," Hawk said. "Play the message."

As the message repeated, Wolf sat down, Laura walked up behind Trey, and Ashron roamed over to the sandwich counter.

When it finished, Hawk said, "What do you think? Trap?"

"Hard to say," Gerard said. "Could be, since they didn't use standard protocol. On the other hand, few people know the *Firefall* code, so there may have been a valid reason not to risk video contact."

"You're a lot of help. Anybody else?"

"I'm just the guy who blows things up," Ashron said, slathering mustard on a piece of bread. "I think the only way we're going to know is to go and find out."

"I'd agree with that," Laura said. "Besides, I seem to remember somewhere in our charter it says we're obligated to respond to an emergency call."

"We are," Ship said. "Paragraph 7, subsection B."

"Obligated, yes," Hawk said. "It's a matter of how cautious we are when we walk in the door." He pointed at Gerard's cybernetic arm. "Can't you use that thing to predict the future?"

"Sorry," Gerard said. "Prognostication with anything beyond the most minute chance of accuracy is mathematically impossible. Too many variables."

"Damn. Ship, did you backtrace that message?"

"Yes, Captain. It had standard Force 13 encoding tagged to it, and it came from Seldon."

"Is the Seldon Excelsior one of Force 13's safe houses?"

"Yes, the Council owns the building."

"And Hostada Sivali is an actual Council Agent?"

"If I had eyes I would roll them," Ship said. "Yes, he is a certified field agent."

Hawk thought for a moment. Things weighed in favor of a legitimate call, but the recent assassination attempt made him more cautious than usual. He had to go. Even if the Knights charter didn't require it, it would drive him crazy not to find out if the message was real.

"Okay, Ship. Plot a preliminary course."

"Already done. We're in luck because we're close. ETA is twenty-six hours, thirteen minutes, plus or minus three minutes. Course is set, simply awaiting Gerard's presence and confirmation."

"Very well. Gerard, get to the bridge and do your thing. Everybody else, into the bunks to get your good time shots. We're going to Seldon."

6

MISSION ACCEPTED

As cities went, Ivaros, Seldon's capital city, looked much like any other Corp city. The corporations had moved in and obliterated any traces of native culture, replacing it with uniform skyscrapers of glass and steel. Not that the buildings matched. Each was as individual as the Corporation it housed, and you could tell from the design which company owned which building, from the black-glassed monolith of Universal Armaments to the asymmetrical gold spire-topped skyscraper of Lithwyn Genetics.

All different, all the same, Hawk thought. He mused that Corporate culture had become *the* culture on many planets. He hated it, just as he hated the traffic jams, the crowds, and the pollution. He was happiest in a place with less than a hundred people. Even that was pushing it.

To Hawk's frustration, what Ivaros didn't have was an unoccupied pit that could accommodate Ship. They had larger berths, but Port Control wouldn't lease time to the smaller craft. Hawk had been forced to dock at one of the three gigantic orbital stations and take a multi-passenger shuttle down to the port. The cramped shuttle, reeking of exotic perfumes and alien odors, had made Hawk queasy and put him in a bad mood.

Station docking also made resupplying a logistical challenge, especially since they were in a hurry. Laura had done an excellent job of convincing the loadmaster to move them up in line. She could, with the help of well-placed credits, be very persuasive. The loadmaster had assured Laura that Ship would be ready no later than 0500 tomorrow morning. Though Hawk bemoaned the wasted time, their hasty departure from Pa'tris Prime afforded them little choice.

Hawk spotted a line of bright yellow groundcabs in the port driveway, patiently waiting for fares to hail their services. Proudly stenciled on the sides of the vehicles were a series of glyphs that Hawk's translator chip decoded as *Seldon Cabs. Your transportation choice for 50 years.* Most of the cabs, even the hovercraft versions, looked like they had been with the company since day one.

Hawk slipped into the front cab and viewed the driver through the glass partition. "Seldon Excelsior," he muttered. His voice filtered through the translation speaker in the glass.

"Sure thing," the Mocklin driver's voice filtered back, his crimson jowls and dreadlocked hair flapping as he pulled into traffic.

"How long?"

"Twenty minutes if traffic is good," the driver answered.

Great, Hawk thought, leaning against the syn-leather seat, its surface covered with patches in various shades of brown. *Well, at least I'm not surrounded by aliens with bad breath.*

As he sat there, eyes staring beyond the towering buildings and speeding vehicles, he thought back to the days when the Knights as a mercenary unit went from a dream to reality. Working for Force 13 had its advantages; the amount of downtime was not one of them. The Planetary Council called in a group like Hawk's, known as a C5, or five-person commando unit, as a last resort. The universe, at least that part of it ruled by the Planetary Council, was a relatively peaceful place, and things didn't get that desperate that often. This left his crew with too much time on their hands and nothing to do but twiddle their thumbs and train.

Never one to twiddle, Hawk decided, after two years with Force 13, to take his crew's cover story as a mercenary unit and make it legitimate. In the last eight years, he had managed to build up both a lucrative side business and gain a lot of good will in the corporate sector. To a corporation seeking a reliable, efficient group of mercenaries, willing to tackle any job that didn't stray too far over the line, the Knights were *the* elite. Force 13 gave its tacit approval to the whole situation. Hawk returned the favor by using his Corporate contacts, if necessary, to aid in the success of Force 13 assignments.

"Here you are, my friend," the driver said, staring at Hawk with large, golden-red eyes.

Hawk came out of his reverie at the sound of the cabbie's nasally voice. "How much?"

"Seven point three Stus."

Hawk held his wrist up to the chip reader on the back of the seat. When it beeped, he said "Ten."

"Thanks," the cab driver said as the credits appeared on his display. "Have a day."

Hawk stepped out of the cab. It drove off as he walked into the Seldon Excelsior. Its easily recognized gold raven emblem seemed ready to swoop down from its place on the gray walls above the double doors, which a blue-suited human doorman opened for Hawk.

Opulence oozed through the lobby. The room ran sixty meters in either direction. Each wall held several paintings surrounded by gold frames. A richly embroidered, multi-hued carpet covered the floor. Woven from fabric that changed color depending on the viewer's angle, it gave visitors the impression they were circled by their own distinctive color that followed them through the lobby.

The registration desk was a meter-high mahogany wall with carved spirals and gold lining. It did an efficient job of separating the guests from the employees. Hawk looked around at the guests, all dressed in the height of local fashion. Lavender and yellow predominated the lady's short-sleeved, gauzy dresses and wraps, while the men's shirts and pants boasted reds and blues in combinations that threatened to give Hawk a headache. His toned-down cyan V-neck shirt and tan frictionless-cloth pants got him a few haughty stares; he didn't care. As much as Hawk enjoyed having money, he rarely associated with the financial elite. He found many of them too full of their own prosperity to be of much use.

A tall, sturdy man with straight brown hair and a hard-edged face walked directly toward Hawk. He stood out worse than Hawk in this crowd. His black jacket and pants, gray shirt, and polished shoes announced him as a Council office jockey.

Hawk didn't recognize the man. When he was within five meters, Hawk lowered his hand to a concealed gun. When he was within three, Hawk said, "Close enough. Who are you?"

"Stearns," the man said, holding out an ID card. "Council, Section T."

Hawk frowned. Section T was the Anti-Terrorist division. They dealt with the fanatics and radicals that cropped up on every planet. Their primary function was to mediate. Hawk couldn't think of anyone he knew who would be involved with or investigating terrorists.

"Throw me your ID," Hawk said. Stearns complied, and Hawk snatched the holder out of the air. A few people glanced at them, but no one interfered.

He examined the ID. It seemed real enough, with all the tell-tale signs and markings in their proper place. "Ship," he said as the ID transmitted to her through the cameras in his contact lenses.

"It's authentic," she said.

"Okay," Hawk tossed the ID back. "What's going on?"

"Yonath Maratai's been kidnapped. The Council wants to talk to you."

"Lead the way," Hawk said, keeping calm despite the twist in his gut.

They boarded the elevator.

"Twelfth floor," Stearns said.

"Twelfth floor," the elevator replied as the doors closed.

They rode in silence as Hawk's mind barraged him with frantic questions and provided him with frightening answers. Yonath and Hawk had gone through the same basic training class at Force 13. When Hawk pursued commando training, Yonath opted for Intelligence. "My friend, the mole," Hawk teased him on the rare occasions when they got together.

Still, Hawk occasionally envied his more sedentary friend.

Yonath's choice allowed him a family and reasonably stable life, two things Hawk had never managed.

Yonath even had Tasha, a bodyguard who doubled as a domestic servant. At a party, a drunk Yonath once said, "I've got a beautiful feline who takes care of my family, and you've got a scaly lizard who blows things up. Tell me now that Intelligence wasn't the better choice."

Hawk had humored his inebriated friend. Despite the occasional wish to settle down, Hawk didn't regret his choice of career. He might envy the idea of putting down roots, but he had too much of a wanderer's soul to ever do it.

The elevator stopped; they stepped out. Hawk followed Stearns until they reached a large oak door bearing a gold plate: Conference Room 2. Stearns knocked twice.

"Come in," a male voice, barely heard through the thick door, said.

Two men stood as Hawk and Stearns walked into the room, richly decorated as the rest of the hotel. Both men appeared to be in their forties, one bald and pale skinned, the other sporting a full crop of iron-gray hair. They wore the same suit style as Stearns.

"Hello, Hawk," The gray-haired man said, extending a thin, well-manicured hand. "I'm Frederick Tudev. This is my associate Hostada Sivali." He indicated the other man, who was shorter and had a thin face Hawk immediately associated with a weasel. "Please have a seat. Care for some lunch?" He pointed to several food-laden plates on the table.

"No, but I would like to see your IDs."

"Of course," Tudev said. The two men fished out their ID folders and gave them to Hawk. Ship found them to be as authentic as Stearns's.

"Do you get this extravagant every time someone's kidnapped?" he asked, handing back the cards.

"Fortunately, kidnapping of a Force 13 agent is a rare event. We own this hotel. No one else uses this conference room, and we have it swept for bugs every day, so we know it's safe."

The two men sat down in the oversized conference chairs while

Stearns took a standing position behind them. Hawk sat and poured himself a glass of water.

"So, what's happened?" he asked, keeping his voice casual.

"Have you ever heard of Unicybertronic Technologies?"

"Of course. Largest cybernetics and robotics corporation in existence. That's where Yonath was working undercover last time I talked to him."

"He was still there," Tudev told him. "For several weeks, UCT executives received threatening calls and postal transmissions from a militant organization called the—" he deferred to Sivali.

"—Tekranese Destruction Force," Sivali provided. "That name ring a bell?"

Hawk thought about it a moment. "Yeah. Three years ago. Big fuss over Tekran joining the Council. Section T wasn't having any luck, so they called us in to make sure the TDF leadership wasn't around to continue blowing up Council buildings and assassinating diplomats. I thought we eradicated them."

"We damaged them badly," Tudev continued, "but terrorist groups are like *carlim* bugs. You chop one into seven parts and you get seven bugs. The TDF is demanding that UCT hand over the plans to a new land-based laser weapons system they have recently completed. They threatened to abduct and torture executives and their families until the company relinquished the plans. According to UCT, security was tightened immediately, with executives placed under constant surveillance. Yonath sent us a message he was coming in. He gave no indication why."

"Was his cover blown?" Hawk asked.

"We don't think so," Sivali answered. "We assume he simply panicked because of the terrorist threats toward families. After all, he was considered a UCT executive. It looks like he may have been right."

"What do you mean?"

Tudev picked the conversation back up. "After he called in, we sent a sweep team to his house. They found two dead bodies and no sign of the Maratais. Evidence on the bodies linked them with the TDF."

Hawk stroked his mustache as he nodded. Standard Force 13

procedure. When an agent decided it was time to come in, they often left in a hurry, so sweep teams went in after them to clean up anything significant they may have left behind. "Was Tasha one of the casualties?"

"No," Tudev said, and Hawk let out his breath.

"The wounds to the bodies indicate she was there for the fight. She's either hiding or working her way back home."

"So, do we know where they've taken the Maratais?"

"We do," Tudev told him. "We began monitoring UCT communications right after Yonath's call. Lights off." In response to his voice, darkness bathed the room. "This message was transmitted to them yesterday morning. Video, play."

The near wall lit up. Five seconds passed, and a man wearing dark makeup, a hat, and sunglasses appeared on the wall. If the situation weren't so serious, Hawk would have laughed.

"My name is Karatel, leader of the Tekranese Destruction Force. We are holding Yonath Maratai and his family hostage. Our demand is simple. We want the plans to the KW-47 Plasma System. We will expect them four days hence at the Candash fortress. You will have a courier deliver them in a hardcopy format at 10:30 p.m. Tekran local time. You will send him in an unarmed shuttle, which will land outside the compound. Both the courier and the pilot will enter unarmed, and we will make the exchange. We will be monitoring them for weapons. If you don't follow these rules, or if the plans are not here on time, we will start with the little girl. Every two hours after that, we will dispatch another. I suggest you show up on time."

The image changed to a dimly lit room, where four figures huddled in one corner. It took Hawk, even with his sharp vision, a few moments to recognize the family. There was a large bruise on Dona's cheek and a bloody rag around Yonath's arm.

"As you can see," the voice continued, "they are still alive. The injuries you see occurred during the abduction. They have not been harmed since. With your cooperation, they will remain alive."

The screen faded to black.

"Lights on," Tudev said. He turned back to Hawk. "UCT has already said they have no intention of handing the plans over. They feel a system that powerful in the hands of an unstable terrorist group would be devastating."

Hawk struggled to keep his anger in check at seeing his friends so brutalized. "That's interesting, since I'm sure they would have no problems selling it to any unstable planetary government with the right amount of cash."

"I think Corporate ethics are a discussion for another time," Tudev said.

Hawk nodded, his mouth set in a tight line. "Any idea why they took Yonath?"

"Bad luck on his part, we think," Sivali said. "It's kind of ironic."

"What do you mean?"

"This assignment was supposed to be a vacation. The only thing we had on UCT were some rumors. Yonath was supposed to go in and keep his eyes and ears open. No active prying, just sit back, collect a salary from UCT and us, and take a breather. If anything happened to come up, let us know. It was as safe as any mission could be."

"So much for that theory," Hawk said. "You want my team to try an extraction."

"Yes," Tudev said. "Since the Maratais are close friends of yours, HQ assumed you would want to be in on the operation."

"Then HQ assumed correctly."

Tudev picked up a small chip lying on the table and handed it to Hawk. "This is the mission briefing. It has all the information you need, including the recommended tactics for a successful extraction."

Hawk picked up the chip and was silent for a moment. He looked at the two men and asked, "How far is it from here to Tekran?"

"Twenty-eight parsecs, give or take an A.U.," Sivali said.

Hawk stroked his mustache. The ripspace drive in Ship boasted a speed of ten light years per Galactic standard twenty-five hour day, although Gerard always managed to coax a little more out of it when necessary. "Two and a half days. We'll be cutting it close. I'll need another agent to act as a courier. They need to be an operator, since all my people will be busy elsewhere, and I'll need him at the ship no later than 0500 tomorrow morning, bay eighty-four."

"No problem," Tudev assured him.

"Very well," Hawk said. "Is that all?"

"Yes."

"Then I'll see you tomorrow morning at 0500," Hawk stood, "One other question—Why the break from procedure? Couldn't you have just relayed this to my ship?"

Tudev spoke. "We've had some security problems lately with hacking and intercepted transmissions. And evidently, there's a leak somewhere within the organization. I think this current situation clearly supports that. Until we can figure out the weak link, direct contact with agents will be standard procedure."

Hawk pondered for a second. "Fair enough." He turned and walked out of the room.

A few seconds after the door shut, a panel in the opposite wall slid open, and a man stepped out of the darkness.

"Good work," Moran said to the two men seated at the table.

"Thank you," Sivali said. "I look forward to working with your organization in the future."

"As do I," Tudev echoed. "This has the potential to be rather profitable."

"Indeed it does," Moran said, smiling. "The accounts we set up for the two of you will show the agreed upon payment. Mr. Stearns already has your next assignment." He looked at Stearnes, who still stood behind the men. "Show them."

Before the men could turn around, Stearns placed a wide focus needle laser at the back of each of their necks and pulled the triggers. The beams cut through flesh and severed their spines. Without a sound, they slumped to the table.

"It's a shame," Moran said with mock sadness, "Council agents used to be so incorruptible. Once someone turns on their employer, you really can never trust them again, can you?" He turned to Stearns. "Any word on that Pralin bitch?"

"Not yet," Stearns told him. "The blood trail ended at the front door. She hasn't checked into any of the local hospitals, and she didn't alert the authorities. No one at the Council has heard anything from her yet. I'd be willing to bet she's making her way home."

"Keep on it. I don't like loose ends." He stared again at the two dead men. "And get someone up here to clean up this mess. Then find an expendable agent to act as a courier."

"I don't understand something," Stearns said. "I'm going to be within a meter of Hawk. Why don't I kill him then and be done with it instead of going through all this trouble?"

"Because I assume you're not suicidal," Moran said.

"What do you mean?"

"His ship has an outstanding defense system," Moran answered with a touch of pride. "I helped design it. The second you pulled your weapon and aimed it at Hawk, no less than three Markland anti-personnel lasers would vaporize you where you stood. So, Hawk would still be alive, and I would lose a valuable member of my force. Besides, if I wanted Hawk dead, we could have killed him here. And there are other considerations."

"Such as?"

Moran smiled. "All in good time. You will know everything. I will tell you this. Before it's all over, I will see Hawk and Gerard suffer."

7

MISSION EXPLAINED

Hawk stepped out of the shuttle and into the spaceport terminal, ignoring his fellow passengers as his mind whirled with plans and strategies. All of them would be dismissed as soon as Gerard took over the planning. Hawk did it to keep from dwelling on the video image of the battered Maratais.

He exited the terminal tube and stepped onto the moving sidewalk that would take him to Ship's berth. As usual, atonal music wafted through the air. A drone circled him, an unemotional female voice playing from its speakers, "Welcome to Seldon Orbital Port. You are currently undergoing decontamination. Please remain motionless until the process is complete. Thank you. We hope you enjoyed your stay on the planet."

The drone scanned as it floated ahead of him. Hawk felt a cool mist, a brief flash of heat, and a scent of lemons wash over him. The ritual of decontamination.

"Ship," Hawk said to the microtransmitter in his collarbone.

"Yes, Captain," Ship answered in his head.

"Dammit!"

"Well, excu—"

"No Ship, it's not you. I just stumbled off the end of the sidewalk again."

"According to my *Book of Galactic Regulations and Other Useless Information,* the approximate number of people in the known galaxy having the required dexterity to manage a moving sidewalk successfully is 27. *You* are not among them."

"The operative word in that speech is 'useless.' Get everybody in the wardroom. I have some important news."

"Aye, Captain."

"Hawk out."

"Ship out."

He wormed his way through the crowded corridor, avoiding the multitude of wandering trinket merchants, and slipped into the white-walled berthing bay that led to Ship. As he walked up the ramp, the hatch opened.

"Welcome, Captain," Ship said.

"Glad to be back," Hawk said. The only advantage to orbital docking was that Ship's docking door was on the top deck, which meant he didn't have to deal with the elevator.

Hawk walked to the wardroom, which often served as the crew's meeting place.

As he opened the door, Wolf, as always, drew his attention first. Wolf sat in his specially designed chair. His broad face stared at a reader while he jotted notes on another screen. He glanced up at Hawk's entrance. His glittering blue eyes smiled in direct contradiction to the perpetual frown on his face.

"Don't tell me, let me guess," Hawk said. "Technical manual and you've found a flaw."

Wolf returned his attention to the reader, his broad face a study in concentration. "I'm working on something."

Hawk knew that he would get no more from the taciturn Uraxian.

"Welcome back," Gerard said, his pale skin reflecting the wardroom lights. He sat next to the Go board, holding a small piece of machinery.

Hawk indicated the board. "How's it coming?"

"Very well. Trey shows a great deal of promise."

"What's the score?"

"Four to nothing, but he's making it harder for me to beat him every time."

"Is that the same cleaning bot you've been working on?" Hawk asked, pointing at the mechanism in Gerard's hands.

"Yes," Gerard answered with a sigh. "These bearings refuse to align for optimal performance."

"So it works," Hawk said. "It just doesn't work like you want it to."

"Something like that."

"Frozen or rocks," Laura called from the bar.

"Frozen," Hawk settled himself in one of the room's comfortable dark blue chairs. Laura walked in bearing a tall glass of frozen margarita in each hand. She gave one to Hawk.

"Don't bother sneaking up on me, Ashron. I can hear your tail dragging again."

"Rats," Ashron said, walking from behind Hawk's chair. "Speaking of which, when's dinner?"

Trey grimaced. "In a half hour. And it's spaghetti, not rats."

Gerard looked at Hawk. "You've returned intact, so the call wasn't a trap. What's going on?"

Hawk took a few snacks from a platter on the table. "Yonath Maratai and his family have been kidnapped."

Hawk explained the situation as the others listened, munching on a few snacks as he talked. Laura got up and made another drink for them. Wolf continued jotting notes. Gerard fiddled with his machinery, and Ashron started a game of chess with Trey.

Despite their seeming lack of attention, Hawk knew that, apart from Trey, any of them could have repeated every word he said.

"Ship," Hawk said when he finished explaining.

"Yes, Captain."

"I'll need everything you have on the Tekranese Destruction Force, and we'll need three-D plans of the Candash fortress. I figured seventy-five hours to Tekran. Give me a real time with Gerard pushing."

"Seventy-three hours, thirty-seven minutes, plus or minus seven minutes. Gerard?"

"Show me the path."

A map of nearby space appeared on the table. A line showed the trajectory Ship had plotted, along with mathematical symbols Hawk didn't even pretend to understand. Gerard glanced at it for ten seconds, then turned his gaze to Hawk. "I can trim two hours without effort. Six hours if I exhaust myself."

Hawk shook his head. "I want you coherent to help us plan, so give me the two, don't burn yourself out." He regarded the rest of the crew. "Study the information Ship has provided. We'll plan during the trip. We're getting an extra agent to act as a courier. He'll be here at 0500, and then we're out of here." He threw the chip he was given at the meeting onto the table. "Here's the Council intel in case anyone cares what their strategy was. Any questions?"

"Yeah," Ashron said. "Where's Dijon?"

"Who?"

"You know damn well who. Dijon, my python."

"Python?" Hawk said. "Oh, yeah. Trey's cooked a special surprise for dinner tonight. Let's go eat."

As everyone filed out, heading for the galley, Ashron said, "I thought we were having spaghetti."

Hawk shrugged. "He had to make the meatballs out of something."

"Going out on the town tonight are we, Captain?" Ship asked as Hawk changed shirts in his quarters. The crew had just finished dinner, which turned out to be vegetarian spaghetti. Ashron found Dijon contentedly wrapped around one of the small trees that decorated the dining room. Hawk gave the crew the rest of the night off since they had three days' travel to plan their assault.

"If I can get anybody to go," Hawk answered, pulling on a coat and slipping a knife into his boot. "Tekran's not known for its nightlife, so this will be the last chance to take in some local color for a few days." He left his quarters and headed for the wardroom.

"Are you sure you want to do that, Captain?" Ship asked as Hawk walked down the hallway.

Hawk paused and looked at the floor. "I have to," he said in a soft voice. "We're going to be traveling for over seventy hours, which is seventy hours I have to wonder and worry about what's happening to the Maratais. My mind is already offering me plenty of visions I'd rather not have. For tonight at least, I need to forget."

"Be careful, captain."

Hawk nodded and continued walking. He didn't bother to tell Ship the Maratais weren't the only thing he needed to forget. He had told her many times, and just as many times she told him to stop being foolish.

As he arrived at the wardroom, he found Trey and Laura enthralled by a game of Scrabble. Putting on a smile to push away his troubled thoughts, he walked to their table and said, "Come on, Laura, let's go paint the town."

"Sorry, I already have a date for ice cream and a movie."

"With who?"

"Me," Trey said, standing up defensively. "Make somethin' of it." Although the boy was teasing, Hawk detected the slightest trace of animosity. Of all the crew, Trey had bonded to Laura the most. Not surprising given his circumstances.

"Please, Trey," Laura chided. "Gentlemen avoid fights whenever possible."

"They also remember whose ship they're living on," Hawk muttered. He turned and walked over to Wolf. The large Uraxian stared at a holo display of Ship's blueprints and made notes on an oversized datapad. "How about it, Wolf?"

"Are we departing tomorrow morning?" Wolf asked, eyes not leaving the display.

"Yeah, but..."

"Then I've got work."

Hawk sighed. "Gerard?" he asked without much hope.

Gerard looked up from the book he was currently reading, *Love's Savage Fury.* "Uh-uh, I'm in the middle of the good part. Plus, I have to help Wolf with some adjustments on the rip drive."

Hawk turned to Ashron, who offered an enviable impression of the Cheshire Cat.

"You want to go?"

"I'd love to," Ashron said. "Let me get my coat."

"No."

Ashron stopped at the sound of Wolf's deep voice and gave an irritated hiss. "What do you mean, no?"

"I'm going to need your help on the rip drive, too."

"It's going to involve large wrenches and slithering into tight places where your lummox body won't fit, isn't it?"

Wolf nodded.

Ashron's scaly green face drooped in defeat. "Sorry, Cap, guess you're on your own."

"I can drink alone here," Hawk grumbled. "What kind of sorry-ass crew is it where the captain has to talk them *into* going out for a night on the town?"

"A professional one," Wolf answered without looking up from his work.

Everyone except Wolf studied Hawk, waiting for his reaction. With a sigh, Hawk nodded. He wouldn't have tolerated an answer like that from the others. Wolf's response stopped short of a rebuke and made it simple fact. They were a professional crew, and he was their captain.

Hawk nodded. "You're right," he said with the barest trace of regret. The siren call of alcohol pulled on him and the desire to sit in a dive and drink until forgetfulness was almost overpowering.

Wolf's somber tone recalled the aftermath of such actions. He would need his mind clear tomorrow, not clouded by a hangover and filled with remorse at his behavior. Even worse, everything he drank to forget would rebound twice as strong, doubled by shame at his weakness.

Even with his decision made, Hawk still felt a great need to forget his problems, at least for a little while. "Can you spare Ashron for an hour?"

Wolf nodded.

"How about a little shoot-out in the simulator?" he asked Ashron. "If I can't get shit-faced, I might as well practice."

Ashron offered his toothy grin. "You're on."

Laura watched as Hawk and Ashron walked away. Once the wardroom hatch closed, she looked at Wolf and said, "Thank you."

Wolf gave her a quick smile and returned to his work.

Trey shuffled the tiles around in his holder. "How come Hawk drinks so much?"

Laura studied the boy's earnest face, one blue eye looking at her, the other perpetually hidden by a bang of thick brown hair. "Hawk has a lot of pain, and sometimes he drinks to forget it."

"What kind of pain?"

"It's complicated," Laura said. "It's your turn."

Trey nodded and stared at his tiles. "I'll never drink," he said with the sincerity of youth.

Laura fervently hoped the boy could hold to that promise. She said nothing about Hawk's past because it too closely echoed Trey's loss, still less than a year old.

Only eight months ago, they had found the frightened boy on the civil war-torn planet of Kel. Laura remembered all too clearly the strange, almost strangled crying sound coming from a burned-out house. Inside the charred shell, they found a barely clothed Trey, his body filthy, his brown hair trailing to his shoulders and matted with dirt and oil. He huddled in a corner, crying as he tried to choke down a piece of rotted fruit. When he spotted them, he snarled and backed away, protecting his treasure.

Despite his threatening manner, Laura's heart had gone out to him. She had approached, trying to soothe him with soft cooing sounds. When she drew close, the terrified boy struck out. Putrid fruit splattered over her face. The child's jagged fingernails raked across her cheek, rendering two bloody scratches. Laura had grabbed at her cheek and backed away; the sight of blood seemed to break something in the boy. His eyes had grown wide, and he had collapsed to the ground sobbing.

"I didn't mean to do it!" he shouted in a voice raspy from disuse. He had curled up into a fetal ball and shook.

Laura had stayed near the boy while the others left to do a quick recon of the two-story house. Still whispering words of reassurance, she had moved closer. He uncurled and lunged toward her. She tensed, expecting another attack. The boy had no fight left. He fell into her arms and bawled.

The others had returned with grim news. The months-old bodies of a male and female lay in a bedroom; a holophoto on the dresser confirmed they were the child's parents.

Laura had insisted they take the boy with them. Hawk had refused at first. Laura, in her only act of open rebellion, had demanded it. She insisted she would stay with the boy and they could leave without her. They had been too late to save the person they were sent to rescue; this was a chance to get something good out of their failed mission.

"Laura?"

"What?" Laura said, her eyes and mind returning to Ship and the present.

"It's your turn," Trey said.

"Sorry, I was lost in thought for a moment."

"What were you thinking about?"

She smiled at him. Eight months ago, Trey had been a mute wraith afraid of his own shadow. Now he was a healthy, eager member of the crew. Even Hawk had admitted his reservations were misplaced. "I was thinking about what a wonderful kid you are."

He squirmed and looked down at his tiles, hair falling in front of his other eye. "Quit being silly and play."

She watched him a moment longer; her heart wrenched with love for this lost little boy they had saved. She refused to consider what would have happened if they had not found him. They did find him, and in the past months, Laura felt she was *meant* to find him. She was being given a second chance, and she prayed nightly that she could protect him better than she had her first son.

Trey glanced up from his tiles to find Laura still staring at him. "Laura, are you okay?"

"I'm fine, Trey," she answered as she pulled her eyes down to her tray of letters. *And with a little luck, I think you will be too.*

"Captain, this is your four-thirty wake-up call. Rise and shine," Ship said in a cheery voice.

"Go away," Hawk said, pulling a pillow over his head.

"Captain—"

Hawk lifted the pillow. "What part of 'go away' did you not understand?" He returned to the pillow.

"I'm only doing what you told me," Ship reminded him.

"Arrgh," Hawk said, throwing the pillow to the floor and dragging himself to an upright position. "I hate getting up this early."

He stretched to work the kinks and stiffness from his lean body. He and Ashron had practiced in the simulator for almost three hours before Wolf had come to claim the Lorothian for help on the rip drive. Hawk felt every hour in every muscle. Despite the soreness, he was much better off than he would have felt after a night of carousing.

He slipped into the shower. "I think I need to quit drinking so much," he said as the hot water, scented with aloe soap, pounded against him, working the aches from his muscles.

"Yes, you do," Ship agreed.

Hawk smiled. Such a thing was easier said than done. Right now, he believed he could do it, even as a voice deep inside told him he was living a fool's dream. Something would send him back to the bottle. Someone else would leave him. It always happened. His mother left him first; then his father tossed him aside like unwanted garbage. Tahorton, his true father, died only eight years after Hawk came to him. That had precipitated his first binge. He and Moran had gone together, pouring drink after drink and slamming them down. Even as the alcohol deepened and sharpened their despair, it also pushed them toward an idea that still seemed sane after they sobered up. Tahorton's will had bequeathed his fleet of ships to his most promising students. Hawk and Moran got the Light Support Cruiser *Paradise Run*. That night, as they drank and remembered, they agreed to form their own business. They would finish school, join the Council Navy, and gain their starship ratings.

Despite the intoxicated origin of their dream, they stuck with it.

Eight years later, with commissions in hand, they had left the Navy, re-christened their ship *The Flaming Star*, and gone into business as mercenaries. A few years later, Force 13 recruited them, and life had been everything they hoped for on that despairing night so long ago.

Then Sara came along.

"Shower off," Hawk said, pounding his fist against the cream-colored plastic wall as the repellers dried him. Old memories best left buried. The very memories alcohol helped to chase away.

He slid the door open and stepped out. Time to put his heart and soul into the mission at hand. The past couldn't be helped. He had a crew in the here and now who depended on him. Time once again to show them he deserved their loyalty.

He dressed in a loose-fitting navy shirt and black pants, trimmed some unruly mustache hairs, and ran a comb through his wavy brown hair, shoulder-length in the true mercenary fashion.

"The agent is here," Ship said.

He made one final pass with the comb. "He's just now walking up to the door," Ship continued. "There's one other man with him."

"On my way." Hawk tossed the comb onto the sink counter and walked out of his cabin. As he strolled down the corridor to the docking hatch, he hummed an old tune off key. With his mind settled and the prospect of work ahead, his mood improved.

Hawk saw the two men on his monitor, waiting patiently on the other side of the door as he stepped up to it. One of them was Stearns, and the other was a short, black-haired human with a wiry build and an expression of extreme anxiety. He wore a dull brown jumper suit. A new automatic suitcase sat beside him. "Open the hatch, Ship."

"Aye, Captain."

"Right on time," Hawk said after the hatch opened. He stepped to one side. "Welcome aboard, gentlemen."

The courier walked in. The suitcase rolled in behind him, keeping a foot behind. "Thomas Wilcox," the man said, extending his hand.

"Captain Sean Grey." Hawk shook Thomas' hand, then turned with an inquiring look at Stearns, who had remained motionless.

"I'm just here to make sure he arrived safely," Stearns said. With a curt nod, he turned and walked away.

"That man makes me nervous," Thomas said after Stearns disappeared.

"That man should make a lot of people nervous," Ship said over Hawk's personal monitor, so Thomas couldn't hear. "He is impressively armed and has an extremely high tech jammer on him."

Hawk gave Thomas a brief appraisal. *A good stiff wind probably makes you nervous,* he thought. "This is your first field assignment, isn't it?"

"Yes."

Great. "Ship, close the hatch."

The hatch began closing. Ashron picked that moment to come around the corner. Thomas let out a little squeal of fright and then blushed.

"Ah, Ashron," Hawk said in the tone of voice that immediately put the Lorothian on his guard. "This is Thomas, our rookie agent. This is Ashron, one of my crew members." The two shook hands. "Ashron is going to show you to your cabin."

"I am?"

"Yes, you are. I'm going to get us away from the station and into a clear field for the rip jump."

"Oh. Okay, follow me."

Hawk watched as they walked down the hall. Thomas followed timidly behind Ashron. The suitcase brought up the rear with robotic precision. Another disadvantage of working for a government agency was the inevitable bureaucracy involved. The kind of bureaucracy that managed to do things like put a green agent on a high-risk assignment.

Hawk sighed. Nothing to be done about it now. It was time to leave and make the best of the situation.

8

DEPARTURE

Hawk checked the screens one last time, and then looked at Gerard, who sat in the pilot's chair, a silver cap on his pale hair, thin wires plugged into his cybernetic arm. "Everything good?"

Gerard nodded. "Just like the first four times you asked me."

Hawk chuckled. He always acted like an overprotective mother when they headed into ripspace, despite Gerard being one of the best rip pilots alive. Both Ship and Gerard constantly checked their calculations, and Gerard handled the physically and mentally demanding task of piloting rip space with greater aplomb than his frail-looking body would indicate. Hawk hated not knowing how to fly the currents, but he didn't have the requisite physical and mental makeup. Once, maybe. No longer.

Hawk shied away from that thought.

"It's all yours, then," Hawk said. "I'm going to the bunkroom. Rip us when we're all bunked in."

"Aye, Captain," Gerard said.

Hawk left the bridge. A seven-meter walk brought him to the bunkhouse. He stepped in to find Wolf and Ashron laid in their "bunks," padded niches cut into the light blue wall. Thomas occupied one of the three extra beds in this room. Two cuffs hung from clear tubes beside each bunk. The devices that would administer the "good time shots" as Hawk called them. Wolf and Thomas already wore theirs around their right arm and Laura stood over Ashron, attaching the thick strips of black plastic to his muscled bicep.

"Where's Trey?" Hawk asked.

"Last minute trip to the head," Laura said. With cuffs attached to Ashron, Laura tapped a keypad on his bunk, setting the dosage she had calculated for the trip.

She turned to Hawk. "You ready to lie down?"

"Let's get Trey strapped in first," Hawk walked to the head's door and tapped. "Almost ready, Trey?"

Trey's tenor voice came out muffled through the door. "Go ahead and jump. I'm going to stay in here."

"You know we can't do that," Hawk said. "Everyone has to be under."

"I'm not coming out."

Hawk turned to Laura and saw his puzzlement reflected in her face. Trey had never shown any disobedience. He knew the importance of this procedure as well as any spacefarer and had done it numerous times without complaint. Hawk tried to open the door and found it locked. "Ship, unlock the door."

The lock disengaged with a soft click.

Laura stepped up. "Let me."

Hawk stood aside as Laura slid the door open. This was one of the smaller heads aboard Ship, a cube barely a meter square with a toilet and sink. Trey, dressed in a loose red shirt and blue pants, had squeezed into the far corner and wedged himself behind the toilet. His bloodshot eyes were wide with terror.

"Stay away!" Trey blurted before Laura moved. "I don't want to sleep."

"You know you have to be asleep when we rip." Laura used the tone of voice Hawk had heard her use to great effect on others in distress. "If you're not asleep, you could die." She took a step forward. Trey tried to push himself even flatter against the wall.

"I'd rather die."

Laura stopped, her face ashen. "Don't say that."

"I'm sorry." Trey squirmed in the corner. His face turned red and eyes puffed as he drew close to tears. "I've tried to be strong. Tried to fight it. But I can't take the dreams anymore."

"Dreams? You don't dream in rip sleep."

"Yes, you do," Trey said, his voice high and eyes haunted. Instead of a child on the verge of his teens, he resembled a terrified six-year-old. "Terrible dreams of monsters that want to kill you and eat you."

"That's not possible," Laura muttered to Hawk. "The trazine doesn't induce normal sleep. Brain activity is minimal. Dreaming isn't possible."

"Unless it is," Gerard said. Hawk turned in surprise to find his pale friend standing behind them, a thoughtful expression on his pale face. "Trey, in these dreams, do you see large creatures swimming, circling you in a void?"

Trey's eyes widened. He nodded. "Yes. They're terrible. They want to kill me."

"If I can tell you how to avoid them, will you come out?"

Trey hesitated, hands clenching and tugging at his shirt. He started to slip from behind the toilet, then stopped. "I can't. What if it doesn't work?" Tears poured from his eyes.

"We don't have time for this," Hawk said. He stepped into the bathroom.

Trey stood up and appeared ready to dig his way through the wall. As Hawk approached, the boy wailed, strangled cries punctuated with shouts of "no." He swung his fisted hands wildly. Hawk grabbed at Trey's thin arms, caught them, and pinioned them against the wall. Trey screamed and thrashed, his efforts to kick Hawk thwarted by the toilet.

"How can he stop the dreams?" Hawk asked over his shoulder.

"Do multiplication tables," Gerard told the boy.

Trey stopped his struggle and gave Gerard a perplexed stare. "What?"

"Multiplication tables. They'll occupy your mind and keep the dreams away."

"That's it?" Hawk asked, giving Gerard a sideways glance, his skepticism matching Trey's.

"That's the short version, but—"

"—The short version will have to do. Sedate him."

"I don't think…" Laura began.

"That's an order!" Hawk said. He kept his face stern even as he winced inside at the anger in Laura's eyes. He hated treating Trey like this, but the lives of four other people depended on the Knights, and time was crucial. He didn't have the luxury of coddling. They needed every minute they could get. Trey understandably had many issues; this was new. Hopefully Gerard and Laura could help the boy after they came out of rip; for now, they needed to move.

With stiff steps, Laura walked into the room. Her face and movements as emotionless as a robot, she pulled a syringe tube from the small medkit on her belt. She dialed in the dosage as Trey flailed.

"Please don't," Trey whimpered as Laura brought the tube to his arm. Hawk saw the briefest slip of her resolve before her detached face reappeared. He detested himself for forcing this upon her.

She hit the inject button. Trey stopped his struggle and stared at Laura with a heart-wrenching mixture of confusion and betrayal.

"I hate you," he said, his words slurred as the sedative took hold and his head slumped forward. Head down, Laura left the room. Hawk picked up Trey's small form and carried him to his bunk, where Laura stood holding the black cuffs.

"You understand, don't you?" Hawk said as he gently laid Trey into the bunk.

"Yes," Laura answered as she attached the cuffs, her voice flat. I understand, even if I don't accept, the tone said.

Hawk looked at Gerard. "You can talk to him when we're in transit."

"If he'll talk to any of us," Gerard said. He left for the bridge.

Hawk knew defending himself would waste the time he was trying to save by his reprehensible action, so he let it go. They were mad at him. They understood his reason, even if they didn't approve of his methods. It was Trey he would have to reconcile with. Time to sleep now and beg for forgiveness later.

He slipped into his bunk. Laura, without a word, placed the cuffs on his arm and dialed in the dosage for the tranquilizer and restorative.

When she finished, she walked to her bunk, attached the tubes to the cuffs already around her arm, and entered her dosage. She plopped into the bed. Her brown eyes still hard and face glum, she gave Hawk the thumbs-up.

"It's all yours, Gerard."

"Engage rip drive, Ship," Gerard said.

"Rip drive auto-sequence engaging," Ship said over the loudspeakers. "Rip transit in fifteen…fourteen… thirteen…"

Ship continued the countdown. At eight, Hawk heard a series of clicks and whooshes as everyone's tranquilizer cuff activated. A slight pressure on his arm told him the compressed air had fired trazine into his body.

"All cuffs activated," Ship said. "Rip is go in five…four…three…"

Hawk succumbed to the drug's effects. The world went black.

Hawk blinked his eyes, slowly waking from rip sleep. It seemed as if no time had passed. A glance at the clock embedded in the top of his bunk told him he had been out almost two and a half hours. He sat up in the bunk, trying to shake off the wooziness of the jump as he removed the cuffs. Hawk weathered the slip into transdimensional space with relative ease. Coming out was rougher. He already dreaded the headache he would have when they ripped back into "normal" space.

A smell of fresh-cut grass came to him, right on cue. Everyone had a scent associated with the void of rip space. Gerard's people had never figured out why and it was different for each person. Hawk's smell was and always would be fresh-cut grass.

"Rip transit successful," Ship said. "We're in the void between."

"Obviously," Hawk muttered. If things had gone wrong, no one would be alive to hear Ship say it was a failure.

The others began waking. Laura had stuck to protocol and allowed Hawk to wake first.

Ashron yanked off his cuffs and bounded from the bunk. "What now?" he said. The jumps never bothered him, coming or going, and Hawk envied his alien physiology.

"Meeting in twenty minutes, in the con—"

A retching sound followed by a distinctive splat against the dura-luminum deck stopped Hawk. Across the bunkroom, a pale Thomas had his head out of his bunk, mouth pointed down. Hawk caught the acrid stench of bile, and his throat gave a reflexive spasm.

"First rip?" he asked Thomas.

Thomas stared up at him with watery eyes and a ragged frown. "Sixth."

Hawk shrugged. Some people just couldn't handle the travel. "Ship, send a cleaning 'bot."

"Aye, Captain, it's on the way."

Trey slogged out of his bunk and tramped across the room, avoiding eye contact with anyone.

"Trey," Hawk said as the boy passed near. He stopped and stared straight ahead. "Sometimes a captain has to insist on things that seem unfair. I had our mission to consider. Do you understand?"

Trey said nothing and continued facing forward.

"Conference room, twenty minutes," Hawk told the others.

They filed out, Laura last, as a trapezoidal robot wheeled in and began cleaning the puddle from the deck. Laura hesitated at the door and caught Hawk's eye. He shook his head, indicating he would handle the situation. With a frown, she turned and walked out.

"Do you understand?" he asked Trey again.

Trey's lower lip trembled. He gave a defiant shake of his head and started to walk away.

"Talk to me," Hawk said in the gentlest voice he could muster.

Trey stopped. "Is that an order?" he asked as he turned his red-rimmed eyes to look at Hawk.

Hawk didn't appreciate the sarcasm, but the sight of the boy's troubled face and pinched lips told Hawk the dream—or whatever it was—had haunted Trey again despite Gerard's suggestion, so he let the caustic remark pass. "No, it's a request. I know you're mad at me, but I want you to try and understand why I did what I did."

"I'll never understand why adults do what they do," Trey said in a soft voice. "Can I go?"

It was a lost cause for now. "Yes," Hawk said. "I need you to do two things. And these are orders."

Trey's face turned hard. Hawk ignored it. "First, I want you to apologize to Laura. Out of the entire crew, she loves you more than any of us, and what you said to her was unfair and hurt her deeply, even though she would never tell you. I want you to do that first thing, before the meeting." Laura would be able to explain better what had happened, her good sense overruling any emotions now that the crisis had passed.

"What else?"

"Sometime before we rip back to normal space, talk to Gerard. He seems to know why this is happening. Now that we have time to spare, he should be able to help you. You *do* understand we can't have a scene like that every time we rip, don't you?"

Trey's face softened. He gave a reluctant nod. "Yes, sir."

Hawk hazarded a smile. "Good man. Carry on."

Trey turned and walked away, his body a little straighter.

"Do you think I handled that okay, Ship?" Hawk asked when Trey had gone.

"I can't say, Captain. Though something is clearly going on while we are in transition. I think you are right to leave it up to Laura and Gerard."

Hawk sighed through pressed lips. "Well, let's get to business. I'll need seven copies of everything I asked for yesterday."

"Aye, Captain."

Hawk made the twenty-meter walk to the conference room and took his seat at the head of the elongated oval table dominating the room's center. Ship had pulled the fortress plans, and the holographic projector hummed as it cast the three-dimensional rotating image a few centimeters above the glass table. Thirty-centimeter-long slots opened on the table in front of each chair. Hawk watched as each slot spit out a sheet of twenty-five-centimeter wide electronic paper, its gleaming front covered with text. Hawk pulled the thin metallic sheet from the slot and laid it on the table. The first two pages appeared to be information on the Tekranese Destruction Force. He tapped the lower right corner of the paper and the text changed to pictures of the Candash fortress from different angles. Another tap brought up more photos and blueprints.

Ten minutes later Trey walked into the room, his hair pulled back and combed and blue eyes much clearer. A small service bot followed him, carrying several breakfast platters. He stopped beside Hawk, and the bot rolled to a halt a half-meter behind him.

"Laura explained everything to me," he said in a contrite voice. "I'm sorry I acted so selfish."

"It's okay," Hawk assured him. "You were scared, and if time hadn't been so pressing, I would have handled it differently. I would never deliberately hurt you, but sometimes there are other considerations besides the crew's feelings." Hawk breathed a mental sigh of relief that Laura had forgiven him too.

Trey beamed his charming smile, and everything was suddenly okay again. "Breakfast, Sir?"

"Yes, thank you."

"Did someone say breakfast?" Ashron bounded into the room.

"Being served now," Hawk said. "Do you think you could eat your eggs without mustard on them today?"

Ashron stopped in mid-stride and stared at Hawk as if the human had suggested he jump out the airlock. "Never speak such blasphemy again."

Hawk sighed. "Fine. The data sheet's at your chair. Look over it and start coming up with brilliant ideas."

Ashron sat down and pulled his paper from the slot. Trey put the breakfast plates in their appropriate places. One by one, the others sauntered in, pouring glasses of coffee and juice. Thomas, wearing a different shirt that was as drab as the one he had puked on, appeared unsure what to do with himself until Trey pointed out a chair and handed him a plate of food. Once the others were seated and had their meals, Trey grabbed his platter and sat down.

Hawk remembered the boy's surprise the first time he had been allowed to sit in on a meeting. "You might have a different perspective," Hawk had told him. "None of us is perfect. If you see something we're missing, mention it. Anything you say will be given due consideration." Though Trey had never made any suggestions in these briefings, he had become comfortable with the process.

"Okay, this is what we've got," Hawk said, holding up his sheet. "Take a few minutes to study it and then we'll start figuring out how to handle this one."

"Excuse me," Thomas said in a soft voice, "What are we looking for?"

The rest of the crew stared at him. After a moment, Hawk said, "Trey, what are we looking for?"

After a brief hesitation, Trey spoke. "The best avenues of approach and possible ambush points for the rest of the team."

"Exactly," Hawk studied Thomas. "Council agent training sure is getting slack these days."

Thomas frowned in misery. "My agent training was somewhat accelerated."

Hawk glanced at Gerard, who shrugged. Warnings flared in Hawk's mind, but he couldn't do anything about it now. "You and I need to talk later," he told Thomas.

Thomas offered a weak nod.

"Okay," Hawk said, "let's see what we can come up with."

They all studied the plans. The only sounds for about fifteen minutes were the tapping of fingers, the clink of silverware, and the soft slurping of beverages.

After glancing at the holograph for the twentieth time and making one final note, Gerard said. "I think I've figured out a plan. How does this sound?"

9

CONSULTATIONS

Hawk sat on the bridge waiting for Thomas and stared out the thick, rectangular front viewport at the flat gray nothing that made up the ripspace void. He knew they were moving. Experience told him that in fifty hours they would take the brief ripsleep nap and awake in normal space almost thirty parsecs from where they entered. The lack of motion outside the craft still unnerved him. There always seemed to be something just beyond the nothing, waiting to reach in, seize the craft, and hold it forever within the monochrome emptiness. Hawk wondered how long it would take him to go insane if such a thing ever happened. "Even after all these years, Ship, I still don't like ripspace travel."

"You don't like it only when you're sitting up here looking at it."

She had a point. Hawk smiled and took a sip from his glass of Aldorian Scotch, enjoying the liquor's woodsy scent and dark flavor. It reminded him of the oak trees that grew on Tahorton's farm, a place of many pleasant memories.

A soft voice interrupted Hawk's musings. "Captain Grey, you wanted to see me?"

Hawk turned and found Thomas standing at the doorway, looking nervous and small as he rubbed a hand over his short black hair. "Yes, take a seat." Hawk gestured toward the chair across from him.

He waited as the man shuffled in and sat, his head down, like a child who knows he is about to be scolded. An urge to reach out and shake the timidity from the man gripped Hawk. He settled for a harsh tone. "I'm curious as to why the Council would send an agent who hasn't even completed his training on an assignment this dangerous."

"Dangerous?" Thomas asked as fear flashed over his round face.

Dear God, what have I gotten into here? "Exactly how much do you know about this mission?"

"They told me we were rescuing some kidnap victims and I was to portray a courier as a decoy. They said it was a simple mission, that your team was the best, and I would be in no danger."

"Someone lied to you," Hawk told him, "or has an exaggerated opinion of our abilities. Who tapped you for this mission?"

"Stearns, Section T. The man who brought me here."

"How much field training have you had?"

"I'm still in the classroom."

"You've had *no* field training," he asked, wanting to confirm he had heard correctly.

"That's right," Thomas said. "My final tests are next month."

Hawk's stomach clenched. He took another drink. An unpleasant conclusion formed in his mind. "Did you apply for this assignment?"

"No. Mister Stearns walked into class yesterday, pointed at me, and told me to follow him."

The glass again came to Hawk's mouth. He swallowed, wishing for a moment he was a teenager again, back before things turned so ugly. "Thank you, Thomas. You can go back to whatever you were doing."

"Thank you, Captain." Thomas stood, hesitated, and then said, "Is everything going to be all right?"

Hawk couldn't outright lie. "I don't know. We'll do everything we can."

A worried frown creased Thomas's face. He nodded, turned, and headed for the door.

"Thomas," Hawk called.

Thomas stopped at the door and turned back.

"I want to be clear, so you know what you're getting in to." Hawk leaned forward in his chair. "We're bringing them all back, or none of us are returning. Our job is to save that family or die trying. And that includes you. You've been dealt a tough hand on your first assignment, and I intend to have a vigorous discussion with Stearns when we return. Until then, you are a part of this team. I want you to act like it."

Hawk pointed to the door. "Now go and learn the action plan. Anything you have questions or concerns about, bring to Gerard's attention. I want your input. Dismissed."

When the door closed, Hawk leaned back, rubbed at his mustache, and said, "Okay, Ship, let's hear his record."

"Wilcox, Thomas H. Employed PC 26. Performed exemplary work as a clerk. Applied four times for agent training and was denied due to personality mistyping."

Hawk nodded. That fit. It was not uncommon for people to apply several times before being accepted. Most couldn't pass the rigorous physical fitness test the first time. Those who did and thought they were past the tough part found themselves running headfirst into the intense psychological testing. If running the obstacle course didn't get them, dodging the mental traps set by Force 13's head doctors often did.

"However," Ship continued, "he was accepted the fifth time."

"I wonder why."

"Maybe they admired his tenacity," Ship offered. "In any case, it appears to have been a mistake, since he has been at the bottom of his class in practically everything. During their last PT, the class had to carry him the last eight hundred meters."

"Was he hurt?"

"No, just tired."

It was worse than Hawk suspected. Someone at Force 13 wanted Thomas out of the way. Hawk needed a decoy courier, so Stearns had found an easily expendable asset: Thomas, a candidate they expected to drill out anyway. If Thomas managed to survive, his comrades would hold him in respect and every effort would be made to help him through training. Problem solved.

If he didn't, the problem was still solved. He would be out of the way, and his parents would get a small pension and a sorrowful letter about his heroic effort for the cause.

Whatever the hell that was. Hawk poured another measure of Scotch. Rubbing his face in his hands, he said, "Damn, I hate this job sometimes."

"What are you going to do?" Ship asked.

"What can I do? The mission's too important to put one of the crew in as the courier. But if I put this guy out there, he's meat within ten seconds after the shooting starts." He sighed. "I guess all I can do is slap some Chem Armor on him, hand him a pistol, and hope for the best."

"You can also warn him what to expect."

Hawk didn't say anything for a moment. "Yeah, but I doubt it will do any good."

<hr>

Sitting in the galley, Ashron caught Thomas shuffling past the doorway with his head low and deep in thought.

That looks like it went well, Ashron thought. "Thomas."

After a few seconds, Thomas poked his head around the corner. "Yes?"

"Care to join me for a Scaly Mudball?" Ashron held up a frothing red concoction.

"Uh, I don't drink."

"Don't fret. It's non-alcoholic."

"However, it is toxic," Laura cut in, walking into the room from the other hallway. Ashron glanced at her and cut his eyes at Thomas, hoping she caught his attempt to cheer up their downtrodden guest. She apparently gleaned his intent. "Come on in anyway, and I'll fix you something good."

"Well..."

"I insist," Laura walked over and took him by the arm.

"Okay," he said, still dejected.

"I can sense right away that you've recently come from one of our captain's little pep talks," Ashron said as Laura sat Thomas down at the table and then walked over to the drink processor. "Let me guess. We're all going to die."

"Well, he didn't say that, really."

"He doesn't have to. He radiates doom. We're going to be chopped up into little pieces and fed to the Anaril."

"The what?" Laura asked, returning to the table carrying two drinks.

"Small flesh-eating fish. All teeth. Very nasty," Ashron took a pull from his drink, tilted his head back and let out a long belch. "That's a good mudball." His forked tongue flicked against his nose, catching errant patches of foaming liquid.

"Pig," Laura said as she handed a glass of bright green fluid to Thomas. "Here, this will make you feel better." She sat beside Ashron. "So, why the gloomy face?"

"I don't think Captain Grey is thrilled with having me on this mission."

"That's just the way he is," Ashron said. "Don't let it bother you."

"He didn't seem real excited about my lack of experience."

"Do you blame him?" Laura asked softly.

Thomas bowed his head. "No."

"Now you know where he's coming from," she continued. "If you were the captain and had the responsibility of this mission over you, you'd feel the same way. Would you blame the recruit?"

He looked up. "No, I wouldn't."

"Hawk doesn't either; he just has too much on his mind to explain it tactfully."

"What's his excuse the other times?" Ashron asked into his drink.

Laura shot him a sideways glance as Thomas chuckled.

"So you can laugh," Laura said. "Put yourself in Hawk's shoes. It's nothing personal. He has a ship to run and a mission to worry about. A mission that involves very close friends. The last thing *you* need to worry about is what our captain thinks of the new addition to the crew."

"I guess."

Ashron downed the last of his drink. "Come on; let me take your mind off it." He stood and walked toward the door.

"Where are you going?" Laura asked.

"I'm going to give Thomas a crash course in weapons handling and firearms skill."

Thomas stopped half in and half out of his chair, "You are? Where?"

"We have a top-notch FATS deck. Boosted by Ship. Most excellent training and guaranteed to make you feel better."

Thomas finished standing and gave Laura a quizzical stare.

"It's a firearms training simulator," she told him. "It's very realistic and a whole lot of fun. You'll see."

Thomas shrugged and followed Ashron out the door.

Trey stopped outside Gerard's door and hesitated before knocking. Even though he liked the pale engineer as much as he liked any of the crew, the small man also intimidated him the most, even more than the massive Wolf. Gerard could call what he did a type of science, but it looked to Trey like magic. He had seen firsthand the devastating effects of such "science" gone rampant.

That was in a past life; a life these people had rescued him from, that he now wanted desperately to leave behind. Just like he wanted to escape the dreams ripsleep brought to him. He knocked.

"Come in."

The door slid open, and Trey stepped inside. Gerard sat at a small workbench, surrounded by an assortment of computer parts, machinery, and tools. The tangy smell of well-used metal filled the room. Every space except the bed seemed taken up by some strange device. Gerard's shiny black, oblong guard robot, which he called ROMANCE, sat on the bed.

Although Trey almost giggled at the thought of a sleeping robot, he found the room's chaos appalling.

"How can you live in here?" Trey asked.

"I don't usually," Gerard said, setting down the sheet of electronic paper he had been reading. "I come here to sleep and that's about it, and I have to do that only four hours at a time. It's also seldom this cluttered, but I'm working on a side project and didn't want to take up space in the workshop. Pick your way over to the bed and have a seat."

Trey took careful steps, doing his best to avoid treading on anything other than floor. Memories of another boy picking his way through a forest of debris tried to intrude. Trey pushed them away. That boy had died on Kel.

He reached the bed and sat down. ROMANCE gave him a friendly beep; Trey petted the robot's rounded metallic side.

"You want to talk?" Gerard asked.

Trey tugged at the front of his shirt. "You said you could help make the dreams go away. You have to help me. I really can't do another jump if I have to see them again."

Gerard frowned. "Did the multiplication tables not help?"

"Sort of." He shrugged. "Not really."

The frown deepened. "What do you mean?"

Trey clenched his hands between his knees. How could he possibly tell Gerard just how bad the dreams were? Giant worms with jaws full of flashing teeth. Red creatures with wings and horns dripping green venom, and so much worse. All of them circling Ship, seeking a way to destroy and get at the precious meat within. The monsters wanted to tear the ship apart and devour them all. Thinking about them made him want to scream. "It's like watching a trideo," Trey began. "The multiplication tables make it fade, but it doesn't go away completely."

Gerard nodded. "That's because my explanation was inferior. We were under stress."

"Hawk was a jerk," Trey muttered.

"No insubordination," Gerard said, his sternness betrayed by a smile. "Hawk is the captain and sometimes has to make calls that aren't agreeable. He does it in the best interests of the mission. I can perhaps offer a better explanation now. I said multiplication tables because I'm aware you know those. The trick is to occupy your mind with whatever repetitive thought works for you. Multiplication tables, a short poem. Algebraic equations. The point is to keep your thoughts occupied. It needs to be short and repeatable, but complicated enough to force you to concentrate."

"Why?"

"Putting your mind in a rhythmic pattern allows it no time to formulate its own thoughts. No thoughts, no dreams. No dreams, no fear. It may take some testing to find what works for you. At the least, you will make the dreams fade. And that's better than having them full force, isn't it?"

It wasn't better. Trey didn't want to have them at all. He couldn't tell Gerard that. "It really works?"

"It will. It has ever since Berolians discovered ripspace."

Trey stared in surprise. "Berolians discovered ripspace?"

"I see someone has been remiss in doing their studies of Galactic history," Gerard said, frowning. "I'll have Ship set up a school course to rectify that. When we go into rip next time, find a pattern that works for you and you'll be fine. Okay?"

Trey nodded, unsatisfied but knowing he wasn't going to get much else. "I'll try. Thank you."

Trey picked his way back to the door. As it opened, he turned and asked one other question that had been bothering him. "Why am I the only one on Ship who has these dreams?"

Gerard hesitated as if he was about to say one thing and then changed his mind. "It sometimes happens to children your age, those on the cusp of puberty. It occurred to me when I was eleven, so be assured that I know what you're experiencing. Does that help?

Trey nodded. It helped, but why did Gerard hesitate? "Thanks," he said again and walked away. He headed for his cabin, where he could make use of Ship's library. He had the feeling there was more to these dreams than Gerard was telling him.

Gerard let out a sigh as the door closed. He had come close to offering Trey the truth before he decided the boy didn't need that burden right now. Trey had done remarkably well since they rescued him from Kel, but his turbulent emotions shone to Gerard, even though Trey tried to hide them. A terrified little boy still formed a large part of Trey. Until he could speak openly about what happened on his homeworld, he would not completely heal. Gerard refused to compound Trey's fear by telling him his dreams weren't dreams at all. They were visions. Scattered glimpses into the true nature of ripspace.

"You want me to lock down any searches on ripspace?" Ship asked. "In case he goes looking?"

"No," Gerard said, much as he might like to do that. "Hiding information would show a lack of trust, and that could hurt him as much as what he might learn. If he has the initiative to search, he deserves the truth. I'll deal with the consequences when that happens."

"Have you ever used one of these?" Ashron asked, holding a pistol up and showing it to Thomas. They were in the large room that did double duty as a weapons training center and racquetball court.

"No." Thomas still sounded miserable. "We hadn't gotten that far in my training."

Ashron flicked his tongue to keep from saying something disparaging. "Okay, let me show you. This is a Colt-Maqasauri LX Series Blaster Pistol. Very easy to operate. You pull the trigger, a charge fires, the capacitor is kicked out, and the next one locks into place. All you have to worry about is pointing at the target and hitting him, her, or it. The clip holds charges for twenty shots, and this model is an autoloader with two spare clips, so you effectively have sixty shots before you have to worry about replacing the mags. This is how you do that." Ashron pointed to a small button near the top of the weapon. "Push that button, and all three clips fall out. Don't worry about picking them up; they're cheap. Besides, you'll be too busy to care." Ashron demonstrated, letting the clips drop to the floor, where they bounced with a plastic clatter.

"Once those are out, simply grab your spares and push them in here." He showed Thomas the empty bottom. "They lock in, and the gun does the rest." He picked the clips up, shoved them back into the pistol, and handed it to Thomas. "Okay, let's see what you can do."

<hr>

Thomas turned and fired. The man ducked behind the window. The supercharged plasma bolt passed harmlessly by. Thomas dropped into the stance Ashron had taught him. He aimed and waited for the man to poke his head back up.

"Pause," Ashron said. The scene stopped.

Thomas turned and looked at him, concerned.

"You're doing great," Ashron said to allay his fears. "I want you to remember two things. Cover and concealment. You currently have neither, and he has one."

To make his point, Ashron drew his weapon. "Play."

He fired through the wall where the man had ducked. They heard a scream and thump from the other side of the window. "Pause." He turned to Thomas.

"These blast charges travel through most interior walls," Ashron said. "That's concealment."

Pointing across the street to a man hiding behind the corner of a building, he said, "That's cover. You can't shoot him through the building. Play." Ashron fired a few blasts in that direction, chipping masonry off the wall and making the man duck back. "Pause. You make him keep his head down, and you move. Moving targets are hard to hit, and cover is hard to shoot through." Ashron stepped back and re-holstered his weapon.

Thomas gritted his teeth and nodded. When he had watched Ashron go through the scenario it had seemed straightforward; he was discovering looks were deceiving.

"Play," Ashron said.

The man behind the building popped out and started shooting. Thomas ducked and fired. The man ran from behind the building to a vehicle. Thomas also moved, running behind a luminary pole and dropping to one knee. The man stood and fired some more. Shots rang out around the pole.

"Damn," Thomas crouched lower and fired. The man ducked back down behind the car. Thomas shot low through the side of the vehicle. He heard a yell.

"All subjects dead," Ship said over the com.

"Good!" Ashron beamed. "You learn quickly." He walked over and swatted Thomas soundly on the back, almost knocking him to his knees. "Let's grab some lunch. We'll come back and work on this some more."

"Great," Thomas said, "and thank you."

As they left the room, Ashron began going into greater depth concerning the differences between cover and concealment.

"Not bad," Hawk said to Wolf. They watched Thomas and Ashron on a monitor from the bridge.

"Do you feel better now?" Wolf asked.

"Some. If he can be trained, Ashron can train him."

Wolf gave a slight, deep-throated chuckle. "Ashron could teach my grandmother to shoot well, and she's blind in one eye. Thomas will do fine."

Hawk watched the monitor as the human and Lorothian left the room. "I hope so. We don't have the manpower to watch him. He'll be on his own out there."

"Yeah," Wolf said. "Won't we all?"

10

PREPARATIONS

Ashron flew fast and low, the *Little Star*'s magnetic engine a bare whisper in the craft. They had blacked the shuttle for maximum stealth. Passersby might hear a slight *whoosh* sound and feel a breeze, but by the time they looked for the source, the craft would be around the next turn.

Ashron glanced at the monitor displaying the crew hold. Laura stood at the ready, dressed in a tight black unitard covered in static pockets that held her equipment. A sniper rifle stuck diagonally to her back, held by electromagnetic tape. She wore her work face: grim, determined, and covered in dark patterned camouflage.

She fidgeted, fingers flexing as she waited for Ashron to reach the landing zone. Two days of training and planning could not erase the crew's anxiousness about the Maratais. They were all keyed up and ready for action.

"LZ in view," Ashron said as he guided the *Star* next to a three-story stone building. "Stand by!" He pulled back hard on the stick and reduced the throttle. The shuttle's soft whir dropped to nothing as the craft hovered. "Go!"

All instruments and cabin lights went dark as Laura tapped a panel and the shuttle door slid open. She jumped from darkness into the night. Ashron flew off before the door finished closing, heading for his landing point. "May Ssarra guide us this night," he said to the air, hoping the Lorothian goddess of fortune listened to prayers so far from her home.

Laura hit the alleyway in a crouch, her landing cushioned by her short-burst gravity repellant packs. She stayed low, checking left and right for any movement. Her multivis contacts, set to light intensifier mode, lit up the lane in a bright green haze. A squat-bodied, six-legged animal rummaged through a can.

"*Cartas*," Ship said, her contralto voice vibrating through the receiver in Laura's collarbone and sounding in her head. "Planetary version of a cat. Harmless."

Laura nodded, even though Ship couldn't see her. The animal hissed at her and its mottled orange-black hair puffed out in a threat display. She stepped toward it; it hissed once and ran into the night, stubby tail flicking in agitation. Laura slipped to the opposite side of the alley and stopped before descending the stone stairway.

"Talk to me, Gerard," she whispered into the com pickup. Gerard monitored the operation from aboard Ship, playing eyes and ears for the crew. He also controlled the light support drones heading for the fortress.

"No electronic devices in the stairwell, and no life forms other than the one you chased away, watching you from the alleyway. You owe me a dinner."

Laura smiled. During the briefing and strategy session, Gerard had pointed out this entrance as the easiest way to the roof. Laura had been convinced it would be monitored in some fashion. Gerard had disagreed; they had placed the bet.

"Roger," Laura whispered. Only a smooth metal door stood between her and the stairwell to the roof. The blueprints had shown a lock. They hadn't shown that it was a one-sided lock with no visible mechanism on the outer side. Even though she'd anticipated this, that didn't make it any less inconvenient. She reached into one of the many padded pouches that lined her pants and extracted a six-inch piece of sturdy metal with retractable hooks on one end. With practiced ease, she slid the bar between door and jamb. A few moments of deft maneuvering produced the desired result. Using the hooks, she pulled the door open.

It stopped after opening eight inches.

What the— Laura thought. She looked through the gap. A length of thick chain looped through the handle and locked to an eyebolt in the wall. It was too far away for her to pick.

"They weren't totally unprepared," she whispered to Gerard. "What's on the other side of the door?"

"One guard standing still inside the stairwell. Can't tell which floor he's on."

Laura knew that meant one of two things. The guard was leaning against a wall somewhere above her, taking a break from the tedious routine of patrolling the stairs, or he had been on the first floor when she opened the door and now stood on the stairs waiting to see what was going to come through.

Can't anything be simple? She thought, reaching into another pocket and pulling out a small camera on a telescoping rod. Lying on the cold concrete, she extended the rod and slid the camera through the door.

Shots didn't ring out immediately; a good start, but it didn't guarantee no one was there. She scanned the hallway, its image projected to her contacts. Switching through the various spectrums the camera allowed, she saw nothing close. The small amount of light leaking in from the open door didn't allow her to view the entire area. She retracted the camera and stowed it back in its pocket. She then pulled a three-inch long box of flat gray metal from her shin pocket and a magnetized wand from her left sleeve. She attached the box to the rod, laid it on the floor inside the doorway, and activated it. A burst of ultrasound fired through the room. The return information traveled up the wand, into a micro-transmitter on her waist, and up to Ship.

"Hallway clear up to level two," Ship responded.

Laura relaxed and dropped into the proper breathing pattern for what she was about to attempt. She had always been a small, lithe woman. This would require her to be more of both. She was using up too much time, a precious commodity, but it couldn't be helped. She concentrated on her breathing.

A minute passed before she felt sufficiently relaxed. She quietly slipped off the rifle and laid it to the side. Grabbing the door with her hands, she pulled her head through the portal and glanced around to make sure nothing had changed. Cool stone and stairs in the hallway. Getting her head in was easy. Now came the tough part. She paused and focused on the task. She exhaled. With a concentrated effort, she condensed her upper torso. With one hand on the door and the other against the concrete, she gave a quick shove and slipped through the opening, her hips and legs following. She rose to her knees, reached back through the door, grabbed the rifle, stood, and quietly closed the troublesome door.

It took a moment to recover from the dizziness that hit her. She rotated her shoulders to loosen them. Once the disorientation passed, she trotted to the end of the hall. With a glance up the stairwell, she treaded up two steps at a time. Her padded shoes and years of training made her so silent she would have amazed a cat, providing it heard her.

"Okay, Laura, your man is still in the stairwell. He hasn't moved more than two meters in any direction."

Laura clicked her teeth twice, the code that indicated a message was received, but the receiver couldn't speak. She continued up the stairs. One flight, pause, look. Two flights, pause, look. According to the plans, the building had five levels. Three flights, pause, look. Four…

She stopped, her body going into a crouch almost before her brain issued the command. She slowed her breathing, escalated from the jog up the stairs, as fresh cigarette smoke assailed her nose and the soft scrape of shoes against stone reached her ears. A slight flick of her wrist released the neuralizer concealed in her sleeve pocket; it slipped smoothly into her hand. She waited, silently cursing every second of delay. The walking stopped. A shoe ground against the concrete as the man extinguished his cigarette. Ten seconds passed, followed by a ruffling of clothes and a poorly suppressed yawn.

Good, he's inattentive. The man did not resume walking. Not having time to wait for him to come to her, she went to him.

He appeared average, just another thug fighting for a cause he did or didn't believe in. A small machine gun rested against his stomach, held in place by a shoulder strap. His eyes were closed. His back rested against the wall. Perhaps he was getting off duty soon, or maybe making the rounds and catching a little catnap. Laura slipped the neuralizer back into its holder. First and foremost, she was a healer and did not kill unnecessarily. This man was not an active threat; she could take him out without his death.

She pulled a black rod from a static pocket on her leg, pointed it toward the man, and squeezed the tube, activating two triggers. With a soft sound of compressed air, a dart launched from the tube. The dart's targeting computer centered on the man's carotid artery and struck. The man slapped at his neck and opened his eyes. They widened as he spotted Laura. Before he could react, the nano-tranquilizer raced to his brain faster than his blood. Nanobots surrounded the hypothalamus and bombarded it with GABA, a sleep-inducing neurotransmitter.

Laura could almost see the man's brain switching off as his eyes glazed and he slid to the concrete, unconscious before his body settled.

There goes two thousand credits, she thought as she slid the rod back in its pocket. She smiled as she recognized Hawk's voice in the thought. When they debriefed, he would grumble about the "wasteful" use of such expensive devices. Laura would give her standard value of human life speech, and he would offer his usual blank—and completely insincere—stare.

That's assuming we survive this thing, she thought as she ascended the final flight of stairs and stopped at the penthouse leading to the roof. "I'm at the roof, Gerard," she whispered. "What kind of welcoming party have I got?"

"Twenty soldiers on the roof. Only two men in position to be an immediate threat. They're at the edge, approximately five meters from the door."

"Twenty? These people are serious. We're not going to get out of this without trouble."

"Thank you, Miss Optimism," Ashron's voice cut in.

"No unnecessary chatter on Tacnet," Hawk said. "That means you, Ashron."

Laura pulled out her silenced pistol. Fortunately, the door hinges were on her side. She grabbed a small tube of liquid graphite from another pocket and applied a generous amount to each hinge. She replaced the container, took a deep breath, and eased through the doorway.

As she closed the door, she spotted two figures directly in front of her, roughly six meters away. Floodlights lined the parapet, creating artificial daylight in the courtyard. The guards faced the quadrangle, oblivious to Laura's presence. Shooting them was the easiest and quickest solution, but also the riskiest. One of them could easily pitch off the roof's edge to the pavement below. She had one more "sleep rod." It presented the same problem, with the bonus of attracting attention from the one she didn't tranquilize and allowing him to cry out before she could stop him. She needed to figure out how to get them away from the edge.

As if to make up for the trouble with the door at the bottom, luck swung her way.

"Damn, it's cold," one of the guards said, his voice coming through in the androgynous sound of her translator system. "You got a cigarette?"

"Nah, I left 'em in my room."

"Go get 'em."

"And get raked because you wanted a smoke? You get 'em."

Laura slid to the side of the pentice and melted into the darkness. Gravel crunched as the unnamed voice headed for the door. With regret, Laura slipped the neuralizer back into her left hand and pulled her silenced slug thrower into her right. The nano-tranq darts were ineffective at this close range.

As the man's hand touched the doorknob, Laura deftly reached out and put the neuralizer against his temple. A small white spark flickered like an arc of electricity. The man dropped, the nerves in his brain instantly destroyed.

Laura wheeled to face the other man, who had realized something was wrong and was bringing his machine gun to bear. She raised her pistol and fired. The weapon gave a soft *thwit* sound. The slug caught him in the throat and punctured his larynx. Moist gurgling noises came from the man as he reached for his throat; blood coated his hands.

He began stepping toward the edge. Laura dashed to his side, dropping him to the ground before he toppled off the roof. He died quickly, and she watched until he stopped breathing. She tried to ignore the half puzzled, half pleading glaze in his eyes. A flicker of remorse rose in her. She pushed it down, remembering why they were here and why she had been forced to do this.

Sure he was dead, Laura moved to her position at the roof's edge. The floodlights did a beautiful job of illuminating the quad and making it impossible to see anything on the roof while standing in the courtyard. No doubt the planners of this little rendezvous wanted it that way, but she doubted they had planned on someone unfriendly to their cause reaching the roof.

The fluorescent lights gave off very little heat, but they obscured her night vision. She closed her eyes and touched her lids once. When she re-opened them, the world stood out in thermographic shades, the bright orange flare of eighteen guards appearing between the aqua glow of the lights. She marked the closest at ten meters. She clicked her teeth five times, her signal that she was in place.

"Roger, Laura. Stand by." Gerard said.

"I'd rather be in Tuscany," she murmured to no one. With a wry smile, she unlimbered her sniper rifle.

Ashron settled the air raft on the roof of the building Gerard had picked as an ideal location, or as ideal as circumstances allowed. Signaling to Gerard that he had reached his position, he settled back and took the lid off a jar of spicy mustard. Grabbing a bag of cookies, he dipped one into the mustard and tossed it into his mouth. Nothing to do but wait until it all went to shit.

Wolf pushed open the door and stepped into the old warehouse that sat adjacent to the back wall of the fortress. He swung his massive weapon out before him, an electromagnetic flechette gun designed by Gerard and dubbed "Wolf's Minigun of Awesomeness" by Ashron.

Wolf scanned the building for inhabitants. Unlikely as it was anyone would be stationed here, he didn't take chances. Bulging muscles, armor-thick skin, and a gun that could chew through steel didn't give him a right to be careless.

The scant light filtering in through cracks in boarded up windows and the open doorway revealed only the shapes of unwanted or obsolete machinery; they took on the aspects of dead mythical beasts in the scarce illumination. Wolf closed the door and sidled through the maze of metal, his large feet stirring up dust. It drifted into the air, creating a shifting haze in the dim light. His bulky body was not exceptionally agile, so he had to be extra cautious not to knock anything over.

He reached the back wall of the warehouse without incident. The warehouse and fortress shared this wall, and it surprised Wolf that the fortress's designers let such a glaring weakness remain. Perhaps they hadn't been residents long enough to make all the modifications they wanted, or maybe the warehouse was added long after the fortress had been abandoned. Either way, he was more than willing to exploit the weakness. Probing the wall with his fingers, he found what he felt to be the weakest spot. Satisfied, he signaled to Gerard that he was in position, then stepped back, relaxed and waited.

11

AMBUSH

Hawk and Thomas sat in the four-person mini-shuttle, five hundred meters from the imposing stone fortress. They had arrived with a few minutes to spare, so Hawk had landed on the side of the road to wait for the rendezvous time.

Thomas scratched at his chest. "This chemarmor smells bad and itches."

"I've got the remover if you want to take it off," Hawk said. "Personally, I'd rather smell like a chemical factory than have a slug or laser plow through my chest." Hawk didn't mention he would have preferred standard kinetic or combat armor, but the chemarmor, applied directly to the skin and adding minimal bulk, stood a better chance of going unnoticed by their opponents.

The faux courier looked at him, continuing to scratch. "Captain Grey, I'm not going to survive this, am I?"

Hawk studied the nervous man. Thomas had spent almost every waking moment on the FATS machine, honing his skill as much as he could in the two days he spent under Ashron's tutelage. In between mission planning and his own training, Hawk had watched Thomas's progress. The man's adeptness and ability to retain what Ashron taught him had impressed Hawk. He had wondered more than once if

Thomas' problems with Force 13's training were because of the trainers or the trainee. "Just remember: once the shooting starts, find some cover. Don't do anything heroic. If someone comes near you, shoot him. Otherwise, stay hidden."

"That didn't answer my question."

After a pause, Hawk said, "No, it didn't. If it's any consolation, none of us may survive this." Hawk stared out the window a moment, then turned and regarded Thomas. "Weapons don't care. They don't care who you are, how well trained you are or how good your physical condition is. They don't care if your cause is just or evil. They simply don't care."

Thomas didn't respond. His face turned pale. He nodded and swallowed.

Hawk frowned. *Your pessimism isn't going to make it any easier for him,* he thought. Thomas was scared, but he was here. "You have a better chance with us than you would with most. We have equipment these guys have probably never seen, and that smelly chemarmor is triple the strength of anything the public can buy. The crew backing us are experts at what they do. Remember, when the shit hits—and it will—stay low, get under cover, and shoot only when you have to. We're all going to die. Let's make sure it's not today." Hawk glanced at his watch. "Showtime. Gerard, we're going in. Positions?"

"Ready and waiting," Gerard's voice told him.

"Be careful," Trey said.

"Always."

Hawk fired up the shuttle and flew toward the fortress. When he was thirty meters away, a harsh spotlight split the night. Its dazzling beam blazed through the windshield. Hawk squinted until the glass polarized, cutting the glare. He landed the shuttle and shut off the engine. The cab grew quiet as the turbines wound down

"Looks like we walk from here," Hawk said, removing his restraining strap. "Turn on your nullifier." He reached back and powered up the small device strapped between his shield dynamo and pistol. It would hide the devices from spying machinery so the terrorists would think the two were unarmed, unprotected little sheep; the exact impression Hawk wanted to present.

"Captain, will the power cell last long enough?" Thomas asked as he powered his on.

"We're not here for lunch. There should be plenty of battery." He fixed Thomas with his eyes. "And from now on, call me Hawk." He offered a reassuring smile, winked and said, "Put on your game face."

Thomas gave a nervous nod, grabbed the sealed tube that served as their fake plan holder, and removed his restraints. As they stepped out of the craft, the spotlight went out.

Abandonment and harsh weather had not been kind to the gray stone fortress; large cracks spider-webbed their way across the building's face. Creeping green vines crawled halfway up the fifteen-meter wall. The road led to a large archway blocked by an ancient iron portcullis. Hawk stopped and scanned the area; he spotted a camera inside the entrance.

"What now?" Thomas asked.

Before Hawk could answer, the portcullis gave out a metallic groan. With a clanking of chain and gears, the iron gate ascended, disappearing into the archway. "Advance to the center of the court-yard and wait," a voice boomed from a speaker below the camera.

When they reached the dark tunnel, Hawk said, "'Once more into the breach, dear friends.'"

The jittery Thomas followed. Hawk moved through the pitch-black arch and stepped into a well-lit courtyard. Spotlights situated on top of the walls brightened the quadrangle like the noonday sun, leaving few shadows. Hawk scanned the courtyard, searching for signs of life. The lights above made seeing the roof impossible with natural vision, so he switched to heat vision. The lighting went blue. Human-shaped blurs of red stood between most of them.

"Gerard?" Hawk asked.

"Picking up eighteen guards on the roof and another eighty indi-viduals gathered in various sectors of the fortress. You want real-time?"

"No," Hawk said. "That many targets on my HUD would blind me. I'll do it the old- fashioned way if I have to."

Ninety-eight people? Hawk thought. *Minus Yonath and his family, that still leaves ninety-four possible dangers.* "Sitting ducks," he muttered. He hoped the element of surprise would suffice, even though 'hope' was a piss-poor strategy.

"What did you say?" Thomas asked.

"Nothing," The short hairs on the back of his neck grew rigid as he approached the courtyard's center. "It just doesn't get any better than this."

Onboard Ship, Gerard monitored Hawk's progress, screens filled with various views from the cameras attached to Hawk and Thomas's clothing, as well as the drones flying above the fortress.

"Gerard?" Ship asked

"Yes?"

"What do you make of this?" A holographic grid map appeared in front of Gerard's monitor.

Gerard studied the control map, which showed all other ships in a five thousand kilometer radius. "I'm not seeing it."

"Let me show you the screen a half hour ago."

When it came up, he immediately saw what she had in mind. "What are those ships up to?"

"They have pulled out of their regular orbit and started on their present course."

Gerard studied the map carefully. "I'd think it was a coincidence if I believed in those. Change your orbit to here." He touched the map so Ship could sense the coordinates. "If they make any course change at all toward our location, we have problems."

Ship maneuvered toward her new course. Gerard turned his attention back to Hawk, intuition telling him things were soon going to turn bad.

In the fortress courtyard, a figure emerged from an opening that the spotlights conveniently left unlit. It was like a black hole in a sea of light, a darkness that seemed to radiate from the man. Though the effect was meant to be dramatic, Hawk had seen the heat signature well before the man drew close. He turned his contacts back to normal vision as the shadow came forward, stepping into the light. Hawk finally learned the identity of One-Eye.

His stomach clenched. Emotions too muddled and complex to sort out chattered in his mind, but he kept his face neutral. "Moran?"

"Surprised?" the man asked, his jewel-encrusted eye patch glittering under the light.

Hawk couldn't let Moran see how this turn of events rattled him. Keeping his voice light, he said, "A little. I assumed you were dead. My mistake. Nice patch."

"I'm glad you like it."

"So much for the formalities. Let's get this over with. Where are the Maratais?"

"Not so fast. I want to enjoy this. The leader of the great Knights of The Flaming Star." He paused and then spit, his face a snarl of contempt. "Helpless. There was a time when I respected your abilities, even to the point of wanting to be like you. Even when we no longer saw eye to eye, if you'll pardon the pun, I still respected you." He put his hand under the eye patch and scratched. "Of course, you never could throw a dagger."

"You'll be happy to know that I haven't gotten any better."

"Of course not. Look at you. You've grown soft. Too much high living from all that money you squandered and never shared."

"I gave you plenty," Hawk said. "Your problem was that you always wanted more than you had."

"You have no right to tell me my problems!" Moran shouted. "Who do you think you are? You're nothing but a Council delivery boy. Useless."

"I see you've done well for yourself. Your own terrorist organization is certainly an upward career move."

"I've done better than you can imagine."

"Yeah, sure," Hawk didn't bother to hide the sarcasm. "Much as I'd love to rehash ancient history, I'd rather take care of the business at hand. Where's the family?"

"Where are the plans?" Moran asked.

"I have them," Thomas said.

Moran held out his hand.

"And you'll get them as soon as I see the family," Hawk said, giving a sideways glance at Thomas.

"You always did have trouble realizing when a situation wasn't under your control. I'm in charge here. Give me the plans, and I'll show you the family."

"First, I want to—"

"SHUT UP! I don't give a damn what you want. You demand nothing. Now give me the plans, or I'll have the family destroyed. Give them to me NOW."

Hawk stared at Moran. His one-time friend had become a man he no longer knew. A man even more over the edge than when they last confronted each other. The lunatic in front of him would carry out his threat, despite the consequences.

"Give him the plans," he said to Thomas.

Thomas drew the metal tube from beneath his jacket and tossed it to Moran.

"You see what I mean?" Moran said, catching the cylinder and pocketing it without even bothering to check the contents. "Soft. In the old days, I would never have been able to intimidate you. You would have shot me, had the team take out the guards, and then found the family yourself. You're pathetic."

It took all of Hawk's restraint to keep from shooting the man now. "You have the plans," he said through clenched teeth. "Where's the family?"

"Yes, I did promise I would let you see them, didn't I? No problem." He waved his hand. The floodlights around the quad dimmed to half intensity. Bright lights flared and illuminated the dark opening from which Moran had appeared. Hawk's mind almost shattered from what the light revealed

Yonath and Dona hung suspended in the air, thick cord looped around their necks, their clothing tattered. Blood-soaked viscera covered the concrete beneath them. Patishi lay on the floor, slumped against the wall. Yoseph hung upside down, his legs held apart by two ropes. A star with flames extending from one end had been neatly etched into the boy's shirtless chest; the skin was carefully peeled from the star's interior. It exposed the muscle beneath, creating a demented badge, a torturous mockery of the Knights' emblem.

Hawk almost froze in revulsion and despair. The lifeless people hanging before him, their bodies hideously violated, had once been living, laughing humans. People with whom he and the Knights, including Moran, had shared a significant portion of their lives. They had been present at the wedding and celebrated in the births of Patishi and Yoseph. Yonath had used his influence in the Council to get the Knights a shot at joining Force 13. The two "families" had often shared dinner together. The sudden non-existence of these people was like witnessing the disappearance of a moon.

Then he realized Yoseph and Patishi were still breathing.

Hawk pushed his horror aside as immediate need took over. Facts slammed into his consciousness in rapid-fire bursts: Yonath and Dona were dead, beyond help, but the children were alive.

And Moran laughed. He stood defiantly in front of Hawk, laughing hysterically.

He was still laughing as three energy bursts from Hawk's pistol smashed into his chest. He stumbled back two meters but remained standing, his singed armor still intact. Grinning, he raised his cybernetic arm and pointed it toward Hawk.

<hr>

As soon as Laura saw Moran through her sights, she expected trouble. A latecomer to the Knights, she had never been privy to the cause of Moran's split from the group. Hawk, Gerard, and Wolf would not discuss it. She knew only that the separation had been hostile; there would be no great feeling of sorrow if Moran died today.

When the lights came on in the alcove, she still had her sights on Moran. She didn't see what caused Hawk's horrified reaction, but she saw Hawk's blasts smash into Moran's chest and dissipate. He was wearing reflective body armor. As Moran raised his arm, Laura pulled the trigger, sending a beam of focused infrared light neatly through his eye patch. A glitter of sparks showered from the patch and Moran dropped.

"Shot out," Laura said through her headset, already aiming for her next target.

Ship sounded an alarm. "They've changed course to match ours."

Gerard studied the map. "Damn. Scan."

"Coming up now. Two class four *Borlan* Frigates, one *Lorothian* Corsair and a *Krizan* class bulk freighter."

"Origin?"

"Good question. There are no exterior markings. I'm running a check of the port to see if they're registered."

"Don't bother," Gerard told her. "They're moving into attack formation. You better strap in," he told Trey. "This could get rough."

As Moran fell with a smoking hole in his eye, Hawk hit the ground rolling. With Moran down, his next priority was to get to the children and protect them. The thunder of gunfire erupted around him. He dashed for the alcove and activated his shield dynamo, but not before one bolt caught him low and on the side, and another smashed into his shin. Immediate, intense pain radiated from the hits. He staggered; the chemical armor coating kept the skin from breaking. Thomas drew his gun and ran for the nook. A blast grazed him across the neck and blood welled out, splashing onto his shirt. Putting his free hand up to the wound, he fired randomly and kept moving.

As Hawk reached the alcove, a man came from either side with his weapons raised. They fired. One slammed into Hawk's shield. His ears buzzed with static overload and he staggered back several steps. The other shot plowed up concrete half a meter from his feet.

Hawk returned fire, taking off one man's head in a splatter of red.

The other man fired again. Heat blistered Hawk's face as the energy bolt glanced off the shield centimeters from his head.

Hawk moved to shoot when a screaming Thomas plowed into the man. They went down in a heap. Thomas put the gun in the other man's face and fired. The backblast shattered concrete and threw the courier against the wall. He slid down, stunned and covered with his victim's gore.

Hawk stood and resumed his interrupted entrance into the alcove. He slid Patishi to the back wall as carefully as he could. He ran to Yoseph, placing himself between the boy and the courtyard. "Don't shoot quite so close next time," he told the dazed Thomas.

"Good advice," Thomas said as he pushed himself up using the wall as a brace. "What do you need?" He activated his shield.

"Stay in cover as much as possible and shoot at anything unfriendly," Hawk said as he worked with a knife to cut Yoseph loose.

Another bolt caught him in the back. Shuddering pain seared through his body. The shield dissipated most of the energy, and the armor stayed intact. Furious noise filled the room as Thomas returned fire. Yoseph came loose. Hawk held him, preventing the boy from hitting the gore-covered floor. As gently as possible, he ran back to Patishi and laid her brother beside her.

"Status?" he yelled to Thomas.

"Intact," Thomas shouted back over the hail of laser and slug fire. A beam struck the wall above his head, showering him with mortar. Spotting a soldier, he took quick aim and fired. The bolt caught the other man in the face; he went down.

The children as safe as they could be in the situation, Hawk took up a firing position at the doorway. Hoping the concrete wall held up under the fusillade of energy raining against it, and filling the alcove with choking dust, Hawk began shouting into the headset.

A burst of racket echoed over his headset. Ashron set his jar of mustard in his cup holder. "It always comes to a fight, doesn't it?" He asked no one as he jerked back on the joystick. The *Little Star* launched into the air, hell-bent towards the trouble area. A small war raged over his headset. Ashron could barely hear Hawk's voice over the din of exploding gunfire. Despite the garbled content, the tone came through crystal clear. It was time to leave.

As soon as the muted *crack* of fired weapons reached Wolf's ears, he powered up the Minigun of Awesomeness, activated his shield, stepped back three meters, and ran at the concrete wall in front of him. Cement shattered and flew out in huge chunks into the adjoining room. Wolf stormed through the wall without slowing his stride. As the mortar dust settled, he opened fire with the MGoA. Twenty surprised men turned from the open bay to face him. They had been crouching behind cover, facing the other direction. They tried to bring their weapons around, but the high-powered minigun ripped through armor, flesh, and wall. A few managed to get off wild shots that struck nowhere near the large Uraxian.

When the smoke cleared, only Wolf stood. He loaded another hopper into his weapon.

From his position against the bunker wall, Hawk hazarded a glance into the courtyard. A slug whined off his shield, the force snapping his head back like a punch to the face. He shook his head and ducked back. He had seen what he needed. He didn't know the exact count of men that advanced on them, but it was enough. If they didn't do something, the sheer weight of numbers would end them. All it would take was a lucky shot or enough structural damage to the building. Hawk shuddered at the thought of a grenade landing in this enclosed space. "Gerard, porcupine."

"Porcupine away," Gerard said.

In a few seconds, Hawk heard a whine from the sky. He chanced another glance out.

A meter-wide half-cylinder screamed through the air, dropped from one of the drones. Jets fired a meter from the ground, slowing its descent enough that it landed with a solid, non-damaging thud. Firing ceased from the thirty or so men as they took in the robot's arrival. Apparently one of them guessed it wasn't friendly. "Run!" he screamed.

It was futile. Hawk felt the buzz in his neck as the machine sent out a pulse of ultrasonic sound, which both identified every living thing within two hundred meters, and tagged the people with IFF responders as friends. He glanced back. A green light at Thomas's waist confirmed he had been identified.

The few men who heeded the shouted command had gone no more than five feet when a hundred small ports irised open on the robot's shell. A whining electromagnetic pulse made it shudder. Hundreds of sixteen-millimeter metallic needles shot forth, blossoming like a deadly dandelion. Every man in the courtyard fell, pierced by the lethal shards of duraluminum through head, heart, and stomach. Those not obliterated in the initial burst went down as the needle sought them, guided by the robot and driven by short-range guidance engines.

One man made it to the alcove before three shards struck him in the back of the head and stopped when they protruded from his face. He collapsed as blood sprayed.

Hawk threw himself over the unconscious bodies of the children. He heard the whine of flechettes and braced for impact, hoping against hope his armor would deflect them if needed.

His neck buzzed. The whine ceased, followed by five metallic *clinks*.

"That's amazing," Thomas said. Hawk saw Thomas staring at the carnage in the courtyard. Five flechettes lay on the ground centimeters from Hawk. His IFF had deactivated them.

"There," Hawk said. "That should give us some better odds."

* * *

Wolf saw the bloodbath in the courtyard and smiled. Much as

he hated the destruction of life, he loved when one of the machines he helped Gerard build worked without flaw.

"Wolf," Hawk's voice came into his head. "I'm in the alcove across from you. Can you see me?"

"HUD," Wolf said. A display appeared over his eyes, outlining Hawk in bright green and offering relative positions indicators on Laura and Ashron. Wolf saw the lighted alcove across the courtyard.

"I see you," Wolf said.

"We've still got unfriendlies, so I don't want to come out until Ashron lands. Can you keep the courtyard clear if anyone pokes their head out?"

"Yeah." Wolf scanned the courtyard.

The startlingly loud thunder crack of medium laser pistols erupted on his left. Several blasts struck his shield, which crackled and gave off a burnt ozone smell. One bolt broke through his shield, so expended that it caused only stinging pain to his naturally-thickened skin. He turned. Five men entered the room twenty meters away.

Wolf roared and returned fire. Smoke and thunder flew from his gun. Concrete shattered as slugs ricocheted off the soldier's shields. Within ten rounds, the gun's harmonic dissipater locked into the shields and shorted them. The yellow glow around the men changed to red mist as their shields collapsed and slugs struck home.

Wolf continued his scan of the courtyard. Nobody had come into the open. His HUD displayed several men hidden behind walls near the various doorways that pockmarked the quadrangle. They took haphazard pop shots at Hawk's position. Wolf's gun whirred to life as he laid down a barrage of suppressing fire. The shapes withdrew, and the gunfire ceased. Bullets still thundered from hidden places, aimed at Hawk's position. Wolf stepped out of the bay doors and hugged the wall. He jogged around the courtyard perimeter, gun ready to provide more covering fire.

He had gone no more than twenty meters when ten more fighters came running out of a large door across from him.

"Ashron, where the hell are you?" Laura demanded. She had taken out six snipers before anyone realized they had an unfriendly on the roof. She dispatched two more in the confusion that followed as they stopped shooting at Hawk and attempted to locate the source of enemy fire. Some of the flechettes from Gerard's porcupine had aimed for the snipers, but had fallen short and rained onto the parapet with their tiny engines expended.

"Thirty seconds out," Ashron said as the floodlight to Laura's left exploded. She returned fire, sending another man down with a hole burned into his chest.

She looked around. In the muddle of combat, she had lost track of people. She had no idea of Wolf's whereabouts. Ten more men suddenly appeared on the ground level. They opened fire in her direction, their aim beneath her, revealing Wolf's position.

"HUD," she said. As she surmised, Wolf's dot put him underneath her. "I'm right over you, Wolf,"

She popped up and shot one of the men. The rest dove for the safety of the doorway as the familiar staccato rhythm of Wolf's MGoA echoed through the courtyard. Two fell to Wolf's fire. Six made it to the door; only two stopped behind the door to return fire. Laura set her crosshairs on one of the men. Before she could shoot, the scene in front of her exploded into a mass of cement chunks, wood, dust, and flesh as Wolf's heavy machine gun chewed up the door and the men behind it.

"Go for the alcove," Laura said. "I'll cover you."

Wolf lumbered across the blood-soaked, body-strewn quad. Three more men stepped out to fire. The one that lived through Laura's return fire dashed back through the doorway. There were no other attacks.

As soon as Wolf reached the alcove, Laura dropped behind the parapet to rethink her position.

Resting on her haunches, she scanned the immediate area. The surviving snipers had disappeared, most likely converging on her position. Rather than wait, she decided to take the fight to them.

"I think they're going to try a Scarplin net attack," Ship told Gerard as he slid into the weapons control seat.

"Really? That's odd. Unless they want us alive," Gerard said. He saw the ships move into position, lines of energy crossing from vessel to vessel, quickly forming a force net. "Launch a salvo of static missiles and slide under the net."

"Aye, aye."

The missiles left their launchers with a soft thud.

A flash of light burst against the energy net. It began to dissolve as the missiles' static charge disrupted the frigates' energy systems.

Ship increased engine power, heading for the widening gap. Gerard saw the Corsair coming in behind them and launching a salvo of missiles.

"Incoming," Gerard said, even though Ship already knew it.

"Countermeasures launched," Ship told him. "E.C.M. on."

He watched the screen as the missiles fanned out. The metal fragments scattered by Ship threw flashes of light as they spun and distracted the guidance systems on the rapidly closing missiles. Two of the eight projectiles made it through the cluster of metallic shards and struck Ship's shields; the thunder of their explosion echoed through the vessel. The vibrations rattled Gerard's teeth.

"Shields at seventy percent," Ship said. "We're through the net."

"Plasma cannon on that Corsair."

"Aye, aye."

Ship's turreted plasma cannon blazed away, arcing yellowish-green spheres of superheated gas toward the Corsair. The two Frigates, recovering from the static missiles, began to reform their net.

"What are they doing?" Gerard asked no one in particular.

"Herding us toward the freighter," Ship told him. The screen showed Gerard that the freighter had maneuvered to a position in front of them, its cargo doors open like the maw of a predator.

Gerard tapped his cybernetic hand against his pale chin. "I'd say things were starting to get interesting."

Hawk, his back to the courtyard and head bowed to minimize target area, heard Wolf before he saw the shadow against the back wall. He turned to find Wolf's massive form above him, gun held at the ready, bright blue eyes studying the slaughter of their friends. The smell of cordite almost poured from the large Uraxian.

"Glad you could make it," Hawk said.

Wolf nodded.

Hawk stood up. Wolf's usually stoic expression changed to one of startled amazement. "They're not dead?"

Hawk shook his head. "They will be if we don't get them out of here soon." He glanced at the disfigured, bullet-pocked bodies of Yonath and Dona. "Cut them down. I'm not going to leave them here."

Hawk took up position against the wall opposite Thomas, facing the courtyard with his pistol ready. Despite the protection of the alcove and the devastation wrought by the porcupine, plenty of firepower had gotten through. His whole body ached from the pounding the energy blasts and kinetic slugs had delivered. His shield was useless, its energy depleted, and his armor penetrated. Blood trickled from his side. He couldn't pass out yet, much as his body told him he wanted to. The assault had stopped, but Hawk didn't know if that was because everyone was dead or just regrouping. "Laura, sitrep."

He heard two sharp clicks. She couldn't talk but was still okay. They still had active enemies.

Hawk looked at Thomas. A dim blue glow crackled around his body; his shield was almost gone too. Other than the shallow gash on his neck, he appeared unharmed. "You okay?"

Thomas gave him a tight smile.

Wolf finished cutting down the bodies as the sound of gunfire returned to the courtyard, followed by the metallic whir of a moving combat robot.

"This just keeps getting better," Hawk muttered

Laura slipped behind a large solar panel and watched as four soldiers stumbled their way from a rooftop doorway toward her previous position, their ad-hoc leader occasionally admonishing them with a whispered, "Shh."

Motion in the sky. She saw the *Little Star* closing in on her position. *Good,* she thought, *this is getting bothersome.*

"Shuttle at twelve high," one of the guards said.

"Open fire."

Flash and thunder lit the night air as the men shot at the shuttle.

"That's pretty damn rude," Ashron said.

Setting down the rifle and pulling out her pistol, Laura stepped from behind the solar panel and fired.

Four shots with heat-seeking slugs, four dead bodies. They never even had time to be surprised.

"Thanks, Laura," Ashron said. He swooped down and flew low enough that she could see him smiling as he skimmed over the wall and into the courtyard.

And a missile flew by from below, barely missing the shuttle.

"They've engaged their tractor beam," Ship told Gerard. "About one minute before we're inside the freighter."

Gerard swore. Whoever planned this attack knew their tactics. After a brief exchange with Ship that left both crafts with their shields exhausted and little else, the Corsair had disengaged. However, it accomplished its mission, keeping Ship occupied while the two Frigates rebuilt their energy net. They encircled Ship, trapping her in a shimmering force web. A web which had slowly moved Ship toward the open freighter until it could capture them in its tractor beam.

As they rapidly approached the freighter entrance, Gerard tried to formulate a way to escape. Hoping against hope, he asked, "Ship, can we fire through the freighter once we're in?"

"Negative. They've got a static field generator inside. Once we're in, I'm out."

"Glanus mukai!" Gerard swore in his native tongue. The static field rendered their energy weapons useless. Beams would scatter, and plasma would dissipate as soon as it stuck. He glanced over at Trey, who sat with his hands clenched and face brimming with fear. Gerard couldn't blame him. Turning back to the freighter on display, he considered a weakness he would have protected that perhaps their enemy hadn't. "Ship, what is the thickness and composition of the freighter's front bulkhead?"

"Ten meters duraluminum steel."

"And is there any shielding or deflection material on it?"

"Negative."

Gerard smiled. "Okay, Ship, here's what we're going to do."

"Son of a bitch!" Ashron yelled as the mini-missile flew by the *Little Star*, close enough he could have read the projectile's model number. He banked away as the *Star's* warning light blared the approach of another missile.

"Now you tell me," the Lorothian growled at the console. The missile passed him and continued into the sky.

He spotted the attacker, a ten-foot-tall combat robot standing in the center of the courtyard. It had determined the shuttle as the most significant threat and launched its missiles. Ashron said a prayer of thanks to Ssarra that the robot was equipped with dumb missiles and not seekers.

"I got this," he said, knowing only Wolf had the firepower to even hurt the armored robot. But the MGoA could be better used elsewhere. Ashron has his own toys. "Drones launch."

Three circular shaped discs detached from the *Star's* underside and warbled in the air.

The robot was bringing chain guns to bear, apparently having calculated the inefficiency of its missiles against the nimble shuttle. The large caliber weapons would bifurcate the craft in seconds if it locked on. Ashron wouldn't let that happen. "Take out the big bad guy."

The drones formed into a triangle, repulsors glowing blue. They fired IR blasts at the robot, blinding it, and followed up with high-powered lasers on its fuel cell. Five seconds later, the robot exploded in a gout of orange flame. The shockwave reverberated across the courtyard. Debris flew. A shard of metal slammed into one of the drones, and it plummeted to the ground. Force rocked against the *Star*. The engines whined as Ashron brought the shuddering craft back under control. "Superior technology for the win," he said. "Someone's going to buy me a replacement for Sylvia."

He swung back around, eased the forward throttle, and kicked in the landing jets. Slug holes and blast burns cratered the walls. Bodies lay sprawled everywhere, many pierced by slender metal spikes. Ashron spotted Hawk, Wolf, and Thomas, and guided the shuttle to land near the alcove, noting with horror the Maratais' bodies lying on the ground. He tried to see if any of them were breathing when the backwash from the jets obscured his vision. A few seconds later the craft touched ground with a gentle thump.

"Touchdown. Let's go." Ashron unstrapped his belt and started to stand. Star-shaped cracks spread across the windshield as kinetic slugs struck. Wondering what was shattering their supposedly bullet and laser-proof glass, Ashron threw himself to the deck. As he pulled his Sub-Lazgun from the holster on his side, the windshield blew inward. Glass showered across the shuttle's floor. Shots smashed into the cabin, sending out muted thuds and electrical sputters as they struck chairs and panels.

Wolf's MGoA filled the air, drowning out all other noise. Ashron smiled as he cautiously reached up and keyed the door open. "Still on the roof, Laura?"

"Yes," Laura answered over the noise of her weapon. "More unfriendlies just arrived."

"Must be the second shift." Ashron started out the door and almost ran headlong into Wolf, who stood outside, a body slung over his shoulder. Hawk stood behind him with another small body.

"Take him," Wolf said, handing over Yoseph. "I'll get the Maratais,"

Ashron took a reflexive step back as he saw the child's raw torso. He recovered and took the boy from Wolf's arm. He gently laid

Yoseph in one of the chairs, yanked off his shirt, and laid it over the child's wounded chest.

Hawk placed the girl in another chair. Cold fury welled up inside Ashron at the site of the unconscious children. He narrowed his eyes and turned to Hawk.

"No time," Hawk said in answer to Ashron's implied question. "Cover Wolf and Thomas. When they get in, dust us off. Leave the drones to do covering fire, but get us out of here." He put a hand to his bleeding side. "I need to sit down." He collapsed onto one of the shuttle's benches.

Happy as it would make Ashron to level this place, he understood Hawk's request. They needed to leave before reinforcements arrived, and the children had to get help in Ship's med bay to have any chance of surviving.

Ashron slipped out of the shuttle and tried to keep eyes everywhere, his Sub LazGun in hand. Wolf had Yonath and Dona in his arms. Ashron did not look at them. He had seen enough as he landed the craft. He noticed Wolf, his shield a distant memory, had no less than twelve wounds. The Uraxian's skin, thick and tough as any combat armor, had kept the damage to a minimum.

Ashron spotted Thomas near a wall. The rookie seemed to be holding his own. "Come on, Thomas."

Thomas disengaged from the wall and ran. As he drew close, he glanced to his right. "Look out!" he shouted. He slammed into Ashron, knocking the Lorothian against the shuttle.

Gunfire erupted. A laser scored the side of the craft.

Thomas, a gun in both hands, returned fire.

"Get in," Ashron shouted as he shot toward the alcove where the men hid.

Thomas scuttled sideways, firing. One of the men went down as Thomas's blast eradicated his face.

A laser drained the last of the rookie's shield. A second beam burned into his abdomen, another struck his pelvis, and a slug slammed into his chest. He dropped with a scream. The holes in his stomach and leg smoked, leaving an acrid stench.

"Bastards," Ashron shouted. He held up his Sub-LazGun and

sprayed energy in the general direction of the assailants. One of them dropped to the ground, his knee burned. Another fell backward, blood and guts spilling from his ruined abdomen. The others retreated.

"Cover me," he shouted to Wolf. The large Uraxian took up a stance in the shuttle, MGoA aimed out the window. Ashron picked up Thomas, not wanting to leave his body behind. The Lorothian almost dropped him when his breath hitched.

"You're alive?" Ashron asked as he walked to the shuttle. "You idiot. I taught you about cover and concealment, and you weren't using either." He laid the wounded man next to the children. "Thank you for saving me."

Thomas gasped and went still. Ashron put his head on the man's chest. A heartbeat. Thin, faint, barely perceptible. "Don't you die on me. I don't want all that time I spent training you to go to waste."

"Get us out of here," Hawk told him.

"With pleasure." Ashron slid into the pilot chair and fired the jets. The shuttle jumped into the air. Five men ran from their hiding spot and fired at the ascending craft.

Ashron's nostrils flared as his eyes narrowed. "It's a shame they don't realize how dead they are."

He brought up the HUD and spotted Laura, outlined in green, and five other targets, giving off heat signatures, twenty meters east. Orange blossomed from weapons as they kept her pinned down. "Laura, heading your way. When I say duck, duck."

"Standing by to duck."

Ashron touched the HUD, highlighting the enemy targets. "Francine, you've been a great drone, but it's time to give your all."

Two beeps in Ashron's ear, and the drone broke from over the courtyard and glided toward the painted targets. A countdown ticked toward the moment of impact. At three seconds, Ashron said, "Laura, duck."

L aura ducked behind a metal conduit that ran across the roof and closed her light-intensified eyes. With a tremendous thunderclap, the drone detonated. Metallic thuds echoed through the conduit as shards of bone struck it, followed by the smack of flesh. A wave of heated, chemical-scented air washed over Laura, and several drops of warm blood struck her clothes.

After a few seconds, she stood and surveyed the damage. Three of the bodies were reduced to bits and chunks. Two had not been as severely mutilated, but were still unmistakably dead. One had been thrown into the pentice doorway, leaving a bloody, body-shaped imprint. His face was smashed inward, and his arms lay at odd angles. The other had been tossed roughly seven meters and somehow managed to become impaled upon a machine gun, the barrel protruding from his back.

"Cable coming down," Ashron said. Laura turned her head to the raft above her. A door in the hull slid open, and a metal cable played out. When it reached Laura, she clipped the carabineer to the duraluminum catch on her belt.

"Attached."

The cable hoisted her toward the shuttle like a fish reeled in toward a boat.

Shots rang out from the roof as a man ran from a doorway.

One of the slugs caught her in the left leg. All the feeling instantly disappeared. She screamed as another struck the inside of her right thigh. She spotted the guard aiming with his machine gun. Fighting off a wave of nausea, she pointed her pistol at the assailant.

"Go!" she screamed as she opened fire. The lurching raft threw off her aim, and only one of the five shots hit her target; it was enough to send the man to the floor and crawling for cover.

The slide locked back as she expended the last of her shots. She tried to re-holster the pistol. Her arm twitched; the gun fell from her grip.

She hung in the air, left leg dangling uselessly, as the cable reeled her toward the shuttle. She looked at the carnage in the courtyard, bodies strewn like carelessly dropped toys.

Moran was missing.

"Fifteen seconds," Ship told Gerard.

"Okay," Gerard paused for five more seconds. "Now!" he said.

Ship's tractor field generator hummed into life, and the beam reached aft, snagging the power net enclosed behind her. A muted roar filled the cockpit as the engines increased to full throttle, and several higher rumbles announced a salvo of HEAP missiles from Ship's two launchers.

Covering his ears at the sudden onslaught of noise, Trey yelled, "I hope this works."

Gerard watched the screens, smiling with satisfaction. The freighter's front bulkhead, unshielded from kinetic attacks, disintegrated in flame and debris under the point-blank missile fire, creating a large, jagged hole. The two Frigates, caught off guard by the sudden increase in Ship's speed, were pulled along by Ship's tractor beam.

As soon as Ship passed the threshold of the freighter, her electrical systems fell dead as the larger craft's static generator went to work. Inertia carried both Ship and the two frigates forward. Ship, having already calculated the approach based of the freighter's tractor beam pull, passed rapidly through the vessel's hold and straight out the newly created portal in the forward hull.

The Frigates did not fare as well. Their energy net, larger than the freighter's opening, struck the outer edge of the ship, unaffected by the electrical dampening field. The Frigates, unable to adequately compensate for the speed increase, continued forward. Like rocks on the end of a bolo, they swung inward, their energy net holding them captive.

They collided with the freighter halfway down its length. Cutting through it like shears through an aluminum can, they rammed head-on into each other. Trey watched the monitor with horrified fascination as two explosions briefly lit up space, followed quickly by a third flash as the freighter's power plant detonated. Within ten seconds the explosions stopped and the fragments of the three vessels scattered into the void.

"Good job, Ship," Gerard said. "Where's the Corsair?"

"Leaving," Ship said, lighting up the Corsair's position relative to theirs on the star map. The dot rapidly moved away.

"Perfect," Gerard said. "Send two missiles their way to drive home the point and then let's head for the planet. It sounds like they're going to need us."

W olf tugged on the cable, pulling Laura toward the shuttle faster than the winch could manage.

On his HUD, Ashron saw ten more armed men pour onto the fortress's roof. Bullets whined by the shuttle. "Laura"

"Stop yelling," Laura said. "My shield is back on. Just hurry up, before I pass out."

"I'm getting tired of these pricks," Ashron muttered. He engaged the autopilot, then reached into his large black bag and pulled out five eight-inch-long missiles held together by a metal rack. With a series of taps on the attached computer panel, he programmed the rockets. A glance back showed Wolf pulling Laura through the hatch. A lucky shot hit Wolf in the shoulder. His skin deflected the glancing strike; the slug hit the roof with a thin clang.

Once Laura was inside, Wolf slammed the hatch door shut. Bullets pinged harmlessly against the shuttle's bottom.

"Okay, we're gone," Ashron said. He pushed one last key on the computer pad, flung the missile pack out of the shuttle's missing windshield, and kicked in the craft's engines.

The missiles detached themselves from the metal pack and headed for five separate points along one of the fortress's outer walls.

The concussion from the small, powerful missiles rocked the shuttle with noise and force. Ashron checked his rear scope and saw that the wall, which had been fifteen meters tall and at least twenty-five long, had become a smoking, leveled ruin. Bricks, brick dust, and two shattered bodies filled the air and rained to the ground. Suddenly, several more explosions lit the night and buffeted the quickly departing shuttle.

Ashron smiled. *Secondaries,* he thought. *What a pleasant surprise.*

Putting his concentration back to piloting the craft, he said, "Guess it just wasn't your day, boys."

"Hawk, Laura, Ashron," Gerard's voice came over the speakers. "Are you there? Hello?"

"We're here," Ashron said as the noise of the explosion died down.

"We thought you were blown up," Trey said.

"No, just me playing with some of my toys."

"Is everybody okay?" Gerard asked.

Hawk sat on the bench, bleeding, his eyes half-closed. "You have command," he told Laura, and then passed out.

"We've got some problems," she told Gerard. "Fly Ship to that large field just beyond the spaceport. The *Star*'s flying erratically and I don't want to take any chances on Ashron landing it in town. No offense," Laura said aside to Ashron.

"No complaints here," Ashron said, fighting the shuttle's sudden urge to bank right.

"Trey, warm up the med bay and have blankets standing by when we land."

"Roger."

They heard the clatter of Trey's feet as he ran from the bridge and Gerard said, "Sitrep."

"Wolf has several minor wounds. Hawk's body armor is punctured near his kidney, and he may have some broken ribs. Yoseph and Patishi are in shock. Thomas has a third-degree burn on his abdomen and pelvis, and a puncture wound through his right lung." She paused. "I'm not sure Yoseph and Thomas are going to make it."

"What about you?" Gerard asked.

"Not bad. My legs are numb, but I'll be moving by the time we get to you. Wolf, get me the medkit." Laura grabbed her knife and cut her black pants away from the wounds, gritting her teeth at the pain. Blood flowed freely from her thigh wound and pooled on the shuttle's deck. She needed to fix it first.

Wolf opened the kit and sat it beside her. Laura grabbed a square pack of synthskin bandaging and a can of sterilizer. She limped over to Yoseph, who lay unconscious beside Hawk. She opened the pack, unfolded the translucent grafting material, and placed it over the boy's chest. He hissed and sucked in a breath as the patch sealed to his chest, coating it with anti-bacterials and painkillers. The hiss encouraged Laura. If Yoseph could feel pain, he wasn't too far gone. Assuming they could return to Ship's med bay, she had a chance to save him. She applied a burn foam to Thomas's stomach and pelvis, and a coagulant to the hole in his chest. He didn't move. It was the best she could do for him until they reached Ship

She returned to the medpack and ripped the can of regenerator from its holder. Popping the top, she sprayed her leg. Yellow foam formed over the cut. Biobots encased in the nutrient liquid burrowed into her skin as they sought out the intrusive metal slug. She took deep breaths and thought of warm sunshine and fresh water, willing the pain away as the tiny organisms did their work with almost magical speed. The foam disappeared as the last of the bots slipped into the injured flesh. Laura grabbed a sealer spray and coated the hole in her thigh. It would stop the bleeding until the biobots could finish their repairs.

"Shit," Ashron said as Laura repeated the process with the less serious wound on her left leg. "We're not out of this yet."

"What is it?" Laura asked.

"Two-seater gunship."

"Gerard, how far away are we?" Laura asked.

"Two minutes from the field," Gerard answered

"What's your position?"

"We're preparing to land."

"Ship."

"Yes, Laura."

"Prepare to fi- damn."

The craft shuddered as a laser blast scored, searing a large hole in the side and sending bits of liquefied metal raining into the cabin. Some hit Patishi; she screamed in pain, waking instantly. Ashron made a sharp bank to the right, the shuttle groaning in protest at the unorthodox maneuver. Warning lights blinked.

"Any more like that and she's going to shut down," Ashron said.

Hawk fell from the bench and woke up to find himself laying on a cold shuttle deck, his chest thrumming with pain and a chill wind whipping through the craft. "What the hell's going on?" He shouted over the wind's roar.

"We've got a light gunship preparing to atomize us," Ashron yelled back.

"Is that all?"

"Sorry to disappoint you," Ashron said. He sent the ship into a steep dive as a missile flew past. A side panel hummed ominously for a second and then blew up, showering sparks and sending a chunk of metal past Wolf's ear.

Hawk pulled himself up to rest against the bench, wincing as more pains called for his attention. "How far to Ship?" he asked.

"About a minute-fifteen."

"Ship, vaporize this thing behind us."

"There are buildings in the way, Captain, and I have no straight line shot. If you can make it to the clearing, I will honor your request."

"Wolf," Hawk said, "get one of the laser cannons out and mount it on the hardpoint. We need to swing around and take these guys down." He started to pull himself up as Wolf walked toward the back of the shuttle. "Whose idea was it to go in with the weapons stored."

"Yours," Laura reminded him. "'In and out. No fuss. Nothing to slow us down.' Remember? Don't move; you're in no condition." The bullet fell from her left leg with a small metallic *clink*. She flexed it slightly and winced.

"Should have had both weapons mounted from the start," Ashron said.

"Yeah," Hawk said, "that wouldn't have raised any red flags." He couldn't see the short Lorothian in the pilot's chair. "Our lives are in your hands, Ashron. Screw up and you're fired."

"I can't begin to tell you how much that worries me," Ashron said. Another laser glanced off the side, sending the ship careening downward. Ashron struggled to bring the raft back to level flight. He succeeded just as the whine of the engines died out.

"Great," Ashron punched the emergency glide key. Short stabilizing wings popped out of either side. "You can leave the laser in the locker; it's scrap metal now."

Wolf slammed the locker door, the giant cannon untouched. Patishi crawled over to Laura, who wrapped her arms protectively around the little girl.

"How far to the clearing?" Hawk asked.

"About another thirty seconds. Without power, we're sitting ducks."

"These guys are beginning to irritate me," Hawk said.

"Funny, I said the same thing a few minutes ago," Ashron told him.

Hawk stood and hobbled to the front of the shuttle, ignoring Laura's protests. He reached into Ashron's bag and pulled out one of his grenades. "What's the delay on these things?"

"Three seconds," Ashron said. He banked left as another laser cracked past the helpless craft. "You don't really think you can hit them, do you?"

"No, but it might shake 'em up." Standing on the co-pilot's chair and ignoring the screaming from his ribs, Hawk leaned out the shattered window and poked his head above the roof; the cold wind whipped his hair into his face. Through the flailing strands, he watched the small gun craft as it zigzagged, trying to keep up with Ashron's erratic maneuvers. Hawk pressed the button on the grenade and tossed it, trying his best to aim at the craft. His side twitched in protest at the sudden movement, and a wave of pain almost pulled him under.

Though the grenade fell far short of the small gunboat, the vehicle's pilot obviously wasn't expecting the massive explosion that flared in front of and underneath his vessel with a cacophonous boom. He peeled his craft upward.

"That should throw him off for a moment," Hawk said as he carefully lowered himself back into the shuttle.

It did more than that. The pilot of the gun craft, in pulling up to avoid the explosion, cleared the highest building, bringing his vessel within sight of Ship's tracking sphere.

"I've got him," Ship said. The air crackled as red fire from her pulse laser briefly lit up the night. The gun craft exploded into chunks of molten, blazing metal. "They won't bother you anymore," Ship said.

"Good." Ashron had followed the laser trail backward and spotted Ship in the clearing. The roof of a frighteningly close and tall building lay between them and the field.

"Strap in, everyone, this is going to be rough." He pulled back on the stick, nudging the craft into an upward angle, painfully aware of the possibility of stalling.

He did not stall; they cleared the roof by less than a meter.

"Now comes the tricky part," Ashron muttered. He launched into a sharp dive and leveled off at ten meters. Gerard and Trey stood outside Ship, next to the large, black armored personnel carrier from Ship's cargo bay. Concern danced on their faces.

The *Little Star* was descending rapidly. Ashron suspected they were about to learn what was meant by the term "controlled crash."

At least, he hoped he could control it.

The shuttle hit hard and slid along the ground, creating a deep trench in its wake as it flung aside mud and grass. They skidded twenty meters before the dead vehicle dug its nose into the side of a small hill and came to an abrupt stop. The unbuckled Ashron slammed against the joystick. The impact snapped it in two, forcing the air out of him. He lay against the dash panel, stunned. They stopped two hundred meters away from Ship.

Laura's legs had finished healing. She carefully stood up, still clutching the frightened Patishi.

Hawk headed for the door, his hand pressed to his side. He pushed the door open, grunting with the effort. The deep hum of the approaching APC drifted into the cabin.

"Wolf," Hawk said, leaning against the doorway and breathing heavily. "Get the Maratais. I'll get Yoseph."

"You get in the carrier." Laura sat Patishi down. "You've probably got some broken ribs, and you're begging for a punctured lung."

"Okay," Hawk said. He was captain, but he trusted his second's diagnostic ability. When she took on her Medical Officer voice, he listened. "Come with me, Patishi." The frightened girl staggered over to him, and they left the shuttle. "Let's get the hell out of here. Ashron, you okay?"

"I'm fine," he answered, giving his head a shake and rubbing a hand across his long snout. "Just a momentary lapse of breathing capability."

"Can you get Yoseph and Thomas?"

"Affirmative." He walked over to the unconscious boy and gently lifted him.

With a stiff gait, Laura stepped out of the raft and passed Trey, who held out the medkit. He quickly turned around and followed her into the ATV. "Trey, help Hawk out of his chem armor."

Hawk sat near the back with Patishi standing beside him, so Trey headed aft.

Ashron stepped into the car, Yoseph's bloody body resting in his arms. Wolf squeezed in behind him, a Maratai over each shoulder.

"Up here," Laura said to Ashron, moving to the front where Gerard waited with a second kit. "Trey, get a blanket for Patishi first."

"Okay." Trey set a small silver can next to Hawk, then grabbed one of the soft blankets off the rack and gently wrapped it around the scared child. Hawk slowly removed his shirt, groaning at the pain.

Ashron laid Yoseph down on the APC's couch and left the shuttle. Laura opened the kit, removed a small diagnostic computer, and attached the diodes to the boy's forehead.

Ashron returned carrying Thomas and put him in a sitting position on the couch. The transport had become cramped

Laura picked up a pressure hypo and extracted a dose of *Metanastin*, an anti-shock drug. Taking Yoseph's arm, she gave him the injection. Gerard hopped into the driver's seat, keyed the door shut, and kicked the APC into drive.

"How does he look, Trey?" Laura asked, catching the acrid smell as Trey sprayed armor remover on Hawk's chest.

"He's got one bullet hole, and I think some ribs are broken."

"That's what I figured." She tossed an insti-dose bottle of tripta-morphine to Trey. "Give him that."

Trey put the small bottle against Hawk's arm and pressed the red button on top. There was a *whoosh* of compressed air as the bottle's contents injected themselves.

"Ouch," Hawk said. "You'd think with today's technology they would have developed a non-painful shot."

Ashron smiled. "You'd think a man who could walk around with a couple of broken ribs and a bullet hole in him wouldn't let a shot bother him."

"We didn't get Moran," Laura said.

"What do you mean?" Hawk said. "You put a laser through his eye."

"And I blew up a fortress around him," Ashron said.

"I saw sparks," Laura told them. "He had something under the patch. And his body was gone."

"Son of a bitch," Hawk said.

"Maybe the building fell on his head," Ashron offered.

"I'm not going to count on it. He's alive until someone proves otherwise. I need a body or a pile of melted bones."

Gerard drove the APC into its cradle and stopped. With a hiss of hydraulics, the cradle began its ascent into ship's hold.

Laura picked up Yoseph and stood by the APC's door, foot tapping. "Everyone to the med bay," she said.

"Okay," Gerard said. The rest of the crew gathered themselves to depart. Ashron picked up Thomas.

As soon as the cradle shuttered to a stop and the APC door slid open, Laura dashed for the elevator, Yoseph cradled to her chest.

1 2

DEADLY RECOVERY

"I think that's the last of them." Laura dropped another piece of metal into the plastic dish that sat on the medtable. It clinked against its brothers before settling in the dish. "Fifteen slugs and eleven laser burns. That's a record for you, isn't it?"

Wolf's mouth straightened in what passed for a smile on his dour face. "It is. I can feel every one of them."

As Laura put her instruments in the sterilizer, Wolf lifted a gallon jug of salt water and drank. As he slept, his body would metabolize the salt and repair the damage to his protective outer skin.

"Put on your shirt," Laura said, "and let's join the others. I could use a drink."

With another straight-mouthed grin, Wolf held the jug toward her.

Laura returned his smile. "Thanks, but I prefer mine with olives."

They had been back on Ship for four hours. Laura had tended to everybody, Gerard assisting after he and Ship took them into orbit. Laura had managed to stabilize Yoseph after an hour and several units of blood, followed by a coagulating agent and a fresh synthskin patch applied to his ravaged chest. She felt confident he would live but would require major surgery to remove the chest scar.

Except for some scratches, bruising and a catatonic stare, Patishi was uninjured. Laura bathed her and administered a mild sedative; she slept in one of the warmed medical bay beds.

She had spent an hour on Thomas, fixing his burns and puncture. Separately, each injury should have killed him, but he was tougher than he looked and had somehow hung on despite all the abuse. Laura had administered biobots to repair the damage. The extent of his injuries would require him to remain under sedated treatment for at least two weeks.

Hawk had three broken ribs, a slug lodged near his kidney, and a nasty gash across the back of his head. A dose of biobots and two hours under the skeletal knitter left him with nothing but stiffness that would last a few days.

Wolf had been last. None of the bullets or lasers had penetrated his thick, sodium-silicon laced skin. Had he gone without treatment, the minor burns would have healed and the slugs would have worked their way out like festering splinters. But Wolf didn't enjoy the discomfort of fifteen globs of metal wedged under his skin, so Laura removed them.

Wolf slipped on his light blue pullover shirt, and they walked toward the wardroom, Laura moving with a slight stiffness. Like Hawk, she would be sore for several days. As they entered the wardroom, Ashron looked at them, then at Hawk.

"Well," the Lorothian said, "I would like to state unequivocally that that plan sucked oranges. What do we do now?"

"As I see it, we need to get word to the Council about what happened," Hawk said. "We'll have to get Yoseph and Patishi to a hospital with their grandparents. We can probably set Thomas there too if he's recovered, and pay for transport wherever he'd like to go. He deserves at least that."

"He did me proud," Ashron said. "I hope there's at least a commendation and a renewal of his training in his future."

At Hawk's instruction, Trey had set out small glasses on a platter, along with a bottle of Scotch from the captain's private reserve. Hawk uncorked the bottle and filled each glass. "Take one."

Everyone reached in and grabbed a glass. Trey stepped away.

"You too," Hawk said. "You were as much a part of this as anyone."

Trey glanced at Laura. She frowned at Hawk.

"He earned it," Hawk told her.

Face still grim, she nodded. Trey picked up the glass.

"'And the fever called living is conquered at last.'" He raised his glass.

"'All that tread the globe are but a handful to the tribes that slumber in its bosom.'" Gerard quoted, raising his glass, a tear running down his cheek.

The others raised their glasses.

"To Yonath and Dona Maratai," Laura said. "May they be forever in our memories, and forever ensconced in the bosom of the Almighty Creator of the universe."

They each drained their glass in silence. Trey grimaced at the taste. They stood, each lost in their thoughts.

A nerve-shattering scream echoed through the hall, smashing the stillness.

"Yoseph," Wolf said.

Laura raced out the door, followed closely by Hawk and Ashron, with Gerard, Trey, and Wolf bringing up the rear. The screams grew louder and more frantic as they rounded the corner to the med bay. Glass and metal crashed.

Bursting through the door, they found Yoseph convulsing on the floor. An overturned cart left, instruments strewn about the floor. Patishi huddled in the corner of the room, wide-eyed with terror despite the sedative. Thomas lay on a bed meters away, oblivious.

Laura ran to Yoseph, trying to grab his wildly flailing arms. His open hand smashed into her nose; she fell back, bloodied and stunned.

Wolf pushed past everyone and grabbed Yoseph, who continued to flail even under the Uraxian's firm grip. The boy's screams were almost deafening.

Laura pulled herself off the floor, wiping absently at her nose as she walked toward the dispensing cabinet.

"What's going on?" Hawk had to yell to be heard.

"I don't know," Laura shouted back. She grabbed a dose of tripta-morphine and injected it into the boy's arm.

The screams grew louder and more frantic. One of Yoseph's hands latched onto Wolf's arm and squeezed with such force that his fingernails bent trying to dig into the armored skin.

"Put him on the bed."

The screams went silent as the boy keened beyond the range of human hearing. Ashron shuddered and put his hands against his tympanic membranes to drown out the piercing screech.

Yoseph stopped in mid-scream, eyes and mouth open, frozen in the act of yelling. Wolf laid him on the bed and stepped away. Trey, hands over his ears and tears pouring down his face, looked once at Yoseph and fled the room.

The rest of the crew stood, stunned and shaken. Laura walked over to the boy, her face ashen. She spoke with a frightening mechanical flatness. "I've got to perform an autopsy. Please leave."

"Should I assi—" Gerard said.

"No," she said, her stricken voice barely above a whisper. "I'll do it. Just leave."

Taking the sobbing Patishi with them, they walked out. She closed the door behind them.

⸻

Hawk sat in a spacious cabin that suddenly felt too confining. A half-finished bottle of bourbon sat beside an empty bottle on his desk. Except for Laura and himself, the crew had long since gone to bed. Hawk had placed Patishi in the guest quarters, where she reacted to nothing he said or did. Hawk had covered her with a blanket and left her with the lights lowered.

Unwilling to be alone in his cabin, Trey slept in Hawk's bed. The boy refused to admit he was upset, but explained that he was "keeping an eye" on Hawk: in case Hawk needed him. Hawk grinned at the boy's bravado as he reached for the glass of bourbon.

Hawk drained the last of the liquor. He saw movement distorted through the bottom of the glass. He set it down and the blur resolved into Laura. "Can I get you something to drink?" he asked her.

"Please. Water would be fine." She sat on the bed beside Trey, careful to not wake him.

Hawk walked over to his small bar and returned with a glass of ice water and another bottle of bourbon. As he handed the water to Laura and removed the seal from the bourbon, the bitter irony of his recent promise to stop drinking came to mind. He had predicted more people would disappear from his life; he never thought it would be so many so soon in such a brutal way.

He refilled his snifter.

Laura gently stroked Trey's brown hair. "You know, my little boy would be about as old as Yoseph was…" She let the thought trail off as she took a drink of water. As Hawk sipped his bourbon, he noticed her trembling hands. He sat back in the chair and waited.

"I don't know where to start." She gazed absently at the reflections in the ice cubes. With a heavy sigh, she began. "I narrowed down the times of death to within minutes. It appears that Patishi, Dona, and Yoseph were strung up, and mother and son beaten. This was over a long period and before Yonath was killed, so I assume it was done in front of him as a form of torture. He was killed first, very slowly over a span of about three hours. After Dona and the children witnessed their father's death, these animals continued amusing themselves with Dona and Yoseph."

Laura stopped, overcome. She finished the water, her hand visibly shaking. Hawk waited until she gained control. He didn't have to ask why they had left Patishi mostly unharmed.

"I place Dona's time of death roughly fifteen minutes before you entered the fortress, so they must have stopped when they knew we would be arriving."

"What killed Yoseph?"

"They planned it very well. Knowing his wound would need immediate attention, they injected a drug in his body that would greatly enhance any coagulating agent introduced to stop the bleeding."

Hawk slowly grasped what Laura was saying. "That would mean…"

"His blood jelled while he was alive and his heart burst," Laura finished for him. "It's a rare drug not programmed in the scanners. I would never have even thought to look for it."

"Moran, you sick sadistic bastard," Hawk said, shuddering as he emptied the glass.

"That stuff is going to kill you," Laura chided.

"Probably not before a laser does. Very few people in our profession collect retirement." Hawk set the glass down and pushed the bottle away. "How's Patishi?"

"She's gone completely catatonic. I think seeing what happened to her brother pushed her over the edge. I'm going to go back and work with her as soon as I take a little break."

"No, you're not," Hawk said gently. "You're going to get some sleep, and you can work with her tomorrow."

"But—"

"No arguments. Captain's orders. I'm not a doctor, but I know that if she's catatonic, she's not going anywhere anytime soon. If there's any change in her condition, Ship will let you know. I need you fresh and rested. We all have a lot of things to discuss tomorrow."

Laura pulled a small plastic bag out of her shirt pocket and tossed it in Hawk's lap. "I found this attached next to Yonath's spine."

An almost microscopically small black chip rested inside the bag. "What is it?"

"I have no idea."

"I know someone who will," Hawk stood. "Sit tight. I'll be right back." As he left his cabin, Hawk said, "Ship, wake Gerard up and tell him I'm coming."

"I'll do no such thing. It's three AM ship time. If you want someone awakened at this ungodly hour, you'll have to do it yourself."

Hawk decided against arguing. She was right; it would be politer to be rude personally.

When he reached Gerard's room, he gave a light tap on the door, not so much to wake Gerard as to let ROMANCE know someone was about to enter. Gerard assured them his Remote Operated Mechanical Annihilator of Nuisances, Creeps and Enemies knew everyone on board and was programmed not to hurt any of them. But Hawk took no chances when it came to a metal trapezoid that could do severe damage to the entire ship on a whim. He knew full well ROMANCE's sensors had him pinpointed and that the robot's laser could slag the wall that stood between them. He hid there anyway.

"Ship, open the door."

The door slid open. Hawk peeked around the corner. Sure enough, ROMANCE sat there with its laser sighted, primed and ready to vaporize. Hawk raised a tentative hand and waved at the stupid thing, convinced the machine hated him out of pure spite. ROMANCE beeped in a contemptible sort of way, almost as if to say Hawk wasn't worth his time. It moved to the foot of the bed. Hawk walked over to Gerard and gently shook him by the shoulder.

Gerard rolled over, and his sleepy eyes found Hawk. "Yeah?"

"Sorry to bother you. Laura found this on Yonath's spine. We have no idea what to make of it. Do you know what it is?"

Gerard sat up and studied the chip. After a moment, he reached into his nightstand and took out a loupe. He fit the magnifier to his eye and examined the device.

"No, it can't be." He sat up and examined it closer. After a moment, he picked up a palm computer off his nightstand, tapped on the screen, and studied the readout. "That's what it is all right," he said, handing it back to Hawk. "It's a body transmitter."

"And that is?"

"A biological transmitting device that picks up all audio within about thirty meters and transmits it to a special receiver," Gerard leaned back against the pillow. "State of the art, extremely rare and expensive like you don't want to know."

"When you say 'biological,' how specifically do you define that?"

"It's an actual living device," Gerard answered. "Unlike biobots, it's totally organic, with no cybernetic parts. It amplifies neural energy for its power supply, uses bone for its transmission conductor, and takes nutrients from blood. The spine is the best place to position it. Since it's not a mechanical device, it's—"

"Undetectable by normal bug monitors," Hawk finished.

"Exactly."

Hawk considered Gerard's information for a moment. "I haven't heard anything about the Council using this. Have you?"

"No," Gerard answered. "The Council wouldn't. Too risky."

"Why's that?"

"The rejection rate is about fifty-fifty. Rejection results in a massive neural overload and agonizing death."

"Thanks, Gerard, you've been a big help."

"Always happy to do it," Gerard said.

Hawk left Gerard's cabin and walked toward his own. As he moved through the hall, he speculated on the origin of the chip. Had Yonath had it installed? No, he wasn't that kind of risk taker, and Hawk could think of no benefits. The Council hadn't done it, which left Unicybertronic Technologies. It was possible that it was standard procedure, but Hawk couldn't picture any corporation risking its executives on an operation which only half the patients survived. Hawk also couldn't imagine many people willingly letting their privacy be so violated.

The only thing Hawk could figure was that UCT knew Yonath was a spy and planted the device on him. Even that didn't make sense, unless they were planning for the long run, using the device to find out what they could about the Council.

Too many questions, too long a day, he thought as he reached his cabin and the door opened. "Laura, I—"

She was sound asleep. Her head rested against the wall; her hand lay on Trey's shoulder. Hawk slipped two blankets out of the closet. One went over Trey; the other Laura. He turned off the desk lamp and headed for the wardroom.

"Why is it people always want to cover up someone who's sleeping when it's obvious they're quite comfortable already, or else they wouldn't be sleeping?" Ship said as Hawk entered the wardroom.

"I'm not keeping you busy enough," Hawk told her. He grabbed a blanket from the closet and headed for the wardroom.

Laura awoke to Trey's sobs. He still slept even as tears ran down his face and a low keening sound issued from his throat. She softly stroked his hair; her heart ached at the torments he must be reliving in his dreams. Though he didn't talk about it, she knew Trey had seen more abominations than a person five times his age should be forced to witness. Laura had brought him to Ship so he would never have to experience anything like that again. It seemed his horror quotient was not used up yet.

"Mom, Dad, NO!" he cried out, pure anguish leaping from his child's voice. The flood of tears doubled.

"Shhh!" Laura shed her tears. She rested her head against the wall and softly rubbed Trey's back. "Shh, honey. Mama's here."

That's what she considered herself. She had lost a son; he had lost a mother. It only seemed right the two of them be together. Trey had never told them how his parents died, either because he didn't want to, or because he couldn't. Whatever the cause, it tormented him in his dreams.

She pulled up the cover and thought of her son, the offspring of a brutal rape by a person Laura had considered a friend. There was no police report or trial. Laura had caught up with him and dispensed her own justice. Though he still lived when she last saw him, the man would rape no other women.

Despite the circumstances of his conception, Laura had loved her little Garritt fiercely. She treated him like the king of the universe, for he was the king of *her* universe. She vowed she would raise him to be a kind, strong man. Her dreams focused on the great things he would do.

Those dreams shattered one afternoon on a city street. A thief, fleeing from the police, ran between her and her boy and pushed him into the street. She screamed a warning, but the car's driver never even saw the small child. She ran to the boy, hoping against hope as a curious crowd gathered. He was dead before he hit the pavement. Even she, expert healer that she was, did not have the power to restore life.

But she did have the power to protect the one who rested fitfully beside her, and she again vowed to do all she could to keep him from harm.

She returned to a fitful sleep, the two of them crying silently at the injustice of the Universe.

THE NEXT MOVE

Wolf rumbled to the wardroom to start breakfast, his thick body almost brushing the passageway walls. As he slid sideways through the hatch, he found Hawk slumped over in one of the dark blue lounge chairs. A blanket lay bundled on the floor, partially covering his leg. Wolf walked into the kitchen, started a pot of coffee, and put two pans on the stove. Ship could have had breakfast prepared before he even woke, but Wolf preferred his cooking. As did the rest of the crew.

Wolf pulled out eggs and bacon—the crew's favored breakfast despite the variety of exotic cuisines available to them—and laid several strips into one of the heated pans. He grabbed a bowl and began cracking eggs, enjoying the quiet solitude before the rest of the crew awoke and wandered in. Calm was a rare commodity on Ship, and Wolf valued every bit of it. Peace had been atypical at his home back on Urax, too. Especially when, on his sixteenth birthday, he announced he would not be following the genotype occupation laid out for him by the *Geneseers* eleven years before. He vowed to pursue his dream.

From that moment, noise had filled his world. Shouts from his mother buffeted him, threats from his father assailed him, and condemnation from many of his friends wounded him. He bore it all with the stoicism of his genetic makeup. Only his eleven-year-old sister supported his decision, and she had no voice in the family councils.

Two years later, the noise stopped as he stunned them into silence by declaring his intention to leave Urax and see the universe. In the current times, younger Uraxians often left, to the chagrin of the elder population. When Wolf did it fifteen years ago, it had been nearly unthinkable. The planetary government punished him with permanent banishment and compensated his family for the "loss" of their son.

Only Hawk and Gerard knew of his scandalous past; Wolf grinned as he wondered what the others would think to discover their taciturn engineer had once been a firebrand of progressive rebellion.

As the brewing coffee passed the halfway point, Hawk stirred. Quiet time would soon be over. Wolf pulled out the half-full pot and filled Hawk's cup. He added an unhealthy dose of sugar and cream. After filling his bowl-sized cup, he replaced the pot in the brewer, walked into the wardroom, and put Hawk's cup within reach.

"Thanks," Hawk said, rubbing the sleep out of his eyes.

Wolf nodded and sipped at his coffee.

Hawk kicked the blanket off his leg and sat up. He groaned as his patched ribs began the first of their several days of dull aching. "I guess I deserve this," he said, cracking his stiff back. "That's the last time I sleep on this chair." He grabbed the coffee cup and took a sip.

"I've heard that before," Wolf said.

"Yeah, but I was sober last night. Well, *mostly* sober."

Wolf grunted. "Why didn't you sleep in the second guest cabin?"

"Because that would have made sense, and I wouldn't be able to spend the rest of the day bitching about my sore back. Correct me if I'm wrong, but I smell bacon."

Wolf returned to the kitchen.

Hawk drank his coffee as he watched Wolf walk away, savoring the warmth and sweetness of the sugar-laced drink. It always amazed him how much more he appreciated the small things after a brush with death. Colors shone brighter, and tastes were more vibrant. The world around him was heightened as if adrenaline pumped through his body for days after the encounter instead of hours.

That's what kept him in this profession. Not the excitement or the money. It was the afterglow, the feeling of euphoria that he survived another day when others didn't. He supposed that's what kept a lot of people doing this work until the day came when they made a wrong move and became one of the others. It would no doubt happen to him one day; that idea hadn't bothered him for five years.

The smell of eggs mingled with the bacon and Hawk's stomach growled. He finished his coffee and stood to get some more. Trey walked into the room, still wearing the green shirt and gray shorts he had worn to bed. Tousled hair and bags under his bloodshot eyes gave testament to a restless sleep.

"Rough night?" Hawk asked.

Trey flopped into a chair. "I dreamed about…home."

That simple statement told Hawk all he needed to know about how bad yesterday's events had upset the boy. "You okay?"

Trey didn't say anything for a moment. "I don't know. I guess…I…there's just so much I don't understand."

"Want to talk about it?"

Trey shook his head. "Not right now."

Hawk nodded. If Trey needed to work it out on his own, Hawk wouldn't force him to do otherwise. He suspected the boy would open up to Laura, or maybe Gerard. He walked into the kitchen and poured some more coffee.

"I'll take a cup," Laura said, walking into the wardroom.

"Okay." Hawk poured another cup and left the kitchen. "Jesus, didn't anybody sleep well last night?" he asked, seeing Laura's haggard expression.

"I don't think I'll be able to sleep well for a year," Laura answered as she took the coffee from Hawk. "How are your ribs?"

"They hurt like hell. My back's stiff, too."

"You fell asleep in that chair again, didn't you?"

"Yeah."

"Sorry we took your bed."

"That's okay. I could have slept in the guest room." Hoping to lighten Trey's melancholy, he said, "You better quit sleeping with this woman. Someone might get jealous."

Trey blushed. "I need some milk." He jumped up and ran to the kitchen.

"You're a very wicked person," Laura told Hawk.

"Any change with Patishi?"

Laura shook her head. "If she doesn't improve in the next few hours, I'm going to have to feed her intravenously."

"Thomas?"

"Good. He is one tough man. He's going to recover. With a proper hospital, he'd be out in a week. I'll keep him sedated and mending until we can get him to one."

Ashron bounded into the room. "Good morning, everybody. I trust everyone slept well?" His teeth showed through his wide-mouthed grin. Four wilting stares met him. Still smiling, his eyes roamed from face to face as his tongue darted in and out.

After a moment he said, "Apparently not." He nodded and changed his grin to a tight snarl. "Get me some coffee, dammit."

He grabbed the proffered cup from Wolf and plopped down into one of the vacant chairs across the room, a stern expression on his face.

"When in Rome, eh, Ashron?" Gerard said from the doorway, having witnessed the entire incident.

Still snarling, Ashron winked.

Trey, a glass of milk in his hand, gave Ashron a puzzled gaze. "How can you joke right now?"

Ashron's return stare was a saurian mirror of Trey's. "What's wrong with right now?"

"People died yesterday. Your friends. A—" his voice cracked, and he paused for a moment. "A kid. Shouldn't they get more than jokes?"

"They did," Ashron said, setting his coffee cup down and holding out his scaled hands. He flexed them and his talons extended.

"What happened to your claws?" Trey asked. Three were missing: two from the left hand, one from the right.

"I pulled them out," Ashron said. "One for each of the Maratais, friends that I failed to protect. I mourned them privately last night and sacrificed part of my body to their memory. The claws will grow back, and the pain will remind me every day of their sacrifice. But I can't stop joking and laughing and living. To do so would be false to myself and a dishonor to them." He retrieved his coffee cup and sat back.

"People mourn in different ways," Laura walked over and sat at the table. "Most of us choose to remember the best of those we've lost and carry on."

"That doesn't always work," Hawk muttered.

"Not always, but most of the time," Laura said. "You grieve for them however you see fit," she told Trey.

Trey nodded, his face thoughtful as he walked into the kitchen.

Gerard emerged from the kitchen with a cup of coffee. "It may have been a dream, but I seem to recall being awakened in the night and shown a rare body transmitter. Someone care to explain?"

Laura described the results of her autopsies and the discovery of the microchip.

Wolf leaned over the bar that separated wardroom from the kitchen. "What does the chip do?"

Gerard quickly went over the workings of the transmitting device.

"How difficult would it be to install one?" Hawk asked Laura.

It would require at least laparoscopic surgery," she answered. "Yonath's appendix was missing, so the chip could have been planted then. But why would anyone bother?"

Gerard spoke up. "How about this? Someone at Unicybertronic found out he was working for the Council. They bugged him so they could monitor the information he was sending to the Council and make sure he hadn't stumbled on to anything incriminating. They would also have a way to discover Council operations when he went back. If he died, it would be blamed on post-surgery infection, and they would be rid of a spy."

"That thought crossed my mind last night," Hawk said. "They were certainly planning for the long run."

"They didn't become the largest cybernetics company in the galaxy by being short-sighted."

"I don't know about this chip," Ashron said, "but I do have a few questions. Who set us up? Why do they want us so badly? Why is Moran involved? And when are we going to eat? The smell of bacon is about to drive me crazy."

Wolf walked back in with a large bowl full of scrambled eggs and a plate of bacon in his hands. Trey followed close behind, carrying dishes and silverware.

"Breakfast," Wolf announced.

"Well, that answers one question," Ashron took a plate and fork from Trey. "I don't think the others are going to be as easy."

"Which one would you like answered first?" Gerard asked.

"Doesn't matter."

"Then I'll start with the easiest. Moran's involvement is simply a matter of personal revenge. He said as much during the confrontation with Hawk. You're aware his split with the Knights was not exactly amicable."

"What happened between the Knights and him?" Laura asked. She and Ashron had joined the group shortly after Moran's departure. Although they knew it was a bitter separation, they were never told the details.

Hawk shook his head. "Not yet. I'm not ready. Someday, maybe."

Laura nodded. "Do you suppose Moran was behind the whole set-up?"

"Interesting thought," Gerard answered. "Though I have trouble picturing Moran as a lieutenant in a third-rate terrorist group, I could see him using one as a front."

"He was behind it," Hawk said. "He may not have been working alone, but I'd be willing to bet Ashron's job that he made the major decisions."

"Thanks," Ashron said dryly.

"So who financed him?" Laura asked. "Their tech wasn't the best, but it was still a pretty big operation we stepped into."

"Ship, is the TDF big enough to support an operation of that size?" Hawk asked.

"Yes and no. They have the connections to come up with that kind of capital. After all, they are known galaxy-wide. However, to do so, they would have to convince their backers that the expenditure would be worth the political gain."

"So what you're saying is that they wouldn't back Moran simply for personal reasons, so there's more to this than meets the eye."

"I wouldn't have been so cliché but, basically, yes."

"So, to sum up," Hawk said, "Moran is involved in a plot to wipe out The Knights. He's involved with the TDF deep enough to get them to devote a large number of their resources to a seemingly personal operation. I see three possible reasons. One: there's something more than personal revenge involved we don't know about. Two: Moran is actually the leader of the TDF, and they will do what he says, or—Three: Moran paid for the operation and used the TDF as a front."

"I think we can safely discount the second reason," Gerard said. "Moran could certainly be in charge of a group like that, but I don't think it fits his style."

Hawk nodded. "Even though I mentioned it, I have trouble with number three. Moran was never what you'd call thrifty. I can't see him having that kind of funding himself."

"Which would indicate he has someone backing him," Laura said. "UCT?"

"I have trouble believing that," Gerard said. "Revenge is not a profitable business."

"Which means there's a reason behind it other than personal revenge," Hawk took a drink from his coffee cup.

Ashron crossed his wide-spaced eyes and turned to Trey, who giggled despite his glum mood.

"I feel like we're running around in circles," Ashron said. "What do we do next?"

There was a moment of silence and Hawk, sensing something was wrong, lowered his coffee cup and peered over the rim. Ten curious eyes stared at him. "What?"

"You're the Captain," Ashron said. He stood up and saluted. "Lead us, O Fearless Wonder."

"Well," Hawk set down his cup. "The first thing I want you to do is step into the airlock and open the outer door. The rest of us are going to travel to ZT-3235."

"What's that?" Ashron asked.

"It's a dead planetoid."

Ashron exhaled from his long snout, letting out a sound between a sigh and a hiss. "I could guess that from its designation. What I meant is: why do we need to go there?"

"It's the nearest place without jumping into ripspace where I can get a direct transmitter link to Force 13. I need to get a message to them."

"Why don't you just relay it?" Trey asked.

"Until we have a better idea what we're up against, I'd rather do it directly. Force 13's relays are tight, but even they can be tapped into. If anyone knows how to do it, it's Moran. Okay, here's the plan. As soon as we're in range, I'll contact the Council and give them a debriefing. In the meantime, we need to determine if UCT is involved and to what extent. They wrote Yonath off pretty quickly, and they're the prime suspects for planting the bug on him. Laura, I want you to find out what you can about that chip. Who creates them, how you get one, what it would cost. Anything that would help narrow down how it got into Yonath."

"I'll check his medical records and find out when he had his appendix removed," she told him.

"Good. We also need to figure out how much Moran is involved in this. Gera—" he stopped at the frown on Gerard's pale face. "What's wrong?"

Gerard removed his baseball cap and scratched his head. "I'm not sure. Something doesn't fit, but I can't tell what it is."

"There are several things that don't fit."

"How many days before we're in range to call Council," Gerard asked.

"Ship?"

"Three."

"Thank you."

"Do you need me for anything right now?" Gerard asked.

"No," Hawk replied. He learned a long time ago that when Gerard found something perplexing, it was because he had noticed a fact the others had missed, but he would never say anything until he was confident it was worth mentioning.

Nodding, Gerard stood up and walked out of the room.

Standing, Laura said. "I have to go see Patishi and Thomas."

"Well then, meeting adjourned," Hawk said to no one in particular, going back to his half-finished plate of eggs.

14

TREY'S LESSON

Hours later, Trey sat in his room staring at nothing. Depression warred with anger for control of his emotions. His life on Ship had begun to give him a sense that the Universe was a sane place, something he had not felt for a long time.

Yesterday's events had shattered that illusion.

Last night, dreams of Kel had returned after months of absence. Friends lived again, only to be slaughtered by glass-eyed soldiers. His parents died again, their plasma-inflicted burns torturing them until they begged Trey to end their suffering. In the dream, Trey always refused, telling them to sleep and it would all be over. At his words, his parents would smile, tell him they loved him, and drift into peaceful death.

The dream had always been better than the reality.

Today's events were little better. He struggled to comprehend the crew's reactions. They seemed casual. As if yesterday never happened. As if three people they knew hadn't been savaged almost beyond recognition. Even worse, he struggled to understand his reaction. The years on Kel had numbed him to the idea of death. Some died, some lived, and the fight went on. Even when his parents left there had been no tears, no remorse, only an understanding that some died, some *killed*, and the fight still went on.

So why did he feel so despondent at the death of three strangers? Why did the crew's seeming lack of compassion bother him so much?

In an effort to chase the thoughts away, Trey pulled out his reader and began doing the research he had wanted to do ever since he sensed Gerard's hesitation about ripspace. The intervening days had been full of school lessons, training, and assisting in mission prep. Now was the first chance he had to get his questions answered. Even though his heart wasn't into doing research, he began hunting down everything he could find.

Four hours later, another emotion joined his mental whirlwind: fear.

Gerard paused outside Trey's door before knocking. He had been trying to figure out what he would say ever since Trey mentioned his "dreams" of ripspace. Trey deserved the truth, but Gerard wanted to present it in a manner that wouldn't rattle the boy too much. Yesterday's traumatic debacle wasn't going to make his job any easier. Gerard fretted—an unaccustomed feeling—and wondered if he would be better served letting Laura explain things.

No. That wouldn't do at all. He was the only one who could do this, and the sooner he did, the less chance the ever curious Trey would discover it on his own. He knocked.

"Come in."

The door slid open. Gerard stepped into the room. He studied the room as the door closed behind him. Considering it belonged to a twelve-year-old boy, the chamber was exceptionally well kept. Perhaps too well. No scattered toys. No underwear or shirts flung carelessly over chair backs. Everything neatly placed on its shelf or in the closet.

Trey sat on his bed, dressed in a loose-fitting green smock and pants. His reader lay across his lap, and one glance at his blank face and bloodshot eyes told Gerard that Trey had already discovered much on his own. He had learned enough to be frightened, but not enough to comprehend. Gerard suppressed a sigh as he pushed back his ever-present baseball cap. He had said he would deal with the consequences. So he would.

He walked over and knelt beside the bed, putting himself at eye level even though Trey wasn't looking at him. "You want to talk about it?"

Trey said nothing for a moment. Finally, he asked, "Where do I start?"

"Wherever you want. I'm here for as long as you need and to answer everything I can."

Still staring at the wall, Trey said, "Why do people have to die?"

Caught by surprise, Gerard paused before answering. "I don't know. That's a question that has confounded people far smarter than you or me."

"Was Yoseph a bad boy?"

"No. He was a typical ten-year-old. A little mischievous, but not bad."

"Then why did he have to die like that? Why did any of them have to die like that? Why did m—" He stopped. His eyes turned puffy.

Gerard reached toward the boy with his golden arm and then stopped. Trey needed warm human contact right now, not the coldness of machinery. With his flesh hand, Gerard pushed aside Trey's ever-hanging brown bang. "He didn't do anything. Chaos is one of the prime foundations of the universe. Good people die young for no reason, while evil people live, become wealthy, and die of old age in their beds. I think you know that already."

"So everywhere is just like Kel?" Trey asked with a voice full of despair.

"Not at all." Gerard sat on the edge of the bed. "There are many beautiful places in the universe. Places where people co-exist peacefully and care for each other. Your life on Kel is behind you. If you stay with us, there will be times ahead that may be as unpleasant. Yesterday was one of those. It was a horrible day for all of us."

"Then how come everyone is acting like it didn't happen?"

"Because that's how we cope," Gerard said. "Trust me, the loss of Yonath and his family hurt us deeply, but we've lost so many good friends over the years that we've learned to keep going despite the grief. As Ashron said, sometimes the best way to honor the dead is to keep living."

"The fight still goes on."

Gerard didn't understand Trey's muttered comment, but he sensed the boy's reluctant acceptance of his words.

Trey's next question caught Gerard entirely by surprise.

"Why did you lie to me?" Trey's hazel eyes fixed Gerard with a piercing gaze.

"I've never lied to you," Gerard said, scrunching his white eyebrows in puzzlement. "What makes you think I have?"

"The dreams about ripspace aren't dreams, are they? What I saw is real." Trey's eyes darted around the room as if he feared the visions might materialize there.

Gerard grasped the boy's tortured logic. "I didn't lie. I left facts unstated. Only until I could think of a way to tell you without frightening you. I should have known you would discover the facts on your own as soon as you could. I suspect you only know some of the story."

"I know that anytime we're in ripspace we're surrounded by creatures that could tear Ship to pieces and try to do so the entire time we're there. I don't ever want to go into ripspace again."

Gerard sighed. "As I thought, you know the truth, but not the entire truth. Where did you get your information?"

"There was a book on the net called—"

Gerard held up a hand. "*Dangerous Journeys: The Fabrications Behind Ripspace.*"

Trey started in surprise. "How did you know?"

"I'm familiar with the book and its 'author,'" Gerard said, not bothering to hide his contempt. "It's sensationalistic pap. The only two words with any meaning in that book are 'ripspace' and 'fabrication.' The rest is wasted bandwidth. Ship, why would you let him read that?"

"Because he asked," Ship said.

And because I didn't forbid it, Gerard thought. *Didn't I want him to find information?* He wondered. *Maybe, but I wish he would have found better information.* He stood up and paced. Between the visions and the hyperbolic "facts" of a book that should never have been published, it was no wonder ripspace terrified Trey. "Do you trust me?"

"Should I?"

"A fair question. I had your best interests at heart in keeping quiet. Perhaps I misjudged. The book's title is accurate, but not in the way the writer intended. Almost everything you read in that book is a lie or a gross distortion of the truth. In the two hundred and twenty years since the Berolians brought ripspace to humans, what are the odds of dying in a ripspace accident?"

"One in one point six million."

Gerard shook his head. "One in twenty-nine point four million. Significantly lower than being struck by lightning."

"Then why would the author write that?"

"Because his agenda demanded such an overblown statistic."

Trey's thin brows bunched in puzzlement. "Agenda?"

Gerard shook his head as he stood from the bed, pulled the rolling chair from Trey's work desk, and sat down. "That's off the point. What I want you to understand is that ripspace is exceptionally safe. Yes, the dimension we travel through is filled with creatures completely alien to us. Yes, they would like nothing better than to destroy the ships that enter; probably out of fear as much as anything, since we are alien to them. When a spacecraft rips into their dimension, it is visible to them for exactly three point five eight seconds. Then phasing kicks in and the ship becomes ethereal, unable to affect or be affected by anything." That four-second span lasted far longer and held considerably more danger to the pilot of those chaotic currents, but that wouldn't be a factor for Trey. Not yet.

"The same is true on exiting," Gerard continued. "The reasons for death in ripspace are crew suicide, engine malfunction, or failure in collision detection, so that a ship phases back in for normal space entry at the precise place and time to intersect with a ripspace entity. Any of these circumstances are so unlikely that—"

"The odds are one in twenty-nine point four million," Trey said. Gerard could almost see the relief spreading over the boy's body.

"Exactly," Gerard said as Trey sat back against his pillow and set the reader aside. "And when you have a pilot with my training, the odds are even less."

"It's still kind of scary, though, knowing those things are around you. What if they ever figured out how to see us?" Trey said.

"That is a frightening thought, but a wasted one. Nothing in ripspace has mechanical or scientific capabilities. They are animals, nothing more."

Trey frowned. "If ships are present in ripspace for such a short time, why would we die if we didn't sleep? The book said the creature's mental em…ema-"

"Emanations," Gerard said. "'The psychic emanations of the denizens within ripspace would overwhelm our primitive brains and rip them asunder, causing instant death.' I believe that's the wording in the book."

"Yes," Trey said, his eyes going wide. "Is that true?"

Gerard feared this answer might drive Trey back into his shell of terror, but the boy deserved the entire truth. "Though the description is overly dramatic, the answer is yes. If the average person was awake in the interim transit time of phasing, the creatures' mental transmissions would most likely kill them or drive them mad."

To Gerard's surprise, the boy seemed to take the answer in stride. "Then why are we kept asleep for hours."

"There are other physical considerations. Anyone could wake immediately after the initial four seconds, but the effects would be unpleasant. Not fatal, just messy."

Trey nodded. "What about you? You're awake the entire time."

"People of my Order are trained for such things."

"Why?"

"That's a story for another day."

Trey nodded. "How come I could see them when others can't?"

"That's the other reason I came here. You can see them because you have potential."

"Potential for what?"

"To be a trans-dimensional manipulator."

Trey frowned. "What's that?"

Gerard smiled and held up his cybernetic arm. "Most uninformed people call us Preternatural Scientists. Or magicians."

"A spellburner? Me?"

"Yes. You see the creatures because your subconscious is revealing the *aether*, the ripspace dimension, to you. Your brain developed with the proper pattern and capacity to accept the *aether*. All you need is the training to unlock it."

Trey picked at his green shirt with both hands. "You mean ripspace and magic are the same?"

"Sort of. We pull the energy we use to create so-called magical effects from ripspace. With mathematics, we use energy from the *aetheric* dimension to create changes in this dimension."

Gerard appraised the boy for a few seconds. Trey had the intelligence and the proper physical and chemical structure. Gerard wondered if the boy had the temperament. "How do you feel about magic?" he asked. "And be honest."

Trey straightened up in the bed and crossed his legs, his feet resting against his thighs. He pushed a button on the box sitting next to his bed. A circular panel slid aside, revealing a hole in the top. Out of the hole emerged an airsteel can of soda. "Would you like one?" he asked, holding out the can to Gerard.

Gerard recognized the stalling tactic. "No, thank you."

Trey popped the top, took a long drink, and let out a healthy belch. He paused, guzzled down the rest of the liquid, and sat the container on the nightstand. The airsteel, having no fluid content to help maintain cohesion, quickly dissolved, turning itself into oxygen. Trey stared down at his lap and said, in a soft voice, "Magic killed my parents."

The confession surprised Gerard, Trey's mention of his parents more startling than the manner of their death. "Do you want to talk about it?"

Even as he shook his head, Trey continued speaking in a flat voice, as if he didn't dare show emotion. "The Tarchis Clan would use magic to take over the minds of men from other clans and make them fight. We called them *enach-sai*, demon soldiers. They always had solid black eyes. A big group of them raided our town and shot my parents with plasma rifles. They…" he stopped for a moment and swallowed. "They died after a long time."

Gerard rolled the chair closer to the bed and leaned forward. "The power of manipulation is like any other. It can be used for good or ill. You have the ability, and I could train you, but it's your choice. You don't have to decide now."

"I want to do it," Trey locked gazes with Gerard, his earnest expression showing even through the hair hanging over his right eye.

"Are you certain?"

"Yes," Trey said. "I want to show the people who use it for evil that they can't do that."

Gerard suppressed a smile. It was a simple motivation, stated with childish enthusiasm. But the well-placed sentiment gave Gerard a solid foundation for Trey's training. "I'm pleased that you are willing."

"When can we start?" Trey rocked on his bed.

This time Gerard did smile. The boy was a creature of severe emotional swings. Though not surprising, it might make training difficult at first. He could only hope time would temper such excesses. It was the conundrum faced by every mentor of trans-dimensional manipulation: potential adepts always revealed ability just before entering the physical and emotional maelstrom of puberty. Gerard suspected such dynamics had played out between journeymen and apprentices for thousands of years. His mentor Genray had alternately threatened to abandon or kill him on numerous occasions. "We can start right now if you want. I have to warn you it's a long process. It will take at least five years for your apprenticeship, and many more years before you can even consider joining an order."

"Five years?"

"Yes."

Trey frowned and his hands continued picking at his shirt. Gerard could almost hear the boy's thoughts. To a twelve-year-old, five years was close to forever.

"You don't have to decide tonight," Gerard reminded him. "The study of trans-dimensional manipulation is not entered into lightly, and we have time before we have to start in earnest."

"Is it dangerous?"

"It can be," Gerard answered. "Manipulation taps into an energy source that has the power to kill, like most forms of energy. By the time you are accessing that level of control, you'll be well-trained and in no more danger than Wolf is when he works on Ship's engine.

Trey didn't speak for several seconds. "I'll do it," he said in an excited voice.

"Are you certain?"

"Yes. I owe it to all of you."

"You don't owe us anything."

"Yes, I do." Trey's thin face grew somber. "If you hadn't saved me, I'd be dead now. If you think I can be a magic-a manipulator, then that's what I have to do. I want Laura to be proud of me."

The boy's maturity boded well for the training ahead. "Laura *is* proud of you."

"Then I'll make her prouder," Trey pushed his hair back and offered Gerard a huge, two-eyed grin.

Gerard returned the expression. "Then we'll start. There are two things you can practice. Hold up your hand." Gerard held up his cybernetic hand; Trey followed suit. "Take your fingers, starting with your thumb, and touch them to your palm, one at a time."

Gerard demonstrated, the *whirr* of the cybernetics faintly audible in the room. "Start out slow at first, because it stretches your tendons. Do it with your right hand until it becomes tired, then try with your left. As the week passes, your—"

"Week?"

"Don't interrupt," Gerard said softly. "A week is a good start. You'll have to continue the exercise all through your apprenticeship, but a week should allow your fingers to become limber enough to start with the basics. When your fingers start getting loose, you can try moving a little faster,"

Gerard once again demonstrated. "The important thing is that each finger touches your palm, one at a time. Show me how you're doing in a week, and we'll go from there."

Trey tried it, grimacing a little as the tendons of his fingers and hand stretched in unaccustomed directions. "Ouch."

"It may hurt a little bit, and both your hands will probably be sore tomorrow. It will go away soon enough."

"What's the other thing?" Trey asked

"Remember when I talked about multiplication tables? That wasn't just to occupy your mind and keep the ripspace visions away. How well do you know them?"

"Pretty well."

"Pretty well won't be good enough. You need to learn them so thoroughly that you can answer a simple equation before I even finish asking it."

"That's not possible."

"Yes, it is," Gerard assured him.

With a mischievous grin, Trey said, "Three times s-"

"Eighteen.

"Seven times ei-"

"Fifty-six."

"Nine times se-"

"Sixty-three."

Trey's eyes widened. "How do you do that?"

"I'll give you a hint. Think about the sounds of numbers. Take two days and let me know when you figure it out."

"Okay," Trey said. "Gerard, can I ask you something personal?"

"I may not answer it, but you can ask."

"How did you lose your arm?"

"What do you mean?"

"You have a cybernetic arm; so how did you lose the real one?"

"I deliberately had it taken off."

"What?" Trey's mouth gaped with astonishment.

"Keep practicing," Gerard said. He glanced over at the clock on Trey's nightstand. "It's late. I'll tell you the story some other time."

"Please tell me now. I've got to sit up and practice anyway." He held out his moving hand as evidence.

"You have to get some sleep. Ship will be expecting you for school tomorrow."

"Tomorrow's Saturday," he said triumphantly. His face suddenly took on a dark expression. "Besides, I don't think I'm going to sleep real well tonight anyway."

"Okay," Gerard said somberly, "I'll tell you."

"Filamentous," Trey said, excited again. "You sure you don't want a soda?"

"Thank you, no."

As Gerard began, Trey leaned back, resting himself against his headboard, fingers still moving.

"I started my apprenticeship at the age of twelve."

"Just like—" At Gerard's stern eyes, Trey halted his comment. "Sorry."

"After three years of training, I was accepted by the Order of the Sterling Arch, one of the most renowned Trans-manipulator Colleges in the Universe. After fifteen years of service, the brothers Zargot and Zehesel—deans of the college—summoned me before the elder members of the Order."

Gerard stood patiently, as his training had taught him, in the drafty meeting room as the seven Elders took their seats, dressed in their multihued ceremonial robes. During his years at the Order's main school, Gerard had seen them all at one time or another, but only Zargot and Zehesel stayed at the school on a permanent basis. The others came and went as it pleased them, pursuing their own goals. All seven gathered at one time was, according to rumor among the apprentices, a rare and ominous thing. Gerard tried to figure out what he might have done, good or bad, to warrant such a gathering.

When all seven had seated themselves, with Zargot and Zehesel in the center, a gong sounded from somewhere. The large doors—gray stone with the Order's silver arch insignia chiseled upon them— closed, seemingly of their own accord.

"Apprentice Gerard," Zargot said, his deep, gentle voice echoing in the chamber. "What is the prime goal of our Order?"

"To comprehend and harness the power of the *aether* to its deepest extent."

"To what purpose?"

"To enrich the existence and knowledge of all sentient beings."

The muscles in Gerard's neck tightened. Had he done something that broke the Order's tenets?

"Outstanding, Brother Gerard."

Zargot spoke in such a matter-of-fact tone that it took a few seconds to register on Gerard.

"Brother?"

"Brother," Zargot confirmed. "You have fulfilled the requirements of your apprenticeship, and are therefore this day accepted as a full member in good standing in the Order of the Sterling Arch, with all the privileges and responsibilities that entails."

Gerard's heart soared. After six grueling years of training so intense only one in three completed it, and nine more years of study and practical application, he was finally a Trans-dimensional Manipulator, recognized and ordained as such by the premiere College in the Universe. He couldn't wait to send a message to Genray.

"In addition," Zargot continued, "you have performed above and beyond the call of your training. We seven have watched your progress, and by unanimous decision, we offer unto you the *Kral-cy-bar*, if you choose to accept it."

Gerard was now convinced he was dreaming. Any moment now the morning gong would ring, and he would wake to another day of study and training. Who was he to think himself worthy of the *Kral-cy-bar*, even in his dreams?

A short time passed as Gerard waited to wake up, when Zargot said, "Are you ill, Brother? You look flush."

"I'm dreaming, aren't I? I'm not worthy of the *Kral-cy-bar*."

"Have you been offered this honor?"

"Yes."

"Then you are worthy," Zargot said. For the first time Gerard could remember, an edge came into his voice. "Or do you presume to question our judgment?"

That convinced Gerard he did not dream. "No. I always defer to the judgment of my Elders."

"Very well. Do you accept? Be aware that there is no shame or insult in refusing. All of this assembly has been offered. As you see, only two are so adorned."

A question came to Gerard's mind then, but he decided to save it for another time. If he asked now, the answer might dissuade him from his decision. "I gratefully accept this honor," he said, bowing his head.

"Very well," Zargot stood. "Let all the Order know that starting tomorrow, Gerard of Berol will undergo the *Kral-cy-bar*.

"The next day," Gerard continued as Trey sat enraptured, the fingers on his left hand moving slowly one at a time. "I underwent a complex ritual to prepare me, and that night they removed my arm and replaced it with this." He held up the cybernetic arm. "They used nothing to dampen the pain. I was expected to overcome it using my abilities to access the *aether* and employ it to bind my flesh with the metal. They told me I struggled for five days, and nearly died twice. What I remember of the experience, I won't discuss freely." Gerard shuddered.

"If it's that bad, I don't think I'd want to hear it anyway," Trey said.

"At the end of five days, I left the ritual chamber, and I was *Kral-cy-bar*."

"What exactly is *Kral-cy-bar?*"

"That's not an easy answer, and I think one story is enough for the evening. You'll be my apprentice for five years. You will have all your questions answered before then, or will know how to find the answers. Try and get some sleep now." Gerard stood up and walked to the door.

"Can I ask one more thing?" Trey said as Gerard started to leave.

"Yes," he said, turning back.

"What was the question you wanted to ask the Elders?"

"I wanted to know how many *Kral-cy-bar* there were."

"Did you find out?"

"Yes. I was the seventy-seventh to survive."

Trey's face went pale. "Survive? How many tried?"

"At the time, four hundred and twenty-three."

15

THREADS UNRAVELED

Three days later, Hawk lounged in his private "think tank," an anteroom nestled beside his cabin with subdued lighting, soft classical music, and a whirlpool that swirled with eucalyptus-scented water. They would be reaching their contact point soon, and he was doing what he could to endure the maddening wait. Even though he usually enjoyed the serenity of ripspace when he didn't have to see its vast blankness, right now too much-needed mending. Every moment of delay frustrated him. He had occupied himself with simulator drills and tactics sessions, but training only took up so much time. The rest he had spent reading or worrying. An acceptable side effect of a well-maintained craft and crew, but maddening nonetheless.

Laura discovered the hospital where Yonath had his appendix removed. As she expected, it resided in the same city as Unicybertronic's headquarters. Though logic dictated Yonath would go there for any procedures, since it was the closest hospital to his home, it also strengthened the argument for their involvement. Using relays and encryption, Laura sent a message to Yonath's physician before they ripped. She would get no reply until they returned to normal space.

She kept busy with her research on the chip, doing what she could for the still catatonic Patishi and keeping an eye on the healing Thomas.

Laura had sent word to Patishi's grandparents that their granddaughter was safe and would be delivered to them as soon as possible. Laura hoped that seeing her flesh and blood would draw Patishi from her fugue.

Hawk absently put his hand in the water, palm up. One of the small, round fish that lived in the swirling liquid settled itself in his hand. He pulled the fish out of the water and stroked its malachite-colored back. It gave a contended burble like a cooing child. Hawk smiled. The *kenquala* had been a birthday gift from Laura. They came from a small planet on the outer reaches of Council control, were outrageously expensive, and emitted a biological chemical with mild calming and restorative properties.

Hawk held the creature for about a minute before it slid off his hand and back into the water. Another one nudged at his leg, begging to be picked up.

"Captain?" Ship said, "Sorry to bother you. Gerard asked to see you in the conference room. We've been doing research and have found out some things you might want to know before you make your report to Grendarin."

"I'm not going to like it, am I?"

"Probably not."

Hawk stood up with a sigh. "I'll be there in five minutes."

He stepped out of the pool and dried off, trying to figure out how the situation could be any worse. His overactive imagination all too willingly provided several possibilities.

Dressed in a pair of loose gray pants and a short-sleeved black shirt, he walked into the conference room to find Gerard sitting in front of one of the table's pop-up monitors, with several sheets of electronic paper laid across the table. "Hello. Have a seat."

Hawk noted Gerard's serious tone. "Am I going to want a drink?"

"Probably."

"Ship, get—"

"Trey is on his way, Captain."

Hawk pulled up a chair and sat beside Gerard. "Go ahead."

"I finally figured out what was bothering me. It didn't have anything to do with our mission. It was the assassination attempt."

"Assassination attempt?" Hawk asked in surprise. "What about it?"

"The whole thing seemed far too elaborate and more than a little inept. Anne, or whatever her real name is, had several private opportunities to kill you, yet she waited until you were on a public street."

"Actually, it was an alley," Hawk told him.

"It was still public."

"Maybe she wanted to use her thugs to distract me."

"Even that doesn't make much sense. These men went on about One-Eye, which we now know is Moran, instead of opening fire. If they had come out shooting, chances are we wouldn't be having this conversation."

"Moran always did have an ego," Hawk said. "I guess he wanted me to know who he was."

"But you didn't until the attack at Tekran. You had no idea who One-Eye was. That's what bothered me. There were far too many times when you could have easily been killed."

"I don't know about easily," Hawk muttered.

"Easily enough," Gerard smiled. "I decided to investigate on the assumption Moran wanted the attack to be public. My findings seem to bear me out. It appears we've been up to some exciting things. Ship, give me the first news story."

"Okay," Ship said. The screen lit up with a printed article. At that moment, Trey stepped into the room carrying a tray with two glasses.

"The kid has perfect timing," Gerard said.

"Great," Hawk said as Trey walked over.

"Your usual." the boy handed Hawk a glass. "And another, because Ship said you'd need it." He set the second glass on the table.

"This just gets better all the time," Hawk said as Trey left.

"Wait," Gerard replied.

Taking a sip from his drink, Hawk turned the screen to face him, and read:

FOUR KILLED IN ALLEY AMBUSH

Pa'tris City, Pa'tris Prime – Four men were brutally slain in a downtown alley yesterday evening, the result of an apparent random act of violence by Sean Grey of Earth (-3.904, -1.426, +3.548), a.k.a. Hawk, leader of the de-licensed Corporate Mercenary Unit The Knights of The Flaming Star.

"We haven't been de-licensed," Hawk protested.
"We'll discuss that in a minute. Keep reading."

According to Ms. Anne Siliar, who was on a date with Mr. Grey at the time of the event, there was no provocation for the incident. "We were cutting through the alley," said a distraught Ms. Siliar, "and these gentlemen asked us for directions to a local bar. (Hawk) said, 'You'll never take me,' pulled out a gun, and shot all four of them." Pointing at a laceration on her arm, she continued, "He tried to get me as I ran, but I got lucky."
This is the second act of violence attributed to Mr. Grey.

"Second?" Hawk asked.
"Give me the next one, Ship," Gerard's smile grew broader. "You'll like this one."
The screen changed, and Hawk turned back to it.

MAN KILLED IN BAR BY MERCENARY CAPTAIN

Pa'tris City, Pa'tris Prime - Violence erupted in a portside bar known as the *Ripspace Grotto* today as a man was beaten to death in an argument over a woman.
Witnesses identified the assailant as regular customer Sean Grey, leader of the Knights of The Flaming Star, a Corporate Mercenary Unit regarded as so renegade by the business community they have been de-licensed.
"It was just a normal day," said bartender Raulf Loraanaw, "with Hawk sitting in his usual booth. This guy walks up to him and starts talking. Next thing I know they're yelling at each other, then fists start

flying and, before anybody can stop it, Hawk has broken this guy's neck. Those mercenaries learn that sort of fighting, you know."

The victim has been identified as local businessman Bray Termain. He is survived by a wife and three children.

Grey is now being sought...

"This is incredible." Hawk shook his head. "No one is going to believe this, are they?"

"I think you'd be surprised," Gerard said. "There are a lot of people who like to see the good guys take a fall. Like it or not, Corporate Mercenaries are in the public eye, and this is the kind of story that may go galaxy-wide. Besides, the ones who don't believe that story will undoubtedly believe the next one, which is dated yesterday and has gone out over the newsnet. Ship."

The screen flickered again; Hawk grabbed his second drink and returned his gaze to the screen. There was a picture of someone Hawk didn't recognize in the center of the article. He didn't look at it long because the headline quickly grabbed his attention.

KNIGHTS IN LEAGUE WITH TERRORISTS

CANDASH (-6.987, +14.381, +2.092) - (AP) Corporate Mercenary Unit The Knights of The Flaming Star are now believed to be in league with a terrorist group known as the Tekranese Destruction Force. According to Cosmos Federated, the Knight's primary employer, the Knights were sent on a routine courier mission to the company's facility on Candash. There, assisted by members of the Tekranese Destruction Force, they attacked a new land-based laser system designed by Cosmos.

When asked for comment, Federated's Chairman Carlton Noaerm said, "As far as we are concerned, (the Knights) are nothing more than terrorists and outlaws. Because of their past service, we were willing to give them a chance even when they lost their license, but they have shown their true colors. We will deal with them in the strictest possible manner. We plan to offer a two hundred million STU reward for anyone who brings them in alive."

Hawk whistled, "Two hundred million Standards. Someone wants us out of the way but good. Hell, I may turn us in. Who is Cosmos Federated?"

"Good question," Gerard said. "There are several Cosmos Federateds listed. All of them deal in their local systems, and we've never worked for any of them. Offhand, I'd say it was a convenient name tossed into the story, and Carl Noarem is an alias for someone we know."

"What do you mean?"

"Look at the picture. Closely."

Hawk studied the photograph he had glanced over earlier. Though the face seemed familiar, he couldn't quite place it.

"Ship, take away the beard, add an eye patch, and darken the hair," Gerard said.

Ship had gone no further than removing the beard when Hawk blurted out, "Moran." Hawk wanted to kick himself for not recognizing his old friend sooner. "Son of a bitch." He downed the last of his drink. "That'll teach me. If I had spent more time practicing with knives, we wouldn't be having any of these problems. Any other tidbits?"

"Actually, yes."

"Well, hang on. Ship?"

"Yes, Captain?"

"Tell everybody to meet in fifteen minutes." He turned to Gerard. "There's no sense in going over the rest twice. We'll let everybody know what's up, then figure out what to do."

"Okay."

"Get whatever you need," he told Gerard "I'm going to let you do the talking."

"So Moran is behind this whole thing," Laura said after Gerard finished his briefing.

"He planned all of it and is certainly deeply involved," Gerard answered. "However, I think we can safely assume there is someone else behind him, funding the operation."

"Why?" Ashron asked.

"As Hawk pointed out a few days ago, Moran was never an expert money manager. Even if he was the best financier in the galaxy, he would be hard-pressed to come up with two hundred million Standards in five years."

"That's just for the reward," Hawk said. "We won't even consider what that little trap on Tekran cost."

"I don't understand," Trey said. He had finished reading the last news story. "None of this is true."

"The people reading it won't know that," Laura told him.

"How can they print it if it's not true?"

"I hate to disillusion you, Trey old chum," Ashron said. "Newspapers reporting lies is as old as newspapers being printed."

"'If you have a choice between the truth and the legend, print the legend.'" Gerard quoted. "Besides, the papers may not know their information is false. It's easy enough to pay people to lie."

"But why?" Trey asked.

"It's actually a pretty clever plan," Gerard said. "I'd be interested to know if Moran set it all up or if he's improvising as things go wrong."

"We'll make sure to ask him next time we see him," Hawk said.

"Excuse me," Ashron said. "You seem to be talking about Moran in the wrong tense. He's dead."

"What makes you say that?"

"He got shot in the chest and through the eye and had a building blow up around him. He may be tough, but I'd say it would be pretty hard to bounce back from something like that."

"I thought he was dead five years ago," Hawk said. "We see what that mistake has cost."

There was a brief pause, and then Trey said, "I still don't get it."

Gerard looked at him. "When you read those stories, what did they make you think?"

"That they were a bunch of lies."

"That's because you were there for one of the events and you know Hawk well enough to disbelieve the other two. Pretend you were someone who didn't know anything about the Knights, and you read those. Then what would you think?"

"That the Knights were criminals."

"And that's exactly what Moran wants people to think," Gerard told him. "He hires assassins to kill Hawk in a public place. If they kill him, no problem. However, if he kills them, it makes it appear that Hawk murdered innocent people. Then if Moran fails to kill us at the fortress, we suddenly become terrorists. That makes Hawk a wanted criminal, which will cause problems with Force 13."

"If they believe the stories," Hawk interrupted.

"Even if they don't believe them, they can do nothing publicly to clear you. So, now the public has it in their minds that Hawk is a loose cannon. Moran sets up his ambush by kidnapping Yonath, and we go on what we assume is a standard rescue operation. Again, if we are killed, no problem. If not, we are suddenly terrorists."

"That's something that's been bugging me," Hawk said. "How could Moran know we would be the team sent in to rescue the Maratais?"

"I suspect he planned that too," Gerard told him. "Remember the message calling us to Seldon was audio only, so anyone with Force 13 coding could have sent it. I'd be willing to bet Moran still has contacts inside Force 13 that would give or sell him the information. He simply made sure we were the unit contacted. It may even have been his altered voice on the message."

"Or perhaps," Laura spoke up, "Moran knew we were friends with Yonath, and had the chip implanted on him in the hopes of finding us."

"Is it me," Ashron said, "or is Moran becoming more and more god-like as this conversation moves along? Next thing you'll tell me he's the one who got our license revoked."

"He's not god-like," Gerard said, "but he's had five years to brood over revenge and make a plan. He seems omniscient only because he knows all the answers, and we're still trying to come up with the questions. And our license isn't revoked. Anybody coming to hunt for us probably won't let that get in the way of collecting the reward, though. If they even bother to confirm it."

Hawk sighed. "So, the situation, in a nutshell, is we are now outlaws with a price—a substantial price—on our heads. We need to find out how much this story has gotten around."

"I can almost guarantee you that every merc unit within a hundred light years has it flashing on their database," Gerard informed them.

"You've been full of cheery news all day," Hawk said. "So, basically, what we have is the entire mercenary community and a sizable portion of the armed and ignorant public sector now looking to hunt us down, and take us in."

"Us against the universe," Ashron said, grinning.

"What's the plan?" Wolf asked.

Gerard spoke up. "Once we finish at ZT-3235, I suggest we go collect the reward."

"Collect the reward?" Hawk asked. "I don't recall you mentioning you knew where to collect the reward."

"Because I hadn't. Ship picked up information off the Mercnet that the general public doesn't have. First off, the reward to mercs is three hundred million."

Hawk whistled. "That's it; I'm turning us all in and collecting the reward. Who's paying?"

"It doesn't say," Gerard explained. "All it says is to bring Ship and us to Meta Brévé and contact Fralor in the city-state of Tralsac. They want us dead or alive, but Ship they want intact."

"Ship?" Hawk said. "Why do they want her?"

"Not certain, but the reward posts are very specific that the craft is brought in intact."

"Where in the hell is Meta Brévé?" Ashron asked.

"Ship?" Hawk said.

"Eighteen parsecs away. The planet is 7,490 kilometers in diameter, a standard atmosphere with slightly high nitrogen content, covered by seventy percent water, and a population of three point eight per square mile. The government is based on the feudal system. The Planetary Council has ruled it a tech-restricted planet. The current technological level is roughly equivalent to 15th century Earth. Worst of all, there is no starport. However, there is a Council monitoring outpost that allows docking for three ships."

Hawk stroked at his mustache for a moment. "This simplifies things a bit. I think it's time we jump into the jaws of the Frandif."

"What does that mean?" Ashron asked in a wary voice.

"He wants us to go to Meta Brévé," Gerard answered.

"Exactly," Hawk said.

"I was afraid that's what it meant," Ashron said. "Do you think that's necessary?"

"What better way to find out who's after us than to go to the source?" Hawk asked him.

"Well, why don't we make it even easier for them? I'll buy the silver platters, and we'll have a courier service deliver our heads on them."

"All we're going to do is scout the planet and see if we can get some ideas."

Ashron said nothing for a moment. "Okay, Ship, Hawk wants you to set a course for Meta Brévé." He smiled. "We're jumping into the jaws of the Frandif."

"Not yet. I still want to contact Force 13. We'll head to Meta Brévé after I make my report."

Ship spoke up. "Captain, I finished the name search for Anne Siliar. There were several, but none matched her picture. If you'd like I can do a galaxy-wide picture to picture comparison to find out her real name. It could take up to seven weeks."

"Go ahead and start," Hawk said. "She could answer a lot of these questions. I don't know why, but I have a feeling she'll find us before we find her."

Trey looked at Ashron as the crew began filing out. "This is kind of like a real-life chess game, isn't it?"

"Yeah," Ashron muttered. "I just hope we're not the ones who end up in checkmate."

<hr>

Hawk stood in his quarters in front of his blank viewscreen. "Link established," a monotone voice, belonging to Force 13's transmitter, said.

"About time," Hawk muttered. He had been waiting twenty

minutes for the tight focus beam to traverse the parsecs between him and his contact. The viewscreen flickered; an image appeared of a tall, thin humanoid with vibrant orange skin, large black eyes, and a wide mouth with thin, almost non-existent, lips.

"Hello, Grendarin."

"Greetings, Hawk," Grendarin said. "To what do we owe the pleasure of this contact?"

Something about Grendarin's tone put Hawk on his guard, even though he had no justifiable reason. The Lokathi were known throughout the galaxy for their honor and trustworthiness. That's why every Force 13 liaison was a member of that race. Then it hit him. Grendarin should have already been apprised of their status and known the exact reason for Hawk's contact. He should be demanding to know what happened.

Full of misgivings, Hawk pressed on. "I wanted to let you know the rescue mission was a bust. Yonath Maratai and his family are dead."

Grendarin frowned, an expression most people found unnerving. "I have to apologize for my lack of information, but I am not aware of any such mission."

Warning flags flashed in Hawk's brain. Either Grendarin was lying or the Knights, Hawk specifically, had been severely duped. Neither prospect held much appeal. "A week ago, I met with three agents from Section T who told me that Yonath Maratai had been kidnapped. W—"

"Which three agents?"

"Stearns, Section T, Tudev and Sivali, both section I. I met them at the—"

"Seldon Excelsior," Grendarin finished for him.

"So you did know about the meeting," Hawk said, although the drop in his stomach told him that wasn't the reason behind Grendarin's knowledge.

"No, but that is where we found Sivali's and Tudev's bodies, slumped over a table in the conference room. The Seldon police want you for questioning since an anonymous party mentioned seeing you leave the conference room."

Hawk knew the exact identity of the anonymous party. "They were alive when I left."

"I accept that. You are not a suspect in Force 13's estimate. The agents were shot in the back of the neck. Assassinated, which does not correlate to your termination methods."

"You only mentioned two. Where's Stearns?"

Grendarin frowned again. "The last anyone saw him, he went into a training class, picked a cadet for a mission and then disappeared."

Hawk nodded. Moran or whoever backed Moran had bought off Stearns. "I think Stearns has gone renegade and he's tied in with Moran."

"Moran? I was on the understanding he was terminated half a decade ago."

"Wishful thinking," Hawk quickly described what they knew and the reasoning behind the doctored news stories. When Hawk finished, Grendarin remained silent for several seconds, his thin lips pursed in thought as he nodded.

"We can do nothing about any mercenary units, but I should be able to discretely assure local enforcement does not harass you," Grendarin finally said. "And I will relay the communication for Council troops to ignore you. We will attempt to have the news outlets issue a retraction. It will take time and may not occur. We will also double our efforts to find Stearns and see how deeply he is involved in this and if there are any others."

"Keep a close eye on Unicybertronic Technologies," Hawk suggested. "I'm convinced they're involved in this somehow."

"I will try, though I do not believe the Council will consider it a high priority. Yonath was implanted for over a year and could find nothing with which to incriminate them; The Council will most likely assume innocence for Unicybertronic and bad karma for Yonath."

Such was the burden of working within a bureaucracy. "Well, do what you can."

"If you provide evidence of their culpability, the Council can intervene," Grendarin said.

"I'll keep it in mind. Right now, I'm a little more interested in tracking down Moran."

"Perhaps one will help you discover the other," Grendarin said. "Do be cautious. Keep me informed, and if we discover the whereabouts of Stearns, I will apprise you."

"Thanks, Grendarin. Hawk out."

"F-thirteen out."

As the image flickered away, Hawk let out a sigh. It was about as much as he expected, even if he had hoped Grendarin would offer two squads of Force Marines and a concerted effort to clear the Knights' name.

"Never hurts to dream," Hawk said ruefully. "Okay, Ship, tell everybody to take an hour and then we'll hit rip. Let's go find out what we can learn at Meta Brévé."

16

OUTPOST ARRIVAL

awk sat on the bridge, staring out the viewport at the blue glow of Meta Brévé and waiting for his ripspace headache to dissipate. The two-day ripspace journey had been filled with training and preparation for their upcoming visit. Even Trey, at Ashron's suggestion, had begun basic weapons training. Though the boy had seemed strangely reluctant at first, he soon took to the challenge of shooting simulated floating discs and was proving quite adept. Hawk didn't know what Gerard had discussed with the boy, but there had been no further instances of trouble before their jumps to ripspace.

Their re-entry into normal space occurred without incident. Hawk's fear that they would find an unfriendly welcoming committee proved baseless. The only space object on Ship's sensors was the monitoring outpost on the far side of the planet. A quick scan and hack into their database told Ship they had not received any information on the crew's wanted status. As near as Ship could tell, they received little in the way of current data from any of the Uninet links. The station didn't warrant the expense of the infrastructure.

Despite his headache, Hawk smiled as he heard the bridge door open and Ashron's tail dragging across the deck. He had been expecting a visit.

"Captain, what the hell just happened?" Ashron asked.

"What do you mean?" Hawk asked, removing his grin and swiveling around in the captain's chair to stare at the irritated Lorothian.

"What do you mean, what do I mean? If we weren't in space, I'd swear you ran into a wall. You almost sent Trey through the viewport."

"So, you're saying the new brakes seem a little grabby?"

"Brakes? Look, I realize I'm only a lowly demo tech, but even I know spaceships don't have brakes." Ashron raised his narrow eyes to the ceiling. "Ship, what happened?"

"I had the hiccups."

"The hiccups?"

"Well, one hiccup."

"I'm not going to get a straight answer from either of you, am I?"

Hawk stared at him, and Ship remained silent.

"Fine. I'm going back to the wardroom."

"Captain," Ship said. "The Outpost Master is hailing you."

"Put him on."

Ashron paused to listen.

"This is Commander Motash of Meta Brévé outpost. Why did you skip the atmosphere?"

Ashron's slitted eyes grew wide.

Hawk looked at him. "Editorial comment?"

"No, not me. I'll just go back to the wardroom now." Ashron turned and moved at a quick pace. Hawk knew that within two minutes the rest of the crew would have the scoop. Nothing he could do about it now, so he turned his attention back to the monitor. A man with a face full of sharp edges stared at him, deep-set black eyes glaring in impatience.

"Sorry about that," he said to the waiting commander. "We had a power fluctuation that messed up our sensors. We're back online now."

The commander stared at Hawk with his hands held behind the

crisp, charcoal-gray uniform with bright red breast patch in the shape of a shield: the uniform of the Council Planetary Protection Service. Hawk could tell by the set of the man's angular jaw that he was weighing the validity of Hawk's story.

"Very well," the commander said, sounding as if his good grace was the only thing keeping Hawk from a fate worse than death. "What is your purpose for coming to Meta Brévé?"

"Research. I have two professors from the University of Zabar, and they're doing a study on Religious and Magical Practices on low-tech planets."

"You have proof of that?" the man asked as if the very idea were ludicrous.

"Yes," Hawk answered. Ship had created the requisite credentials yesterday; Laura and Gerard had taken a crash course on Zabar and the University, on the minute chance someone on the outpost would know about either and asked them questions.

The man again paused as if pondering the fate of worlds. Hawk put his hand over his mouth as if rubbing his mustache, and keyed off the outgoing audio. "This guy's either a pompous ass or a real slow thinker," he said.

"I vote for the former," Ship said.

"You may dock at port three," the commander said in a tone that suggested Hawk should fall to his knees and worship the man for his benevolence.

Hawk keyed the audio back on. "Roger that. ETA in," he glanced at the display, "two minutes, thirty-seven seconds." Hawk closed the channel before the man could say anything else. "Go ahead and dock us, Ship."

"Aye, Captain."

"I'm going to the wardroom and do damage control on Ashron. Let me know when we've docked."

<hr>

"You're kidding," Laura said. "He bounced off the atmosphere?"

"Yep."

"What would make Hawk skip the atmosphere?" Laura asked.

"I don't know. Ship said it was a hiccup, and Hawk tried to convince me Ship had brakes."

"She does have brakes, after a fashion," Wolf volunteered.

"Nothing that would make us bounce around like that." Out of the corner of his eye, Ashron saw Hawk walk into the room. "I think he's been nipping at the bottle again."

"Not bloody likely," Hawk said, walking over to the bar and pouring a shot of tequila.

"See, there he goes now," Ashron said, "sucking it down like a sponge."

Hawk ignored him. He downed the liquor. "We'll be docking in about two minutes. Gerard, Laura, ready to be university professors?"

"As ready as two days can make us," Gerard said.

"I don't think Mister Personality will take much bluffing. Let me go talk to this squink, and I'll call you in once I have the situation assessed."

Hawk left the wardroom and made his way to the airlock, arriving as the dull metallic thud and slight jarring indicated they had docked.

"Docked, Captain," Ship said.

"So I noticed. Open the airlock."

The airlock door irised open. Seven meters away, the entrance to the station opened. A man wearing the Planetary Protection Service uniform stepped through the doorway and greeted Hawk. A green vertical bar above the shield emblem marked him as ex-marine; it showed in his proud bearing and arrow-shaped haircut.

"Welcome aboard." the man offered a sharp salute. "My name is Waren. Please follow me." The man turned and all but marched back into the station. Hawk followed.

Waren led Hawk halfway around the circular, white-walled station. They stopped at a gray door on the inward side of the hub, and Waren knocked.

"Enter," a voice said from the other side. The door slid open to reveal a small, windowless chamber. The man Hawk had met over the viewscreen sat behind a plaswood desk, a smug expression on his face.

His black hair appeared even oilier in person than it had on the monitor.

Hawk stepped through the door as Waren saluted, turned and left. Hawk walked over in front of the desk. Putting on his most disarming grin, he offered his hand. "Commander Motash, pleased to meet you. Damn fine outpost you have here."

The Commander regarded Hawk's hand as if he saw something disgusting, and made no effort to reciprocate the gesture. "I'm sorry, did you expect anything less?"

"Of course not," Hawk said, his smile slipping a notch. *Time to get this over with*, he thought. He dropped his hand. "What do I need to sign?"

"One moment, Captain…" the commander glanced down at the screen on his desk, "…Grey?"

Hawk nodded.

"Right. I will need to meet these professors and anyone else that will be going down to the planet."

Hawk nodded and activated his collarbone transmitter. "Laura, bring everyone on board."

"We'll be right there," Laura said in his ear.

"They'll be along in a moment."

"Fine," the commander returned his gaze to his desk and began shuffling through papers on one corner. Hawk pulled the chair out from the front of the desk and sat down. The commander glanced up, said nothing, and returned to his paperwork.

Hawk thought about trying to start a conversation, decided his social skills would be too severely tested, and remained silent.

To pass the time, Hawk studied the room. To call the chamber Spartan would have been kind. Aside from the usual equipment necessary for any governmental office, there was nothing in the chamber. No pictures of family, no plaques or certificates. Not even a plant to add a little cheer.

Dismal room for a dismal personality, Hawk thought. He surmised that the boredom on a station like this for any length of time might sour one's outlook on life. Especially being cut off from the rest of the universe for whatever reason. Hawk knew he wouldn't be able to handle it for more than a day.

A few minutes passed, and Hawk was about to call again to find out the delay when the chamber door opened. The Commander looked up to the door. Hawk stood. The rest of the crew walked in. Hawk wondered what the commander would think of Ashron and Wolf. He wouldn't be surprised if the man demanded that only the humans go planetside. An uncomfortable memory tried to surface, a flash of another place where the non-humans stayed behind, resulting in disaster. Hawk quickly pushed it down.

"Commander," Hawk said, again offering his killer grin. "Allow me to introduce—"

"Thank you," the commander said. "I will handle this." His gaze took in the crew. "Who are the Professors?"

Laura stepped forward. "Doctor Laura Benzing at your service." She offered her hand and received the same repulsed sneer that greeted Hawk.

"And what exactly are you a Doctor of?"

"Socio-anthropology and medicine."

"Your credentials, please."

Laura produced the forged documents and handed them over. The commander studied them at length.

After five minutes passed, Hawk said, "What exactly are you looking for?"

"These documents are forged."

"I beg your pardon," Laura said.

"These are forged documents," the commander repeated. "You are no more a doctor than I am."

"I can easily believe you are not a doctor," Laura said with ice in her voice, "but I can assure you I have been one for ten years, and have studied planets far more important than this one. As you can see, I have unrestricted access to all planets in my field of study. Are you aware of what the penalty is for obstruction of that privilege?"

"I can't say that I am. I'm sure it's something quite severe, and you may bring the full wrath of the law on any time."

Laura, with a glance at Hawk, said. "Well, are you aware of the commission attached to a Research Survey?"

"Commission?" the commander asked. His eyebrows lifted slightly, and Hawk suppressed a groan. The conversation had just turned expensive.

"Yes," Laura continued, "in consideration for the inconvenience to a station Commander during our surveys, the University offers a commission of—" she looked at Gerard, "—what is it these days, Doctor Pretari?"

"Somewhere in the area of five thousand, I believe," Gerard answered without hesitation. Hawk wanted to kick his pale-skinned friend. He didn't mind spending money; he hated giving it away.

The commander reconsidered the documents.

"That commission is, of course, in advance," Laura said.

The commander returned his attention to the group. "What about these two?" he indicated Ashron and Wolf. Wolf had a large backpack in one hand.

"Actually, I think the commission was closer to six thousand," Laura offered.

"Very well," the commander said after a moment of hesitation. "And the child?"

Surprised, Hawk saw Trey standing with the crew, almost hidden behind Wolf.

"The child is my valet," Laura said before Hawk could say anything.

"I don't think the planet is safe for a child," the Commander said. For once Hawk heard something other than imperiousness in the man's tone. It sounded almost like concern.

"It is my responsibility," she said, flashing Hawk a warning glare when she saw him about to speak. Hawk kept quiet, but someone would have to offer him a damn good explanation for Trey's presence when they got a moment alone.

"Yes, he is," the Commander told Laura, his brief moment of openness gone. "May I see your papers as well, for the record?" he asked Gerard.

Gerard handed over the papers with his left hand, keeping his cybernetic hand in his pocket, his arm hidden beneath a long sleeve shirt.

The commander gave Gerard's documents a cursory inspection before handing them back. He kept his hand out and Hawk, taking the hint, handed over his credit stick. The commander slid it into a slot on his desk and deducted the appropriate amount. He handed a printed receipt to Hawk. "For the University's records," he said.

He pushed a button on the desk. "Arlan, please get the shuttle ready. Destination?"

"The city-state of Tralsac will do for a start," Hawk said.

The corner of Motash's mouth turned up in what may have been an evil smile. "The city-state of Tralsac."

"Yes, Commander," a disembodied voice answered.

"What do you have in the pack?"

"Trade goods," Laura said. "Do you want to inspect it?"

"That won't be necessary," Commander Motash said as he walked from behind his desk. "Follow me." He marched through the open doorway. They followed him down a short, white hallway. The commander paused before two doors, one on either side. "You will find proper clothing in here, although the child and the large one may be difficult to outfit. Men on the left, women on the right. I will wait here."

Hawk opened the door and found a surprisingly large room filled with various articles of clothing. Unlike the rest of the outpost, this room appeared unkempt and smelled musty and disused. He stepped inside. The others followed. When the door closed, he turned on Trey. "What do you think you're doing?" he asked in a low voice.

"I'm going with you," Trey said, not moving. "I didn't want to be left alone."

"You wouldn't be alone. Ship would be with you."

"It's not the same," Trey protested. "Laura said I could come."

"Well, Laura and I are going to have a talk when this is done. This is a dangerous situation and no place for a child."

"I'm not a child," Trey said through clenched teeth, surprising Hawk by balling his fists and taking a step forward. "I haven't been a child since…"

He stopped and stared at Hawk, his pale face a strange mixture of anger and sadness. "I can take care of myself." He walked away and began rummaging through the clothing.

"Let him go," Gerard placed an arm on Hawk's shoulder and guided him toward clothes on the opposite side of the room. "He has a valid point. He *did* survive on Kel for months without our help."

"That's not *my* point," Hawk looked at the dusty clothing hanging on thin wire racks. "He needs to ask my permission. I run an open ship, but I'm still the captain. He needs to learn that. Laura should know better, too."

"Speaking in defense for both of them, Trey was rather adamant, much like when he refused to go into ripsleep. Laura is strong, but in his way, Trey is even stronger. He has willpower that will serve him well if it's properly channeled. I think you can help by treating him less like a child and more like a member of the crew."

"But he is a child," Hawk insisted.

"Physically, yes. Mentally and emotionally? I think he's teetering. You'll get a better response if you approach him as an adult. Think about how Tahorton taught you." Gerard moved away and began pulling clothes from the rack.

Hawk considered Gerard's words as he studied the clothing, everything a muted shade of yellow, brown, or red. He suspected all the clothes were at least a decade old.

Maybe Gerard's right. Hawk pulled a brown linen tunic and rust-colored pants off the rack. Trey was always seeking ways to show he could be part of the crew. The few chores they gave him he did with no complaint. In many ways, the young boy was the perfect crew member, far more mature than most twelve-year-olds. Only certain things set him off, and most of them could be traced back to Kel. His fear of being alone was apparent. His reluctance to enter ripsleep had been discovered and overcome. There were other, more minor things Hawk could remember. In all of them, someone else had solved the problem, while Hawk had only reacted—and poorly—to Trey's seeming childishness.

As he put on his new clothing and tried to shake off the smell of dust and mildew, it occurred to Hawk that he and Trey were much alike in certain ways. Both stubborn, both used to things their way, and both with a fear of being left by the people who loved them.

Hawk grabbed a pair of brown boots that were his size and slipped them on. Finished, he turned and saw the others already dressed: Ashron in red, Gerard in yellow, and Trey in an overlarge brown shirt, rust-colored pants that he had cinched to his waist with a strip of cloth, and dusty brown boots.

He picked the same colors I did, Hawk thought. Whether he did it before or after he saw Hawk's choices didn't matter. Hawk experienced a sudden closeness with this orphan child he had never felt before, despite their similar situations. He smiled, and Trey offered a tentative grin in return.

Wolf, finding nothing that fit, had fashioned a toga from several yellow shirts and wore it draped over his massive grayish body. Hawk broke out into a laugh and said, "You look like a mutant canary."

"What's a canary?" Wolf asked.

"Never mind," Hawk walked over to a woefully understocked rack of weaponry and said, "You have a choice: broadsword or scimitar."

Hawk passed out the weapons, giving a scimitar to Ashron and a broadsword to himself. Wolf took a broadsword, which looked like a metal toothpick in his large hand. Gerard accepted a dagger as Hawk handed them to everyone, even Trey.

When he finished, Hawk said, "Let's get out there and see if Laura looks as stupid as we do."

Ashron opened the door. They stepped out to find Laura waiting for them. She wore dark blue pantaloons with fluted leggings and a cream colored shirt with bloused sleeves. A slender rapier in a black sheath hung from her side. Hawk thought the outfit suited her, unlike the rest of the crew, himself included; they reminded him of rejects from an acting troupe.

The commander stood nearby. "Is everything okay?" he asked, his tone full of derision. Hawk suspected he had overheard some of their dressing room conversation.

"Fine," Hawk answered, eager to get out of the station and away from this petty bureaucrat. "We're ready to go."

"Follow me."

They walked another twenty meters around the hub until they reached the round hangar airlock on the station's outer side. The door opened as they approached and the Commander stopped at the portal. "Arlan will take you planetside. Exactly how long will you be on planet?" he asked Laura.

"No more than a week," she answered.

"Very well," he said, then turned and walked away.

"'Rudeness is the weak man's imitation of strength'" Gerard quipped as they headed for the shuttle.

"All civil servants are not like that, Trey," Laura told the boy.

They walked across the hanger and into the open shuttle, which, like the rest of the station, was exceptionally well-maintained and clean.

"Does the phrase anal retentive strike a chord with anybody here?" Ashron asked.

"Commander Motash can be a bit of an ass sometimes," a voice said from the cockpit doorway. All heads turned to see a short, slender man with thick, black hair and a bushy mustache leaning against the doorframe. Like Waren, his Protection Service uniform marked him as ex-Marine. "But he's a good officer and a decent person once you know him."

"That's what they said about Atilla the Hun," Laura murmured.

The man frowned, looked prepared to say something in defense, and then seemed to reconsider. The ends of his mustache curled up as he grinned. "I'm Arlan. If all of you will strap in, I'll launch us. The trip will take about twenty-five minutes."

"Why so long?" Hawk asked. A standard shuttle trip from station to planet lasted ten to fifteen minutes.

"The cloaking generator is an older model; it takes ten minutes for the shielding charge and noise mufflers to disperse evenly." He turned, stopped, and turned back to the group. "Don't think too badly of the commander. He has things to consider you wouldn't understand." He walked into the cockpit and the door shut behind him.

"Well, that was cryptic," Ashron said as the others stared at the closed door.

"Why do we need a cloaking generator?" Trey asked.

Hawk started to answer. Gerard stopped him. "Why do you think we need a cloaking generator?"

"Is this a psychological test?" Ashron asked, smiling. "Can we play word association next?"

"No," Gerard offered Ashron an annoyed glance. "This is an exercise in reasoning ability."

He turned back to Trey. "A good manipulator must be like a detective. If you can learn to draw conclusions from the known facts and order your thoughts accordingly, it will make learning manipulation much easier."

As the others took seats, Trey's eyes narrowed in concentration as he thought things through. The shuttle was designed to hold twenty passengers, so they had plenty of room. Although Wolf had to content himself with sitting on one of the benches along the wall since the standard seats were too small. He used two separate belts to strap in.

As the low whine of the engines reverberated through the cabin, Trey sat down between Laura and Hawk and his face lit up. "We're going to a low-tech planet, so they have to hide any sign of technology," he said triumphantly. "The cloak will cover us up, and the noise mufflers will disperse the sound so if anybody is nearby it will sound like distant thunder."

"Very good," Gerard said. "From now on, before you ask a question like that, see if you can come up with your own answer."

"Kind of like when I ask Laura for help with my homework and she tells me to work it out for myself."

"Very much like that," Gerard said, smiling.

The engine grew louder, vibrating the cabin and making conversation difficult. Trey closed his eyes, swallowed, and grabbed Hawk and Laura's hand. Hawk knew once they were in open space Trey would be fine, but takeoff and docking always made the boy nervous. Hawk didn't know if this was a symptom of his experiences on Kel or merely the same reaction many people had to shuttle flight.

Hawk regarded the boy, dressed like a miniature version of himself, with his head nestled against Laura's shoulder, and realized they had become the boy's surrogate parents. Trey relied on them. It was a startling revelation that made Hawk feel, surprisingly, good. He sat back and grinned, wondering if this was the feeling Tahorton had gotten from all his adopted children over the years.

With a slight lurch, the craft pulled away from the station's docking ring. After a brief acceleration, the engine noise dropped to a moderate level, allowing conversation to resume.

"Gerard, would you clear us?" Hawk asked as Trey released his hand.

Gerard nodded, spoke an equation, and moved his cybernetic arm around the cabin. "We're sealed."

Free to speak without fear of being overheard, Hawk said, "I'm going to have to talk to Ship. Her forging skills are slipping," Hawk told them.

"No, they're not," Gerard assured him. "The commander had no clue if our papers were forged or authentic."

"Why do you say that?"

"Number one, Ship's forgeries are not perfect, but the flaws are so minute that just the naked eye would reveal nothing. Our commander did not have a cybernetic eye so that rules out any visual enhancement. He made a pretense of studying them for a long time in the hopes of making us nervous. Number two, he had a credit slot on his desk. And even though the administrative setup of Protection Outposts is not my specialty, I'm positive desk-mounted credit slots are not standard issue."

"What about accepting research commissions?" Ashron asked. "I know those exist."

"True," Gerard agreed. "They're handled through the Sector Command. The outposts never see the money."

"So that was a bribe?" Trey asked.

"A rather tactless word but, yes," Gerard told him.

"You mean we could have gotten away without paying him?" Hawk asked.

"Doubtful," Gerard said. "He would have found one way or another to keep us there until some money changed hands. Be thankful. We got off paying only six thousand."

"Only," Hawk said.

They spent the rest of the trip to the planet discussing trivial matters. As Trey went back to his finger exercises, Hawk considered reprimanding him for his belligerent behavior in the dressing room, then decided to let it slide for the moment. Even though he better understood the boy's behavior, he could not condone it. He would deal with it back on Ship, away from the others, showing Trey the same courtesy he would any other crew member.

"Doesn't that hurt?" Ashron asked, watching Trey.

"It did for the first couple of days, but my tendons have stretched out, so it's not a problem now."

Arlan's voice came over the shuttle's intercom. "We're about to hit the atmosphere; there may be a little chop."

As the shuttle began vibrating, Trey's breathing suddenly became ragged. "Why is the air so thick?"

"How do you mean, thick?" Gerard asked Trey.

"My head feels stuffy and my chest hurts. Everything is tingling." Trey shook his head as if trying to clear it. He suddenly looked startled. He glanced around and, noticing everyone staring at him, blushed as he placed his hands over his crotch.

Hawk suppressed a smile and thought about telling Trey that none of them could see anything in the loose clothing he wore. He decided that would only embarrass the boy further.

"What's happening to him?" Ashron asked.

"He's sensing *aether*," Gerard said.

"Does it always feel like this?" Trey asked, his voice hoarse, as if he had a cold. "It's getting worse." He laid his head back against the shuttle.

"Ripspace is thin here," Gerard said. Hawk sensed that wasn't the full reason for Trey's reaction. "The planet is saturated in *aether*. That explains why it's restricted."

"I'm glad that explains it for you," Ashron said. "I don't have a clue."

"Do you know what the Trans-Federation is?"

"Sure." Ashron offered his pointy-tooth smile. "It's an evil coven of witches and warlocks."

Gerard sighed. "It's an offshoot of the Planetary Council in charge of laws and regulations concerning Trans-dimensional manipulation.

They can place *aether*-heavy planets on a tech-restricted list so no outside technology can be introduced."

"Why?"

"With a few exceptions, such as my arm and the ripspace drive, *aether* and technology mixed can create unpredictable results," Gerard said. "The more *aether*, the more volatile—and potentially dangerous—the consequences. There is also a balance problem. Too much technology too fast will destroy the *aether* and could have its repercussions. Therefore, to keep things simple, the Council puts such planets off limits and allows them to advance at their own pace. As they develop, the *aether* will recede, or may remain such a strong presence that the planet never develops past a certain level."

"When you say dangerous, what do you mean?" Ashron asked.

"The most extreme result would be a tear in the divide between normal space and *aetheric* space, which would allow things into our space that you don't want to meet."

"No, you don't," Trey said with a chill in his raspy voice.

"What about this shuttle?" Ashron asked.

"It's a matter of scale and time," Gerard explained. "If a colony ship landed here loaded with technology and settled in, there would be problems. A shuttle landing for a few minutes doesn't create enough disturbance to be significant. The truth is no one knows where the boundary is, so that's why these planets get a blanket restriction. That does lead to a concern, though. The commander ignored our backpack after our 'donation.' We could have any manner of contraband in it. If he's done this with others, it could eventually lead to problems. We may need to report him and have him watched."

He turned back to Trey. "How are you feeling now?"

"It's getting better," Trey answered. Thankfully the strange battle occurring in his head had lessened. It was worse than the ripspace visions. This time the voices of angels sang in his mind even as the demonic creatures tried to overpower their beautiful voices. It made the demons more furious, and they howled louder.

Trey had held himself together, saying nothing, not wanting to seem frightened even though the noisy conflict made him want to scream. If Gerard thought he couldn't handle something like this, he might no longer want to teach him to be a manipulator.

As the shuttle drew closer to the planet, the voices faded away, leaving only the congested prickling in his head and a faint tingle throughout his body. He relaxed. Gerard had said the creatures couldn't reach them as long as the barrier was intact. If it had already been breached, they would all be dead.

The craft hovered over a large clearing in a clump of forest comprised of huge trees with bright yellow-green leaves and muted red bark. Trey stared out the window and saw a small medieval style town, complete with castle, several kilometers away. "Why..." he started. Then he remembered what Gerard said about thinking it through.

After a few moments, he reached a conclusion. "We're landing a few klicks from town so we don't appear to come out of thin air," he said with great authority, even though no one had asked for an explanation. "We'll walk in like we came from some other town." He grinned, pleased he had figured it out on his own.

"Very good," Gerard said. "Although people appearing out of nowhere may not be uncommon on this planet, considering the potential for manipulators. A distant landing also reduces the chance of the shuttle being spotted by a local inhabitant."

"It's invisible," Trey said.

"It's cloaked," Gerard corrected. "It can still leave noticeable ripples in the air, especially if you're close to it."

As the shuttle descended closer to the planet, the cabin once again filled with vibration and thunderous noise as the landing jets kicked in. Trey quickly grabbed Laura's and Hawk's hands.

"Apparently the noise mufflers don't do a damn thing for the inside," Ashron yelled over the cacophony.

They thumped down softly, and the cabin filled with blessed silence as the jets powered down. Trey let go of Laura and Hawk, and they all began unbuckling and gathering themselves.

"Lady and gentlemen," Arlan's voice said over the loudspeaker. "Welcome to Meta Brévé."

17

WELCOME TO META BRÉVÉ

The cockpit door opened and Arlan stepped out with a small yellow coin in his hand. "This is a transmitter that resembles the local currency. Press it, and we'll return to pick you up. Don't spend it or let it get stolen. In any event, I'll return here in five days. If you aren't here, you'll be in violation of the Council Accords."

Hawk took the coin. "We'll be here."

"Good luck with your research," Arlan said. He returned to the cockpit. With a slight hiss the shuttle door opened and a set of stairs descended to the ground. Bright sunlight and a fragrant aroma that reminded Hawk of cherry blossoms drifted into the cabin.

"Looks like it's going to be a warm walk," Hawk said as he stepped out of the shuttle.

Trey held up his finger. "Eighty-five point six degrees. Humidity forty-eight point four percent," he continued as the others departed the shuttle. "Wind from the Northwest at six kilometers an hour. Baromet-"

"We get the point." Hawk favored Trey with an arched eyebrow. "Pray tell, is this some mutant ability you possess that you haven't told us about?"

Tugging at his brown shirt, Trey said. "I read the shuttle display."

Gerard chuckled. "Very resourceful."

They stepped away from the shuttle as the door closed.

"All clear?" Arlan said over the loudspeaker. Hawk moved into view of the cockpit and gave him thumbs up, then stepped back as the thrusters fired and the shuttle lifted off the ground.

"Filamentous," Trey said as the group moved out of the radius of the cloaking generator. To the crew, the vessel disappeared, leaving only a vague ripple in the air, and the noise became no louder than a slight rumble.

"Head 'em up, move 'em out," Hawk said.

"Which way?" Ashron asked. "I guess following that dirt road there would be a good start, huh?"

"That's an annoying habit, you know?" Laura told him.

"What?"

"Answering your own questions."

"I'm just following Gerard's advice. I thought it through while I was asking." He gave a playful flick of his tongue.

"Don't blame me for your idiosyncrasies," Gerard said.

"While we're young, people." Hawk headed for the road. The others followed, taking up defensive positions. Ashron moved ahead to take point.

"How is your breathing?" Gerard asked Trey.

"I still feel like I have a cold, but it's getting better."

"You should be fine in a few minutes. The initial shock is the worst, and you came through it okay. It could have been a lot worse for you, considering the amount of energy floating around here."

They had gone no further than a hundred meters when Gerard paused. "Ashron, wait."

Sensing the edge in Gerard's voice, Ashron drew his scimitar while he scanned the area. Hawk and Wolf followed suit, placing themselves between the wood line and the others.

"What is it?" Hawk asked.

As if on cue, a large force of soldiers stepped out from the trees and surrounded the small group.

"This looks bad," Ashron muttered.

One section of the soldiers parted. A tall man with pale yellow skin and straw-colored hair stepped into the clearing. He wore a black and gray, well-tailored modern suit that would have been entirely out of place, except that his soldiers also wore state-of-the-art polymesh body armor and sported light-caliber assault rifles.

"Drop your weapons," the man in the suit said. "We've got you surrounded, outmanned and—" he paused, smiling slightly, "outgunned."

Ashron slowly backed up to the others. "I don't know if anybody's noticed, but those aren't crossbows."

"Appears our Outpost Commander has had a very profitable week," Laura added. "Hawk?"

"Gerard?"

"There's a force shield around them. I could punch it, and take out half of them in the blast, but the other half would open fire before I could establish a shield of our own."

"Why not—"

"—Enough talk," the suited man interrupted Hawk. He made a gesture, and the soldiers leveled their weapons. "Three seconds."

"Drop 'em," Hawk said.

Grumbling, Ashron threw his sword to the ground. "How cliché. We brought knives to a gunfight."

The others complied, and the group disarmed in short order.

The leader motioned to two of the soldiers. They moved toward the group. One held a pair of manacles that he tossed to Gerard, who sidestepped and let them clatter at his feet.

"Don't play games," the leader said. "Put on the cuffs."

Gerard glared at the man, who stared back impassively.

"I have all day," the man said. "Face it; you have no choice. Your finger waving won't do you any good here. By the time you took out my sorcerer," he nodded toward a small man wearing purple robes, "we'd gun you down. If you don't put them on, we'll gun you down anyway. Makes life simple, yes?"

Slowly, Gerard bent down and picked up the manacles. His face became pained as he felt the anti-enchanted metal start to sever his connection to the *aether*. He clamped a cuff over his left hand. He began to put on the other and stopped. "I can't do this." He held his hands out to Wolf.

Mouth set in a grim line, Wolf clamped the manacle shut. He jumped back as a flash of silent purple light blazed across Gerard's cybernetic arm, leaving behind a smell of burnt air. Gerard stifled a cry of anguish. Trey grimaced and put a hand to his head.

Gerard's only comfort was that the manacles were made of *aculary*, a relatively weak anti-*aetheric* material. Unlike *triclum*, these cuffs only severed his contact while he wore them. If he could remove them, his power would return.

"I'll trust the rest of you to behave," the leader said. "Not that you need to know, but my name is Fralor. Let's go."

The soldiers formed up around the small crew, and they started down the road for the castle.

Hawk decided to see if he could get some information from Fralor. "So—"

"No talking," Fralor said, walking away.

Hawk started to retort. A threatening glare and raised rifle butt from a nearby guard changed his mind.

The robed magician walked next to Gerard, his saffron face almost painfully thin and devoid of hair on his pointed skull. "I am Partulas, High Magician to Lord Fralor and Ranking Thaumaturge of the Brévé City-States. What is your title?"

Gerard curled his mouth in a contemptuous frown. "Gerard."

"That's all? Gerard? That's no title for a magician of any worth." Partulas studied him as if appraising a peasant or slave. "It's just as well you didn't try to challenge me. I wouldn't have broken a sweat." He rapped on Gerard's cybernetic arm. "How good could you possibly be, with this abomination destroying your connection to the flow?"

When it became apparent there would be no reply from Gerard, the man walked away chuckling.

They marched two miles in a silence broken only by the tramping of booted feet. Sweat trickled down Hawk's forehead as he considered a way to escape. He soon concluded that they didn't have one yet. With Gerard incapacitated magically and the rest weaponless, they were outmatched. He needed to create a change in their situation.

They reached the keep, a squat, square fortification constructed of brownstone which sat on the outskirts of a small farming village. Sitting in the middle of a plain without a moat, the building seemed utterly indefensible.

"Force field," Gerard said.

"Completely impenetrable," Partulus crowed, his high voice filled with pride. "The only way in is for me to open it."

They paused at the doorway and Partulas opened the force field with extravagant gestures and a booming voice. Gerard shook his head at the overblown display.

As they continued into the keep, Partulas turned and repeated the procedure, closing the field. They walked through a narrow hallway and into a courtyard filled with pale green grass. Orange feathered birds with long necks and shovel-shaped bills scattered with a raspy caw of alarm as the group entered.

Fralor dismissed all but four of the guards and led the others down a narrow stone staircase. They continued through a dank hall dripping with mold-scented water and into a large room that contained chains, manacles, and numerous implements of torture.

"Chain them up, except for the woman. She'll come with us."

The guards manacled the crew's feet and performed a quick search, finding Ashron's concealed dagger. The guard who discovered the weapon gave Ashron's elongated snout a jabbing punch.

Recovering from the blow, Ashron offered the man a menacing smile full of gleaming teeth. "I never forget a face."

The guard took an involuntary step back. Ashron flashed a glance at Hawk, his expression begging permission to engage. Hawk gave the barest shake of his head. Ashron's snout curled in a sneer as the guard recovered and shackled him to the floor.

They clamped Wolf's calves in a pair of waist restraints attached to a heavy chain. "Lay down," Fralor told him. Wolf did, and two of the guards grabbed the handle on a large winch. They began cranking, the ratchets letting out loud pops in the stone chamber. With much grunting and puffing, they lifted Wolf until he hung three meters in the air, suspended upside down. The other two guards pushed a heavy iron plate covered with eighteen-inch titanium spikes underneath. The spikes glistened green with poison.

The guards stepped back from their task. Fralor looked at Hawk, chained against the wall with his arms and legs spread. "Uncomfortable?"

"A little," Hawk admitted.

"Good," Fralor said. "We'll be talking again soon, I'm certain."

"I wouldn't bet on it," Hawk said.

Fralor's brows bunched for a moment. Then he gave a vulpine smile. "Of course. Bravado in front of the lady." He turned to Laura. "You will come with me."

Laura frowned. The guards formed around her and marched her from the room. Fralor stopped at the door and turned back to the imprisoned crew. "Until later, gentlemen."

He left the room; the gleaming metal door closed with an ominous *boom*.

"What an asshole," Ashron hissed, spitting at the door. "You know, this walking into traps is getting to be a bad habit. Any ideas on getting out of here, O clueless one?"

"Pretty rude talk for someone who hasn't collected his last month's paycheck. These are obviously the people who are after Ship. Now we need to see if we can find out why."

"What are they going to do to Laura?" Trey asked, shackled next to Hawk.

"Laura can take care of herself," Hawk said.

"That's not an answer."

"She'll be all right." Gerard listened at his internal com unit. "They're still walking and not saying anything," he told Trey. "They want something from us. Considering the contraband tech, I suspect they know about Ship. They're not going to do anything to jeopardize our cooperation."

"Don't you mean anything *more*?" Ashron asked. "I'm way beyond any desire to cooperate."

"We'll cooperate until we find out what's going on," Hawk told him. "Then we'll leave."

"Just like that?" Ashron asked.

"Just like that."

"Well, okay, I feel much better about the situation now." Ashron sat on the floor with his chin in his hands.

"If you're going to sulk, go sit in the corner," Hawk told him.

"I would, but the chains aren't long enough."

"Don't worry," Gerard said. "We've got it planned out."

"Whatever it is," Wolf said, staring at them from his inverted position, "I hope it won't take long."

"Ashron, do me a favor," Gerard said. "Listen and see if there are any guards on the other side of the door."

"On it." Ashron stood and walked as close to the door as his chains allowed him.

"Everybody quiet down," he said, even though none of them were making any noise. He tapped lightly on the side of his head and Laura's voice disappeared as the implanted communications unit deactivated. He closed his eyes and focused solely on the sounds that came to him. Echoes from the roof filtered down as people walked on the floor above. Snatches of muted conversation drifted in. The scuttling of a creature in the far corner of the room screamed for his attention. He did his best to block those out and concentrate on any noise that might be beyond the door seven meters ahead of him. He listened for well over a minute. Nothing indicating soldiers presented itself to his acute hearing; no shuffling of feet or clink of armor. Ashron opened his eyes and focused on Gerard. "There's no one out there."

"Are you absolutely certain?" Gerard asked.

"Not *absolutely* certain." Ashron hissed in irritation. "As certain as possible considering the charming acoustical properties of this cellar and the foot-thick door between us and the hall."

"But you're reasonably certain."

"Look, unless this plan of yours requires firing a cannon, no one beyond the door is going to hear us, so let's go. These chains are chafing my scales."

Gerard stood up. "Are all Lorothians as impatient as you?".

"We live on a planet with ten hours of daylight and an eighty-six-day year. What do you think?"

Gerard moved the seven fingers on his cybernetic arm in a complex sequence. With a high-pitched whine, a concealed cover on the arm popped open. Out of the recess rose a four-inch silver tube mounted on a swiveling rod. A small carnelian sat at one end of the tube. Several strands of thin copper wire wrapped around the stone and wound over the cylinder in a delicate, intricate pattern, terminating with the end of each wire facing the tube opening.

Gerard pulled his arms apart until the chain holding his manacles was held taut. As Gerard flexed his fingers, the silver tube rotated until it faced the mid-point of the chains. He curled his thumb and forefinger until they made contact. The gem pulsed once and a bright red beam silently fired from the tube. The chain parted under the brilliant flare.

Gerard used the arm-mounted laser to slice the shackles off his legs. Leaving the anti-magic manacles on his wrists, he freed the rest from their restraints, except Wolf.

Once loose, Ashron ran to the door, prepared to take out any guards unlucky enough to step into the room.

When Gerard had freed everyone on the ground, he told Hawk, "Everybody will have to wait. As soon as I take off these cuffs, I'm going to be disoriented for at least a minute." He walked over to the corner and prepared to cut off the manacles.

"Is Laura still okay?" Trey asked Hawk.

"Laura, you good?"

She responded with two clicks.

"She's fine," Hawk told Trey.

Steeling himself, Gerard cut the manacle off his left wrist first, then his right.

The *aetheric* energy that had been denied to him by the metal in the manacles washed over him in an exhilarating wave of power. The force of it, potent on this power-rich planet, numbed his brain. He felt drunk and giddy. His knees buckled. He sat down hard on the floor. The room spun. It was hard to see through the scintillating lights that danced in front of his eyes.

"Are you okay?" a deep voice he thought he recognized asked him.

He tried to answer. Nothing coherent would form in his brain. His thoughts consisted of shapeless colors and meaningless pictures.

"I'm okay," a higher voice said in slow motion.

"Yes, I'm okay," Gerard echoed weakly after several interminable seconds. He wiped a hand across his pale face. "That's what happens when your connection to power is taken away and then suddenly given back." He sat up against the rough wall. The short-term assault had passed and he already felt himself gaining strength. He frowned when he saw Hawk helping Trey stand up. "What happened?"

"Trey suddenly got dizzy and fell," Hawk said.

"I'm alright," Trey assured him. "I felt like something punched me in the stomach."

Gerard considered the implications of Trey's extraordinary mental senses as the boy helped Hawk push the pallet of spikes out from under Wolf. It could make his training much easier...or infinitely harder.

Hawk turned the winch, lowering Wolf to the floor. The winch did not pop as it had going up, but it emitted a sharp *twang* every third or fourth turn as the thick cable smacked the edge of the feeding wheel.

"Someone's coming," Ashron hissed from the doorway. Hawk stopped turning the winch. Ashron tensed, ready to attack anyone that walked through. Gerard stood up.

They waited as Ashron listened. The others could hear nothing through the thick wall and door. They relied solely on Ashron's heightened auditory capabilities.

Seconds passed. They all heard the sound of a key inserted into the lock. Nothing happened for several more seconds, then the door swung open slowly. Two guards stepped in, sub-machine guns held to their sides. A third guard followed with a tray of food.

Before the sentries could even register that their captives were loose, Ashron leaped on them. He pushed his way past the two startled guards in front, forcing them to stumble forward and almost lose their weapons. Using one hand, he grabbed the food bearer by the throat, cutting off air and keeping him from screaming.

With the other hand, he snagged the tray before the guard could drop it. Yanking both tray and guard into the room, he used his tail to slam the door shut. The guard grabbed futilely at Ashron's muscled arm, trying to break the hold on his throat. Ashron slammed the man's head against the stone wall. The impact made the soldier go limp despite the brass helmet that sat on his head; he ceased struggling.

Hawk launched himself across the room toward the other two guards. As they raised their guns he slammed into them, his arms spread. They all hit the floor. The weapons fell from their hands. One of the guards received the full impact of Hawk's tackle and lay stunned from the collision. The other flailed wildly and started to scream. Hawk smashed the heel of his hand into the man's jaw. The force of the blow knocked the man's helmeted head into the stone floor. The flat ring of metal on stone echoed through the chamber; the man quit yelling. Both guards lay stunned on the floor. Hawk rendered them unconscious.

Ashron set the tray of food on the floor and cracked open the door. The key still sat in the lock, so he removed it. After a few moments, he said, "No one's coming. Let's get Wolf down and get out of here."

Hawk returned to the winch and continued turning the crank. "Not yet. We have to wait for the right moment."

Ashron walked over to Hawk. "What right moment?"

"*The* right moment."

"You're deliberately abstruse just to irritate me, aren't you?"

Hawk smiled at him.

They soon had Wolf free. He swooned a little as his blood returned to its regular circulation.

Ashron hauled the guards next to the winch and gagged them. Tying their feet with the cable, he hoisted them into the air until they hung suspended upside down. "See how you squinks like it," he said

Meanwhile, Gerard had begun chanting an equation and waving his arms with his eyes closed.

"What's he doing now?" Ashron asked.

"Wait," Hawk took off his shoe and removed a large silver disk. Laying it on the floor, he said, "Good thing they didn't check our feet."

As Gerard's chanting quickened, the coin glowed bright red. Its intensity increased in syncopation with the volume of Gerard's voice. After about thirty seconds, Gerard moved both his arms in a downward gesture and pointed at the disk. *"Pascare."*

The disk gave a bright flare and disappeared, replaced by a rectangular metal crate, roughly a meter by a meter and a half. It had fins on all four sides and a small jetpack on the back.

Gerard leaned against the wall, hand to his head.

"You okay?" Trey asked.

"Yes, but it wasn't the wisest thing to do that so soon after regaining my connection."

"What is that?" Ashron asked.

Hawk walked over to the crate. "Remember when I bumped the atmosphere?"

"Yes."

"That was a distraction so I could let this go," Hawk explained, opening the top of the crate.

Inside were four auto lasers, Wolf's Mini-Gun of Awesomeness, spare clips and belts, a handful of grenades, and a field medical kit.

"You know, sometimes you're a genius," Ashron said as Hawk began distributing the weapons.

"No, I'm a genius all the time; I only let it show sometimes."

"What about the introduction of technology thing?" Trey asked.

Gerard shrugged. "Sometimes you have to take chances."

Ashron cocked the weapon "So, what next?"

"Now," Hawk said, smiling at Ashron. "We wait for *the* right moment."

Ashron hissed derisively at him.

FORCED HOSPITALITY

Laura kept her intentions hidden as she walked with her head down. She bent her entire thought on figuring out a way to escape, despite the guards on either side that held her arms, their hands gripped tightly around her biceps.

As they trod the drab stone corridor, she glanced from left to right, searching for side halls or anything else that would facilitate her getaway. She spotted a few branching passages, but until she had a better idea of the fortress, the thought of flight was little more than an exercise to occupy her mind.

With Fralor leading, they ascended a long flight of stairs, through a small, bare anteroom, and into a spacious and opulently decorated throne room. Large, elaborate tapestries embroidered with scenes of bloody battles and gentle landscapes of verdant hills dotted the walls.

An imposing throne covered in silver and filigreed gold occupied the center of the end wall. Intricately carved pillars of blue stone held up the roof, which towered ten meters above the floor. Guards dressed in shining chain mail stood between each post. Red tabards emblazoned with a stylized, six-legged animal covered their armor coats. She counted twenty soldiers standing at attention, the machine guns slung over their shoulders incongruous in the medieval surroundings.

Fralor walked up the dais steps and sat in the silver chair. As she waited, Laura wondered if Unicybertronic Technologies was funding this highly illegal corruption of the planet, what their purpose was, and why they had involved the Knights or, more specifically, Ship.

Fralor clapped his hands. From the shadows of the throne, a young man and woman emerged to stand beside the dais. Laura judged them to be between eighteen and twenty. Dressed like the guards, minus the chain mail, they both had honey-colored hair. The boy's short and straight: the girl's long and wavy. Their bright green eyes stood out from their buff-colored skin, the predominant hue of Meta Brévé's inhabitants. Laura guessed them as brother and sister. They seemed well cared for, though their haunted expressions made her think they lived in constant fear. Suspecting Fralor would be a harsh master, Laura could well understand their countenance.

Fralor looked at the young man. *"Fertä stala tûe viztu."* To the young woman, he said. *"Lugew vin en pradeca."*

The two servants ran off on their errands. The guards released their grip on Laura's arms and took a few steps back. Laura flexed her arms and hands to shake away the guards' grip. She stopped when she heard the ring of cold steel behind her.

"Not a wise idea to try and cast magic when twenty armed men surround you," Fralor said with a smirk that couldn't completely hide his brief flash of fear.

Laura said nothing. Though she had no powers of manipulation, letting them keep their misconception might give her an advantage.

They waited in silence until the servants returned. The boy carried a plain wooden chair with a dark blue cushion. The girl bore a large silver tray which held two goblets, a pitcher, and a bowl filled with pink and purple fruits. While the girl placed the tray on a small table beside the throne, the boy sat the chair down behind Laura and stepped away. Laura continued to stand. At a motion from Fralor, one of the guards stepped up behind her. He put a hand on her shoulder and exerted gentle downward pressure. She didn't budge.

Fralor sighed. "I'm doing my best to make this civil. You're my prisoner and will continue to be so for several days. Why don't you accept the fact and try to enjoy what you can of it?"

"If you want me to enjoy it," Laura said, "put me back in the dungeon with my friends and out of your sickening presence."

Fralor gave a tight smile. "Don't try my patience. The only reason I haven't let my men take a turn amusing themselves with you is because I've been informed you are a gifted healer, which makes you worth more than you would be as a whore."

"And who told you such a thing?"

"A friend," Fralor said, still grinning. His teeth were almost the same color as his skin. The girl poured wine from the pitcher into the two goblets and offered one to Fralor.

After taking a long drink, he said. "I assume the young boy downstairs is your son or someone you're fond of. Unless you want one of my guards to bring him up and cut him open in front of you, I suggest you sit down."

He stated it with so little emotion that Laura almost didn't believe him. The cold stare in his dark eyes convinced her he meant every word. She sat.

"Have a drink," At a motion from him, the girl offered her the other cup. Stiffly, she accepted the proffered goblet and swallowed a portion of the liquid, not even paying attention to the taste. The girl withdrew to stand near her brother.

"I'm not your enemy," Fralor told Laura as he picked up a triangular shaped purple fruit with light green dots. "I'm simply a small noble on a small planet whose eyes have been opened to the beauty of commerce with other worlds." He popped the fruit into his mouth.

Laura let out a bitter laugh. "Looks to me like you're a petty little chieftain on a backwater planet who's been corrupted by money and technology."

Chewing, Fralor spoke around the fruit. "Why is it the people who've lived with money and technology all their lives think it hasn't corrupted them, but anyone just being introduced to it must be? The people who want your ship are the corrupt ones. They're the ones bribing protection outpost leaders and killing innocent people. I'm simply the—," he paused a moment, swallowing. "—broker."

"So, what's your commission for bringing us in?"

"For bringing *you* in? Nothing but what I can get for myself. Which is why I was so pleased to learn of your medical abilities. However, bringing your vessel in is another matter entirely."

Laura tried her best to sound casual. "What does our ship have to do with anything?"

"I honestly don't know," Fralor answered, "The company is interested in whatever special capabilities it has."

"What company?" Laura asked.

Fralor chuckled. "I may just be a 'petty chieftain on a backwater planet,' but I'm not stupid."

"If you're going to keep us prisoner and sell me away as a slave, what's the harm in telling me?"

"If you're going to be a slave, what's the point in you knowing?"

"It'll be much easier if you tell me now, instead of having it forced out of you."

"Forced out of me?" Fralor asked with an amused expression on his face. "You don't seem to be in a position to force anything. Now, why don't you drink some more wine before I become upset?" His face took on a dangerous frown.

Laura lowered her head and quietly said, "I'm getting tired of this pompous ass, so anytime you guys are ready."

"Give us the word," Gerard said.

Picking up the wine goblet, Laura said, "Are you sure you don't want to tell me who's after Ship? After all, you're not my enemy."

"No, I don't think it's that important, and you shouldn't either," Fralor answered.

"Does anyone else know about this company?" Laura asked.

"A few others. Why?"

"I wanted to make sure the knowledge didn't die with you." She smiled, then whispered, "Go ahead, Gerard."

Fralor gave her a curious cock of his head. "You have a strong will, and I admire that as far as it goes. We'll have to break you of that before we se-"

A deep rumbling originating somewhere under the floor stopped him. Fralor's eyes dropped toward the floor, his face uneasy. "Go see what that is," he snapped at one of the guards.

"Goodbye," Laura said. She jumped from her chair and backed away.

Fralor looked at her, head still cocked. As she smiled at him and the rumbling grew louder, his mouth and eyes widened in a wash of fear. "St—"

The floor underneath him erupted like a long-dormant volcano suddenly gone active. Shattered stone flew in all directions. Flames belched forth like the fires of Hell. Fralor had no time to scream, his body instantly immolated. He burned like a piece of dry tinder as he fell through the hole created by the fountain of fire. The throne cracked in half. The gold and silver filigree turned into molten globs before vaporizing.

Laura dropped to the floor, trusting Gerard to avoid her as the intense heat washed over her. The conflagration arced a meter over her prone form and caught the two guards standing behind her; their tabards and leggings burst into flame and chain mail melted into their skin. They ran a short distance, blind and screaming in pain, before toppling over, their skin still burning.

The guards positioned between the pillars turned to run. They reacted too late. Spikes of orange-white flame sprang from the central column, which now scorched the stone roof ten meters above. With unerring accuracy, the flaming spikes found the soldiers, spearing them through the chest and igniting them like paper. Their dying screams echoed through the chamber with the crackling of the flames, blending into a concerto of the doomed.

The sound attracted Fralor's elite guards. They ran into the throne room to discover what was happening to their liege. Witnessing their comrades' fate, many of them turned pale, sickened by the sight and stench of burning flesh. Though shaken, they did not retreat. They drew pistols and hefted their small metal bucklers.

Partulas, Ranking Thaumaturge of the Brévé City-States, was disturbed not by the noise of the flames and dying men in the throne room. Those sounds were too far from his opulent chambers to be heard. But the bright, loud tone of powerful magic being wielded sang to him like a *palla* bird chirping boisterously upon his shoulder. He jumped up from the tome he was poring over, grabbed his bone staff from its ebony rack, and chanted.

A few seconds later he teleported to the throne room, which had become an inferno. He stepped back and threw his hand up, trying to shield himself from the intense heat. At the same time, he barked a command. His staff flared, and a light green nimbus encompassed his body, protecting him from the fury of the flames.

He studied the scene. Several charred bodies lay on the floor. A white-hot spire of flame reached to the ceiling, burning where the throne once sat. The woman they had taken from the clearing crouched nearby, the fire arcing well above her head. Other than the sweat that beaded her forehead, she seemed unaffected. Either she was magically protected, or the mage wielding the flames had exceptional control.

Ten of the lord's elite guard stood nearby, weapons drawn and shields in place. They milled about, unsure what to do. The woman had not noticed him yet. Partulas moved toward her, darting from column to column until he stood in range to cast an enchantment and bring her to him. He had no fear she had caused this destruction; somehow the other magician had been freed from his bonds. His only hope was to catch this woman and use her as a hostage. Despite his boasting, he could not win in a contest of will with the metal-armed mage.

He had taken only one step toward her when something in the flame caught his eye.

Like a demon rising from the depths of the Abyss, Gerard floated through the hole in the floor. He stood in the center of the pillar, the flames coursing around him with no effect. Ascending until he stood level with the floor, he stepped out of the burning column as calmly as a man would leave an elevator. There was a determined set to his colorless face and a cold gleam in his pale eyes. He waved his hand; the incandescent shaft behind him winked out of existence, creating an audible pop as air rushed to fill the vacuum. His eyes locked with Partulas and he said. "Do you wish to challenge me now?"

Terrified almost beyond the ability to speak, Partulas shouted, "Guards, kill him." He hoped his voice didn't sound as weak to them as it did to him.

The guards moved forward, taking up the positions their training instilled into them, and raised their guns. Gerard calmly turned and faced the soldiers, his back to Partulas. Raising his cybernetic arm and flexing his fingers in an intricate pattern, he said, "Surrender or die." He did not scream it theatrically, his voice booming, but stated it in a manner so soft Partulas barely heard him.

The men halted, uncertain, and turned to their captain. The captain considered the destroyed landscape that had been the throne room. His lord Fralor was gone, nearly twenty soldiers lay in ashen heaps, and the man responsible for the cataclysm bore no scars, nor even seemed strained from the effort. The captain holstered his gun and lowered his shield. The soldiers, relief evident upon their faces, followed suit.

"Gerard, watch out," the woman shouted. During the guard's indecision, while Gerard had his back turned, Partulas had drawn a slim dagger from under his robe. It was enchanted to fly true and strike with deadly precision. Partulas launched the missile. It sped toward Gerard, aiming for the spinal cord at the base of the brain.

Without even turning, Gerard waved his hand, touched three of his fingers together and muttered a word. The blade struck him. With a flash the magic discharged, and the dirk shattered. The handle clattered uselessly to the stone floor, followed by the slivers of metal that didn't get snagged in Gerard's clothing.

Gerard slowly turned to face Partulas. Sensing his doom, Partulas chanted, hoping to teleport away before the other could stop him.

"Silence," Gerard said. He threw his hand forward, his thumb and seventh finger touching with the others flexed back. Partulas's tongue went numb. He tried to continue the spell; no coherent sounds would come from his mouth. Knowing he had lost for the moment, Partulas laid his head on his bone staff.

"There it is." Ashron pointed to the large wooden doors. Unable to levitate like Gerard, they had to reach the throne room by walking. They were all armed from Hawk's cache box. Trey, in addition to his knife, carried Laura's rapier, an auto laser slung over one shoulder, and the medical kit over the other.

Wolf pushed at the doors. They flew open, attracting the attention of everyone in the room. He stepped aside, and the others walked in. He came in last and closed the doors, throwing down the wooden bar that sealed them shut.

Hawk took in the room's destruction. "Bit messy, but very impressive. Wolf, disarm the guards. Trey, take the weapons and toss them into the hole." He pointed to a door about seven meters left of the throne's previous location. "Laura and Ashron, check that room and make sure there're no surprises waiting for us. Gerard, you and I are going to talk to our new friend."

Trey handed Laura her equipment. "Are you okay?" he asked her.

She grinned. "That's my line," she said as she slid on the medical kit. "You trying to take over my job?"

He smiled back. "No, I was just worried."

"I'm fine," she assured him. Looking where the throne once stood, she said, "If he hadn't been such a bastard, he would have been a real gentleman." She turned back at Trey. "Go help Wolf."

"Put down the shields and take off the weapons," Wolf rumbled at the soldiers, waving his MGoA as Trey walked over.

"Let's go," Ashron said to Laura as the soldiers stripped off their weaponry under Wolf's gaze. Laura strapped on her weapons, and the two of them headed for the mystery door.

Trey gathered the discarded weapons and tossed them into the hole created by Gerard's fiery entrance.

"Against the wall," Wolf said. The soldiers moved to comply. "If I find any concealed weapons..." He left the threat unfinished. The glower on his sizable gray face persuaded three of the soldiers to relinquish hidden daggers.

Gerard and Hawk stood in front of Partulas. The mage's eyes were wide with terror. "If I free your tongue," Gerard said, "will you try to formulate an equation?"

Partulas bunched his eyebrows. Remembering where he was, Gerard rephrased the question. "Will you try to cast a spell?"

The scared man shook his head vigorously; droplets of sweat flew from his forehead.

Hawk drew his sword. Partulas backed up, holding up his hands.

"Stand still!" Hawk commanded the man, and he stopped. "This is insurance."

Gerard moved his hand. "*Losoda.*" He looked at Partulas. "You can speak. Now, what should we do with you?"

"I'll tell you anything you want to know."

"Yes, you will," Hawk said. "Let's start now, and then we'll decide on an appropriate punishment afterward."

"Punishment?" Partulas asked, swallowing. "For what?"

"You severed my connection to the *aether*; took away my power to manipulate," Gerard said, his voice slightly raised, a sure sign to any who knew him that he was close to seething. "You imprisoned my friends and me, and insulted me. With some manipulators I know, instant death would be your fate.

"However," Gerard continued as he surveyed the room, "current circumstances aside, I am opposed to wanton destruction. We will think of something appropriate."

Shifty-eyed desperation passed over Partulas's face. "You cannot be my punishers," he said brazenly. "I demand an audience before the Council of Mages in Yerefstat."

Despite himself, Hawk was impressed with the man. It took guts to stand amidst this destruction and demand anything from the person responsible for it.

Impressed or not, Hawk had grown dangerously short of patience. He put his sword up to the mage's chest, forcing him back against a column. "You'll get what we give you, nothing more."

The man started trembling again.

"We're not going to kill you. You can thank Gerard for that, but you better answer some questions, or I'll make sure there's a great deal of pain."

Partulas licked his lips. Hawk could almost see the man's mind working behind his beady eyes, and wondered what he could be thinking. Partulas's face suddenly became placid, and he quit shaking. He had made a decision.

"The consequence of revelation is death," Partulas said in a flat voice, "So I will tell you this."

Before Hawk or Gerard could react, Partulas rolled his eyes upward, flicked both wrists, and muttered a word. With a slight smile on his face, he collapsed to the floor.

<hr>

Laura opened the door. Ashron slipped in, body low in case anyone decided to send knives, bullets, or any other sort of projectile his way. He scanned the area and found himself in a large kitchen. A wooden table dominated the center of the room, surrounded by cooking pits, bread ovens, and various other culinary implements. A sizable hock of raw meat sat on the table. Its fleshy odor flared his nostrils.

One other door sat nestled between a wall rack full of pots and a stained wooden wash tub. Ashron motioned toward the door. Laura sidled next to it, gun at the ready. He joined her, avoiding the pots that hung next to him. He listened for a moment, then pointed at the door and held up two fingers. Laura nodded and signaled that it was probably the young servants. Ashron gave her a questioning stare for a moment and then nodded. He pushed open the door and eased in, gun poised.

It was a pantry, filled with food-covered shelves. A young man and woman huddled in the farthest corner, shivering with fear. Ashron relaxed. He didn't wholly lower his guard, but he dropped the gun to his side. The two youngsters appeared more terrified than dangerous. "Clear," he said.

Laura stepped in. Slinging her auto laser, she stepped closer to the pair and spoke in a soothing voice. "It's okay. You're safe."

Whimpering, the girl tried to push further away, shoving the boy out in front of her. He stood and, revealing a substantial meat cleaver he had concealed behind his back, took a resolute fighting stance.

Laura stopped. "We're not going to hurt you," she said softly. "Put the weapon down."

The boy advanced, holding the cleaver out and waving it menacingly. Laura stepped back as Ashron walked into the pantry.

"*Nakali!*" the girl screamed. The boy backed up, stark terror on his face, but he still held the weapon.

"What does that mean?" Ashron asked softly.

"No ideas here," Laura whispered back. "Friends," she said to the two, who stared at her with fear and incomprehension. "Did you download a translation program before we left Ship?"

"Yes," Ashron said.

"Now might be a good time to use it."

"I was hoping to avoid that." Ashron clicked a button on his belt, and the program kicked in. Words displayed in his brain, inserting themselves in his synapses. In ten seconds, he became fluent in a language it took most people years to learn. He already dreaded the headache he was going to have later.

"*Nakali* means demon," he explained to Laura. He turned to the two frightened youths. "*Seleé ta Nakali. Isva sa acami.*" He pointed to Laura. "*Isvé sa mekalic, tu acami.*"

The boy and girl looked startled for a moment. "*Nê nakali?*" the boy asked Ashron, sounding uncertain. He still hadn't lowered the cleaver.

"*Nê,*" Ashron said. He pointed at himself. "*Isva sa* Lorothian." He once again indicated Laura. "*Isvé sa* Earthling."

"Lor...othian," the boy said, the word finding it a tough time in his mouth.

"I'm going to go see if they need any help out there," Laura told Ashron. "See if you can convince them we're friendly and get them to leave here. We might need them to help us."

"No problem," Ashron said, smiling.

"Whatever you do," Laura said, walking out the door, "don't smile at them."

FRIGHTENING REVELATIONS

Gerard bent down to the prone magician and checked his pulse. "Damn," he said.

"What?" Hawk asked.

"He committed suicide."

"How?"

"He overloaded his brain with *aetheric* power. I'm afraid he won't be telling us anything. Sorry I couldn't stop him."

Hawk shrugged. "Not like you had any way of knowing he would do something like that. I wonder who had him so frightened he would rather die than tell us anything."

"What happened?" Laura asked as she came back in from the pantry.

"He killed himself," Gerard said.

She turned to the unarmed soldiers "Are any of you hurt?"

They stared at her in incomprehension, then the commander turned to his men. They held a quick, whispered discussion. He turned back to Laura.

"We..." he paused, obviously not as fluent in Standard as the better-educated nobles.

Still, she mused, *considering the restrictions on the planet, none of them should even know the language.*

"We…okay. What…do with us?"

"That's a good question," Laura said. "What are we going to do with them?" she asked Hawk.

"That depends on them."

Ashron returned from the kitchen, followed by the two young servants. As everyone turned toward them, Ashron said, "This is Kalae and his sister Kerlai, and I think they may be able to help us. They've seen some strange things in the past couple of weeks, in addition to the usual oddities like guns and hovercraft. They've been telling me about mysterious objects being carried into an 'unholy place' behind the castle, followed by people being carried into the dungeons, followed by loud screams at night, followed by objects wrapped in sheets being brought back out. I don't know about you, but my interest is certainly piqued."

"Sounds like what we came here to find out," Hawk said. He eyed the soldiers. "If we let you go, will you try to attack us or will you leave us be?"

The soldiers stared at Hawk, while the captain's yellow face grimaced as he struggled with the words.

"Allow me," Ashron said. "Might as well get the most out of this before it leaves my brain."

He spoke to the captain, who responded with his own words and a shake of his head. Kalae joined the conversation, pointing at Ashron and the others. The captain appeared unconvinced; Kalae and Ashron persisted. Eventually, the captain nodded to Hawk.

Ashron translated. "He said they'll remain in the castle and not hinder us. Kalae convinced him we were here to destroy the 'unholy place' and stop the destruction and chase away the demons. That seemed to do the trick."

"Demons?" Gerard asked. "Is that figurative or literal?"

Ashron stared at Gerard. "Try again in words I understand, please."

"Are they saying demon because of the strangeness and the killing, or have they seen creatures they would consider demons?"

Ashron looked at Kalae and the captain. *"Avtu vivû nakali?"*

The captain shook his head, and Kalae said, "*Nê. Balo stalos casol tánakali.*"

"They haven't seen the demons," Ashron said, "but Kalae says only demons could make they screams they've heard.."

Gerard relaxed. "As long as they haven't seen one."

"What does it mean if they have?" Laura asked. To her surprise, Trey answered.

"It means the technology here has created a hole to ripspace and the creatures there have come here." Trey shivered.

"That's right," Gerard said. "And that would not be good. We may be in time to stop this from getting any worse if we can go to this 'unholy place' and destroy any technology in there."

"Then let's get a move on," Hawk said. "I guess it would be too much to hope the guards would want to help us, so tell them they're dismissed and thank them for being so cooperative."

Ashron translated. The captain gave an open-handed salute and the men, in orderly fashion, opened the throne room door and departed.

"Okay, Ashron, take point. I've got your back. The two locals can stick with me and give you directions. Gerard, Laura, and Trey take middle ground. Wolf, you've got rear guard. Let's go."

Ashron translated instructions to Kalae and his sister as the others took up their positions. They left the throne room and, following Kalae's directions, marched toward the courtyard. Unconcerned about attacks from the surviving guards, they made good time and soon stopped at the edge of the courtyard. Ashron and the servants held a quick conference, Kalae pointing as he talked.

When they finished, Ashron turned to the rest of the crew. "We have a choice. We can go out the front or the back. The back is closer to the building, and there's a wall that can provide some cover, so I suggest we go that way."

"They have a back door?" Hawk asked.

Ashron shrugged. "So they aren't big on defense."

"With the force field they have around the wall, they didn't have to worry," Gerard said. "If they hadn't wanted us in here, it would have taken me days to breach the defense."

"What about getting out?" Hawk asked.

Gerard shook his head. "Shouldn't be a problem. All the energy is directed outward. Once we leave, we won't be coming back in."

"That's fine; I wasn't planning on spending the night anyway." Hawk turned to Ashron. "Tell them we'll take the back door."

"*Rada tu akess*," Ashron told Kalae. Nodding, the boy pointed across the courtyard. They started marching again, crossing the yard and entering another doorway. A trek down a hallway put them at the keep's rear wall, where they found a wooden door.

Ashron cautiously opened the door and peered out.

"*Tesvê sa urhöla*," Kalae said, hovering over Ashron's shoulder. He pointed to a structure that had been set up in a large field of purple vines. Ashron nodded. Though the building didn't appear particularly "unholy" as Kalae put it, it didn't belong on this planet.

"Single story structure about twenty-five meters away," Ashron reported to the others. "Two guards, two heavy laser emplacements. There's a stone wall five meters away, surrounding the field. If we stay low and quiet, we can reach it without being spotted."

The castle wall exploded two meters from Ashron's head, grey stone showering outward. Ashron ducked back into the hallway as Kerlai screamed.

"I think we've been spotted," Ashron shouted above the ringing in his ears.

"Move," Hawk said. "Low and fast."

Ashron dashed out the door, dropping into a crouch. He felt the searing heat of the laser fly over him as another section of the castle wall disintegrated. Flecks of stone dust peppered his back as he raised his Sub LazGun and fired, crab-walking until he reached the low stone wall.

Wolf came next, mini-gun in hand, and laid down suppressing fire as Hawk ran to the wall and dropped behind it. A blast chewed up the ground in front of Wolf; he flung his large body sideways.

Hawk peered through a low spot in the wall and spotted one of the guards standing behind the large laser panel. He prepared to rise and fire when the guard slumped and fell to the ground. A quick peek toward the other laser revealed the guard there doing the same thing.

"Gerard," Hawk called back over his shoulder, "was that you?"

"Yes," Gerard said from inside the castle.

Hawk stood and turned to Gerard and Laura, who waited at the doorway of the keep wall. "Stay put. We'll reconnoiter the building and call you when it's clean. If we need help, we'll scream."

"Roger," Gerard said.

Nodding, Hawk turned back to Ashron and Wolf. "Everyone okay?"

Ashron reached around and poked himself in the back, "Medium rare, I think, but otherwise good."

"Wolf?"

Wolf nodded, brushing out clumps of dirt stuck in his black hair.

"Move out," Hawk said.

They stepped over the wall and made a cautious approach toward the structure. They scanned the surrounding field, focusing most of their attention on the building's single doorway.

"Smart," Hawk said when they reached the building.

"What's smart?" Ashron asked, also looking at the building. "I know you're not talking about the baby-puke-green paint."

"That's not paint, that's part of the building," Hawk said. "It's a pre-fab organotech lab. The whole building is suspended microorganisms. Activate them, and they consume themselves and anything inside the building within hours. No trace, no evidence, no crime. Moran and UCT have certainly covered their bases."

"You're convinced it's them?" Wolf asked as Ashron moved to disarm the unconscious guards.

"I've been convinced since day one," Hawk said. "I'm just searching for the smoking gun."

"Well," Ashron said, standing by one of the large laser cannons. "That explains why they couldn't hit us. These are just excavation lasers. Lots of power, no accuracy. You realize everybody inside is probably aware something happened out here, right?"

"Yes," Hawk said, "So it's by the numbers. You're on point, Wolf is rear guard."

They nodded. Ashron, standing to the side, pushed open the door.

When no gunshots, laser blasts, or explosions were forthcoming, he chanced a glance.

It was not at all what he expected. The sun shone through the structure's micro-organic layer, spreading pale green light through the building. It revealed a space devoid of anything except a set of stairs leading into the ground near the entrance. Ashron sniffed. The building had a stale, unused smell. He detected an undercurrent of something less pleasant, a whiff of decay emanating from the stairs.

He stepped inside; the others followed. They all moved silently across the micro-organic floor. He felt the scratching roughness of the material through his soft-soled boots. It gave him the creeps.

He started down the concrete steps, thankful to be off the strange floor. Every few steps he would pause and listen, testing the air to see if everything "felt" right. The dim green light quickly died out, leaving the stairwell in darkness. He could see well despite the lack of illumination, but he knew Hawk and Wolf would be activating their enhancement contacts soon. He continued down the stairs in his routine. Move, stop, test. Move, stop, test. All of them were careful to stay centered on the stairway and not near the walls, although Wolf had to move sideways to do so. A piece of equipment scraping on stone acted like a beacon in the dark.

Ashron paused again, kneeling down to get a different perspective. His eyesight enabled him to see deeper into the infrared spectrum than even the technology available to the crew members. This visual acuity allowed him to notice the thin beam of light running across the opening at the foot of the stairs. The beam ran about thirty centimeters off the floor. Easy to avoid, as long as you knew it was there. Ashron assumed it was a system to alert the people within the compound, similar to devices used in stores to notify staff of a customer's arrival. This group of customers, however, wanted their visit to be a surprise. Ashron had already seen all the selling points of an excavation laser he cared to know about.

Motioning with his hands, he outlined the laser and then cautiously stepped over the beam. The hallway ran about seven meters in both directions, each path terminating at a closed door. A quick scan proved both ways clear. He waved the others down.

At a signal from Hawk, Ashron moved down the right-hand corridor. Wolf took up a position at the foot of the stairs, obtaining what little protection the wall offered his bulk. He covered the unsecured left hallway while Hawk followed Ashron.

They reached the door and Hawk signaled for Wolf to join them. As Wolf backed down the hallway, Ashron examined the door. It was dull gray metal except for a bar-shaped handle. He saw no traps, but they had no way of scanning the room beyond. Ashron put his ear to the wall and heard the sound of muffled machinery. A scream of agony followed. Hawk's lips thinned and turned white beneath his mustache, and Ashron knew his captain had also heard the sound. Ashron put his hand on the handle and Hawk nodded.

Ashron turned the handle and pushed the door open. He ran through the doorway, followed by Hawk. Wolf stormed in behind them.

No one took notice of them for a few seconds, which gave them ample time to scan the room. The more they saw, the more horrified they became.

The room was, roughly thirty meters long by fifteen wide. Ten men stood at various metal tables, and three sat at a large computer console. The men at the tables wore long coats that had been white at one time, now stained with blood. Another man, wearing a black robe, chanted and hovered around a large glass sphere filled with sickly orange light.

Around the tables sat pieces of equipment that looked as if they had been borrowed from Satan's antechamber. Gore covered blades and spikes dominated. On the tables lay what could only vaguely be described as people, each lashed to their table with thick metal straps. Wires ran to various parts of their bodies, trailing across the floor over to the computer console. Most of them had been completely stripped of their skin. Several had sharp metal prongs sticking half a meter out of their arms. Hanging down from the top of these prongs were four thin metal wires that ended in hooks. Lying over these hooks were strands of muscles that had been pulled up from the forearm; sinew torn away from the limb.

Hawk's mind whirled. Like the vital piece in a jigsaw puzzle that makes the rest fall into place, this scene put all the recent events into their proper order. The reason behind Moran's insanity became crystal clear, and Hawk almost wept at the depravity caused by his old friend's twisted logic.

Hawk didn't want to consider it right now; refused to consider it. All he wanted to do at this moment was stop it. Destroy it. Make it burn.

One of the men in the blood-splattered robes noticed them. Before he could say anything, Hawk opened fire.

The technicians looked up for the cause of the noise. Blood and charred flesh flew as five of them fell dead under Hawk's gunfire.

Caught off guard, Ashron and Wolf hesitated. When one of the men sitting behind the computer console drew a small pistol and aimed it at Hawk, that hesitation disappeared. Ashron unloaded his gun, firing until all three of the operators lay slumped in their chairs. One ended up sprawled over the console as sparks leaped from the destroyed machine.

The other five technicians had managed to find cover. They had no weapons, so they could do nothing but gibber as Wolf moved in and shot them.

Hawk focused on the glass sphere with its churning amber glow. The mage stood behind the globe. His eyes slowly grew alert, as if he woke from a dream and realized too late something was amiss. Hawk fired at the mage and struck the globe. Laser light refracted as the glass shattered, sending shards whickering through the air at deadly speeds. Released from its containment field, the stored *aether* flew outward with a cry of banshees. As orange light struck nearby equipment, pieces exploded. Metal scattered with a cascade of orange and blue sparks. Several shards slammed into the mage, and he staggered back, wounded.

Hawk and the others ducked, avoiding the lethal slivers as they buried themselves in the walls and the dying flesh on the tables.

Hawk kept his head down as sound and fire flooded the room. The smell of burning wire hit his nose. Shaking off a sudden chill, he saw the vague outlines of creatures from a nightmare vision of hell. Horned, winged, and scaled, they resembled a madman's mash-up of a snake and bat. Orange and blue fire limned their long, legless bodies. Sharply curved teeth hung in their giant round mouths as they roared in silent fury. They smashed at the equipment, their strikes destroying anything they touched. As their incorporeal forms passed through the tables, the mangled flesh on the metal slabs screamed a sound of agony almost beyond endurance. Hawk lowered his head and covered his ears, waiting for the bad dream to pass. He had seen these beings years before and had prayed never to see them again.

The explosions soon died down as the energy expended itself. Hawk stood up with the others. Flames and smoke packed the room and equipment lay in scattered pieces. Where the manipulator had stood there was little more than splashes of blood on the walls and floor and a few shreds of black cloth. The creatures trapped in the *aetheric* sphere had extracted their revenge. Hawk shuddered.

"We'd better go," Ashron said, sneezing as the acrid electrical smoke irritated his sensitive nose.

"In a minute," Hawk said in a shaky voice. He went to each of the masses of flesh. Some were dead; he put a shot through the heads of any still twitching. Seared flesh joined the mélange of odors in the room.

When he finished, Hawk's eyes played over the burning, destroyed lab for a moment. "Now we can go."

As they left the room and started back up the stairs, Ashron said, "Would you like to tell me what that was all about?"

"Later," Hawk said.

They ascended the stairway and exited the building to find five concerned faces staring at them.

"I thought I told you to stay in the castle," Hawk said.

"We heard explosions, and Gerard said he felt the tainted energy of a *malevolum*," Laura explained. "We were about to come down. What happened?"

"I'll explain on the way up." Hawk looked at the two servants. "Do these two have a home?"

"Kâmil doma?" Ashron asked Kalae.

The boy nodded and pointed in a direction across the field. *"Doma sevil wës."* He quickly explained to Ashron that they were taken in lieu of a tax burden their parents could not pay. Ashron relayed all this to Hawk.

"Tell them they're free to go," Hawk said. "They won't be bothered by the screams anymore."

As Ashron did so, Hawk said, "Ship?"

"Here, Captain," she responded. "Good to hear from you again. Do you realize the people up here have run a coded override on all my systems? They're holding me prisoner." Ship sounded insulted.

"That doesn't surprise me. Can you break them?"

"Of course, their coding is sloppy. However, I don't think you want me to."

"Why not?"

"To lock me down, they had to feed in a signal from their system, which allowed me to log in, so I have the run of the station. By the way, they've been sending a distress signal, saying that we shot up the station and have corrupted the planet. I've been sending replies saying help is on the way from several sectors."

"Good girl. If you override, you'll lose the connection with their system, and they'll realize they've been duped."

"Affirmative."

"Send down their shuttle, would you? They'll realize something's wrong, but they won't be able to do anything about it." Hawk said with a wicked grin.

"Affirmative," Ship said. "The shuttle will be there in twenty-three minutes."

As Hawk turned back to the group, Kalae and Kerlai were running, smiles on their faces.

"They're going back to their home," Ashron told him. "They said thanks."

"Okay," Hawk told the group. "Our ride is here in twenty. Ashron, I want you to take some of those incendiaries, go back down there, and make that place burn. I don't want anything left. The rest of us will be at the front of the castle."

"Why not just activate the microorganisms?" Ashron asked.

Hawk gave Ashron a dead-eyed stare that made the Lorothian shiver. "Because I want it to burn."

Ashron nodded. As the others jogged toward the front of the castle, Ashron ran toward the building, confused and unnerved by Hawk's demeanor. He had no problem with Hawk's decision to kill everyone in the macabre lab they stumbled upon, but the captain was usually more level-headed. *I'm the one who would go in guns blazing,* Ashron thought as he reached the stairwell and began his descent. *And then have Hawk mad at me because I didn't leave someone alive to interrogate.*

And while burning such a grisly scene seemed more than fitting, it erased a major piece of evidence. Again, something he, not Hawk, would do.

Ashron reached the lab, trying to focus on nothing as he set a twenty second delay and popped the tops on three incendiary grenades. He had seen enough of the lab's contents the first time around.

He lobbed them into three areas of the room and dashed back to the stairway corridor. He waited at the intersection until he heard the *whompf* of the grenades detonating. A gust of heated air passed him, and he saw reflections of the orange-white flame as it danced through the room. He tossed another grenade down the other hallway and then ran up the steps. He didn't want to get caught in any secondary explosions.

Though Hawk had put his question aside for the moment, Ashron expected an answer soon. The crew never questioned orders, but they were encouraged to question motives. Although Ashron understood Hawk's reaction to such pronounced evil, it seemed they had missed a prime chance to discover and eradicate the greater evil behind it all.

He reached the others and found them standing or sitting near the castle front. A glum expression was on every face. He also understood that reaction, though he had trouble condoning it. Gloom was for the dead or dying, and they were still alive and kicking. "Well, it's burning like a hundred-year-olds' birthday cake," he said. "So, Hawk, I was won—"

"Later," Hawk said, giving Ashron another chilling glare.

Ashron flicked his tongue in thought and remained quiet. He kept his concerns to himself as they waited for the shuttle.

THE COMMANDER'S EXPLANATION

"Docking in sixty seconds, Captain," Ship informed Hawk as the shuttle glided toward the outpost. "Engaging auto landing tractor in ten seconds. Ashron, adjust your vector twenty- seven degrees and fire your back thrusters."

"Roger," Ashron said, hands moving the joystick.

As Ashron maneuvered, Hawk stared out the shuttle's window and studied the outpost. Its blue-tinted metal gleamed in the sunlight, and the red Planetary Protection Services logo shone in stark contrast. Little of that gleaming façade revealed the corruption within. Despite his promise to explain, Hawk had gone to the cockpit without a word to the crew. Sitting beside him, Ashron had said nothing as he piloted the shuttle from the planet.

The station's four gun pods hung limp, giving the vessel a sad, droopy appearance. No lights shone forth, and none of the monitoring dishes that normally rotated on the station's surface were moving.

"You did leave them with life support, didn't you, Ship?" Ashron asked.

"Of course. I'm not a barbarian. However, I do have all the bulkhead doors locked down, and I can pinpoint every crew member for you. Auto tractor engaging...now."

There was a small thumping sound followed by an electronic whine that lasted three seconds before tapering off. Ashron let go of the flight controls and leaned back.

"What about weapons?" Hawk asked.

"Nothing has been taken from the station's armory; I can't account for any personal armaments."

Ashron looked at Hawk. "This should be a cakewalk."

"We'll treat it like a boarding of any other hostile vessel, just in case." Hawk stood up. The door separating cockpit from cabin slid open; Hawk walked through, followed by Ashron.

"We're docking in thirty seconds," Hawk told the crew. "Ship has the station's crew buttoned down and can give us their locations. We don't know if they're armed or if they've rigged any improvised traps, so this is a hostile boarding as far as I'm concerned." He looked at Trey. "I need you to remain here on guard in case things go wrong and we have to retreat. Got it?"

"You want me out of the way, you mean?"

Hawk shook his head. "I want you to follow orders, like any crew member, and your orders are to remain here until we come back or you get the all clear. Is that understood?"

Trey stood straighter and had little success in suppressing a grin. "Yes, Captain."

With a nod, Hawk turned to the others. "Stand by to move on my mark."

"Hello old boy," Hawk said as he walked into the station Commander's office with a gun pointed at the man's chest. Commander Motash was visibly shaken to see Hawk standing in the doorway.

Despite Hawk's concern, Ashron's assessment of the situation had been correct. None of the men had been armed with anything more than a pocketknife. Ship had cut power and locked them down before anyone thought to move to the armory. They had personal sidearms in their cabins, but the Commander didn't allow them to be carried on the station since he saw no practical reason for it. The Knights simply walked through and collected the scattered members of the crew, who meekly let themselves be huddled into one room. No one had even managed to get a message to the Commander that his station was being overrun.

"You," the Commander exclaimed with a slight quiver in his voice. "I thought you were…"

"Dead?" Hawk finished for him. "Sorry to disappoint you."

Hawk stopped in front of the Commander's desk and leaned forward. His gaze and pistol demanded Motash's attention. "I'm about to teach you an important lesson. As an anonymous twentieth-century philosopher of the Southern Red Neck tribe once said, 'If you can't run with the big dogs, stay on the porch.'"

"What are you talking about?" Commander Motash asked, regaining some of his composure.

"I'm telling you not to bother buzzing for help. The button you've been frantically pushing since I first walked in has been disconnected. Besides, the other seven members of this station are currently lounging in a workroom, guarded by one of my crew."

The Commander took his hand out from under the desk. "What is it you want?"

Hawk sat down and propped his feet up on the Commander's desk. His gun never wavered. "I want some answers, and I want them now. Who paid you off?"

"What makes you think I was paid off?"

"Don't play games with me. I'm in no mood to play, and you're in no position to win. Once again, who paid you off?"

"Your position isn't as strong as you'd like to think," the Commander said. He also assumed a comfortable posture in his chair, though his eyes revealed that he was painfully aware of the pistol pointing at him. "You do know what the penalty is for entering a restricted area, don't you?" His voice had taken on the same pompous tone that had greeted Hawk when they first spoke. Hawk didn't like it then and, considering recent events, found it even more annoying now.

"Death," Hawk answered the man's question. "The same as for embezzling funds at the expense of those very people you are supposed to protect. Not to mention the importation of technology to a restricted planet. We could also talk about torture, murder, extortion, and the fact that you're pissing me off. Now, one more time, who's paying you?"

"Why don't we wait until the authorities arrive? Then you can question me all about your little charges," the Commander's sharp face took on a self-satisfied smirk, his black eyes gleaming with some secret delight.

"I don't think you're getting the big picture." Hawk sat up and leaned his elbows on the desk. "There will be no cavalry coming to your rescue, no knights in shining armor, and no chance of your leaving this station alive if you don't start answering my questions. We have complete control of your station and all of its facilities and have had control ever since you tried to take over my ship. Your transmissions never left the station." Hawk paused a moment to let the Commander digest the new information.

"I don't believe you," the Commander said, although his voice revealed otherwise.

"If you had control, why didn't you stop the shuttle from coming down to pick us up or shoot us down when we came back."

"We had a temporary power failure," the Commander answered, seemingly unwilling to face the truth. "Everything is back online now, and you are under arrest."

Hawk shook his head. "Let me explain your options. We banish you and your crew to the planet's surface and destroy the station, or we destroy the station. My patience is wearing thin."

"I don't believe you," the commander leaned further back in his chair.

"You have a real fondness for that saying, don't you? Fine." Hawk stood. "Wolf, come in here, please."

The door opened, and Wolf walked in. "Yes?"

Pointing at the commander, Hawk said, "Space him. I'm through playing around." He stepped aside.

Wolf crossed the room in two quick steps and reached for the Commander.

With a squeak of fright, the Commander slid his chair back against the wall and reached for a dagger stashed in his boot.

Not missing his stride, Wolf kicked the desk. It slid across the floor and pinned the Commander against the wall. Reaching across the desk, Wolf backhanded the man's outstretched arm and sent the knife flying across the room. With his other hand, he grabbed the Commander by the face and lifted him over the desk. Kicking and screaming, Motash frantically tried to free himself from Wolf's powerful clutch. Wolf held him out at arm's length and left the room.

***

"What's that?" Waren said, standing and walking forward as they heard the screaming.

"At ease there, soldier." Ashron pointed his gun at the man's chest. "I'll check for you as soon as you sit back down."

Waren sat on the workbench beside one of the other members of the outpost's crew. The seven of them had been sitting uncomfortably and grumbling ever since being forced into the small workroom by the Knights.

Ashron walked over to the doorway, cracked open the door, and peered out. Closing it after a brief glance, he turned to the others and said, "It looks like your commander is about to be spaced. Guess he didn't answer Hawk's questions correctly."

"You can't do that!" Waren said indignantly.

"*I'm* not," Ashron informed him.

Waren turned to the others. "We've got to save Commander Motash! Let's rush him!" He motioned his eyes at Ashron and moved his hands toward a steel rod that lay on a shelf.

"Screw that," one of his comrades answered. Also indicating Ashron, he said, "That's a Lorothian. An *armed* Lorothian. He could take us out without breaking a sweat."

"Well, actually," Ashron said, "nothing makes me sweat because I can't." He smiled, showing his teeth. "But the gist of your statement is most accurate."

Waren stared at him briefly, seeming to debate the wisdom of attacking, and then studied his feet, muttering. His hand moved away from the pipe.

Still smiling, Ashron leaned back against the door.

***

"Put me down!" Motash screamed, the sound muffled by Wolf's massive hand. Wolf stepped up next to the airlock and pushed a button on the wall. With a hiss of escaping air, the inner door opened. None too gently, Wolf tossed the Commander into the small room, where he slammed into the outer wall and slumped to the floor, stunned. Before he could recover and scramble out, Wolf had the door closed and locked.

The Commander, eyes teary and wide with panic, pounded at the airlock door. "Let me out."

Wolf keyed in a sequence on the airlock panel. With a loud sucking sound, vacuum tubes began removing oxygen from the sealed room. Wolf wouldn't have believed it possible, but the Commander's eyes got even wider as he realized he only had about ten seconds to live.

"Please!" he screamed, his voice getting hoarse. "I'll tell you everything. Do you hear me? Everything!" With one last feeble pound, he slumped back to the floor, utterly defeated.

At the last possible moment, Wolf canceled the exit sequence. The vacuums went silent, and the chamber refilled with air.

When the pressure had stabilized, Wolf opened the inner door, grabbed the still prone and gasping Commander, and dragged him back toward his office.

***

Ashron heard the dragging sound and glanced back out the door. "Good news," he told the dispirited outpost crew. "A new high-pressure system moved in and made the climate favorable for discussion, ensuring continued life for your Commander."

"What's going to happen to us?" Waren asked.

"My guess is you'll be exiled to the planet. I hope you can get used to cooking over a fire."

Waren leaped at Ashron, a half-meter long pipe with a gear attached to one end in his hand.

Although the attack was sudden, it was not unexpected. Ashron was flattered that intimidation of his race had held them this long. As the pipe whistled down toward him, he fired and stepped out of the way. The pipe clattered to the ground with a loud noise. Waren's eyes stared in wide-eyed surprise at the hole that had appeared in the space between his thumb and forefinger. Both fingers danced wildly as severed nerves tried to adjust to their new condition. Blood ran down his wrist, soaking into his uniform.

"That was a warning shot," Ashron said calmly. "Anybody else?"

Waren, with the help of two of his comrades, sat back down, his eyes never leaving his hand.

Ashron pulled down a small first aid kit attached to the wall. "Here," he tossed it to one of the men. The man opened the box and went to work on the injured hand.

"What was that?" Hawk's voice said in Ashron's ear.

"Nothing," Ashron assured him. "Just the natives getting restless. Could we accelerate the process?"

"Wolf's bringing in Commander Motash now and he appears ready to have a nice friendly chat."

Hawk had taken up a seat behind the Commander's desk and tapped at the keys on the in-desk computer as Wolf sat the still limp Commander in the chair facing Hawk. "You see, Wolf. The careful application of terror is also a form of communication."

He eyed the Commander. "No wonder Ship couldn't find anything. There's nothing in here out of the ordinary. In fact, most of it is downright boring." He turned off the computer. "How did you manage that?"

Commander Motash tried to speak. His throat and tongue moved; nothing came out. Hawk poured him a glass of water and handed it over. The Commander gulped it down with shaking hands.

"Calm down," Hawk told him. "Do you have any records of what's been going on?"

The Commander nodded. "Bottom right desk drawer," he said, his raspy voice getting stronger.

Hawk reached down and pulled on the drawer. It didn't budge. He looked back at Motash.

"Cubbyhole. Left side under the desk."

Hawk felt the underside of the desk until his fingers found a small niche in the board. He pushed and a small panel dropped, spilling a tiny circuit card into his hand. He inserted the key into the drawer. There was a soft *click,* and the drawer slid open. He saw a bound notebook lying in the bottom of the drawer.

"Paper?" Hawk said, lifting the book from the drawer. Motash nodded. "Very clever."

In a galaxy of electronic communication, paper was rare and, on some of the more arid worlds, unheard of except as rumors. It was seldom used for anything of importance since it was messy, prone to having things spilled on it, and easily destroyed. Its one advantage was that no computer in the known universe could locate information written solely on it.

Hawk flipped through the pages, scanning the numbers. "You've made quite a little enterprise for yourself, haven't you?" As he flipped through the pages, one name stood out above the rest. "So who is Seladyne Propulsion and what do they want with my ship?" Hawk asked, tossing the notebook onto the desk.

Commander Motash glanced briefly at the notebook. "I can't help you with the 'why' because I don't know, but I can tell you who. Seladyne Propulsion is a company that has been paying my crew and me to allow certain ships free passage on and off the planet, no questions asked. They also are the ones who set it up for you to be allowed on the planet with little or no fuss."

"I suppose that little six thousand credit donation was your idea."

"I didn't want it to seem too easy. Anyway, we were supposed to let them know when you arrived at the station and then set you down at the ambush site. After that, we were to notify the home office that we had the ship. The rest you know."

"I assume you weren't supposed to just call them up and say you had the ship. What was the code?"

"Quite simple really. We were to tell them that Bill called and the package had arrived and was ready for pickup."

"Bill?" Wolf asked.

"Makes sense," Hawk said. "When was the last time you met someone named Bill? Was that it?"

"Yes."

"Who was the message to be delivered to?" Hawk asked.

"The owner, Ms. Rianna Selan."

"And where is this 'home office' located?"

"I don't know. All of the currency has been transferred through different channels but with the same name. Not that I was going to do any tracing anyway."

"Well, if you don't know, where were you going to send the message?"

"Relay station Prometheus XJ5 with a destination code of Spin-ward 42-46-28 D.A."

"Ship?"

"Checking it now, Captain."

"Thanks. Do you have anything else you'd like to tell me?" he asked Motash. "Anything I need to know?"

Motash's eyebrows gathered in thought for a moment. "I know it won't matter for me but would it help my crew any if you knew they had no choice in the matter whatsoever."

"How do you mean?" Hawk asked.

"We were given no choice. This wasn't exactly a career move on my part, but to get the whole crew to go along, we were told that this station might fall to some 'natural disaster.'"

"Like getting hit by a comet?" Hawk asked.

"With a plasma warhead," Motash answered flatly.

"I see," Hawk said. "I imagine families were also mentioned."

"Only to one of the crew members. The rest were satisfied with the original threat. Again, I know it's of no help; I wanted you to understand the situation. The money was part of the deal I negotiated for us so we could get something out of this other than death threats."

"You realize they would have killed you anyway. An operation like this is too important to have witnesses."

"We knew that all along. That's why the money was put into trusts in our survivor's names."

Hawk heard no hope in the Commander's tone. What the man had just told Hawk wasn't some last minute fabrication or attempt at avoiding guilt. Hawk stared at him a long moment. "Look at me," he said in a tone that would brook no resistance.

Commander Motash lifted his head, his black eyes lifeless as they locked with Hawk's.

"Tell me one thing. What were they doing with all of that equipment?"

"I forbade any of my crew from going down to the planet. I didn't want any of them to know what was going on and I didn't want to know. I hoped the less we knew, the higher the probability of us leaving alive."

Hawk studied him a moment longer and then smiled. "I believe you."

"Good luck," Hawk said, shaking Commander Motash's hand. The Commander stood in an open field with his crew gathered behind him. "You too. Whatever your mission is."

Ashron leaned out the doorway and looked at the injured Waren. "Sorry about the hand. Business, you know. Let's go, Cap'n, we're burning daylight."

"Now remember, don't wander off. Should we succeed, someone will be back to pick you up in a few years. Who knows, you might even grow to like the place."

"Who knows?" The Commander smiled back as the door to the shuttle started to close. "It's better than the alternative."

"You all strapped in?" Ashron asked as Hawk sat down next to him.

Hawk didn't answer as he buckled himself into the co-pilot's chair. As the thrusters took hold, Hawk allowed himself one final glance at the eight men they left behind. Standing there with his men proudly in formation, the Commander looked up at the shuttle and saluted. Hawk saluted back, then turned to Ashron. "How long will it take you to set the charges?" he asked.

"Depends," Ashron said. "Setting it to blow will take about half an hour. If you want it to look like an accident under intense investigation, then about two hours."

"Go ahead and take the extra time. It'll take us that long to pull any relevant information from the computer, find out what we can about Seladyne Propulsion, and set the quickest course to their headquarters."

"Are you sure blowing up the station is absolutely necessary?"

"It is if we don't want anyone coming to search for the Commander and his crew. Whoever is looking for us will try revenge unless he thinks they're already dead." Hawk cocked his head and arched an eyebrow. "Since when have you been squeamish about destroying something?"

"I realize we're supposed to have *carte blanche*, but wiping out Council property seems to be pushing the boundaries a little."

"If we make it out of this, you can let me worry about the Council. For now, just set the charges."

"Okay. Do you have any idea why this company would want Ship?"

"Yes," Hawk said guardedly.

"Why?"

"They want to recreate the past."

They were quiet for a moment. Ashron, sensing a chance, said, "Does this have anything to do with those torture—" he stopped. Hawk's eyes told him this still wasn't the right time or place to pursue it. "Never mind."

They made the short trip back to Ship in silence.

A PAST REVEALED

Hawk sat in his think tank and stared at nothing. A glass of tequila rested on a small tray next to a half-empty bottle; beads of condensation ran down both.

After watching the outpost station explode, they had set course for Jeran Seven, the planet that hosted Seladyne Propulsion's home office. Feigning fatigue, Hawk had retired to his room and crawled into the whirlpool. Now that the action was over he had time to brood about what had transpired. He had been thinking and drinking in the luke-warm pool almost two hours. The alcohol, so good at dulling the pain, had no power this time.

"What's wrong, Sean?" Ship asked.

"At some point, I'm going to have to explain my actions on the planet, and that means I'll have to explain about you."

"What's wrong with that?"

"Nothing. It's just that…" Hawk paused, uncertain. "It's painful. Do you really want them to know?"

"I've wanted them to know all along. It's getting harder and harder to differentiate between 'me' and the ship that is me. 'I' need some interaction, and now would be as good a time as any to start."

"Sara, I don't know what you feel anymore," Hawk looked up to the ceiling with a tear running down his cheek. "*Do* you feel anymore?"

"I have emotions, but it's more difficult than it was. I have to remind myself at times that I'm supposed to feel a certain way."

"Do you have to remind yourself about us?"

"Never. That feeling will always be there."

Hawk rubbed his hands across his eyes. "Christ, Sara. This all started out as a game. Remember? A group of friends out for adventure and glory. We were immortal then. No one was supposed to get hurt, especially you." He drained the glass and poured himself another shot.

"You've got to quit punishing yourself, Sean," Sara said, her voice anguished. "You did all you could. You have to let go of the past."

"Let go?" Hawk asked, incredulous. "How can I let go when every time I hear your voice it tells me how much I failed you?"

"You didn't fail me. Because of you, I still exist." Her voice lightened. "What more could a girl ask?"

Hawk squeezed his eyes shut as more tears flowed. "I want *you* back. I want to feel your touch again, look into your eyes, feel your breath on my cheek. I can barely remember the sound of your laugh," he said quietly.

He threw his drink across the room; the glass shattered against the far wall. The small *kenquala*, sensing his distress, gathered around him and nudged, demanding his attention. He ignored them.

Hawk heard his cabin door open and waited for the knock at the inner door as he listened to Laura's light tread across his room.

"Are you okay?" Laura asked after giving a soft tap. "I thought I heard something break."

"I'm fine," Hawk said in a flat voice.

"Are you sure? Can I get—"

"Just leave me alone!"

There was a pause, and then the shuffle of feet.

"You've hurt her feelings," Sara said as the outer cabin door shut. "She really does care for you."

"Not like you did."

Softly, she said, "Yes, like I did. It will never be like it was, Sean. Never."

Hawk slumped back, his head resting against the side of the pool. "I know."

"You need to start living again. It's been five years. The Sara you knew is gone."

"Don't say that," Hawk whispered, "I…" he couldn't continue.

"It's true. There are times I wish I had truly died that day because of all the pain I've caused you. If I had known you would suffer for all these years, I never would have fought so hard to come back. If I had died that day, you would have mourned me for a time and then gone on with your life. I'm happy to still be a part of your life, and I want *you* to be happy. It hurts me to see you so self-destructive. You are not the same man I fell in love with."

Hawk looked over at the bottle, thinking back over the past years: his sudden fondness for drinking, the one-night stands, the almost suicidal way in which he threw himself into things. "I have changed, haven't I?"

"Yes. And not for the better."

Hawk felt a bitter smile on his lips, hearing the simple truth from Sara. He replaced the bottle cap.

"I think you're going to be spared the pain of telling them," Sara said.

"What do you mean?"

"Wolf is telling the crew about us."

"What?" Hawk yelled, standing. He started out of the pool, sending water sloshing to the deck.

"Sit down." Anger tinged Sara's voice. Hawk stopped, shocked.

In a softer voice, she continued. "There's no reason to be mad at Wolf. He's doing what should have been done years ago. If you want to be mad at someone, be mad at me. I gave him permission."

His shoulders sagging, Hawk slumped back into the warm water. They said nothing else as Hawk lay there; conflicting emotions— anger, regret, self-loathing—washed through him.

He had no idea how much time passed; seconds, minutes, hours. As he thought, remembering the past, both good and bad, one thought rose to the top of his muddled contemplation and stood above his all-too-clear memories.

For five years, ever since that terrible day, he had wallowed in self-pity, hiding it behind a bottle and reckless abandon. Though he was the leader of the Knights, he hadn't been acting like much of a commander. His slipshod attitude was affecting not only the Knights' reputation but the crew as well. They had managed, with skill, talent, and a little luck, to get out of the situations his flaws had gotten them into. He knew that would only get them so far. Skill and talent ebbed, and luck ran out. It was time to return to using his brains, and he couldn't do that through a cloud of liquor and misery.

"Okay, Sara, you win." He stood up purposefully and grabbed the half-empty bottle. Striding to the trash receptacle, he dropped the bottle and pushed the small red button on the side. There was a *whoosh* of air and Hawk smiled. He could almost hear the bottle breaking as it landed in the large garbage hold. He had told himself many times before that he would quit drinking, and every time something had pushed him back into the corner, shoved him beneath the bottle. There would be no setbacks this time. He had slogged through the worst and lived to tell about it. Enough people had disappeared from his life. *I'll be damned if I'm going to disappear on myself.* "Crew meeting in fifteen minutes, Ship. It's time to get our act back together."

"Aye, Captain," Sara answered.

Catching her tone, Hawk smiled and got dressed.

"What's wrong?" Wolf asked as Laura entered the wardroom on the verge of tears.

She looked at him as she walked over to a chair and sat down. "Something's wrong with Hawk."

"You mean aside from his penchant for going berserk at a moment's notice?" Ashron asked.

At Laura's puzzled stare, Ashron quickly recounted their grisly discovery in the dungeons of Meta Brévé and Hawk's subsequent violent outburst. "I would have done the same thing, but I would have kept someone alive and made them tell us what they knew and what they were trying to do."

"Hawk already knows what they were trying to do," Wolf told him. "As do I."

When it became apparent Wolf wasn't going to say any more without prompting, Laura said, "Would you care to elaborate?"

"Ship, with your permission."

"Certainly," Ship said. "It's time the air was cleared anyway. I'll get Gerard and Trey."

Laura and Ashron exchanged a perplexed look, and then gazed back at Wolf. Ashron started to speak.

"Wait for the other two," Wolf said.

After a minute, Gerard and Trey walked in.

"What's up?" Trey asked, leaning against the doorway.

Wolf looked at Ashron, Laura, and Trey. "I guess it's time you three knew something about the Knights before you joined, so I'm going to give you a history lesson."

"You mean you're actually going to speak more than two sentences in a five-minute period?" Ashron asked.

"Yes."

"Grab a seat, Trey. This could be good."

"Some of this you may already know," Wolf began. "Hawk and Moran were friends from childhood, having grown up under the care of the same man."

"Tahorton," Ashron interjected. "Hawk told me about him."

"You mean Hawk is an orphan, too?" Trey asked.

"Not like you were," Wolf answered. "His mother died when he was seven. His father didn't die until five years ago."

"So why did he live with this other man?"

"His father used him as a bet in a poker game and lost him."

"Lost him?" Trey asked. "You mean he just gave him away?"

"Yes. According to Hawk, his father was happy to do it."

Laura spoke up. "I remember Hawk telling me that he would never forget the look on his father's face. The bastard was grinning."

Trey squirmed and moved closer to Laura.

Wolf continued. "Hawk went to live with Tahorton, and he met Moran and the other boys who lived there. According to Hawk, he and Moran instantly became friends."

"Not a great surprise if you knew Moran before he went insane," Gerard said. "He was a very genial person."

"Using the skills Tahorton drilled into them, they both made it into Force 13. Hawk quickly showed his aptitude and was given a chance to form his own C5 unit, although he was able to talk them into letting him get seven members."

"Why seven?" Trey asked.

"He talked it over with Moran, and they decided on seven. They were both romantics at heart..."

"Hawk a romantic?" Ashron snorted. "Yeah, and I'm a three-headed Gundite."

"There is a slight resemblance," Laura said.

Wolf glared at Ashron and Laura.

"Please continue," Ashron told him.

"They were both romantics, so they named their group the Knights of The Flaming Star. Zerus, a star in the night sky where they lived, was the inspiration for the name. It's a red star with seven points; there appears to be fire leaping off of it in the night. That's why they wanted seven members, so there would be one for each point.

"The original members were Hawk, Moran, Gerard, Sara, Terafin, Alexander and me. After two years working with Force 13, Hawk talked them into letting us work as mercenaries when we weren't on assignments.

"We started out small. Over the years we managed to build up a reputation as honest, expedient, and proficient; traits not always easy to find in mercenary units. Ship had been a gift from Tahorton, bequeathed when he died. Things were going well for the Knights, but even then there was tension between Hawk and Moran. They both had definite ideas about how things should be run. And then there was Sara."

"Sara? Hawk's never mentioned anyone named Sara," Laura said.

"No, I don't imagine he would," Gerard said.

Wolf continued. "Sara was the medical officer before Laura and the main source of contention between Hawk and Moran. They both loved her; she wasn't at all interested in Moran. I'm sure that's what ended up driving him over the edge."

"Why do I get the feeling we're about to hear a Shakespearean tragedy?" Ashron asked.

"Because you are," Wolf said, letting the humor fall flat. "Her last mission was on a planet much like Meta-Brévé, six months after Hawk had kicked Moran out of the Knights."

"Last mission?" Trey said. "Did she retire?" he asked, without much hope.

"No," Wolf said. "The mission was fairly standard, as such things go. A group of dukes had taken hostage of the king and his heirs. The corporation who hired us had contracts with this king to mine the planet's resources, so they wanted this king alive and in power. We were sent in to extradite them and eliminate the threat. Since Hawk, Sara, and Alex were the only humans, they would go into the castle alone. The rest of us would be too conspicuous."

"If the rest of us had been there," Gerard said, "things might have gone differently."

Nodding in agreement, Wolf began his story.

Hawk glided across the floor, careful to avoid the roaming eyes of the guards on the balcony. Sara moved in unison with him. As they approached the door, he held up his hand and signaled to her. She nodded her head.

He hated these low-tech missions. A robust communications rig was so much easier than hand signals and vocal imitations of local wildlife. But one learned to take the good with the bad. Hawk had signaled he wanted ten seconds, so Sara waited ten seconds and threw the flash powder grenade toward the back of the hallway. It landed and fired off with a roar and a burst of brilliant white light. It distracted the balcony guards, allowing Hawk and Sara to enter the chamber room unnoticed, and it was a signal for Alex to move in.

Hawk kicked open the door and walked in. When he saw what lay before him, he stopped. Sara moved in behind him and gasped.

Moran sat on the throne, dressed in his full Knight uniform, black with red flashing. A loaded crossbow rested in his lap, and four dead bodies lay on the floor: the King and his two sons lay to one side, and at Moran's feet rested the thin, pale body of Alex.

Stunned, Hawk barely heard the sound of rattling armor as the guards moved in behind them, cutting off their escape.

"What have you done?" he asked. His friend had betrayed him and killed one of their crew. Hawk could not have said which twisted his stomach more, Alex's death or Moran's betrayal.

"Alex never could keep his mouth shut," Moran said. "He mentioned this little mission to me when I saw him a few weeks ago, so I told your employer's competition about it. They were very interested. By the way, I hereby consider this a formal separation of the Knights," Moran stood up, stepping over the bodies. "You know, assassination pays much better than extradition."

"We had a code, damn you," Hawk said.

"What code?" Moran threw back at him. "The only code I saw was we went to the highest bidder and then justified our actions with some twisted philosophy about justice and morality. That's all I've done. These three were despotic weaklings who deserved to die, and I found someone willing to pay me to do it."

"What about Alex?" Hawk asked. "What was his crime?"

Moran shrugged. "He tried to stop me."

"And who is your employer going to put in place of those three?" Sara asked. "Some corporate puppet."

"Of course not, darling. I'm going to rule."

"You?"

"Yes. I'm going to be king." He looked at Sara; the madness in his eyes softened. "I would like for you to be my queen."

Sara stared back at him. "You really are insane, aren't you? I would rather die than be your queen."

Moran grabbed the crossbow and pointed it at Hawk. "Would you rather he die? Come here, or I'll put this through his heart."

Sara stepped in front of Hawk. "You'll have to send it through me first."

Moran looked at her, his face a mask of anguish that slowly twisted into insanity. "So be it."

He fired.

Hawk screamed as the bolt sunk into Sara's chest. The force of the impact knocked her back. Hawk caught her as she fell to the floor, the color draining from her face. She looked at Hawk. "I..." she started. She gasped and collapsed in Hawk's arms.

"Guards, take him alive," Moran said.

In one fluid motion, Hawk stood, drew a dagger, and threw it. It whistled end over end. Moran ducked; the knife still smashed into his eye. It struck hilt first; there was a popping sound as his eye was crushed. Viscous blood poured from the socket.

Screaming, Moran put his hand over the gaping hole. "Kill him!"

The armored guards drew their swords. Without even looking back at them, Hawk raised his left hand and uttered three words. Flame leaped from his hand and shot back into the courtyard. The heat incinerated five of the seven guards. The other two ran.

Hawk, blood pounding in his ears, drew his sword and rushed toward Moran. With almost inhumanly quick speed, he leaped through the air, slashing at Moran's head. Moran raised his left arm to ward off the blow. The sword bit into flesh and Moran's arm parted from his body, severed at the elbow.

Blood gushed from the separated limb as Moran screamed. Hawk pulled the sword back, preparing for another swing. Moran raised his right arm and fired a shot from the palm blaster concealed in his hand. The bright blue beam struck Hawk square in the chest. It caught him off balance and sent him tumbling to the floor on his back.

Moran ran behind the throne and struck a hidden switch. With a soft grinding sound, a portal revealed itself in the wall as the stone panel slid aside.

The throne burst apart in a spray of splintered wood and shredded cushion, destroyed by a blast of *aetheric* power from Hawk. Before he ran down the secret hallway, Moran glanced back. Hawk stood, sword in hand, arm extended, a smoking black hole in the breastplate of his armor. The steel suit had absorbed most of the blast from Moran's weak weapon.

Moran fled into the hallway, tripping the switch that resealed the secret door.

"Moran!" Hawk screamed at the top of his voice as the secret door slid shut. He started to run forward. The force of the blaster, coupled with the drain from the energy bolt he had fired, disoriented him. He stopped for a second as his internal senses realigned, then continued toward the wall, passing through tufts of padding floating in the air.

Hawk wasted no time looking for a switch. He swung his sword at the wall, infusing the blade with a burst of *aetheric* energy as it struck. Mortar shattered and the stones tumbled outward from the force of the blow. Hawk continued the swing downward until the blade hit the floor, burying itself three inches into the stone. A two-foot-wide ragged gash lay before him; he stepped through. He saw nothing of Moran but a trail of blood marking his path. With grim determination, Hawk started forward. A sound stopped him cold.

A gasp of pain.

All thoughts of Moran fled as he realized Sara still lived. Dropping his sword, he dashed back and knelt beside her. Her eyes were open, and she smiled weakly as she saw him.

"Hi, lover," she said, coughing at the effort. A trickle of blood ran from her mouth.

"Shhh," Hawk said, lifting her from the floor. A grimace of pain crossed Sara's face, and she closed her eyes. As delicately but quickly as possible, Hawk headed for the castle's exit.

Sara opened her eyes one last time and said, "I love you, Sean." She closed her eyes; her body went limp.

Tears ran down Hawk's face as he continued forward, hoping against hope that he could still save her.

As he crossed the courtyard, Hawk saw a whole platoon of soldiers standing in front of the drawbridge that led to the outside of the castle. One man stood in front, the markings on his armor declaring him as a sergeant.

"Stand where you are and..." the man started. He never got to finish.

Hawk spoke an equation that projected all his anger and grief at the thirty men before him. The sergeant stopped, a startled expression on his face. As one, the soldiers dropped their weapons and reached up, clutching their heads with their hands. As one, their heads exploded, and their lifeless bodies toppled to the ground. Hawk crossed the gore-stained courtyard and left the castle.

Tears ran down Hawk's face as he struggled back to his hidden ship. He lost any hope he could save Sara from death. It was taking too long. Her body grew cold in his arms. Hope gave way to despair. Despair soon gave way to an idea, an idea that could save her. An idea that bordered on being both insane and blasphemous. His grief quickly seized upon it and would not release it from his mind.

Despite his blind stumbling, Hawk eventually found his way back to the vessel. In the intervening kilometers, the tenebrous strands of his idea had welded themselves into a firm conviction. He could save her. To do so, he would have to attempt something that, to his knowledge, had never been done. There were rumors of complex equations, formulas too difficult for most minds to comprehend, but nothing had ever been confirmed.

As he entered the ship, the others gasped as they saw the dead body of their companion. They tried to question Hawk. He ignored them and walked past, heading for the medical room. He had made up his mind. If he stopped to explain, his resolve might weaken, and he would never again find the courage.

He closed and locked the door on them, leaving their questions unanswered and their pleas unheeded.

He lay Sara gently on the bed and removed the bolt from her chest. As he bandaged the wound, he mentally prepared himself. Not for the actual act, but for the consequences of what would follow.

Putting his hands over her heart and head, he concentrated. Her soul had already fled; he planned to bring it back. He would open a hole to the *aether* and, by sheer force of will, use it to infuse life into her body.

He spoke the first equation learned by every manipulator: the invocation that created the link between the *aether* and the mind. He spoke it again, widening the breach and bringing in more power. He spoke it again. And again. His head pounded as energy surged through him, almost too much for his mind to contain. The creatures of the *aetheric* plane glided at the edge of his vision, silent and ravenous.

He mentally reached out and found a lingering thread of Sara's soul; it glowed in front of his vision with a dim silver radiance. With equations of his own formulation, he slowly wrapped layers of energy over her soul, securing it to her body. When he felt he had enough power surrounding the slender strand, he gave a firm tug, pulling her soul back from its destination. The soul was strong. The very universe balked at what it was being denied. The aether creatures fled. Even they seemed to reject what he attempted. Hawk continued, determined to have her back.

Sweat drenched his clothing. He became unaware of the passage of time. He did not hear the pleas of his companions to open the door. He was oblivious to the door being ripped from its hinges by a concerned Wolf. He noticed nothing of the confused looks and whispered apprehensions of his crew. Though none of them knew what was happening, the golden nimbus surrounding Hawk kept them at bay; they were afraid any contact would injure him.

After an eternity, he saw her soul, a pulsing amorphous form glowing a dazzling silver-white. Now came the final effort. Reciting improvised equations never before uttered, he gave his power to latch on to her soul. He offered his essence and with it, forced Sara's soul back into her body.

Without warning, fire engulfed Hawk's nerve ends. Electric arcs of light with the vague shapes of winged creatures flew from his body, each emanation a torment on his spirit. They passed through Sara and struck the walls, ricocheting from corner to corner; the crew ducked and scattered from the room.

Hawk screamed, dropping to his knees as the *aetheric* power raced from him and dissipated itself in a blazing spectacle that left the air heavy with ozone. His clothes burst into flames and incinerated so quickly his body remained untouched. The same happened to Sara. Her body hitched as she breathed in air. He'd done it!

As she exhaled, silver strands flew from her mouth, wound through the sizzling arcs of power, and struck the walls. Instead of ricocheting, the glittering filaments faded into the metal, disappearing as quickly as they had appeared.

As the last of the energy dissipated, Hawk sprawled to the floor, weeping.

"Are you all right?" Wolf asked. Hawk made no acknowledgment. How could he tell them that nothing was right and never would be? He had failed. He had forfeited all his mortal power to the universe in exchange for the life of his lady. The universe had taken his power and laughed in his face.

"Ship," Trey said, his face lighting up through his tears. "Ship is Sara, isn't she?"

"At your service," Ship said.

"What?" Ashron said.

"Sara's soul didn't go into her body," Trey explained, "It went inside Ship. Ship is alive." As he wiped his eyes, Trey's grin threatened to break his face. "How?"

"I don't know," Gerard admitted. "I'm still studying to try and figure it out."

"Wait a minute," Ashron said. "Maybe I'm a little slow. Are you saying Ship is a sentient being, inhabited by the soul of one of the original Knights?"

"That's pretty much the idea," Gerard said. "Laura, Ashron, Trey, meet Sara."

"It's very nice to meet all of you," Ship said.

"So what do we call you?" Ashron asked.

"'Ship' is fine. Sara as some of you knew her is gone, and I think we would all be more comfortable if I remained Ship."

"How come you never told us this before?" Laura asked with an accusing look at Wolf.

"Would it have changed anything?"

"No, I guess not, but it would have been nice to know."

"Hawk used to be a manipulator?" Trey asked.

"Yes, the power of which I have never seen," Gerard said with a trace of sadness in his voice. "Now if he even tries to formulate an equation his head pounds and his vision turns blurry. He went as far as to pass out one time. We found him unconscious on the floor with blood coming from his nose and ears."

"Well, I guess I was wrong," Ashron said, "Hawk *was* an old romantic."

"He still is a romantic," Wolf said. "I told you there are always seven Knights. How many of us are there on board?"

"Six," Ashron answered.

"Sara is the seventh."

A lump formed in Trey's throat as the significance of what Wolf said came to him. They considered him a Knight. They might not always treat him like an adult, but Hawk thought enough of him to consider him a crew member. Surprised and touched by a sudden feeling of genuinely belonging, he ran over and hugged Laura, afraid it might all disappear.

MORAN'S MOTIVES

"So now you all know," Hawk said, walking into the wardroom.

The crew watched him as he came toward them. Laura said, "You know you could have told us before."

"Yeah," Hawk sat in his chair.

"Okay," Ashron said. "That explains Ship, but I still don't understand what that has to do with the horror show we saw downplanet."

Hawk said nothing for a moment, uncertain where to start. Trey walked over and handed him a drink.

"No thanks, I'm on the wagon."

"Since when?" Ashron quipped.

Hawk gave Ashron a steady gaze. Ashron, realizing he had stepped over the boundary, muttered an apology.

Hawk continued. "I will take some water, though. Moran was over the edge. He had been going downhill ever since Gerard came on board."

"Gerard?" Trey asked as he poured a glass of water. "What did he do?"

"He's a cyborg, and Moran was intrigued by anything related to technology. He began studying everything he could find on the effects of body implanted hardware. I think part of it was that Moran always had a feeling of inferiority, even when we were kids."

Hawk took the water glass from Trey and drank half of it before continuing. "He was easily the smartest of the seven of us, but all he saw was himself in league with two very powerful manipulators, a walking tank," he pointed at Wolf, "two outstanding warriors, and me. He constantly looked for ways to make his own physical and mental capabilities greater. It started with minor enhancements, but he soon had major hardware being implanted."

"I thought cybernetics were illegal except for medical or religious reasons," Ashron said.

"Off the top of my head," Laura said, "I can name at least twenty-five doctors who will happily give you two ultra-boosted legs and swear on their mother's grave your real ones were gnawed off by a Chihuahua."

"Not to mention," Gerard added, "the military and any number of scientific companies that will take volunteers, legal or otherwise."

"Well, fork my tongue," Ashron said, his tongue flicking.

Laura looked at Hawk. "So, Moran was a victim of *cyberpsychosis?*"

"I don't think so," Gerard spoke up. "I noticed his interest and kept a close eye on the number of enhancements he had. He was nowhere near what I would have considered the danger zone. Besides, even doctors who will do illegal implants will only go so far. If they think you're too close to the edge, they won't operate no matter how much money you throw at them.

"Why not?" Trey asked.

"I'd like to say professional ethics, but I'd be lying," Gerard said. "The fact is the doctor who did the operation is most likely going to be the first person the patient sees when he wakes up. If the patient has tumbled into psychosis, chances are the doctor won't survive the attack."

"So, what do you think happened to Moran?" Laura asked.

Hawk took over. "I think he was borderline from the beginning and kept it well hidden. He did some things when we were younger that might be considered psychotic. I chalked them up to being young. After all, I did some pretty crazy things, too.

"Be that as it may, his fascination soon became an obsession. We told him about our concerns, and he assured us he had it under control. At that time, I believe he did. He told us he had gotten everything he wanted and his other research was merely so he could work on his own inventions. I believed him because he was worse than Gerard when it came to tinkering with things, but also because we were friends and I was still young and naive enough to believe friends stayed that way forever.

"Obviously, he got more enhancements we didn't know about. He started becoming withdrawn and moody. He became envious of Gerard and began experimenting with ways to infuse *aether* into cybernetics. None of his attempts were successful, and that made him even more withdrawn. He started steadily becoming more and more irrational. It finally came to the point that I couldn't trust him on missions anymore. I told him and, as you can expect, it turned into an argument."

"One that I'd just as soon forget," Gerard said.

"Why?" Trey asked.

"Hawk's understating it quite a bit. Moran became violent. He broke Terrafin's arm, and we ended up having to restrain him and remove him from the ship."

"That was the last time we saw him until the day that..." Hawk stopped.

After a pause, Ashron said, "I'm still a bit confused about what this has to do with Meta Brévé."

"What we saw on Meta Brévé," Hawk answered, "was an extension of Moran's experiments infusing *aetheric* energy into cybernetics."

Ashron continued giving him a blank stare.

"I guess that is a little vague," Hawk said.

"A little," Laura agreed.

"One of the things Wolf neglected to tell you was that while I was working my way back to the ship, Moran linked into the computer and attempted to download everything he could. Gerard discovered it about the time I got back with Sara and started trying to cut off his access."

Gerard cut in. "At that time, Moran had the advantage, because one of his enhancements was a direct neural net link, which I didn't know about."

"What does that matter?" Ashron asked.

"A direct link is faster and harder to break. In fact, it's almost impossible short of shutting down or overloading the system."

"So Moran's mind was hooked up to Ship when Sara entered it?" Trey asked.

Smiling at the boy's insight, Gerard said, "Sort of. Moran was connected to the ship when Sara died."

"But Sara didn't die," Trey protested.

"Moran didn't know that," Gerard told him. He paused a moment, then looked at Hawk, a glint of realization in his eyes. "All he felt through his connection was a massive influx of *aether*, a scream of pain, and then the connection being abruptly severed. Moran must have thought Sara was dead. Something has happened to make him find out otherwise."

Hawk nodded, indicating Gerard's line of thought was correct.

"Sorry, me again," Ashron said, "I missed the pain thing somewhere along the line. What pain?"

"Imagine," Hawk said, "having your soul ripped out while you were still alive."

Ashron was quiet a moment, then said, "Tough to do, but I think I see your point. Sara wasn't dead when she went into Ship."

"She *was* dead, and I thought I could bring her back. I tried to play God in my own fumbling way," Hawk paused a moment. "Getting her soul back worked, barely, but once I had it, I was at a loss. How do you weave a soul back into a body? I didn't know what to do, so I used a hammer on crystal and forced it back to where I thought it belonged. It went against all that is natural. Her body awakened, she took a breath and screamed. The universe wanted to show me it was not to be denied. Her soul was torn out of her body and thrown violently from my grasp. It shattered and fled, trying to escape…"

Ship said, "I couldn't find the light anymore. I had nowhere to go."

The crew was silent, until Trey, in a small voice, said, "Why?"

"The first time was easy, like following a lighted path with someone holding your hand. The second time there was so much energy and so many emotions it was like trying to swim upstream in a strong current. I didn't have the strength to fight it, so I went where I could rest, and I never found my way out. I quit trying a long time ago."

"I think I get it," Ashron said. "Moran thinks the pain combined with the magic trapped Sara, so he's trying to duplicate it."

"That, or he thinks I did it on purpose," Hawk said. "Regardless, he's trying to reproduce the conditions."

"To what end?" Ashron asked.

"Strictly from a monetary standpoint," Gerard said, "a vessel like Ship is priceless. We work with the *only* self-aware computer in existence. Companies would give us planets to have her."

Trey said, "I don't want any planets. I like Ship."

Gerard smiled. "I think that may be the other reason. Moran may still love Sara and could be working on a way to reverse the process. That's a question we'll have to ask him."

"Ask him?" Ashron repeated. "Assuming he's still alive--which I'm beginning to accept as a distinct possibility, by the way--we don't even know where he is."

"We don't yet," Hawk told him. "When we get to Seladyne Propulsion, we're going to see if someone there can tell us."

***

In another part of the Universe, Alexic Salakon sat at his desk, looking at the beautiful body of another anonymous boy, this one with pearl-colored skin and curly ebony hair. He chose to ignore the haunted glaze in the boy's eyes. Just as his father had ignored the look in his eyes. These boys basked in his affection, even if they didn't know it yet. Much as it had taken him decades to understand the depth of his father's love.

"Come closer, boy," Salakon said.

The boy took a hesitant step forward when a chime sounded on Salakon's desk.

"Sir, Moran is here to see you,"

Salakon sighed. "One moment." The boy's evident relief disturbed him.

"Return to the waiting room," he snapped. When the secret panel had closed, Salakon punched the pad that unlocked his door. "Come in," he said and turned to face the window as if he had been staring over the city in contemplation.

Moran's reflection appeared in the window as the dark-haired man, bruised and battered, walked in and stopped in front of the desk. Moran looked perturbed, or as perturbed as his almost emotionless face could.

"You have seen the report?" Moran said.

Salakon wheeled around in the chair to face Moran. "I have. I was going to call you when I finished my...meditations." Salakon tugged at the skin on his neck.

Moran's eyes, the real one and the new cybernetic one, replaced after the skirmish on Tekran, flickered toward the wall. A moment's panic touched Salakon. Did Moran know about the secret room?

The man's gaze returned to him with no change of expression, and Salakon relaxed. No doubt it was a reflexive glance around the room. The ever-paranoid Moran had continually darting eyes.

"I have trouble believing they would destroy their own station," Salakon said. "All the analyses indicate a failure in the reactor. The resulting explosion destroyed the station and all aboard. Are you sure they did it themselves?"

"Positive," Moran told him. "We have been unable to get a reply from the laboratory, and I have no doubt we'll find it also destroyed when our ship gets there."

"This is beginning to become an expensive proposition. Are you sure this vessel is worth it?"

Anger flashed in Moran's good eye. "Don't back out on me now. These losses are nothing compared to what we will gain. When it comes down to the final battle, you had better accept losses, because there will be plenty. What we get in the end will make it all worthwhile."

"I'm not backing out on you," Salakon assured him, "but some of the board members are becoming a little edgy."

"If any of those weak-willed fools are having second thoughts, send them to me. I'll persuade them to change their way of thinking."

Salakon cringed to think of Moran's methods of persuasion. He changed the conversation's focus. "Do you think they killed the station crew?"

"I doubt it. Hawk has too much sympathy for that. Have your crew look for them on the planet. If they find them, kill them. Don't expend a lot of resources. We have more important things to worry about."

"You think Motash talked?"

"I'm certain of it. You had better alert our people on Jeran Seven to be prepared for visitors."

23

A VISIT TO JERAN SEVEN

Laura sat in a large booth near the back of the Whysky Café, drank her iced *selaba* tea, nibbled on fresh vegetables, and waited for Hawk. The remainder of the trip to Jeran Seven had been uneventful. Ship easily found Seladyne Propulsion's headquarters located in the planetary capital of Jeranos. While Gerard arranged transportation for Patishi to her grandparents and the still recovering Thomas to the local hospital, Laura had spent the last hour probing the company's defenses, or lack thereof. It quickly became evident to her that the corporation was a business and only a business. The receptionist had been friendly and helpful, and Laura's later calls had been routed without delay. She didn't know what Wolf could do with some of the parts she ordered, and she could already picture Hawk wincing at the price, but it was evident from the ordering process that Seladyne was a legitimate company.

As she took a sip of tea, she spotted Hawk's silhouette stepping into the doorway and waved to him. He walked over and slid into the opposite side of the booth.

"How did it go?" Hawk asked.

"Hang on. Here comes the waitress," Laura indicated with a nod.

251

After ordering a *selaba* tea for himself and sandwiches for both of them, he said, "Well?"

"It seems legit. I posed as a buyer for Firefall, Inc. and told them I wanted to upgrade our control systems and add some custom elements. The sales rep I talked to was knowledgeable and helpful. He already had some programs that would fill the immediate needs of the problem I laid out for him and said he would get back to me on our long-term goals. I followed up about an hour later and got the same treatment. I also contacted their shipping, receiving, parts, and accounting departments. Everyone was helpful and eager to do business. I think we're dealing with a legitimate operation here."

"That's my impression, too," Hawk took a vegetable chip from the basket on the table. "I grabbed a tool belt and a datapad and went in through the loading dock. No one even gave me a second glance. I walked around everywhere, looking busy and making notes. I'm no expert on shipping and warehouse procedures, but nothing seemed even remotely out of place. When I left through the front door, the receptionist asked me if I had found everything okay. If anything, they should have tighter security. I could have walked out with a thruster under each arm, and someone would have held the door open for me." Hawk tossed the chip into his mouth.

"So, why didn't you ask the receptionist why the company wanted Ship?" Laura said with a smile.

Hawk swallowed. "That may not be a bad approach. I've been trying to decide the best way to go about this and haven't come up with much. How about you? Any thoughts?"

Laura considered for a moment, playing with the straw in her tea. "We could go in posing as a buyer and ask. Of course, we'd have to use some ploy to get in front of someone in the know. Since I've already made the initial contact, it shouldn't be too difficult. We just need to come up with a plausible reason." She stopped as the waitress brought their sandwiches and refilled their glasses.

As soon as she left, Hawk said, "The problem is that there *is* a plot to kill us and capture Ship. We know Moran is behind it, and all indicators point to this company as the source of our problems. I'm not sure how smart it would be just to walk in and ask. We might be stepping into another elaborate trap."

Laura leaned across the table. "What does your gut tell you?".

Hawk thought for a second. "That we have a legitimate business being used as a front, possibly without their knowledge." He paused a moment. "I don't know how well I should trust my gut instincts anymore."

"Your instincts are fine, just rusty. When we finish lunch, I'll make a call and see if I can set up a meeting for tomorrow."

Hawk nodded and spoke around a mouthful of food. "Just us. We'll use the rest for backup and support."

"Let me get this straight," Ashron said as the crew sat in the wardroom. "You're just going to waltz in, walk up to the head honcho, and, nice as you please, ask him why he wants our heads."

"That's pretty much it," Hawk replied. "And it's she. The head of Seladyne Propulsion is a woman.

"Ship!"

"Yes, Ashron?"

"Place an ad in the local paper. Captain wanted, brains preferred but obviously not necessary."

"I think it will work," Gerard said. "From what you've told me and from my research here, there appears to be no danger whatsoever."

"No danger, he says." Ashron slumped into his chair. "For the last month or so, people have been hell-bent on making luggage out of my hide, and you say there's no danger."

"I would stress the word 'appears,'" Gerard said.

"Lovely," Ashron said, sinking lower into his seat.

Hawk turned to Gerard. "We're a hundred percent the funds for the Meta Brévé project originate from this company?"

"One hundred. And, I might add, a large quantity of funds. Looking over their tax records, I'd say much more money than their product output could account for."

"We're definitely looking at a front," Laura stated. "Have we found out who Bill is?"

"No," Gerard answered. "It's not a common name, and there are no Williams or Bills in their personnel files. They have a secure access system for upper management. Ship and I are working on getting into it."

"Unless you can crack it, we'll have to ask at our meeting tomorrow and play it by ear," Hawk said. "Although I'm guessing Bill is a code name precisely because it's so uncommon. We'll give this a shot. Everyone will be close, and if need be, we can evacuate in a hurry. Ashron, I expect you to have a nice diversion planned should we need one."

"Not to worry, Captain. I'll be there to save your butts when you get into trouble again."

"Hopefully, you won't be needed," Laura said. "If everything goes well, we'll get the information we need without any trouble."

"Let's hope," Hawk said without much conviction. "Remember, Moran is still out there. Blowing up the outpost at Meta-Brévé may have thrown him off our trail, but I wouldn't count on it."

***

Gerard pulled the crew van up to the front of the building. "I'll be nearby," he said. "Give a shout if you need me."

Hawk opened the door. "Let's do this."

"Good luck," Gerard said as Laura closed the door.

They watched Gerard pull the craft back into the flow of traffic and disappear around a corner, in search of a free space where he could park and stake out the building entrance from across the street.

Hawk turned to Laura. "Shall we?"

"Let's."

They walked toward the ten-story building, the smallest in a cluster of beige-colored high-rises, and strolled into the lobby. The reception desk sat in the center of a foyer, comprised of a semicircle with two hallways leading toward the back of the building around either side. Hawk noticed several monitors and a communications panel behind the desk. None of them were currently operating. He assumed the counter did double duty as a security station at night.

The receptionist acknowledged them with a smile and held up one finger as she spoke to someone on her headset. After transferring the call, she looked up and said, "Welcome to Seladyne Propulsion. How can I help you?"

"I have a ten-thirty appointment with Talec. Would you tell him Laura Benzing is here, please?"

"Certainly. I believe he's expecting you. One moment." The receptionist pressed a button on the console, and a holograph of Talec's pale blue face popped up on the desk. "Yes?"

"A Laura Benzing to see you," the receptionist said.

He looked at his watch. "Is it ten-thirty already? Tell her I'll be right down."

The receptionist disconnected and looked up.

"I heard," Laura said. "Thank you very much. We'll wait over here."

They moved over to a waiting area and sat down in two of the several chairs gathered around a small table. Various magazines lay on the tabletop. Hawk picked one up and flipped through it. "It's nice to be on a planet that still believes in printed material."

"You have to admit the accessibility of information on a monitor and the lack of advertising have their benefits," Laura said.

"I like the advertisements," Hawk said. "It gives me an idea of what people are interested in."

"You just like the pictures," she said, scanning the page he had turned to. A beautiful humanoid woman stretched across the page. Though Laura couldn't quite discern the model's race, she was a prime example of the species. The print advertised some type of mind-altering drug that was supposed to be ingested with cold fluid. The attractive model stood on a beach of black sand playing Taldé, a game requiring great skill and dexterity. Laura seriously doubted anyone would be able to play it while consuming the product advertised.

"No, really," Hawk said, "This is intellectually stimulating."

Before Laura could reply, Talec approached from the hallway to their right.

Smiling, she stood and held out a hand. "Good to see you again."

His small ears twitched as he smiled and offered his own cerulean hand. "Good to see you," he said in a soft voice as he looked up at Laura. "I have the specs you wanted to see."

"Good. I'd like you to meet my associate, Sean Grey. Sean, this is Talec...I'm sorry, I don't remember your last name."

"Wicktorick," Talec said, taking Hawk's outstretched hand, "Talec is fine. Please follow me. We'll go to one of the conference rooms and see if what we've prepared is satisfactory."

They followed him down the viridian hallway toward a pair of lifts. Talec's bluish skin almost disappeared against the similarly colored walls. A shiver of apprehension hit Hawk.

When they reached the silver-colored lifts, Talec's skin tone changed, his face and hands taking on metallic glints to match the doors.

"You're a Chameleon," Hawk said, voice level despite his sudden unease.

Talec smiled as the lift doors opened. "Our race is called Slandarnis, though we are commonly referred to as Chameleons." He stepped on to the lift. Hawk and Laura followed. Wondering why Laura hadn't mentioned Talec's race, Hawk balled his hands into fists, ready in case something bad happened.

"Fifth floor," Talec said. As the door closed and the elevator rose, Talec turned to Hawk. Splotches of brown, matching the compartment's paneling, had appeared on the small male's face. "I'm only half-Slandarnis. As you've probably noticed, I can't control the color shifts."

Hawk nodded, keeping his relief hidden as he loosened his fists. Chameleons often served as spies and assassins, where their color-shifting abilities gave them a distinct advantage. Half-breeds lost the capability, retaining only the capacity to mimic portions of their surroundings unconsciously. Laura hadn't mentioned it because it wasn't important, and Hawk realized how edgy he still felt despite the seeming innocuousness of their environment.

"I'm sorry you had to wait," Talec continued, smoothing his lemon-colored shirt, a strange match against his skin. "I was working on the price sheet when you called up. It's a rough draft, but the numbers will be pretty close to the final total."

The upward movement stopped, and the doors opened. They stepped out into a carpeted hallway that led off in two directions. They followed Talec, passing the doorways of several spacious private offices, most occupied with busy salespeople and upper executive types. Consumed with their work, most didn't even notice their passage.

This is no trap, Hawk thought. The whole situation seemed too permanent. The carpet, though nice, showed at least two years' wear. The chairs downstairs had also seen their fair share of use. The place had not been hastily put together.

Talec opened a set of double doors into a large meeting room. An oak colored table occupied the center, surrounded by twenty chairs and topped by a holo-unit. Each position around the table also had a terminal with a separate monitor and e-paper slot.

"There's the information," Talec said, pointing to two sheets of electronic paper lying on the table. "Take some time to look over the information provided. If you have any questions, I'll be back to answer them in just a moment." He left the room, closing the two doors behind him.

Hawk and Laura seated themselves at the chairs. Hawk pulled a black cube from his pocket and sat it on the table. While they waited, Hawk and Laura studied the schematics and numbers in front of him. "These look pretty good," Hawk commented.

After about a minute, the cube turned bright green on all sides, indicating the absence of electronic listening devices.

"So, what do you think?"

Hawk placed the cube back in his pocket. "I think this guy is going to be disappointed when he finds out why we're really here. It's a shame, too. From what little I've seen of their work, it's quite good.

Laura smiled. "I think we can both be happy."

Hawk waited.

"Wolf sat me down one day and told me about some improvements he and Gerard wanted to make to Ship's main and ripspace systems, ways to make them more efficient and faster without increasing the mass. The conversation was over coffee and just casual chatter, but when I found out we were coming here, I pressed him for more information. He had some specific ideas and even drew up some plans. He, Gerard, and I sat down yesterday and reviewed the preliminary work-ups Talec had done. They both agreed that if Seladyne Propulsion isn't what it claims to be, they had gone to great lengths to find knowledgeable people in this particular area of engineering."

"Continue." Hawk had noticed the gleam Laura got when one of her plans came together, especially behind his back.

"Well, we worked into the night trying to decide if these plans would work and if they would be an improvement. I didn't do much. Not my area of expertise. Wolf and Gerard did all the work, and they concluded that we were on to something. They did another work up, and we sent them to Talec last night."

Hawk held up his hand. "This is all well and good, but it has no bearing on why we're here."

"It does, sort of."

Hawk raised his eyebrows.

"I'll get to the bottom line. Gerard and Wolf feel that if this is a legitimate company, and I think we all agree it is, then we have devised a marketable item. In other words, we could make some money out of this and improve Ship at the same time." She settled back in her chair, crossed her arms, and waited for a response.

"Make money, huh?"

She smiled.

"And all three of you feel this is a good venture?"

Laura nodded as a knock sounded at the door. Talec opened it. He stood there with a human female at his side.

"Please forgive the intrusion," Talec said. "If you need more time, we'll be glad to return later."

"No," Hawk stood. "We were just finishing."

Talec approached the table. "I'd like to introduce my boss and the owner of the company, Ms. Rianna Selan. Rianna, this is Laura Benzing and Sean Grey."

"The pleasure is mine," Rianna took both of their hands warmly. She was a short, older woman, barely coming to Hawk's chest. She appeared to be in her mid-seventies. The authority of age shone through her bright green eyes. Her well-lined face radiated an air of regality and power, and the wrinkles around her mouth proved she still knew how to smile and laugh.

Hawk spoke to Rianna. "Tell me, does Talec have your full approval to speak for the company?"

"Well, yes," she answered with a questioning tilt of her head.

"The reason I ask is because I feel you and I may have more pressing business, and I would like to let Laura and Talec handle this deal while we talk."

"I'm afraid you have me at a complete disadvantage, because I haven't a clue as to what kind of business you could be talking about."

"Please humor me for a moment," he said with a friendly smile. "Do you have a secure place we could talk and leave these two alone to hammer out the specifics?"

For a long moment, she studied Laura and Hawk. Hawk felt sure she was gauging them, trying to puzzle out his request. Did she know anything about Ship? Was she attempting to decide how best to break away and warn someone? Or was she afraid? Nothing in her warm face and friendly eyes gave him any clues.

Finally, she nodded. "All right. But my people have put a lot of energy into this project, Mister Grey." She fixed him with a cool stare, her warm eyes turning emerald hard. "Don't let me find that it was all a waste. Follow me."

With a reassuring nod to Laura, he followed her out of the room. They walked in silence to the lifts. "My office," she said to the speaker as they stepped through the doors.

"I know you have a lot of questions," Hawk said as they ascended, "and I hope to be able to answer them all. Rest assured, I don't mean any harm to you or your company."

"I run a tight ship here, Mister Grey, and I don't like surprises. Lately, some things have happened that are out of my control. Forgive my caution, but I don't need any more of those types of dealings."

Her words put Hawk on his guard, even as it gave him hope. She had unwittingly confirmed her company's involvement with Moran; she obviously didn't care for the partnership.

The doors opened, and they stepped into a large and lavishly furnished office. Hawk noticed artifacts from many planets he had visited and many others he had not. A large desk, devoid of any clutter, nestled near the all-glass back wall. The wall overlooked a stunning botanical garden that contained a variety of rare and exotic plants. Hawk thought a small animal moved through the growth.

As Rianna took a seat behind her desk, Hawk paused to admire a case of ancient weaponry from the Zincon region of Rega, a giant planet populated by a race of fierce four-armed warriors.

"I have a passion for travel, Mister Grey, and I collect something from everywhere I go."

"You have exquisite taste," Hawk said as he admired a case of artwork.

"Thank you. But we digress. You mentioned something about business we need to discuss?"

Hawk walked over and sat in one of the overstuffed chairs in front of her desk. "I'm not quite sure where to begin," he said, leaning back against the soft cushion. "We— meaning you and I—have a problem."

"And what would that be?"

"I am the captain of a Light Support Cruiser named *The Flaming Star*. Laura is one of my crew members, first officer and ship's doctor. We have a talented engineer who came up with the drive unit improvements, but we are not a company, and that is not our purpose in being here. We originally came to your company for information."

"Corporate espionage?" she asked, seeming more amused than alarmed. "We're not a very big fish, Mister Grey."

"No, and neither are we," he said pointedly.

She offered no readable expression.

"I'll cut to the chase," Hawk continued. "My crew and I just came from a planet called Meta Brévé. Ever hear of it?"

"Yes."

"Have you ever been there?"

"No. Why do you ask?"

"It's part of the problem I'm talking about. Are you familiar with the restrictions on a tech level one planet?"

"I am. No advanced technology whatsoever. No exceptions and

they are well monitored. I went to one on an art-buying trip many years ago. I found the hassle and expense of getting the permits too onerous and haven't done it since."

"And you're certain you've never been to Meta Brévé?"

"If you have the time, I'll name off the sixty-seven planets I've been to. I can assure you Meta Brévé will not be on the list." She leaned forward in her chair, placing both thin-fingered hands on the desk. "Why don't you tell me what's going on."

"It seems a company on this planet is supplying one of the nobles on Meta Brévé with weapons and technology, and that company is yours."

"Mine?" she scoffed. "Hardly. We don't have the capital to finance an operation like that, and we don't deal in arms tech. Even if we did, to what end? The Planetary Council would never allow it, and the punishment for getting caught is death. That is a very harsh accusation, Mister Grey," she stood up. "And I won't have it. If you're trying to blackmail me..."

Hawk held up a hand and said, in the calmest voice he could muster. "Please, Ms. Selan. I have no intention of blackmail. I'm not some rogue captain with information looking for a quick Standard. I have a message for you. Bill sent me. The cargo has arrived, and is ready for pick up."

The color drained from her face. She almost fell back down in her chair, suddenly looking much older. "I had no idea."

"What do you mean?" Hawk asked.

"All those things you said, are they true?"

"Yes," Hawk answered. "So what happens now?"

"I'm supposed to contact a Mister Farkinan and relay the message you just gave me."

"That's it."

"Yes. It's one of the favors I've been asked to do." Her green eyes regarded him. "How are you involved in all of this?"

"My ship is the cargo that's ready for pick up. Someone is going to a great deal of trouble to get it, and I want to find out where they are. I don't suppose you have direct access to this Farkanin."

"No, I'm supposed to send the message through a relay station."

"The money to finance the Meta Brévé operation is coming from your company accounts. Why is that?"

"Why someone wants your ship I can't explain. The money I can. Years ago, my husband and I financed this firm and eventually took over its operation. I had my own marketing firm, so Bill, my husband, ran this one. Well, he wasn't much of a businessman and got into financial trouble. He also had a drinking and gambling problem that didn't help matters."

Hawk shifted in the chair at the mention of the man's drinking problem. She paused; he gestured for her to continue.

"We were going to have to sell the company until a man named Carl Noearm came to Bill and offered to help the company back on its feet. And all we would have to do was an occasional favor. Nothing that would interrupt the company's business and nothing illegal, just things the man might be too busy to do himself. I tried to talk Bill out of it because there was something about the man I didn't like."

"Did he have black hair, a cybernetic arm and a patch on his right eye?" Hawk asked.

"He had the arm and a cybernetic right eye. No patch."

"Your instincts serve you well. His real name is Moran, and he's deadly dangerous."

"I couldn't dissuade Bill, so he agreed to this man's deal. Technically it was his company, and he could do it. Unfortunately, he died three years ago, and I'm still stuck with the deal. I have to admit not much has been asked of us from his end other than delivering the message that you mentioned. I swear to you I know nothing about the money being funneled to Meta Brévé. I would never agree to do anything like that."

"Which is probably why you weren't told about it. Moran did it and neglected to mention it to you." Hawk was silent a moment, thinking. "Why would they do that?"

"I beg your pardon," Rianna said.

"Why would they use you to send a message? Why not transmit straight from the Meta Brévé outpost?"

"I don't know. Paranoid."

"They're getting too paranoid for their own good. The more links in a chain, the better a chance it will break. Ship?"

"Yes, Captain," came the reply in his ear.

"Can you tap into this computer's message base?"

"I could. It will be politer if you ask for the code."

"That's what I meant." He looked at Rianna. "Would you be willing to give us a code to your message base?"

"Certainly. What are you going to do?"

"We'll need you to send the message you're supposed to send, and my ship will have a stringer attached to it so we can find out its destination. I think I have a good idea where it's going though." He paused a moment. "I'm sorry to tell you this. I think Mister Farkinan is someone in your own company."

"That's impossible," she declared.

"Nonetheless, I think that's the case. Someone has to be controlling the money from this end."

"That could be done by a computer."

"Computers keep records that can be hacked and stolen unless someone is around to do a core dump if necessary. As you've seen, these people are paranoid to the extreme. They're going to have someone who can wipe the system if things get bad."

"I don't believe anyone in my company is capable of that."

"I hope you're right," Hawk said. "If you are, I'll apologize. However, I fear you're going to be disappointed."

While waiting for the trace, Hawk returned to the conference room to find Laura and Talec discussing the fine points of a working contract. He sat in on the talks, adding input when necessary. After about two hours, they had an agreement.

"I'll get this to our lawyers, and they'll have a final draft ready by late next week," Talec said.

"Great," Hawk told him. "We need to wait for something from Mrs. Selan. Can we wait here?"

"Certainly." He gathered up the electronic papers and placed his datapad in its case. "Speak with you later," he said as he walked out the door.

"How did it go?" Laura asked as soon as the door closed.

"Almost as well as could be expected when I told her she has a mole in her company," Hawk said.

"She has a mole?" Laura asked in surprise.

"Almost certain." Hawk explained his reasoning.

"Makes sense. You don't think it's her, do you?"

"I doubt it, but I dropped a motion monitor as a precaution. Ship?"

"Yes, Captain."

"Has Ms. Selan left her office?"

"Of course not. I would have told you."

"That's my girl. If she *is* guilty," he told Laura, "she's being very cool about it."

"So, what do you think of all this money we've made you?"

They spent the next half hour going over the plans and contract. Despite recent events, Hawk found himself well pleased with what Laura told him. Wolf and Gerard's plans were going to pay off handsomely for everybody involved, provided they all survived.

"Captain."

"Yes, Ship."

"The stringer has come back. You were right. It's someone in the company."

24

EXTRACTION

Jonas Wilkinson, Vice President of Seladyne Propulsion, sat in his office and stared at his monitor. The message that the package had arrived finally showed up. He expected to see it sometime this afternoon and was not disappointed. A tag tracer had been attached to it, which he also expected.

He anticipated these events because his employers had informed him the group they sought might show up on his doorstep; he had made a point to keep a watch out for them.

Sure enough, they had arrived yesterday, strolling in as if they had not a care in the universe. Jonas immediately recognized both of them from the holos the Corporation had sent him, so he knew the other four and the ship must be nearby.

As soon as he spotted them, he sent a high priority message. The reply came back this morning, telling him a capture team was en route. He needed to wait for their arrival. If any of the vessel's crew approached him, he was to feign ignorance.

Jonas chose to overlook the last part of the message. He would confess ignorance before no one. With confidence born from a taste of power, he knew he could deal with any rag-tag mercenaries, no matter how exceptional their spacecraft. He would set these insignificant pawns in their place and show those above him that he deserved their admiration.

Soon after he received the message there came, as also expected, a knock at his door. Before he could reply, the door flew open and the man and woman from the holos walked in, followed by the bothersome Rianna.

Determined to take the upper hand, Jonas glared at Rianna and, in a hard voice, said, "Rianna, what's the meaning of—"

"Shut up," the man he identified as Hawk told him in a voice of steel. "I have a few questions, and you have a few answers. It's very simple. I ask, you answer."

"Now look here—" Jonas started again.

"I haven't asked you anything yet," Hawk said in a deadly tone, staring into Jonas' eyes.

Jonas' pride warred with his fear. Even though he knew mercenaries could be brutish, he refused to let this mustached thug, with his insultingly long mercenary-styled hair, push him around. Help would arrive soon, so he had to stall and let the bully think he had cowed Jonas. "Very well, ask away."

"How long have you been funneling money through this corporation for your operations?"

"About a year and a half. They're not my operations."

"No," Hawk agreed, "the operations are financed and run by Unicybertronic Technologies."

"You catch on quick for a Neanderthal mercenary."

The man appeared unfazed by the insult. "Why do they want my ship?"

"I don't know."

"I don't believe you."

"I don't care. Torture me, if you think it will help."

"That option hasn't been ruled out," Hawk's eyes narrowed in a manner that Jonas would have laughed at were it not so intimidating.

"Why?" Rianna said, whimpering like a child.

"Why what?" Jonas didn't bother to hide his disdain.

"Why would you do this to my company?"

"Your company?" Jonas laughed. "You seem to forget it's our

company and, before long, it will be *my* company. Once Unicybertronic's plans are completed, I'll have the money and the power to take over. We already have very lucrative contracts drawn up. Unfortunately, there's no place for you in my plans."

"I won't let you do this."

"You won't be able to stop me. When the time comes, you can walk out or be carried out."

"There's a flaw in your plan," Hawk told him.

"Oh." Jonas favored Hawk with a haughty stare. "What's that?"

"It relies on UCT capturing our ship, and that's not going to happen."

"Of course it is," Jonas told him. "There are already interdiction units moving in. You're trapped."

"Thanks for the warning." He looked at the woman named Laura. "Guess it's time for us to leave." He turned back at Jonas. "You're coming with us."

"I don't think so."

"Then you thought wrong."

Laura spoke up. "I can immediately think of four Council edicts you've broken, and I'm sure they'll find others once we turn you in."

"There's no bounty on me, so you have no authority to take me in."

"You can explain that to the Council," Hawk said.

"Look, I don't know who you think you are, but I'm not going anywhere with you. It doesn't matter what edicts I've broken because very soon after Unicybertronic has your ship the Council will cease to exist."

"That sounds a lot like treason to me," Hawk walked up to the desk and stood directly in front of Jonas. "I've heard enough. To use your words, you can walk out or be carried out."

Jonas stood up. "You can't threaten me."

I t was time to end this man's pretense of control. Hawk lashed out over the desk with a ridgehand and struck Jonas across the temple. The man's knees gave out, and he plummeted to the floor. His jaw made a loud clacking sound as it struck the top of the desk.

"Now then," Hawk stared down at the stunned man, "let me introduce myself. I'm Captain Sean Grey, Commander of EC Team Seven, attached to Force Thirteen. You are under arrest for suspicion of treason, violation of the Tech Restricted Planet Code, and whatever else we can come up with."

"Force Thirteen?" the man mumbled, only semi-conscious.

"That's right." Hawk walked behind the desk. He helped Jonas stand up, twisting his right arm behind his back at an uncomfortable angle. "You picked the wrong person to spill your guts to. I imagine your fellow conspirators forgot to mention that." He forced the still dazed man over to the door. Turning to Rianna, he said, "Thank you for the help."

"What's going to happen to him?"

Laura answered. "The Council will be interested in what he knows, so I suspect they'll question him quite thoroughly. Once they've finished, he'll be sent somewhere far away for a long time."

Rianna stared at Jonas, her expression pained. She opened her mouth, closed it; paused a moment, and then said, "Please get him out of here."

Hawk pushed Jonas out the door.

"I'm sorry about this," Rianna said to Laura.

"Don't be," Laura told her. "None of it was your fault. The people you dealt with are masters at manipulating others." Laura smiled at her. "They've been doing it to us quite well, so you're in good company."

Rianna smiled back. "Good luck."

"Thanks," Laura said as she started to leave, "we're going to need it."

Laura and Hawk walked down the corridor, Jonas in front of them. A few people gave them curious stares. Something in Hawk's gaze told them not to interfere. A buzz of whispered conversations started in their wake. Hawk and Laura paid no attention.

Halfway to the lobby, Hawk sensed a change in Jonas's posture; a slight tensing of the muscles told him the man had recovered from his stun and was considering doing something stupid.

"Don't even think about it," Hawk told him calmly while applying pressure to the bent arm. "I'll stop you cold before you get two meters."

Jonas's shoulders slumped.

"Hawk, Laura, you there?" Gerard's voice said in their ear.

"Yeah," Hawk answered. "We're on our way out."

"You might want to slow down a moment. There's a minor problem out here. I'll see if I can take care of it."

"What kind of problem?"

"Rough estimate, seventy men, armed with assault lasers."

"Boy," Laura murmured. "They're not even *trying* to be subtle anymore."

"Ship, keep your sensors open," Hawk told her. "You might have some company too."

"Aye, aye, Captain. Nothing so far."

"Anything we can do to help, Gerard?"

"Walk on through and keep your hands on Jonas. You'll have to trust me; I'm going to be busy."

"Problems?" Jonas asked, his voice a mixture of sneer and hope.

"It looks like your rescue party has shown up."

"You're trapped." The triumph returned to Jonas's dark eyes. "Why don't you give up now and save yourself some pain?"

"Your powers of underestimation are staggering," Hawk informed him. "How did you get so far ahead in the corporate world?"

"Obsequiousness," Laura said. "He's willing to bow down before the great overlords at UCT."

"Only as long as it suits me."

"That may be longer than you expect," Laura told him.

"Or not as long as you might hope," Hawk said. "If we're going to be captured, we won't have any more use for you."

Hawk left the rest unspoken. The fear visible on Jonas' sallow face told him the meaning had gotten through.

Gerard studied the situation from his vantage point a block away. Everything had been calm, with nothing to break the monotony other than the usual traffic of a typical workday. Gerard had begun to hope they had gotten a step ahead of their antagonists.

He should have known better.

The first hovervan had pulled up in front of Seladyne Propulsion's dull glasteel building about fifteen minutes ago. Gerard saw nothing unusual about it, which immediately made him wary. Gray metal, with no company logos, no fancy designs. Bland enough to be suspicious.

His suspicion grew when the van settled to the ground, and no one exited the vehicle.

Other vans, identical to the first, pulled up one by one. By the time seven duplicate vans sat parked in front of the building without one person having emerged, Gerard had moved from suspicion to absolute certainty. He sent a tiny "bumblebee" drone buzzing past the vans. A dash with the robot into an open window which emitted cigarette smoke showed ten armed and armored men piled in back. The drone retreated before the smoking passenger noticed it.

Gerard considered pulling in Wolf and Ashron, then decided he might be able to help Hawk and Laura leave less conspicuously and with no bloodshed.

As he listened to Hawk talk to their prisoner, he prepared for the task ahead. Within the confines of the van, Gerard closed his eyes and recited equations; the world around him faded to silence as he opened a breach into the *aether*. His senses traveled through the gray, swirling void, passing into the building and searching until he located Hawk and Laura.

In the *aether*, they appeared as colored, humanoid-shaped patterns. Laura was a swirling, sparkling white cloud. Hawk looked muted red that moved sluggishly but occasionally showed the spark of the manipulation ability he once possessed.

Once he tuned to them, he used Hawk's physical contact to link to Jonas's murky brown pattern. When he had them established, he opened his eyes and brought outside stimuli back to the front. Holding the patterns was easy once he had them fixed. The actual manipulation he planned to invoke was incredibly draining. Especially on this high-tech planet, where the connection with the *aether* was tenuous and hard to maintain. He wanted to wait until the last possible moment to activate it.

Perhaps another thirty seconds passed before the men in the vans piled out of the vehicles, armed and ready for action. With a soft sigh, Gerard went to work.

A s they moved down the hallway, a tingle started at Hawk's scalp and crawled down his body. Seconds later, the world around him drained of color and transformed to shades of fuzzy gray and black. People changed from firm flesh to pulsing shapes of dazzling white, punctuated by areas of darkness where clothing or hair concealed skin. Sounds dimmed, overlaid by incessant, deep whispering voices, a ritual chant filtered through static.

"What's going on?" Jonas struggled against Hawk.

"Stop it," Hawk gave Jonas's arm a sharp tug, which made him yelp. "A friend is watching after us."

They walked in the *aether*, no longer solid in the "normal" dimension, invisible and silent to everyone around them. Though able to move across surfaces in the same space, they were incapable of affecting the physical environment. The solidity of the floor beneath them and the walls around them had become malleable, changeable with a thought.

Jonas shook, and Hawk almost felt sorry for him. It was unnerving to walk through this monochromatic, out of focus landscape with demonic voices circling and a constant feeling of something hovering beside you. Hawk had been close to terror the first time he did it. He didn't feel especially comfortable now. He drew his sidearm. Laura looked at him, her raised eyebrow glistening ebony against her glowing, eyeless face.

Hawk shrugged. "It makes me feel better," he said, even though it was a foolish notion; the gun wouldn't work in this reality. Even if it did, it couldn't injure anything that existed here.

They rounded a final corner and walked through the lobby. As they moved across the foyer, the glass doors at the front of the building opened. A group of about twenty armed men stormed in, wearing the uniform of local law enforcement special forces. Hawk and Laura both instinctively skipped a step, but continued walking.

"I sure hope Gerard knows what he's doing," Hawk noticed several more men running outside the building, presumably moving to the back to cut off any escape routes. No doubt someone had informed the police that the "wanted fugitives" were in the building, armed and extremely dangerous.

As the men spread out in the lobby with guns raised, bystanders sought hiding spots. Their screaming and yelling broke through as high squeals that briefly punctured the whispers.

"Here we are," Jonas yelled.

"Shut up," Hawk said. He put his gun against Jonas' head, knowing the man would be unaware of the weapon's inoperability. "Keep walking."

The police spread through the lobby in a skirmish formation that revealed their familiarity with such tactics. Some of the officers looked right at them; no one tried to halt the trio as they shuffled through the lobby, every muscle taut.

Hawk noticed the extra tension in Jonas a split second too late. Before he could do anything, the man slammed the heel of his foot down on Hawk's toes. Not painful, it still distracted Hawk enough that Jonas broke free from Hawk's grasp and ran toward the nearest commando.

"Shit," Hawk shouted as he tried to catch the fleeing Jonas. There was no danger of the commandos seeing them, but they needed to remain in close proximity for Gerard to keep them *aetheric*. If Jonas suddenly appeared in front of the police team, Hawk feared they would shoot before questioning.

"Help me," Jonas shouted, waving his arms at the men who couldn't see or hear him. "Help me."

Hawk had his hands out, prepared to grab Jonas, when the fleeing man turned colorless in a flash of brilliant red light that momentarily blinded Hawk.

"Gerard lost him," Laura shouted.

Hawk felt more than saw the high-watt blaster bolts as they fired off, sending throbbing pressure waves through the *aether*. His vision cleared as Jonas flew backward. His vibrant white skin turned black as he died with three burns in his chest.

A man with a smoking blaster and sergeant's stripes shouted. "They're invisible. Waste everything."

"Let's go," Hawk said as auto blasters opened up around them, bursts of sizzling blue energy ripping through the drab. Screams pierced the air as frightened civilians dug for further cover; a few got caught in the crossfire.

They ran as the lobby turned into a shredded charnel house. Several bolts passed through Hawk. It did little more than leave a strange tingle as energy disturbed the *aether*.

They reached the double glass doors and jumped straight through them. This had less to do with their *aetheric* state than with the volley of blaster fire. It had destroyed every plate of glass in the lobby; beads of molten glass lay scattered on the sidewalk.

As they landed on the sidewalk, Gerard pulled up in the crew's van. Hawk thought of the van door and mentally pictured it as not solid, hoping Laura remembered to do the same. He leaped, passed through the vehicle's outer body, and landed on the wide bench seat. Laura followed behind, slamming into him.

The van pulled away. Color and sound returned with stunning fury as Gerard yanked them from the *aether* and back to the normal dimension. Hawk's head swam. Nausea clenched his stomach.

"That could have gone better," Gerard said, sweat beading his pale forehead. He entered the flow of traffic, unnoticed by any of the forces destroying Seladyne Propulsion's lobby.

Hawk was holding his own against his queasiness. The fresh cut grass smell helped, making him think of calmer things. Laura wasn't so lucky. Gerard turned up the van's conditionalizer, and the bile odor quickly subsided.

"Agreed," Hawk said when Laura's stomach had stopped rebelling. "My mistake. I let Jonas get the drop on me."

"That wouldn't have mattered," Gerard assured him. "I had him until he ran into an anti-*aether* sphere. All of those police had *Triclum* powered *aether* sweepers on their belts. As soon as Jonas came into range, there was no way I could keep him phased. Gave me a brutal headache. Lucky they were short range, and you kept away from them."

"*Aether* sweepers?" Laura brushed her hair back from her face. "I don't imagine those are standard issue."

"Not exactly," Gerard agreed. "They were well-informed of our capabilities."

"No great surprise there," Hawk muttered.

Laura rested against the back seat. "I wish we could have gotten out with Jonas; we could have learned a lot more from him."

"I think we've got plenty to work with," Hawk leaned back as fatigue struck him, a side effect of moving in the *aether*. "At least he confirmed my suspicions. Now, all we have to do is decide what we're going to do with the information he gave us."

Hawk glanced over at the deep breathing Laura to find her fast asleep. He turned to Gerard. "She must be—"

He got no further before his eyes closed and he sank into sleep.

THE LARGER SCHEME

They returned to Ship without incident, although Gerard had a few tense moments when police cars passed by the van and then continued on their way.

"No visitors, Ship?" Gerard asked as he drew close to the port.

"All clear," she assured him. Gerard frowned. Something didn't add up. If their hunters knew the Knights were on-planet, then logic dictated they knew Ship would be in port. He expected to find the area crawling with soldiers and tanks, and had been prepared for a brutal fight to escape. Instead, the port looked no different than when they left.

As Gerard rolled onto the van's cradle underneath Ship, Hawk and Laura stirred, awakened by the bumping of wheels on metal.

"Bring us up, Ship," Gerard said.

"Aye."

The van rose off the pavement, lifted by the cradle.

Hawk rubbed his eyes. "I'm starving. I knew there was a reason I didn't like traveling *aetheric*."

"I have a list of reasons," Laura said, yawning as she stretched.

"We made it to Ship without a fight?" Hawk asked.

"Yes," Gerard answered. "Once I left downtown, it was as if nothing ever happened."

"That's suspicious."

"That's what I thought," Gerard said.

The cradle settled and Ship's hull closed. As they stepped out of the van, Gerard activated a thin, saucer-shaped robot and set it to cleaning the van's interior.

They said nothing as they rode the elevator to the main decks. When the doors opened, Ashron and Trey greeted them, both grinning.

"Glad you're back. Did you remember my mustard? Where to now?" Ashron asked.

"What did you bring me?" Trey added, glancing at Ashron and giggling.

Hawk sighed. "Ashron, quit teaching Trey your bad habits. Everybody settle in for takeoff." He headed for the bridge. "Meeting ten minutes after we leave the atmosphere."

The others followed Hawk.

"Another meeting?" Ashron asked. "Boy, you'd think we work for the government or something."

"We do," Trey reminded him.

"Oh, yeah."

"Where's Wolf?" Hawk asked.

"Doing maintenance on the ventilation intakes," Ship answered.

"Then let him know the drill," Hawk seated himself in the pilot's chair.

Everyone else strapped into their chairs. Trey grasped Laura's hand.

"Someday I won't have to do this," he promised her.

"It's okay. You can do it as long as you want."

Five minutes later, Jeran Port Command cleared *The Flaming Star* for take-off. Five more minutes put them clear of the planet's atmosphere, and everyone began removing their harnesses. Trey tossed his aside and dashed off the bridge.

"Going to get ready for the meeting," Laura answered to Hawk's quizzical stare. She smiled. "I think finding out you consider him part of the crew did him a world of good."

Hawk nodded. "I always assumed he knew it. Ship, start flying in random directions and change course at random intervals. Once I have a destination, I'll let you know."

"Aye, captain."

"Okay," Hawk said to the others, "let's go decide our next step."

They arrived at the wardroom to find Trey laying out snacks; a cart loaded with beverages hovered behind him. The famished Hawk and Laura dug into the various sugary confections spread on the table.

"You know," Ashron said, "you've got a great future in the food services industry."

In his most haughty voice, Trey said, "I'm going to be a powerful magician, and if you make me mad I'll turn you into a toad."

"Isn't that nice, Ashron?" Laura smiled through lips covered with sugar glaze. "Trey's going to take you a step up on the evolutionary ladder."

Ashron stuck out his forked tongue as Wolf walked in.

"Salt w—" Wolf stopped as Trey walked toward him with a large glass of salt water.

"Thank you," Wolf sat in his oversized chair.

The crew had listened through Ship's speakers to the events that transpired at Seladyne Propulsion. Once everyone settled, Hawk wiped his hands on a napkin and said, "Ship?"

"Yes."

"Did anyone approach close to you in the port?"

"Four people passed within a three-meter perimeter at different times; they all moved on to other ships."

"Do a hull surface scan and see if you find anything that shouldn't be there. Check the landing gear, also."

"Aye, aye."

"You think there's a tracker on us?" Laura asked.

"That's the only reason I can think of that they didn't send an army to take Ship, since they knew we were here."

"Maybe we're starting to strain their resources," Ashron said brightly.

"That's wishful thinking," Gerard told him.

"So, what's the game plan?" Ashron said.

"An excellent question," Hawk picked up a cookie. "What would you do in this situation?"

"Great." Ashron turned to Laura. "He doesn't have a clue."

"No, no. I know what I want to do, but I want your input."

"Yeah, right. I've heard that 'surround yourself with good people' spiel before. You want to hear our ideas and then claim they were yours all along."

Hawk stared at the ceiling. "Are you sure we can't replace him, Ship?"

"I don't think we could find another Lorothian crazy enough to work with us."

Hawk sighed. "Oh, well." He took a drink of fizzwater before continuing. "Jonas's little tirade about the Council ceasing to exist has me concerned. Even though it may have been an empty threat, it certainly sounded like he believed it."

"Come on," Ashron said. "You don't really think there's anyone out there with the guts and power to take on the Council, do you?"

Gerard spoke up. "There are several corporations with the resources to make a good effort at it. UCT is among that group. If any two or three of the bigger Corporations banded together, the Council would no doubt fall within a few months."

"So why hasn't anyone done it?" Ashron asked.

"There's been no reason for that sort of cooperation or action," Gerard told him. "Think about it. For as large a governing body as it is, the Council is reasonably benevolent. It places surprisingly few restrictions on the Corporations."

Ashron picked up a piece of wrapped lettuce filled with meat. "So why does someone suddenly want to do it now?"

Hawk spoke up. "I think we can safely replace 'someone' with 'UCT.'"

"Okay, why does *UCT* want to do it now?"

"Because Moran is pushing the buttons," Gerard answered. "And he has somehow convinced them his personal vendetta is profitable. If they take possession of Ship and duplicate her, he could well be right."

Ship's voice piped up. "Excuse me. I detected a foreign object on the secondary support strut of the port stern landing gear. It's transmitting a signal."

"Can you scramble the signal?" Hawk asked.

"Negative. It's a broad beam transmission so I would have to flood the area around me, which would interfere with my equipment. If you patch me to it, I could send a false image."

"Okay. Cancel the random flight pattern and head for..." Hawk paused, looked at Ashron. "Loros. We'll do a patch after a while and make them think we're still heading that way while we head somewhere else."

"Aye aye, Captain."

"Thanks," Ashron said dryly. "If they blanket my home planet with radiation, you and I will have a little talk."

Ignoring him, Hawk said, "Okay, this is what we need to do. We'll go ahead and relay what we know to the Council. I suspect they're going to want more proof than the rantings of one not very reliable and now very dead person. However, his warning plus what we already know times the fact Moran seems to be heading it up equals a high probability the threat is real." He picked up a piece of bread and placed slices of cheese and salami on it. "Now all we have to do is figure out how real the threat is."

"That should be easy, shouldn't it?" Trey asked. The others turned to him.

"Go on," Gerard said.

When he realized he had unwittingly put himself in the spotlight, Trey squirmed as if his chair had turned into a bed of warm coals. Picking at his shirt as he wiggled, he said, "Well, to go after the Council you'd need a whole bunch of ships, wouldn't you?"

"Yes," Gerard answered.

"Well, someone has to build them or buy them or something. There's got to be records of all that, right?"

"That's true," Hawk told him.

"So can't we just look at UCT's records and see if they've been putting out that kind of money to ship companies?"

There was a brief silence. Then Laura leaned over and hugged Trey. "Have I told you today what a wonderful kid you are?"

Trey blushed furiously.

"That's a great idea," Hawk said. "Hacking into their system may take some work. You, Gerard, and Ship can work at it while we head to Red's."

"We're going to Red's?" Ashron asked.

"Yeah," Hawk said. "Strangely enough, it's one of the safest places I can think of that will still allow us to pull together the resources we need."

"Yeah, because things went so well the last time we were there," Ashron said with a roll of his eyes.

"Resources for what?" Laura asked.

"When we get to Red's we're going to disguise ourselves and Ship. Once we find out the threat is valid, we're going to pay personal visits to the various heads of UCT, starting with the chairman of the board, and put a stop to the threat. Any questions?" Hawk looked at the five of them as they turned to each other, brows furrowed in concentration.

After about fifteen seconds, Ashron said, "Well, no, I guess not."

"I think you stunned them, Captain," Ship said.

"The fact he even has the inkling of a plan stunned the hell out of me," Ashron told her.

"I have a question," Trey said.

Hawk looked at him. "And that is?"

"How do you disguise an entire ship? Or Wolf?"

"Fair question," Ashron said. "They're both about the same size."

"I guess disguise was a bad word. How about 'hide'?"

"How do you hide a ship?"

Gerard held up a finger to keep Hawk from speaking. "Think about it."

Trey thought a moment, his eyes darting rapidly around the room and a frown on his face. Then his expression brightened. "You put it in a bigger ship."

"That's right," Hawk said. "And, much as I hate to do it, we're going to give her a paint job. I'm thinking bright red with black highlights."

"Won't she kind of stand out?" Ashron asked.

"Yes," Hawk agreed. "She'll stand out so much that no will even consider that it's the same vessel."

"Hide in plain sight," Gerard offered

"Exactly. Any more questions?"

"Yeah," Ashron said, "What am I supposed to do for the next two days?"

Wolf stood up with a grin. "Glad you asked. To start, there's a transmitter on a landing gear that needs patching. Then there's more."

"It was a rhetorical question."

"I know," Wolf said.

Muttering, Ashron stared at the table.

"We'll do ripsleep in ten minutes," Hawk said. "When we're back, Gerard and Trey can get busy on those corporate records."

"Captain, good news," Ship said.

"Great. I could use a little."

"I found a picture and statistics match for Anne. A most interesting woman."

"Dump it in my room," Hawk said. "I'll look at it on the other side of rip."

Hawk whistled in amazement as he finished the information Ship had placed across the terminal. "I lucked out again, didn't I?"

"Yes, you did."

Anne Siliar's real name was Madrin Abarla. Judging by her past work, she easily ranked in the top echelon of assassins floating around the galaxy. They had no way to get an accurate count of how many beings she had killed; the rumors Ship could find had it in the neighborhood of a hundred.

"So, Ship, in the past five years, how many times do you think sheer blind luck has saved me?"

"Thirty-two. Of course, that's just a rough estimate."

"I need to start relying on more than luck, then. I'd say mine's about run out. Do we have any way to track her down? I'd like to have a chat with her."

"There are channels I could go through if you'd like me to put out a false feeler."

"Do that. It may not matter, but I don't like the idea that she's running around out there and we have no inkling where she is."

"Aye, Captain.

"That was a good call, Trey," Gerard said. "They are definitely building up for something big."

They had been working with Ship for the past day, searching, locating and compiling information on purchases made by Unicybertronic and any of their subsidiaries. What they found staggered Gerard. In a little over three years, the company had purchased ten thousand ships for a total cash outlay of roughly four trillion Standards

"I didn't know companies made that kind of money," Trey said.

"Many of them don't," Gerard told him. "UCT is one of the rare exceptions. That's no doubt why Moran approached them."

"If they're that rich, why do they want to overthrow the Council?"

"For a lot of people, money isn't enough. They want power, too, and they think by overthrowing the Council, they'll have the power they want. People will do horrible things for power."

"I know," Trey stared down at the table.

Gerard patted the boy on the back. "I know you do. But I don't think the executives at UCT have fully thought it through."

"What do you mean?"

"The Council is only able to exist because the planets involved let it exist. If UCT takes over, the only way they'll be able to continue ruling is through force. Ten thousand ships may be enough to overthrow the Council, but it's nowhere near enough to make two hundred and eight planets bend to your will."

"What about ten thousand ships like Ship, only bigger?"

"Ten thousand sentient ships?" Gerard considered it. "It's possible.

And if they ever learn how to do it, they could build as many as they want. Ship, download this to Hawk. Come on, Trey, we need to show him what we found."

As they moved down the hallway toward Hawk's cabin, Gerard asked, "So, the ripspace visions have stopped?"

"Not totally," Trey admitted, "but I can handle them now."

Gerard nodded. "And your finger exercises and multiplication tables."

"The finger stuff is easy now; I'm getting better with the math."

"Five times seven?"

"Thirty-five."

"Six times six?"

"Thirty-six."

"Three times ei-"

"Twenty-seven. No, twenty-four."

Gerard smiled. "Keep working at it. You're doing well."

Trey returned the grin.

When they arrived at Hawk's door, they saw it already open. Hawk sat in a blue fabric chair. Trey liked Hawk's cabin. It was a neat, well-kept room, unlike Gerard's machinery-strewn wreck, or Ashron's, where his discarded clothing served as a carpet.

Trey approved of Hawk's cleanliness. He didn't like messes. Life had shown him it was messy enough without adding to it. The walls were a shade of blue that was almost black. Much darker than the other walls in Ship. A holo-picture of a beautiful woman with short brown hair and tan skin sat on his nightstand. Trey had never asked who she was. He now realized it had to be Sara. Her hazel eyes, even in the static picture, took Trey's breath. She resembled Laura; Trey decided he probably shouldn't say that.

Another holo hung on the wall, this one of Ship, a younger Hawk, and a black-haired man Trey suspected was Moran.

Trey wondered why Hawk kept such painful memories where they could torment him. Trey had left everything behind on Kel, wanting to take nothing with him. The memories had followed him anyway. He suddenly wished he still had a picture of his parents. Maybe seeing the memories helped. He would have to ask Hawk sometime.

Hawk broke into Trey's thoughts. "Ship told me you were coming. Show me what you've got."

Gerard explained their discoveries while Hawk followed along with the information Ship put up on the monitor.

"It certainly looks like a nice little coup attempt to me," Hawk said when Gerard had finished. "I think Grendarin will be able to get the Council to act on this."

"I believe I'll mention this to my Order, too," Gerard said.

"Why?"

"That size a force might have some manipulators connected to it and my colleagues should know that. Plus, they might be able to find out more information for us."

"Okay," Hawk said. "Never hurts to have a flock of spellburners on your side."

"Flock?" Gerard's pale eyebrows quirked in amusement. "I'll refrain from telling them you said that."

Hawk's face reddened. "I'd appreciate that."

Moran brooded in his dimly lighted office, the ebon walls a reflection of his mood. Despite the painkillers and bone menders, his sternum still ached from the impact of the lasers. The cybernetic eye destroyed by the sniper's blast had been replaced immediately with no complications. The skin around it, shredded by the exploding metal, still healed and itched constantly. Moran dared not scratch it.

That he should be dead never entered Moran's mind. He had come close to death and survived by sheer will so many times he felt he couldn't die. Each close encounter with the grim specter had resulted in the loss of some portion of himself, which he replaced with a machine part. He would simply become more and more machine until the only human element left was his brain. He knew a machine, properly maintained, could run forever.

He intended to make sure he was properly maintained.

The pain in his ribs was only a minor annoyance. The major

anguish came from knowing Hawk—a seemingly indestructible survivor like himself—was still alive with the ship in his possession.

Moran cared nothing about the ship itself. Sara, trapped inside, was another matter. He would free her and make her his. The fools at Unicybertronic could babble about overthrowing the Council all they wanted. Moran would help them, since ruling the known universe had a certain appeal. But he would do it with Sara at his side. He would continue with the experiments and the project as long as there was no chance she would come to harm. The destruction of their research lab on Meta Brévé had been a setback, nothing more. They had other labs making progress. When the starships were ready, Moran would be ready, too.

A knock on the door intruded into his melancholy thoughts. "Enter," he said.

The door slid open, and one of the nameless, faceless corporate flunkies walked in. "Sir, we have a tracking lock on the vessel. As you suspected, they patched the broadband transmitter to send a false reading."

"Did they find the secondary?"

"Apparently not, sir. Here's the data and projection information." The technician walked over and handed a small cube to Moran.

"Is that all?"

"Yes, sir."

"You may go."

The technician turned and left. Moran looked at the cube. His face contorted into what he thought of as a smile; most would have seen it as a grimace.

I'm still smarter than you are, Hawk, he thought as he dropped the cube into its slot. They had found the decoy, which he fully expected, and completely missed the real transmitter, which had been his hope.

It was a tiny piece of equipment, no bigger than a thumbnail, so small and low-powered that not even Ship's hypersensitive apparatus could detect it. Its drawback was that it could only send data over a short distance, usually no more than ten kilometers. Moran had modified the device; instead of a constant transmission, it sent out a static burst every six hours, which were intercepted by powerful scanners tuned to its pattern. The power cell on the device allowed for four such bursts. Ordinarily, this would have been useless for figuring out a vessel's projected course, but Moran knew enough about Hawk's mindset that he felt confident he could fill in the blanks left by technology.

Moran turned on the screen, viewed the line of static discharges, studied the routes projected by the computer, and laughed. Hawk was almost making it too easy.

"Back to Red's? Well, I'll make sure what you meet there keeps you entertained."

26

A BAD NIGHT AT RED'S

Hawk pushed through the batwing-style double doors. They clattered behind him, swinging smoothly on well-oiled hinges as he let go. He scanned the tavern with its motif of Old Earth West and felt a brief disappointment the crowd hadn't gone instantly silent when he walked in. A few people did glance at him before returning to their business. The two-man band didn't even pause in its playing. He would have to talk to Red about that later.

He shuffled to the bar, sat down, and placed his back against the edge of the bar's wooden railing so he still faced the crowded room.

"What'll it be, stranger?" the boisterous Red asked from behind him.

"Banana shake," Hawk said. He felt more than saw Red's puzzled expression. Without turning around, he added, "I'm on the starship."

"Good," Red said.

Hawk grinned as he rested his elbows on the bar and studied the crowd. To Hawk, the Galaxy consisted of two types of individuals: hunters and prey. Hawk considered himself the former. Recent events had shown him a view of life as the latter. He did not enjoy it and was ready to resume his place in the ranks of the predators. Places like Red's drew hunters as inevitably as blood attracted sharks.

Red had informed Hawk earlier that one of the major predators had shown up hunting for him, much as he had been seeking her. He decided to turn the tables and flush her out before she had a chance to take him down.

Hawk found his mark. She sat in a far corner staring at him. She diverted her attention and continued to study the room as if the eye contact had been incidental. He continued to stare at her. She gave no indication that she noticed.

A hand touched his shoulder. Without turning away, Hawk held out his hand. A cold glass pressed into it.

"Any luck?" Red's voice said behind him.

"The fishing's fine, thanks," Hawk answered, staring at the female. She studiously avoided his direct gaze. A tactical error. Hawk hadn't been sure she was the one. Her continued evasion of his stare confirmed it.

He glanced away to another part of the room. In a small booth beside the fireplace sat another female. Feline in appearance, with multi-hued chocolate fur and dark green eyes. She sat in an alert posture, her claws sliding in and out as her hands flexed. She left no doubt about her place on the hunter/prey scale. She gazed at Hawk and, with minute gestures, gave him the all clear.

"Tasha looks much better now than when she first arrived," Red said.

Hawk took a drink of his shake, enjoying the creamy cold as it went down his throat. He almost didn't miss the vodka he used to put in them. "Do you think she's ready?

"Oh, yes. I saw her workout this morning. She's more than ready."

Upon their arrival yesterday, Hawk and crew had been surprised to find Tasha waiting for them at Red's cabin, alive and well. Tasha told them about the kidnapping and how she struggled to find a way to Red's, not knowing whom to trust and forced to avoid medical attention lest her name show up in official databases. She finally managed to stow away on a freighter heading to the right system and steal one of the escape pods, which she immediately charted for GH-5955.

Later that night, Red told Hawk she had arrived near death, and it was a miracle she made it at all. The poison from the needler could not kill her outright like it did humans, but without any antidote, it continued to weaken her system. Unable to eat and barely able to drink, she arrived malnourished, dehydrated, and incoherent. How she piloted the escape craft into the hanger without crashing was still a mystery, since she remembered nothing about it. Red had told Hawk that when she first arrived, the odds on her living through the night were about a hundred to one.

"It's amazing," Red said as Hawk stood up from the bar. "If you had told me four nights ago she would be up and back to normal within a week, I would have thrown you in the hole for being a liar."

"Well," Hawk said, "maybe Pralins have nine lives, too. Showtime."

He gave one last glance at Tasha. Nodding, she stood and slid to a better position, ready to back up Hawk if he needed it.

With his drink, Hawk strolled toward the table where the woman sat. Noticing his movement in her direction, she smiled and took a casual sip from her drink, a dark green liqueur that smelled of mint and fresh grass.

"Hello, Sean," she said as he reached the table. "It's been a while."

"Hello, Anne," Hawk pulled up a chair and sat. "Or should I call you Madrin."

She started at the use of her real name—a hesitation so brief only someone trained like Hawk would have noticed—then smoothly regained her composure.

"Either is fine," she said. "I see you've been doing your homework."

"I think I liked you better as a brunette."

"I'm sorry to hear that," she said, touching her short, tawny mane. "This is my natural color."

"Is it?" Hawk asked. Ship's file had included every picture of Madrin that could be found. An expert in disguise, she had one feature she could not change. The keen vision of her race relied on a chemical composition that made their eyes highly sensitive to any touch. Colored contacts would have her writhing in pain within thirty seconds. Color correction surgery would have blinded her. The golden eyes Hawk remembered so well had given her away. "I'm disappointed you didn't stick around that night so we could have said proper good-byes."

"I had a pressing engagement."

"Fair enough," Hawk said. "Moran can be a little impatient." She offered no reaction to the name other than a quizzical frown.

She's good. Hawk thought. Standing, he said, "Then I'll say good-bye now."

"So soon? I was hoping we could dance."

"Funny, I thought we just did."

She smiled and sipped her drink. "Some other time then."

Hawk smiled back. "I look forward to it." He offered a slight bow and left the bar, turning his back on her.

Madrin watched him leave, sliding her needle gun back in her boot. She could have taken him then, but it was hard to collect a fee on suicide missions. As soon as she shot Hawk, the crowd would have grabbed her, she would have been found in violation of Red's code, and they would have tossed her in "the hole."

The hole was just that, a ten-meter wide, twenty-meter deep concrete pit that contained absolutely nothing. By Red's decree, anyone found guilty of killing someone on GH-5955 was lowered into the hole. Lowered with them was an eight-legged creature known as a Spiner. It immediately latched on to the trapped convict, stunned the victim with a nueropoison, and laid eggs in various appendages. The Spiner died shortly after impregnating its host. The eggs took years to gestate, and they fed on the host, causing pain so mind-crushingly intense the person went insane within a year. If anyone was caught helping any person try to escape the hole, they also received the same treatment. It was a brutal, effective punishment. Word had spread, and there had been no murders on GH-5955 in ten years.

She watched as the Pralin female who played back up left behind

Hawk. No murders in ten years. She planned to change that tonight. She would take as many as she thought she could safely get away with. Hawk was the priority. If she could manage the whole crew, all the better.

She downed the rest of her drink and walked toward the exit. She needed to be even more cautious than usual, since Hawk obviously expected danger. Experience and common sense dictated she should wait a night or two, lying low so they would assume she had left, but she had no way of knowing if the Knights would even stay that long.

Besides, she grew tired of the cat and mouse game. She had deigned to work this last job for Moran after he agreed she could go it alone and do it quietly instead of grandstanding. The pay, though excellent, was by the head and not the hour. She was ready to move on.

Walking down the hall, she headed to her room. She would wait a few hours until things had quieted down and people were asleep. She had enough preparations to keep her busy until it was time to move.

After slipping through the easily bypassed airlock security, Madrin crouched on the ground and remained still. Her preternatural eyesight picked out every detail in the subterranean darkness. Despite the entire colony's underground location, it managed to have a pale imitation of day and night, marked by differing illumination. A thin fungus covered the various caverns' walls. It reflected and amplified the weak light of the nearest star that managed to slip through cracks in the surface or openings carved out for ships. When the star moved to the far side of the planetoid, the fungus went dark, and the inhabitants called it night.

Red's cabin, far from the hub of commerce, was bereft of the luxury of outside electric light. Pitch black surrounded the dwelling, broken only by the faint lights of the main cavern, which sat at Madrin's back.

To Madrin, everything appeared as if it were bright day on a salt flat. She didn't have much to see other than a modest two-story structure, built from dull gray stone carved out of the surrounding cave.

She cocked her head, listening for movement, her hearing augmented by a directional audio amplifier. There had been no real activity for the two hours she had crouched here, motionless as ice. She decided to wait a little longer. She wanted this to be done, but she wouldn't throw away all caution.

After another half-hour, she had waited long enough. Moving from her crouch, she lay down on the ground. Inch by inch, she belly-creeped across the cavern floor. *Lift on the fingertips and toes, rock forward and down, listen, look, repeat.* She could almost hear her instructor standing over her.

"Training will keep you alive" he used to tell them. "Do it right every time, or you're dead."

Though fingertip crawling was excruciatingly slow, it attracted almost zero attention from people or cameras. Her black clothing had a thermal coating that hid her heat signature and a transmitter to confuse audio devices listening for life signs. She was as camouflaged as technologically possible.

She did not let the tedious pace bother her. Training had drilled into her that real life rarely tolerated incompetence. She listened and looked. Nothing new. *Up, rock, down.*

She continued this pattern for thirty minutes, covering twenty-five meters at an ant's pace. As she moved, she wondered why anyone would pump oxygen into such a large area when their front yard was only stone.

Ten meters out from the house, she saw a small infrared beam running across the floor of the cavern. *Weak,* she thought. Not much of a defense. Then again, Red wouldn't need much since he was already protected in several other ways. Very few people knew this cabin's location. Most of those who did had no real reason to harm him.

Besides, there was that nasty doomsday device rumor.

Still keeping her movements small and deliberate, she lifted herself over the beam, avoiding it with childlike ease. Once past that obstacle, she watched for the Knight's defenses, knowing they wouldn't trust their safety with Red's standard security.

As soon as she thought it, she spotted the vibration of the waves.

Ultrasound. Very nice. If the waves were disrupted in any way, an alarm would trigger. Either movement or an object in the path of the waves would do it. Motion sensors were easy. They could be fooled by moving at the snail's pace she set. Ultrasound presented a more significant challenge. Even with the advantage of being able to detect the waves, Madrin needed a little help to avoid this sentinel.

She reached into one of her many pockets, pulled out a small silver sphere, and activated it. Holding it toward the waves, she gave it a few seconds to tune to the pattern. A minuscule green light informed her when the device had duplicated the rhythm. She could now move through the waves without disrupting the pattern. The handy device was heavily used in the spy and assassin trade. The same corporation that manufactured the ultrasound wave emitters also conveniently sold the equipment to bypass them on the black market.

She resumed her trek, passing through the waves with no problems. She reached the front door and paused. Although she could see nothing on this side, Moran had warned her Red always had an alarm on the front door and the windows.

Rising from her prone position, she crouched and sidestepped, careful to stay below the windows and avoid touching the walls, in case they were wired.

She reached a midpoint of the house where there was a reasonable distance between windows. Going over the engineering plans for Red's house in her head, she oriented herself to the inside. According to those plans, she stood on the other side of the guest bathrooms. She listened to the wall with her augmented ears and caught the sound of heavy snoring. She allowed herself a grin. Someone's peaceful dreams were about to be shattered.

She retrieved a small vial from her breast pocket, stepped back a foot from the wall, and gulped the contents of the vial. The acidic taste made her grimace. After a moment, the world turned monochromatic and deep buzzing filled her ears. As instructed, she pictured the wall before her as insubstantial and moved forward. An unpleasant tingling sensation crept over her as she passed through the stone barrier. She thought she saw winged figures in the corner of her vision.

A few seconds after she slid through the wall, color and quiet returned as the elixir wore off and she phased back to normal space. She glanced at the wall behind her and felt a thrill of relief she had moved through as fast as she did. The potion was an expensive and rare mixture, and Moran had only given her one. Had she not been able to use it to slip in through the house's walls, her job would have been much tougher. She didn't even want to consider what would have happened if she had returned while still walking through the wall.

She suddenly caught an odor of *batras*, a pungent herb from her homeworld used in preserving the dead, and wondered why Red would have such a thing. Then she recalled the phantom smell phenomenon Moran had told her about. As she swallowed the bile that rose in her throat, she remembered his mention of nausea, too. *If he had been this precise the first time I worked for him, I wouldn't have to be here now.*

Her recall of the house plans had been correct. She stood in the guest bathroom, a dull room with dark green walls and teal fixtures. She stepped to the open doorway and listened again. Still no movement, but the snoring had gotten louder. She glanced into the hallway. The likelihood of any further security devices was small, since people needed the freedom to move around their home at night.

The hallway branched off in both directions with a door at either end, three doors on the opposite wall, and two doors on the same wall as the bathroom. According to Moran, Hawk always took the bedroom at the north end of the hall. Wolf had a room specially designed for him at the other end, and the rest of the crew would be in the various rooms along the hallway.

She glided down the hallway, her stealth aided by the simple beige carpet covering the floor. The snoring emanated from Hawk's room. She reached into another pocket and retrieved a small atomizer. Shaped like an innocuous perfume sprayer, it held a vicious poison. Sprayed into the target's face, it was inhaled into the lungs, where it rapidly expanded and foamed, causing an excruciating, silent death. The victim's eyes would snap open in horror, and their mouths would flex as they tried to scream. The fast-acting poison kept thrashing to a minimum. Madrin had access to quicker and less painful methods, but she liked her victims to see her as their killer. She wanted to stare into their eyes and smile at the moment life fled.

As a precaution, she scanned for any alarm devices and found nothing. She pushed open the door and slipped into the room in a crouch. The loud snoring came from an oversized bed placed against the far corner of the room. On top of the bed lay Hawk's sleeping form. She crabbed toward the bed and then stopped. Something was wrong, although she couldn't determine what. A closer inspection revealed no heat signature coming from Hawk's prone body. *Damn.*

She spun for the door and ran right into Wolf's massive frame. *How?*

Everything went black.

She awoke sitting on the same bed where she had seen Hawk, or the illusion of Hawk, earlier. She had been stripped to her undergarments and couldn't move, although she could see or feel no physical restraints. Her stomach knotted and head spun. She wondered if she was having a bad reaction to the potion.

The entire crew stood gathered around her. Red leaned against a far wall with his large arms crossed, emotions unreadable on his heavily bearded face. The Pralin that had been shadowing Hawk in the bar was also there, her reaction plain to see; she wanted to rip Madrin's guts out and hand them to her.

Things looked grim. She felt like a hovertruck had run over her. Still, she hadn't gotten her reputation and status being a quitter. "Now what?"

Hawk turned a chair around and straddled it, his arms sitting on the backrest. "Why don't you tell me? After all, unless you can convince Red otherwise, you're headed for the hole."

She thought for a moment, fighting back the bile that rose in her throat. "Information," she said at last. "I want promises in return." She hadn't gotten where she was by being loyal either.

"What kind of information?" Hawk asked.

"Let's not play games. You know what's going on here. People don't arbitrarily go after a faction of Force 13 without a reason or cause. Moran has both."

"We already know that he wants Ship. And my head on a platter."

"You don't know why."

"But we do. I guess I have you to thank for him finding out. Your damsel in distress act was quite convincing. Moran knows I'm a sucker for a pretty lady. Try again."

"I can tell you where to find him."

"Okay. Tell me."

"Promises," she repeated. "My life and a one-way ticket off this backwater rock."

Hawk turned to Red. "It's your call."

"It's your life," he answered. "She's an assassin and her profile is she works alone, so more than likely no one else except Moran knows she's here. Therefore, my reputation is safe. The question is, do you trust her information enough to let her live? You're the only one who can make that decision."

Hawk turned back to Madrin. "Well? Can I trust you?"

"Yes," she answered immediately. "I have nothing against any of you personally. Moran offered good money. I don't owe him anything." She grimaced as her stomach gurgled, reminding her of its displeasure with the recently ingested contents.

"Fair enough," Hawk told her. "I give you my word. If the information proves accurate, you'll be spared the hole and banished. If not..." he shrugged.

The Pralin's shoulders sagged, and her cat face frowned. "I'll be in my room," she told Hawk. With a dagger-loaded glare at Madrin, she turned and stalked out.

"What's her problem?" Madrin asked when she had left.

Ashron spoke up before Hawk. "She has an even lower opinion of assassins than we do."

Madrin considered asking him what he thought the Knights were, if not government-sponsored assassins. She decided she was in no position to argue philosophy.

"Information," Hawk prompted.

"Very well," she said. "Can I at least get a robe or something? And could you let me go? This position is uncomfortable, and it's not like I'm going anywhere."

"Sure," Hawk said after a moment. Red moved across the room to a closet. Gerard, with a slight hand gesture, released the bonds that held her to the chair.

Rubbing her hands, Madrin said, "He's on Kalaros Three, Unicybertronic's corporate home, staying with Salakon. They're having a…"

She stopped and cried out in pain. Her body shuddered; she doubled over, gripping her stomach.

<hr>

"What's wrong?" Hawk stood as Laura moved toward Madrin. Wary of a trick, Hawk held up his hand to stop Laura.

Madrin had gone ghost white and drenched in sweat. "I…don't… know." She convulsed.

Before anyone could react, Madrin's stomach started melting through her fingers. Flesh foamed as it hit the floor. She let out a bone-chilling scream as she fell off the bed. It spread rapidly from her stomach; her body boiled off its frame in a pink froth.

"Get back!" Gerard yelled, his arms a flurry of movement.

Compelled by Gerard's tone, the rest backed away. As one of Madrin's arms flung out, throwing gouts of foaming flesh toward the crew, Gerard enveloped her in a glittering dome of *aetheric* energy.

Hawk ducked as a clump of hissing flesh passed him. It struck Ashron square in the chest.

A piece flew straight toward Laura. She flinched as a small hand came into view. Trey had reached out and grabbed the oozing gob just before it hit her face.

He started to smile at her. It changed to a scream of pain and horror as his flesh rapidly disintegrated from his hand. His eyes went wide; his cry became inaudible as the destruction to his hand quickly worked its way up his arm.

Snatching the half-meter-long knife Ashron always carried out of its scabbard, Hawk spun and shoved Laura out of the way. He grabbed Trey's arm at the bicep and swung the weapon, cutting at the elbow.

As his bubbling arm fell to the floor and sizzled, Trey stared at Hawk with a wide-eyed mixture of hurt and confusion. He went ashen and collapsed. Hawk grabbed the front of the boy's shirt and lowered him to the ground.

Laura dropped to Trey's side as she pulled the ever-present medkit from her belt and set to work to stop the bleeding.

Hawk turned at Ashron, knife raised.

"You better get away from me," Ashron said, backing up.

Lowering the weapon, Hawk asked, "Are you okay?"

"I think so," Ashron crossed his eyes to look through his destroyed shirt at the spot on his chest where he had been struck. His scales had turned a slightly lighter green, and the area felt tender. Other than that he was unharmed.

When Hawk determined there were no further injuries, he observed the dome that contained what had once been Madrin. His stomach clenched. Bubbling pink flesh oozed down the side of the shield wall, rapidly disappearing. Steam rose; a large mass of entrails and skeleton lay near the center.

Hawk had seen enough. "Wolf, grab Trey," he said, noting that Laura had covered the wounded stump arm. "Everybody out. Gerard, seal the room. Everybody to the decon chamber, pronto."

The crew moved. Even Red jumped at the sound of Hawk's voice.

"Decontamination isn't necessary," Gerard said to Hawk as he closed the bedroom door.

"You know what that substance is?" Laura asked.

He nodded. "I've never seen it until today. It's called *kataverin*. It's a flesh-eating virus that, as you've seen, completely consumes any living organism it touches."

"Not that I'm complaining," Ashron said, "but how come I'm still alive?" He pointed at the spot on his chest.

"I can only surmise that your top scales are dead and non-porous. The virus must have never had an opportunity to enter your body."

"Why don't we need decon?" Hawk asked. "We've all been exposed, at least indirectly."

"It's short-lived and doesn't survive in the air. It devours any flesh it touches. If you make contact, you're dead. Your quick thinking is the only thing that saved Trey."

"Who we need to get to the sick bay," Laura turned and headed toward Red's underground hanger. Wolf followed, carrying the barely conscious child.

"Let's get back to Ship, too," Hawk said.

"I'll be along in a minute," Gerard said. "I need to get a sample for Laura."

"I gotta see this," Ashron said, following Gerard back into the bedroom.

He stared at the crackling energy dome where Madrin once stood. Still sizzling chunks of flesh clung to the sides.

"I thought you said that stuff was quick," Ashron said.

"It is if it has oxygen," Gerard explained. "The dome doesn't allow oxygen in or out."

"Looks like someone went wild with a food processor."

Gerard gave him a disgusted frown. "You're a sick individual."

"It keeps me sane."

"Certainly," Gerard said, his tone indicating exactly what he thought of that statement.

Gerard moved to the dome and studied its surface. Finding a still active area on the inside face, he spoke an equation and motioned with his golden arm. A bubble pulled away from the dome, bringing the flesh with it. As the bubble separated, the remaining portion of the dome pinched itself closed.

Gerard turned his hand, and the small sphere hovered approximately three inches above his fingertips. The glob inside continued to sizzle and pulse. Gerard brought his other hand up, held it over the globe, and spoke another equation. A hissing issued from the sphere and it changed from transparent to opaque and then solid white.

Crystallized condensation formed on the outside and cold vapor rose from it.

"Freeze dried and ready for storage," Gerard said, standing.

"Do you think that will help?"

"I think it will answer some questions." He turned and walked through the door, the sphere floating along behind him. Ashron followed, watching the bobbing globe.

27

THE KNIGHTS REBORN

After a brief discussion, the crew agreed that a return to Kalaros Three was in order. They wanted to make their arrival in a discreet manner. With Red's help, they secured an empty spot on the *Mazil Daqim*, a vessel transporter heading for the planet with a load of ships for Unicybertronic's growing armada. Kasta, the transporter's captain, was an old pirate gone legit. In his checkered past, he had occasionally found Red's Tavern a convenient spot to disappear.

"He's a rogue," Red had told Hawk. "But he's an honest rogue. If the pay's right, he doesn't ask questions, and once he's bought, he stays bought."

Red had contacted Kasta, and a price was agreed upon. There had been some concern from Kasta that the rendezvous and docking would be noticed by anyone at UCT looking over the Ship's flight computer. Hawk had quickly assured the former pirate that Ship was more than up to the task of altering the carrier's recorder and manifest.

As Red's men worked on Ship's new paint job and the crew attended to other duties, Hawk sat on the bridge and plotted the course to the rendezvous with the freighter. They were meeting in-system so a ripspace jump would not be required. Hawk agreed to do the calculations required for their trip so Gerard could contact his Order and let them know about recent events.

The sound of footsteps entering the bridge made Hawk turn. Laura walked in.

"How is he?" Hawk asked.

"He'll be okay. I've sealed and bandaged the wound. He'll sleep for a while."

"Should we drop him at a hospital when we get to Karalos?"

"I can treat him here on Ship. The *kataverin* destroyed his nerve ends so thoroughly there's no way to regenerate the arm. We'll have to find someone to give him a cybernetic."

Hawk took a moment to study Laura. Bloodshot eyes, drawn face, brown hair in disarray, she looked like a person who hadn't slept for several days.

"How are *you?*"

"I'll be okay." She rubbed her eyes and pushed hair off her forehead. "I've already done the mom thing and cried about it."

"Nothing wrong with that. It's been a rough couple of weeks, especially for him."

Laura walked over to the padded navigation chair and leaned back in it. "It's times like this when I wonder if I shouldn't have left him on Kel."

Hawk leaned against the console in front of her. "If you think about that a moment, you'll realize you're too hard on yourself."

"I know. But he's so vulnerable. I don't want to fail him like I did Timothy."

Hawk took her hand. "Now you're shortchanging both of you. Remember how he was eight months ago. You could barely get near him without him running into a corner and whimpering in fear. Today, he put himself at risk to save your life. I think he would have done the same for any of us, even grumpy old me. You haven't failed him."

Laura's eyes glistened. "He could have died today. He could have died on Meta Brévé. He's not safe with us." She paused. "I think we should let him live with someone else. Maybe Red." Tears ran down her face.

Hawk walked around the console, knelt, and gently lifted Laura's head until he could stare into her soft brown eyes. "We're in a dangerous profession. Trey will be in danger as long as he stays with us. We can leave him with Red if you want. Do you think that would be any better?"

"He'd be safe."

"But what kind of life would he have? Since he's come aboard Ship, he's been to fifteen different planets, he's gone a long way toward recovery from serious emotional problems, and he's gained respect and trust from all of us. What do you think it would do to him if we suddenly said, 'You can't stay with us anymore, we can't trust you to care for yourself.'?"

"That's not fair." Laura's eyes flared behind the film of tears.

"That's what you'd be telling him, isn't it? He doesn't have to grow up overnight, but he does have to grow up. He's eager to be treated like an adult. Gerard showed me that. If we sent him to Red's, I don't think he would ever trust anyone again."

"At least he'd be alive."

"Would he be living?"

A new voice spoke up. "What's makes you think sending him to Red's would make him any safer?"

Hawk and Laura turned. Tasha stood in the hatchway. "Yoseph and Patishi should have been safe at home," she reminded them in her silky voice. "You can only do so much to protect them. Even if you do everything you can, it's not always enough." A tear fell on her arm, darkening her brown fur. "Think about it, Laura. Are the people who go to Red's the type you would want Trey around? Some are okay, but plenty wouldn't think twice about kidnapping Trey for their own use."

"Red would protect him," Laura insisted.

"The only way he could completely protect him would be to lock him in the cabin. As Hawk said, what kind of life would that be?"

Laura stared at the ceiling and said nothing for several minutes. Tasha walked into the room and sat down, while Hawk remained kneeling in front of Laura. They both waited without speaking, allowing Laura to sort out her emotions.

Laura wiped her eyes. "You're both right. I'm upset and not thinking straight."

"Have you thought about talking this over with the person it affects the most?" Tasha said.

"Trey? Not yet. Part of me hopes he'll ask to be somewhere safer; another part of me is afraid that's exactly what he'll ask."

"You know he's as safe with us as he is with anyone," Hawk said, "and I honestly think you'd have to pry him off Ship to get him to leave you. If it's any consolation, the only place he's going to be when we go to UCT is right here on Ship, far away from any danger."

"I think Hawk's right," Tasha said in her soothing tone. "I don't know Trey. I do know children." She paused a moment. "On the whole, they're very loyal to the people they care about. Talk to him. If you feel strongly enough he should be somewhere else, he'll go to please you."

"He doesn't need to go anywhere else. I was being fatuous."

"No, you were being concerned," Tasha told her. "Like any good guardian. But concern can also be smothering. You have to learn when one has crossed into the other. Trey's a bright child. He'll decide what's best for him."

"You're right, but I'm going to wait until I'm a little more level-headed about it." She gave Tasha a sharp look. "Have you ever thought about being a parent? I think you'd be very good at it."

Tasha's tail twitched in surprised. "I thought you knew. I have four grown children and two grandchildren."

"No, I didn't know," Laura said. "Tell me about them."

Hawk stood up. "That's my cue to leave. I'll be in the workout room if you need me."

Several hours later, Laura walked into the wardroom, where the rest of the crew, except the still sedated Trey, had gathered. "Moran's sadism constantly amazes me."

"What do you mean?" Hawk asked, looking up from the Go board that sat between him and Ashron.

"I finished analyzing the virus that killed the assassin. It's exactly what Gerard said it was. It consumes any flesh at a rapid rate and then consumes itself until only a few cells are left, and they die in the air."

"So it's an organically harmful version of the bug that eats the degradable labs?" Hawk asked.

"Exactly. As long as it has sufficient oxygen, it will continue to feed." She shuttered and looked at Hawk. "If you hadn't cut Trey's arm off, he would have been dead in less than forty-five seconds."

Hawk gave a low whistle. "How did it get Madrin, though? It wasn't in the room, or at least one of us would have gotten it."

"It's not an airborne virus," Laura said. "There was residual Geber Fluid in the virus."

"What's that?" Ashron asked.

"A fairly rare elixir," Gerard answered. "It's essentially *aether* suspended in our plane. It allows...magic potions, I guess you would call them. The liquid can be worked to duplicate a specific manipulation. The creation of such things is its own sub-science of manipulation."

Gerard looked at Laura. "She drank a potion that took her into ripspace. That's how she got in the cabin without setting off the door or window alarms. And the liquid also acted as a time release for the virus."

"That was my hypothesis," Laura agreed.

"So the assassin kills us and then dies herself," Hawk said. He shook his head. "And to think Moran used to be my friend."

The next morning, Hawk stood back and admired Ship's new paint job, gleaming under electric lights strung through the cavern. It shone a dazzling red and yellow, loud and almost obscenely bright. Hawk hated covering up her crystal blue, but her scheme was too well known to pass undetected once they landed on Unicybertronic's home planet.

Red joined him, and they walked in silence across the landing pad. Once they reached the gangplank, Hawk turned and offered his hand. "Good-bye, my friend. Sorry to leave in such a hurry."

"We won't even mention the mess," Red said, a smile breaking through his crimson beard. He clasped his friend's hand and slapped him on the back. His voice took on a more serious note. "Kasta is at the rendezvous and expecting you in a few hours. Be careful and take care of the young one."

"We will. Tell Nora not to worry. We'll be back for the anniversary celebration," Hawk said, referring to the yearly gathering Red and his wife had celebrating the founding of Red's Place.

"I will. By the way, I think she left you all a present in the galley."

"Yes, she did," Ashron said, walking up with his nose in the air. "I can smell the three egg cake from here." He shook Red's hand. "Good to see you again, you must excuse me. I have pressing business inside." He started up the steep ramp.

"Hold it," Wolf's voice rumbled from near Ship's aft.

Ashron's eyes narrowed, and his tongue flicked. "What?"

"I need some help getting to one of these thrusters."

Ashron glanced at the airlock, then down at Wolf, then back to the airlock.

"We're leaving soon," Hawk said. "You can be inside Ship or strapped to her."

With a dramatic sigh, Ashron moved back down the ramp.

After a last pat on Hawk's back, Red turned and stomped back toward the colony.

Hawk called to Wolf. "How long?"

"Fifteen minutes."

"Good. We leave in twenty." Hawk walked up the gangway and headed for the bridge.

Six hours later, Hawk watched the monitor as a crew of robots finished sealing up the compartment where Ship anchored. Thought compartment seemed a strange word for something so large, it was the only thing that came to Hawk's mind. The *Mazil Daqim* appeared almost the size of a small planet. Ship was simply one of a multitude of assorted craft bound for Kalatos Three and other destinations.

"Ship, what's our ETA to Kalatos?"

"According to the freighter's computer, approximately sixty-eight hours. Once we've entered ripspace, I'll get a more accurate reading."

"Moran's there, waiting for either his assassin or us to show up. Do you think we'll finally be able to put an end to this?"

"I think so, Sean," Ship said, her voice soft. "I just hope it ends the way we want it to."

Hawk didn't say anything for a moment. "Well, I think now is as good a time as any for the Knights to be reborn in full form."

"Long overdue," Ship said.

"Perhaps," he said thoughtfully. "However, it may be a short rebirth." Hawk stood and headed for his cabin.

Gerard walked into Trey's room with a food tray and found him propped against the back of his bed with his knees up. A blank stare revealed that he gazed at something far beyond the wall of his room. A large bandage covered the stump of his severed arm. He looked over as Gerard entered.

"Hi," Trey said, giving Gerard a weak smile.

"How are you feeling?" Gerard asked as he dropped the tray's legs and set it on the bed.

Trey's smile disappeared. "Not good. I can still feel my arm. It itches, and I can't scratch it."

"That's called phantom pain. It's your nerves not yet realizing your arm is no longer there. It never completely goes away, though it gets less severe. How's the cut?"

"Laura says it's clean and will heal okay. It hurts like hell." Picking up the cup of tea awkwardly with his left hand, he took a small sip.

"The pain will go away too. I knew you'd be fine physically. You're a tough person and Laura is a good doctor. But how are you *feeling?*"

Trey didn't say anything as he picked up the spoon, hand wrapped around it like a baby's fist, and ate some soup. A large part of it ended up on his chin, so he set the spoon into the bowl and wiped his sleeve across his face. "I was mad at first, but I'm okay now."

"Mad? At whom?"

Trey's eyes turned to the soup. "At Laura," he said in a low voice. "At Hawk. At all of you."

"Why?" Gerard asked gently.

"I don't know," he said. "I guess because I thought it was your fault I was there. I was being stupid, because if you had made me stay on Ship or back in my room, I would have been mad at you and begged to come along, just like I did on Meta Brévé. So I'm not mad anymore."

"How do you feel about your hand being gone?"

Trey looked back up at Gerard. "I was mad about that, and sad too. Then I thought about all the people I knew—" he stopped again, "—back home. I thought about Yoseph. Compared to them, I'm lucky. I thought about that woman, too." Trey's voice choked. "I know she wanted to kill Hawk, but no one should die like that."

"I agree. Anytime you want to discuss things, you know you can talk to us. Any of us."

"I know," Trey leaned back and stared at the wall.

Gerard examined the boy a moment. The invitation was there; Trey didn't take it. Gerard frowned. The boy seemed to be accepting things *too* calmly. Gerard didn't expect him to be throwing fits or rolling around with insane laughter. He had expected more than this composed discussion, as if they spoke about nothing more than a bad night's sleep.

Maybe he needs more time, Gerard thought. *Or perhaps you aren't the person he wants to talk to.* He wasn't going to force the issue. He also wasn't going to let Trey brood over things. "Since you're going to be stuck on Ship for a while, now would be a good time to start your reading."

"Reading?" Trey asked, his eyes coming back into focus.

"Yes, there are seven books you're going to have to read."

"Seven? That should be easy," Trey said. He seemed happy to be discussing something other than current events, exactly the reaction Gerard had hoped for.

"I'm glad you're optimistic," Gerard said. "However, not only do you have to read them, you have to understand the concepts. Some of this may be tough going. However, when you get stuck, I can help you."

"Okay," Trey said. He picked up his spoon again. "Where do I start?"

"The first book is *The Fundamental Order of Aether Explained* by Zargot of Meladosta. Ship has already downloaded it to your reader."

"Okay. Is that the same Zargot that's in your order?"

"It is," Gerard said with a smile.

A knock sounded at the door. "Come in," Trey said.

The door slid open, and Laura walked in.

"Well, I have some things to do," Gerard stood. "Get to work on that book as soon as you can."

"Okay," Trey set down his spoon. He went to wipe his mouth on his sleeve. Seeing Laura, he grabbed the napkin from the tray instead.

Gerard walked out. Laura took his place on the edge of the bed. Her heart almost broke as she watched Trey struggle to flip open his napkin with his off hand. She gently took it from him, opened it, and handed it back. "Been a rough couple of weeks, huh?" she said, trying her best to keep her tone light.

After wiping his mouth, Trey said, "I saw a lot worse on Kel."

"But you've never had anything this bad happen to *you*."

Something passed through his mind at her words. She saw it in his loss of focus, the distant gaze of remembrance. He took a deep breath and then locked her with his deep hazel eyes. "I would rather lose both arms than fail someone I love again."

Laura didn't speak as her eyes blinked and she wiped at them. She wanted to ask him what he meant about failing, but she had to know something else first. She swallowed the lump in her throat. "I was wondering if you felt like maybe you weren't safe with us. Would... would you feel better if we let you live with Red or someone else, where you weren't always in such danger?"

Trey's face turned serious, and Laura got a glimpse of how he would look as an adult: handsome and possessing that indefinable quality of leadership she saw in Hawk. People would someday turn to Trey for guidance, knowing they could trust his wisdom.

When he spoke, he sounded much like an adult also. "I haven't felt really safe since...I left my parents. But I would rather die tomorrow knowing I had the time with you I did than go somewhere and live a long life knowing I wouldn't be with you. I love all of you. I would do anything for you. Please don't make me leave." His chin quivered as his eyes pleaded his case.

"We won't make you." Laura leaned over and hugged him tight as the tears cascaded down her face. "I just wanted you to know you had a choice," she said in a raspy voice.

"I know," Trey hugged her back as best he could.

Neither spoke for a long time. Trey suddenly leaned back, his face lit with a laser bright smile. "However, you *don't* have a choice. You're stuck with me whether you want me or not."

Laura laughed. "I could have been stuck with worse."

Hawk's voice spoke over Ship's intercom. "I need everyone in the wardroom right now."

"Trey's finishing up lunch," Laura said.

"It can wait. This is important, and I think Trey will want to be here."

"Do you feel up to it?" Laura asked Trey.

"Yes, if you'll help me get out of bed."

When they had all gathered in the wardroom, Ashron flicked his tongue and turned to Gerard. "So, what's going on? Everyone's here except the person who called the meeting."

"I'm here," Hawk said from the doorway.

"About t—" Ashron started. Hawk's uniform stunned him into silence.

The entire outfit was black, so black it appeared devoid of color and almost seemed to be drawing in the light around it. Through this darkness, there appeared pinpoints of illumination so subtle they were almost illusory, like stars viewed in the night sky. The silken shirt had bloused sleeves and a V-cut collar that tapered to mid sternum. Richly embroidered above the right breast was a seven-pointed star of sterling thread. Bright red and orange flames leaped upward from the top of the star. When light touched the insignia, the colors flashed in brilliant contrast to the black cloth, as if the star were bejeweled.

The pants were fashioned of the same black, slightly flared at the bottom. Thin red piping ran down the outer seams. The outline of the star was laser pressed into each leg, so subtle it remained invisible until the light struck the correct angle. The high-topped boots gleamed ebon; a jeweled knife hilt protruded from the top of each one.

The cape came straight from a medieval fantasy. Black and flowing, with red satin lining on the inner side, it moved on its own accord, as if a breeze blew through the room even though the air sat still.

The real beauty lay in the cape's star.

It was a larger version of the emblem on the shirt: seven-pointed, with flames leaping from the top. Like those on the pants, the design had been laser pressed, but subtlety had no place in the creation of this symbol. The silver forming the star's lines flared with the brilliance of freshly minted, newly polished metal. The flames leaped off the fabric, the colors almost blinding in their intensity. As the cape shifted, the flames moved, flickering and dancing around the star.

An elaborately decorated broadsword fastened on the belt

completed the uniform. Gems covered the pommel, and the sword itself gave off a faint glow. A pearl-handled pistol rested opposite the sword.

The whole outfit radiated power and an almost overwhelming presence.

Ashron's mouth moved; nothing came out.

"Wow," Laura said after a full twenty seconds.

"Filamentous," Trey chimed in.

Wolf and Gerard grinned broadly, and Gerard said, "Does this mean I need to break mine back out?"

Hawk smiled, and then looked at Laura, Ashron, and Trey. "This uniform was last worn the day Sara died, and no Knight has worn it since. However, since we are now going to face the person most directly responsible, Sara and I decided it was time for the Knights to be as they once were. Laura Benzing, step forward."

Laura walked up in front of Hawk. He drew the broadsword and touched the sword to her forehead. "Touched by the sword of Zerus, blessed by the fire of Zerus, witnessed by the son of Zerus, Laura Benzing, your service has made you worthy to wear the uniform of a Knight of The Flaming Star. Do you accept?"

"With all my heart," Laura said, smiling at him.

"Ashron, son of Ashon, step forward."

Ashron stepped up next to Laura. Hawk placed the sword on top of Ashron's head. "Touched by the sword of Zerus, blessed by the fire of Zerus, witnessed by the son of Zerus, Ashron, son of Ashon, your service has made you worthy to wear the uniform of a Knight of The Flaming Star. Do you accept?"

Despite his best efforts, Ashron was grinning like an idiot. "Are you kidding?" he said. Laura elbowed him in the ribs. Composing himself, he said, "Yes, of course, I would be honored."

Hawk nodded to him and then winked. Looking at Trey, he said, "Trey of Kel, step forward."

With a nervous glance at the others, Trey moved next to Ashron.

Putting the sword on Trey's head, Hawk said, "Touched by the sword of Zerus, blessed by the fire of Zerus, witnessed by the son of Zerus. Trey of Kel, your service, bravery, and willingness to sacrifice yourself for others has made you more than worthy to wear the uniform of a Knight of The Flaming Star. Do you accept?"

Trey couldn't handle it. He burst into tears. Overwhelmed, he saw in the other crew members love and caring he had almost forgotten existed. Love and caring he didn't know if he deserved. Not trusting himself to speak, he merely nodded.

"Let these three stand forth as proud members of the Knights of The Flaming Star." Hawk sheathed the sword.

Ashron couldn't control himself. "When do we get the uniforms?"

"They're right over there," Hawk said, pointing to three boxes on the kitchen counter.

"Yes!" Ashron ran over and grabbed the box with his name on it.

"Put it on in your room," Laura said as Ashron began kicking off his boots.

"Oh, yes, of course." He scooped up his items and ran from the room.

"Come on, Trey," Gerard said, "I'll help you try yours on."

Still not speaking, Trey tucked his box under his arm and walked out, followed by Gerard.

Laura walked over to Hawk. "Very nice," she said. She tilted her head up and kissed him on the cheek.

"Thanks," he said, smiling.

As Laura left to try on her uniform, Wolf looked at Hawk and grinned.

"What?" Hawk asked.

"Nothing," Wolf answered, his broad face still grinning.

ARRIVAL AT KALATOS THREE

"This is Kalatos Three Port Authority to *Mazil Diqam* holding compartment seven six two."

"Hold sivin ses two har," Laura answered back. Kasta's ship held so many vessels that unloading protocol used no names, only cargo hold designations. That suited Laura and the others fine.

"You are cleared to disengage and begin descent. Follow beam twenty-nine."

"O'ger tat. Beam tenty-ine, argeted and locked," She keyed a different com frequency. "Kear mo-rings."

"Moorings cleared," came the reply from one of the freighter's crew. "Hey, Dellan, bring us up a couple of bottles when you come back up."

"I'll tink about et," Laura replied. "Clear the bay. Preparin fer throsters firing." For this trip, Laura became Dellan Kortel, a female Tralan who served as a member of the freighter's crew. Her brown hair now glowed fiery red and her ordinarily bronze skin had been dyed a few shades shy of sheet white. She was also doing a passable job of imitating a Tralanese accent.

"Bay empty," another voice told her. "Fire thrusters at will."

Laura entered the proper sequence. A dull roar filled the cabin as

Ship's thrusters came to life. As soon as she cleared the freighter, the voice from the Port Authority spoke again. "Ship seven six two, you are clear to switch to automated landing sequence."

"Switching to otto now." Laura punched a sensor on the control pad.

"Automatic lock established. Landing in fifteen minutes. Sit back and enjoy the ride."

"Tank you," Laura told him. "Sivin ses two oot." Laura turned off the microphone. She spun around in the chair and looked at the rest of the crew, who had been sitting silently behind her.

"Good job," Hawk told her. "I like the accent. How are you doing, Ship?"

"Fine, Captain," Ship said. After a moment, she said, "They're scanning us now."

"Port Authorities are so predictable. How's the distort?"

"Holding nicely," Ship answered. "The only lifeform they're reading is Laura."

"Well, this lifeform is going to go get her pack ready."

"Okay," Hawk said. "Ashron and Tasha will leave with the freighter's crew in…?" he looked at Laura.

"Two hours," she told him, knowing full well he already knew the answer and was testing her.

"And you're going to rendezvous at…?"

"The grocery store two klicks from the compound."

"And you're going to…?"

"Infiltrate the compound, get pertinent incriminating data, and get out."

"And the whole operation is going to take no longer than…?"

"Thirty minutes."

"Boy," Hawk said. "I'm glad you're so smart. I'd be lost without you."

"I'm going to go pack now."

"No need," Trey opened one of the cabinets on the bridge. "I already packed it for you."

Using his good hand, Trey pulled out her black jumper suit. He pushed the locker shut with the stub of his arm. Holding the jumper up so it wouldn't drag the floor, Trey walked over to Laura and handed it to her. "Check and make sure everything is there."

She opened the various static pockets and made a quick examination of the contents. Everything in place and expertly packed. "Thank you," Laura said, smiling. Trey's condition, both physically and mentally, had improved dramatically during the transit time.

"Okay," Hawk said. "We'd better go hide."

"Be careful," Trey told Laura.

"I always am," she said, leaning down and kissing him on the cheek.

Hawk and Trey left the bridge and headed for Hawk's quarters. Ashron and Tasha were with the freighter's crew, offloading the ships. Since they were the stealthiest and, ironically, least recognizable of the people who were on Ship, they would ride down with the rest of the work crew and back up Laura on her midnight invasion of Alexic Salakon's house. The rest would stay on Ship. Hawk and Gerard would help with coordination of the assault. Wolf obviously could go nowhere without causing heads to turn and would stay aboard for that reason. Trey would remain aboard because they had ordered him to.

As they walked into his room, Hawk said, "Open it up, Ship."

"Aye, Captain," she answered. There was a click and the secret door that sealed off Hawk's "think tank" opened up.

"Filamentous," Trey said. "I never knew that was there."

"That's the idea," Hawk said, starting to remove his clothes. "If anyone comes snooping around, they won't know it's here either. You might want to strip to your shorts. The water gets warm."

Trey started undressing, hampered by his missing arm. "If someone inspects her, won't they notice Ship's been lived in?"

"Been taken care of," Hawk tossed his clothes into a hamper. "Manifest reads she was confiscated from a group of pirates and sold to UCT. There are so many ships no one is going to check that closely. You ready?"

"Yeah," Trey said, also tossing his clothes into the hamper.

Gerard and Wolf were already inside as Hawk and Trey settled in.

It made for a tight fit. The small *kenquala* darted from person to person, doing their best to relax the tense crew members.

———

Laura watched the monitors as Ship, guided by the tractor beam, landed. She let out a low whistle at what she saw. Hundreds of starcraft of all sizes stretched out for at least three kilometers. According to Gerard, this was only one of about twenty such sites. The amount of money being laid out on this operation astounded her.

With a dull thump, Ship landed. Laura quickly ran through the shutdown sequence and unstrapped herself, relishing in the quiet as the engines died away. Since she could say nothing to Ship, she took the elevator to the lowest deck and hit the pressure switch to drop the stairs.

As the bottom of the steps settled to the concrete, she saw, not unexpectedly, a small Gralin standing in front of Ship with a datapad in his indigo colored, three-fingered hand. He wore a pair of coveralls with the UCT logo laser pressed on the front.

Laura strolled down the stairs and into the heat of Kalatos. She shielded her eyes from the glare coming off the landing pad and saw the technician tapping at his datapad.

The Gralin looked up at Laura as she stopped at the bottom of the ramp. "Seven six two?" he asked, voice modulated by the translator he wore on his throat

"Yes," Laura answered, still mimicking Dellan's accent. "Et's all yurs."

The Gralin glanced at the hatchway, and then scanned the field with his solid yellow eyes to see if any of his superiors were watching. He turned back to Laura, and his small blue mouth moved. "Everything look good in there?"

"Loks like any uther ship," she answered.

"Okay," he said, tapping on the datapad.

Laura relaxed inwardly, surprised at how concerned she had been that they would board Ship and inspect her. She wasn't going to have to offer their contrived explanation.

As the Gralin started to waddle away on his stubby legs, Laura said, "Perdon me."

He turned back.

"I'm uff duty and need to peck up some tings from a shop. Is tere one around?"

"The city is twenty kilometers away. A shuttle leaves in two hours when the rest of the crew is down. That building there." He pointed to one of the large metal sheds that dotted the field. Laura hoped they had air conditioning here or the building would be a boiler box.

"Tank you," Laura said. "O, ere's the keys," She handed the Gralin a metal cylinder with three different buttons on it. The man pushed the top button and Ship's stairs began to fold up.

As she walked away, Laura smiled. If anybody tried to open the hatch, it would develop a mysterious short. By the time they figured out there was nothing wrong with it, the mission would be over, and Hawk could take off with Ship, leaving everyone standing with their jaws open.

Laura moved across the field to the large shed the technician had pointed out. Even though she didn't relish the idea of waiting around for two hours, she didn't have much choice. She couldn't walk the twenty klicks to town, and she had a feeling this operation would frown on cabs being called.

She stepped into the open doorway and looked around. The building was sparsely filled. A few benches and some tables occupied one corner. The rest was taken up by the long shuttle, a craft whose door was presently closed and guarded by two beefy fellows with large rifles. These people were serious about no one leaving before the shuttle was ready to go. Thankfully, the building had air conditioning. It did nothing to hide the metallic odor of shuttle fuel.

With a sigh, Laura sat down at one of the benches and resigned herself to waiting.

29

MIDNIGHT INVASION

"Jesus," Laura said under her breath. "It looks like a castle."

Ashron watched as Laura approached the outer wall of the compound to Salakon's estate. She didn't exaggerate. The place was huge, made mostly of stone with an outer wall roughly ten meters high. From his vantage point, Ashron could see the entire courtyard, patrolled by several heavily armed men. A Bolor Mark 7 tank sat in front of the gate, its large barrel pointing down the road leading to the manor.

"This guy's ready," Ashron said to no one in particular. "You know, just once I'd like to assault a place that was guarded by one poodle armed with a pea shooter."

"Sound check," Laura said.

"Clear," Ashron, Tasha, and Gerard answered in order.

"Clear," Laura repeated back. "I'm hitting the rounds."

That was the signal for everyone to go online. From here out they would run by the numbers.

Back on Ship, Gerard oversaw the mission. He had control of sound and visual from Laura's headset and monitored vital signs from the biochip implanted in each crew member. The latest toy from Gerard's lab, the headset had several micro-cameras; they covered a three hundred and sixty-degree sphere around her. He could change them to look in various spectrums, including infrared and ultraviolet. The microphone could pick up an ant walking at a hundred meters if Gerard so desired, He could watch her back while she performed other tasks, and also observe things she would be unable to see with her contacts.

Trey, wearing his Knight's uniform, sat in a nice soft chair Wolf had brought in for him. He watched in amazement that Gerard could keep up with the dancing screens as he went through the various spectrums. The best Trey could do was follow what he thought was every third one.

Wolf sat nearby, his face unconcerned as he settled in for the show.

Hawk perched over Ship's controls on the bridge one deck above the others. If necessary, he would act the instant anything went wrong. He had Ship sitting like a cat ready to pounce, all systems powered and weaponry on auto. Now that she had been assimilated into the shipyard, no workers bothered to show interest in her.

"How are things on your side, Tasha?" Laura asked, her voice pouring over Ship's speaker.

"As well as we expected. No new players."

"You're clear to move anytime, Laura," Gerard said. He glanced over at Trey and keyed off his transmit. "You enjoy chess. Want a lesson in tactics?"

"Sure," Trey answered.

"I'm going," Laura said.

"Roger," Gerard said, then returned to Trey. "In a building assault, you give each face of the building a number. One is the front, and you go clockwise from there," Gerard pointed at a glowing form that represented Tasha. "Tasha is covering the three/four corner, and Ashron has the one/two position. Those positions let them cover Laura in case things go wrong."

Laura slipped on a pair of malachite colored gloves and began climbing the vertical face of the wall almost as quickly as walking.

"Wow, she's good," Trey said.

"One of the best," Hawk said, his pride carrying through the speakers.

"Her gloves help," Gerard said. "They're made from ciliaside and stick to rough surfaces. But there's no doubt Laura is one of the most adept at their use."

"See anything out of the ordinary, Gerard?" Laura asked, now on top of the wall and peering over the edge.

"Not yet," he answered, fingers flitting over the various controls.

One of the cameras stopped on something at the bottom of the wall. "What the hell is that?" Trey gasped.

"A *trosh,*" Gerard answered. "Laura?"

"See it. It's a big one."

The camera revealed a two-hundred-pound doglike creature with six legs and extra teeth. Its skin, the color of moss-covered lead, glistened, as did its black eyes, which protruded from three-inch longs stalks.

"How are you going to handle it?" Gerard asked.

Staring down at it from her position on the wall, Laura considered her options. She didn't want to shoot it. Even at this range, a shot could go astray and not kill it instantly. An unexpected bark or yelp of pain from the animal would cause trouble. She also had no idea *where* to shoot it. Logic dictated its brain would be located in its large, hairless head, but she had seen creatures before that defied logic.

"I'll have to neuralize it and hope it works," she answered. The neutralizer ran through the entire body instantly and fried nerve endings. Quick and hopefully, quiet. Hopefully.

"Good luck," Gerard said. "Who has a bead on it?"

"I do," Ashron said, "although I have no idea where to shoot it."

Laura couldn't help but smile as she attached a cable to the top of the wall and prepared to lower herself to the *trosh.*

"Aim for the chest," Hawk said. "I read they have a large heart and a small, sturdy ribcage. That cannon of yours should take care of it if it comes to that."

Laura fervently hoped it wouldn't come to that. She hung upside down and descended the titanium fiber wire like a spider on its thread. Good luck had the creature staring into the courtyard with its small, rounded ears laid back. As she drew closer, she caught the animal's odor. It reminded her of a horse that has worked up a good lather; unpleasant but reassuring in its earthiness. Not at all the scent she expected from such an ugly beast. The smell also told her she was downwind, another piece of fortune.

She came within striking distance. If the *trosh* turned now, she would have almost no chance to escape before it attacked or raised the alarm. She pulled the neuralizer from her pocket with exaggerated care. With equal caution, she extended the weapon. Once it touched the animal's back, she discharged it. The *trosh* unceremoniously collapsed in a dead heap. Its slimy yellow tongue flopped from its mouth and thumped against the ground.

"Good work," Hawk said. Laura flipped over and placed her feet on the ground.

As she paused to let the blood drain from her head and get Gerard's assessment of her surroundings, she scanned the compound. Two guards stood nearby, highlighted by the dim light from Kalatos Three's silver moon. Floodlights beamed down the wall at irregular intervals.

"Clear," Gerard said. "Nothing unusual in any spectrum. No nearby alarms or traps."

"Roger," she said. "Keep an eye out for more critters."

"Roger."

Laura slid from shadow to shadow until she reached the stone wall of the house, fifteen meters from the outer wall.

"Off sight," Ashron said, letting her know he no longer tracked her visually.

"I'm on," Tasha affirmed. She now covered Laura's approach, ready to aid with well-placed firepower.

Laura glided along the inner wall until she reached the back corner, keeping herself in Tasha's visual field. She put a hand on either side of the corner and concentrated. With a deep breath, she began to climb, pressing the ciliaside gloves and shoes against the house's rough surface.

She reached the second floor and moved horizontally, shoving her feet into the tiny mortar crevices. Even with no ledge to use, she moved quickly, seeking to reduce her exposure time on the sheer surface. It had to be her imagination, but she could feel the eyes of a guard staring at her, trying to determine if the movement on the wall was shifting shadows or a camouflaged intruder. Though her suit chemically adapted to the patterns of her surroundings, it wasn't perfect. An alert observer could notice discrepancies. Sweat born of tension and exertion trickled down her back. After five meters she reached her destination and stopped. "Anything?" she whispered

There was a pause as Gerard checked his monitors. "Nothing."

Laura pulled out a black box, no bigger than a sugar cube, and set it against the window. It vibrated for half a second, sending receptor waves through the room. While she waited for Gerard to analyze the data, Laura shifted position to keep her rapidly tiring leg muscles from cramping.

"Looks good," Gerard said. "The window is real glass, and the room has no photosensitive receptors on any spectrum."

Putting the alarm detector away, Laura pulled out a small plastic vial with a mist applicator and sprayed some of Gerard's special concoction on the top panes. The glass bubbled, turned to liquid, and ran down the window. As the liquid touched the other panes, they too bubbled and turned liquid. When the last of the glass melted away and ran down the wall, Laura used a mirror and then one of Gerard's cameras to check the inside of the window for any triggering devices. Finding none, she removed the windowpane framing and attached it to the wall with a small glob of adhesive. Slowly, very slowly, she slid into the open window.

She found herself in a well-decorated study full of dark paneling, darker furniture, and ornate curtains. All of it spoke of money and vanity. A large holo-painting of a fearful-looking gray-haired man with domineering eyes towered over the faux fireplace. A placard on the spiral gold frame read, "In memory of my loving father." Laura thought the man in the painting wouldn't know the meaning of love.

The room had two doors. Laura knew from the plans she had studied that she wanted the closer one. The one across the room led to a hallway, but the one on the left-hand wall hid Salakon's office.

Fearing pressure sensitive alarms, which the trap detector could not find, she swung around and clung to the wall, avoiding the floor. She pulled the interior window frame back into place with one hand and secured it with the gelatinous glob. She couldn't do anything about the melted glass. She had to hope the frame would serve for a casual inspection from outside.

She crept along the wall, no mean feat considering most walls were cluttered with ornaments and not designed to be walked on. This one was no exception. She also had to apply more pressure to get the ciliaside material to dig into the smoother surface.

"Hold," Gerard said. "I hear something. Switching to enhanced x-ray."

She froze on the wall and heard a noise behind her, in the hallway.

After a second, Gerard said, "Guard making his rounds. He's moving on; give him a moment, and he'll be out of range."

Motionless, Laura waited for Gerard's signal. Her muscles throbbed like overwound guitar strings, and her breathing had quickened. She didn't know how much longer she could fight against gravity and fatigue.

Suddenly, her cramping muscles loosened, her body cooled, and her breathing turned even and easy. She felt as if she had just emerged from a cooling shower.

"Your vitals were getting ragged," Gerard said.

Laura nodded, knowing Gerard would see the motion in the monitors. She didn't like using boosters since she knew too much about the long-term damage they caused. She accepted this as a unique situation. Better to allow future harm than invite immediate disaster.

"He's clear," Gerard said. "Go."

She continued inching on the left-hand wall, slid around a short green flowerpot, and reached the door. After going through the usual checks and scans, she reached down and tried the doorknob. Locked. *Damn. Oh, well, it was worth a try.*

She pulled out her lockpick set, chose the appropriate pick, and went to work on the door. She didn't consider picking with one hand while clinging to a wall an ideal situation, and knew she wouldn't have been able to achieve it without the enhancement coursing through her blood. She soon heard the click of tumblers falling into place. Smiling, she secured her pick and reached for the knob. She stopped short. *What's wrong with this picture?*

Not finding an answer, she quietly posed the question to Gerard.

"What do you mean?" he asked.

"I don't know, but my 'hunch' went off. Something's not right, and I can't place it."

Hawk's voice slipped in. "No alarms."

"You're right," Gerard said. "There hasn't been a single one yet, has there?"

"And not for lack of looking," Hawk said.

"Do we call the mission?" Gerard asked.

"Your choice, Laura," Hawk said.

She considered the options. They should have spotted some alarm, even a simple motion detector, by now. The lack of any interior security meant one of two things: either they expected someone to break in and planned to spring a trap, or Salakon felt confident that the walls, guards, *troshes,* and tanks on the grounds would dissuade any intruders.

She could go back and forth with the pros and cons all night with her only accomplishment being to make herself paranoid. "We've gone too far to back out now. I'm continuing."

"Affirmative," Gerard said.

Laura studied the door. Taking a calculated risk, she stepped down in front of the doorway. No alarms or traps went off. She crouched, reached for the knob, turned it, pushed the door open, and did a quick scan.

"Looks clear," Gerard said.

She slipped inside the office, which she found decorated much like the study. Warm colors permeated the room, soft browns and muted reds. Bookshelves lined the walls, filled with paper books, a true sign of wealth. Several thickly-cushioned chairs were placed strategically throughout the room. The air smelled of exotic cigars and strong cognac, another ostentatious sign of affluence. The russet carpet, though worn and well used, was made of a very expensive weave. Several statues and objects d'art adorned the chamber. A fist-sized silver globe rested on a pedestal in one corner, providing illumination. It lit the room in a subdued fashion, even though the sphere itself seemed to have no light coming directly from it. Laura found something disconcerting about its glimmering, dark surface. After a moment's glance, she turned away.

A large wooden desk dominated one end of the office. Laura glided to it and searched it for anything out of the ordinary. Finding nothing unusual, she pushed the chair aside and discovered her target underneath the desk. A thin cable ran down from the desktop computer to a hole in the floor. Most systems were wireless and used encrypted digital radio waves to send their information and code. Those signals could be intercepted and deciphered with special surveillance equipment. People concerned about that sort of thing used wire since intercepting them required a physical splice in the cable.

Laura pulled out a small black strip of "tape" coated with thin metal pins and a transmitter. She applied it to the cable, splicing into the signal. Mission accomplished. It almost felt anti-climatic after so much effort to get in here. She started to stand up.

"Look..." was all she heard Gerard say before everything went black.

"...Out" Gerard yelled into the microphone, knowing even as he said it that he was too late. The world viewed through the monitors tilted crazily as Laura fell back underneath the desk.

"Laura's down," Gerard said, his voice even but urgent. "Go." He was surprised Hawk hadn't already launched Ship.

"She's not dead," Hawk said.

Gerard glanced at the display of vital signs and saw Hawk was right. The indications all showed she was merely unconscious.

"So what?" Trey said in a tight voice. "She's in trouble."

"She's not in trouble yet," Hawk said, trying to project calm over the speakers. "If we go charging in without knowing what's happened, then she *will* be in trouble. We need to be calm and wait."

"What's that?" Trey asked. One of the monitors had gone dark, its source camera smashed. Another monitor showed a small silver globe floating in the air.

"That's what hit Laura," Gerard told him. "I have no idea what it is."

As Gerard talked, the globe floated back to its pedestal and settled down, again throwing its strangely muted glow across the room.

A second later, Gerard heard a sound in the room. He touched a few buttons on the panel and increased the sensitivity of the external microphones. Another control sent the audio to Ship's speakers.

The soft tread of someone walking across the carpet, followed by the heavier steps of several people. One camera caught the bottom of a shoe as a person stopped next to Laura. A hand came into view, and the world moved rapidly as Laura was pulled from under the desk. A face came into the cameras' view.

Moran.

Only two monitors showed anything, which meant that Laura was lying on her stomach. Gerard frantically worked the controls, trying to get a better view of the entire room. They could hear voices. One of the monitors soon revealed Salakon, the head of Unicybertronic, flanked by several armed guards. The image shifted as Laura was rolled onto her back. Moran's expression changed to one of maniacal delight, and he let out a victorious laugh.

Salakon's gray eyebrows shot up. "What have you got?"

Moran reached down and unceremoniously snatched the headset off of Laura. He held it up close to his face and grinned. "You lose."

The monitors went blank as he dropped the unit and crushed it under his boot.

"Son of a bitch!" Hawk's voice reverberated through Ship's passageways. Footsteps echoed as he came down the ladder from the bridge and stormed into the Operations room. He stopped beside Gerard. Punching the panel with a finger, he said, "T.L. to Hawkeye one and two. If you haven't already, get the hell out of there."

"Roger," Ashron said.

"Roger," Tasha echoed.

Hawk kicked a nearby chair, sending it rolling across the deck. "Dammit!"

Plopping down in another chair, he leaned forward and put his head in his hands. "Damn," he said softly.

Trey looked over at Wolf, who sank back in his chair with his arms folded across his broad chest, square face devoid of any readable emotion. Trey turned his attention to Gerard, who seemed to have lost focus and looked at the dark monitors with a blank stare. The expression of defeat on Gerard's pale face scared Trey.

He was about to speak when Hawk jumped out of his chair.

"Okay," Hawk said, drawing everybody's gaze. "Ship, did we get it?"

"Yes, Captain, everything. It's very interesting."

"What we expected?"

"And then some."

"Zip it and ship it. *Firefall* priority."

"As we speak," Ship said.

"Good girl." Hawk hit the microphone button, then took his finger from the panel. "Not a good idea. Gerard, how far?"

Gerard spoke an equation as the fingers moved on his gold arm. He closed his eyes for a few seconds. "They'll be here in twenty minutes."

"Good. I'll be in my cabin." Hawk started for the hatch.

The other three glanced at each other and then Gerard said, "What's the plan?"

Hawk turned back. "We wait."

Unable to contain himself, Trey said, "Wait? How can we just wait while he's got Laura? He might hurt her." His throat and face hitched as he held back tears.

Hawk crossed the room and knelt in front of Trey. "What else can we do?" he asked gently. "The next move is Moran's. He's not going to do anything to harm Laura. We have something he wants, and he's going to use Laura as a bargaining chip. She's safe."

"Are you sure?"

"Yes," Hawk assured him, "because Moran knows if he hurts Laura, two things will happen. He won't get Ship, and we'll spend the rest of our days hunting him down."

Trey struggled to accept that, and as he did, something else occurred to him. "We're going to wait here?"

"Yes."

"Won't they be searching for us?"

"Of course, but this is one of the last places they would expect us to be. Plus, we have the new paint job. And if they get too close, Gerard can manipulate us into invisibility."

"I don't know about that," Gerard said.

"I have faith in both you and Moran. He'll organize a half-hearted search which will look for us in all the places *he* would hide, and he'll contact us by noon tomorrow."

"How will he contact us if he doesn't know where we are?" Trey asked.

"Laura's headset."

"I thought he crushed it."

"He did," Gerard said, taking over for Hawk. "It's a simple enough matter to take apart the transmitter and get the frequency we were using. All he has to do then is broadcast. He knows we'll be listening."

"He could also contact us through Laura herself," Hawk said, "if he realizes she has an implant."

"Oh," Trey said. He hated doing nothing but realized there was nothing he could do.

"Ship, I'll be in my quarters. Let me know when Tasha and Ashron arrive."

Moran pointed to two of the guards standing beside Salakon. "Tie her to that chair," he said, indicating a sturdy armchair sitting against the far wall.

The two soldiers snagged Laura and tossed her into the seat. They glanced at each other and then quickly scanned the room.

"What?" Moran asked, noticing their confusion.

"There's nothing to tie her with," one of them said.

"Check the pockets on her jumper. She'll have something you'll be able to use."

One of the men found the black disc attached to her wrist that held her titanium fiber cord. He yanked the disc off and used the cable to bind her arms and legs to the chair. The other started to tear off a strip of cloth from her jumper sleeve.

What are you doing?" Moran asked.

"I was going to use it as a gag," the guard answered.

"Don't. I want to talk to her."

Nodding, the guards moved back and rejoined their comrades.

Moran strolled over to a small recessed bar and poured himself a three finger shot of Parathian Brandy. Downing about half, he walked back over to Laura's inert form and threw the rest in her face.

Laura sputtered and shook her head. With a gasp she squeezed her eyes shut as the liquid burned into her orbs, the acrid liquor searing in its intensity.

"So sorry," Moran said in mock sympathy. "I imagine that stings a bit."

"A little," she answered.

Moran waited until she could open her eyes. He paced the room as he spoke. "You look different than your picture, but I still recognize you. The infamous Laura Benzing. I'm glad to finally meet you, although I feel like I know you already. Born on Earth in a little nowhere place called Fayetteville. Graduated high school at age fourteen. Went to Duke Medical School and graduated top of your class at eighteen. Went onto advanced neurology at the University of Charon. You had one son who is, unfortunately, dead. You have been a member of Force 13 for seven years and with the Knights four years. You function as ship's doctor, second in command, and sometimes assassin." He said the last with an edge of contempt that Laura found humorous coming from him.

"It's a living," she said.

He paused in his pacing. "And what drew you to this particular line of work?"

To her surprise, Moran sounded genuinely interested. However, she had no stomach for idle conversation. "Why don't you cut the shit, you psychopath? What do you want?"

Cold fury lit up his dark face. Flesh and cybernetic eye narrowed as he glared at her. "Very well. I want Ship, and you're my ticket to get her."

"How so?"

"With you alive, he won't leave the area. It's only a matter of time before I find them."

"Possibly," she said, "But when the Council—"

"To hell with the Council!" he shouted back at her. "Why do you think I want Ship in the first place?"

"Infatuation?"

Moran flung his glass at her. She ducked, barely avoiding it, and it shattered against the wall behind her. He stormed across the room and grabbed her jaw in his cybernetic hand. Laura winced in pain as he squeezed.

"Your plan failed." Moran held up the small strip of transmitter tape Laura had attached to the computer. "By nightfall, I'll have Ship in a hanger and Hawk chained to a wall. By year's end, I will *be* the Council. It's over." He shoved the strip of tape in Laura's mouth and pushed her away. "Strip her down and toss her in a cell."

Two guards, followed by a third, dragged Laura's chair down a flight of stairs. Each bump jarred her until she began to see stars and thought she might pass out. They reached the bottom and things smoothed out as they towed her down a dimly lighted corridor. Her vision cleared; her head continued to pound. They pushed open a large metal door that opened into a closet-sized room, a little over two meters to a side. Although it looked like a medieval dungeon room, it did not surprise Laura to find its existence underneath Salakon's ultra-modern house.

They sat her in the room. With his knife, one of the guards slit her jumper suit down the center and along each arm and leg. He yanked it away; she closed her eyes against the pain as the fabric abraded her skin in several places. She opened them again when she felt a hand on her bra. The knife slipped between her breasts and cut the fabric.

"Not bad for an Earthling," the guard said, squeezing one of her breasts. "Shame it's only two."

Rage rose up in Laura as she flashed back to an earlier time, when another man took advantage of her. A man she thought of as a friend. The guard's leering face in front of her became Wynick's face, his groping hands Wynick's hands. She felt helpless now, just as she did then.

She had to fight back, even though she knew the outcome would be the same. With a snarl, she spat the wad of transmitter tape at him. It struck him in the eye; he gasped in pain. As he pulled back, his hand left her breast and came by her mouth. Straining her neck, she lunged out and clamped down. Her teeth dug into the meat of his palm.

He screamed as she tasted his blood, a bittersweet taste, like charcoal-tainted honey. With his good hand, he punched her face. The force knocked the chair over. Her head bounced against the wooden backrest as it slammed into the stone floor. She again saw stars; she smiled as she pushed chunks of palm flesh from her blood-coated mouth.

"You whore," the guard screamed, his voice breaking with pain as he cradled his mangled hand. He kicked at the chair's bottom, sending a jolt through Laura's spine. She continued to smile.

"Come on, Jonak," one of the others said. "Leave her be unless you want to deal with Moran. Let's get your hand fixed up."

Jonak leaned over, grabbed her by the hair on either side of her head, and kissed her on the lips. She tried to bite him; he quickly pulled back.

"That's just a little sample," he promised. "When Moran's done with you, I'm going to make you wish you had never been born."

"Bring it." Her eyes aflame, she spat blood back in his face.

Despite Laura's disadvantage, she spoke with such ferocity that a moment of fear passed over Jonak's face.

"Let's go, Jonak," the other guard said with a nervous glance down the hallway.

Jonak looked ready to do something else, then appeared to think better of it. They left and closed the door. The *chink* of the lock slamming home echoed in the small room.

Spitting more blood out of her mouth, Laura wiggled, fury still burning through her. The tight cable dug into her wrists as she squirmed; her anger wouldn't allow her to submit. Determined not to be left helpless when the guards returned, she vowed to get free, even if it meant cutting herself to ribbons doing it.

The pain eventually broke through her rage. She stopped, recognizing her irrational behavior. Calming herself, she spat a few more times. The blood that had tasted sweet in her fury now almost gagged her. She longed for some water to alleviate the foul taste.

Calmed, Laura took stock of her situation. A study of the cell revealed no apparent cameras. Her hysteric wriggling had accomplished something: though still tight, the cable had loosened. It would take effort and concentration, but Laura thought she might be able to slip free of her entrapment. All she had to do was get the first loop free of the chair back, and the rest would come easy. Even though she had no way to escape the room, she could offer the guards an unpleasant surprise when they returned to fetch her. And she felt certain Jonak would be among them. *Come on. Get yourself together. Trey is counting on you.*

With the thought of Trey focusing her, she closed her eyes, lowered her heartbeat, loosened her muscles, and started her slow push toward freedom.

———

Back on Ship, Hawk and Gerard sat in Operations staring at a monitor, both unable to sleep. Trey lay in his chair, dozing fitfully and occasionally muttering Laura's name.

"God, I could use a real drink right now," Hawk said as he sipped his glass of melon soda.

"It looks like we kicked a beehive," Gerard said as they watched the monitor. A chronometer in the upper left of the screen clicked off the seconds: two A.M local time.

"I expected nothing less," Hawk didn't take his eyes off the frenzy of dots flitting across the screen. Each dot represented a planetary craft; most of the dots were running search patterns. "Do you think she's all right?"

Gerard glanced at the monitor displaying Laura's vital signs. They had lost verbal contact with her, but whatever jammed the internal communicators didn't affect their bio-implant sensors. "Her heartbeat seems to be slowing down. Maybe she's trying to get some sleep. Something we should consider ourselves."

"I couldn't even begin to sleep now," Hawk said, rubbing his eyes.

"Me neither," Gerard agreed. "We should try anyway. We're doing no one any good getting ourselves fatigued. There's nothing we can do until Moran contacts us. Ship will let us know if anything changes."

"I know," Hawk said. He made no move to leave the room. Neither did Gerard.

Laura pushed away the last bit of cable and rubbed at her shoulder, abraded by the stone floor as she wriggled her way out of the chair. She pushed herself across that same floor, finally free of confinement, and rubbed her hands together, trying to chase away the damp chill of the bare stone room, uncomfortable but not life-threatening.

She flexed her jaw to open her internal comlink and said, "Can anyone hear me?" She got no response and tried again, with the same result.

No communication and no weapons other than her body. She pushed away the despair that tried to intrude. She still had a heartbeat and a brain and had used nothing more than that many times before to escape dire situations. She also had friends nearby, a factor not always present in earlier times.

Though she had seen no cameras, she ran through the modes on her contacts, searching for any electronic signals that might indicate surveillance equipment. She found nothing. Another sign of Salakon's overconfidence. She wanted to laugh at his incompetence until she considered what she had missed that put her in this cell.

She had no idea when her captors would return. To make use of the time, she picked up the thin titanium cable that had so recently held her and twisted it, forming it into a whip. When she finished, she began scraping the braided wire against the stone floor, working to fray the edges along the weapon's length, creating dozens of jagged barbs. As she worked, she smiled, thinking about the little surprise she would offer her escort when they returned.

"Hawk, wake up," Gerard said.

Hawk stirred in the chair. Despite his assertion he wouldn't fall asleep, the pattern of the searching ships on the monitor had turned hypnotic, forcing his eyes closed.

"Sorry," Hawk rubbed at his scratchy eyes as he looked at Gerard. "Guess I dozed off."

"It's okay, you needed it," Gerard said.

Hawk thought about pointing out Gerard's bloodshot eyes—a strange sight against his pale skin—as evidence he should also have been sleeping, but kept silent. "What's happening?"

"Ship just picked up a blanket broadcast from Moran on an old coded Force 13 wave." He tapped a few numbers on the control panel. When he finished, the center monitor went static white for a second, and then resolved into an image of Moran.

"so don't wait too long or Ms. Benzing will be nothing more than a puddle of flesh."

The image disappeared, replaced by a black screen. Five seconds later, the image reappeared, Moran's head and shoulders backed by blackness, offering no clues to his location.

"Pause and record, Ship," Gerard said. Moran's image froze in a grimace.

"Why are you doing that?"

"I told Ship to wake the others. We might as well all hear it at the same time."

Hawk nodded and looked at a yawning Trey, who had begun stirring at the sound of Moran's voice over the Operations Room speakers.

"What's wrong?" Trey asked, his face blanching as he saw Moran's oversized sneer on the monitor.

"It's okay," Hawk said in a soothing voice. He explained the situation to Trey as Ashron, Wolf, and Tasha, all briefed by Ship and alert despite the early morning hour, walked in. As they all turned to the center monitor, Hawk said, "Run it, Ship."

The video started again. Moran's grimace turned into a cold smile. He had removed his eyepatch, revealing a gleaming black cybernetic eye with an emerald green pupil. "Hawk, old friend. I have to assume you are out there somewhere receiving this broadcast since I know you won't go far. I also know you won't answer, for obvious reasons, so I'll get to the point. I have something you want, and you have something I want. Cliché perhaps, but aren't most of the great truths? The question is: where do your values lie? Are you willing to give up Ship for Ms. Benzing? I'm betting you are, but I'm not as patient as I used to be, so I'm moving up the time frame a notch. I've injected the young lady with a time-release capsule of *kataverin*. I know you've seen the effects, so I won't bore you with a description. It's set to go off in twenty-four hours. It can't be removed so she must have the antidote before its release. I want you to bring Ship to a nearby airfield. Follow beacon four seven six point seven six and land there. In case you decide Ms. Benzing will have to make a noble sacrifice so you can leave with Sara, I want you to know I've mobilized my entire fleet and cut off all avenues of escape. As we speak, the net grows tighter and time is getting short.

"Now I have no delusions about the ship's capabilities. I know that should you wish to make a fight of it, I would suffer heavy casualties. Be warned. Heavy casualties or not, you would lose, and Sara would die; something neither of us wants. I offer your doctor and safe passage in exchange for Sara and the ship. I consider this an extremely generous offer con—"

"Don't they always?" Ashron said.

"—sidering you're trapped and I will find you anyway. So don't wait too long or Ms. Benzing will be nothing more than a puddle of flesh."

The image faded out.

"Recording stopped," Ship said.

No one spoke, looking at each other with morose faces, until Gerard said, "He's worried."

"Right!" Ashron said. "I could see the fear radiating off of him."

Gerard turned to Ashron. "Don't analyze what he said but what he didn't say."

Ashron's tongue flicked. "I'm listening."

"You and I both know he has no intention of keeping his word. As soon as he gets Ship, he'll kill us all. Probably with the same virus. He also knows that we know this."

"Yeah, and we know that he knows that we know this, what's your point?"

"My point is, why make the offer in the first place?"

"To save time?" Trey asked.

Gerard turned to Trey. "Yes, but why?"

Trey shrugged. "I don't know,"

"Why indeed?" Tasha asked, stroking the fur on her cheek "Time is on his side."

"Is it?" Gerard asked. "He made several mentions of time running short. I think he was speaking for himself as much as for us. He feels pushed for time. Why?"

There was a pause as the crew considered possibilities.

"He found the transmitter," Wolf said.

"Exactly," Gerard confirmed. "He found the transmitter, and we have to assume he found it right away. But he doesn't know how much information we got."

Trey had a puzzled frown. "Wouldn't he have intercepted the transmission to the Council and know what we sent?"

"No. Our transmission was like a shot in the dark. By the time he heard the shot, it was too late. The message was sent."

"That's why he's worried," Tasha said. "He knows we have information on his organization and that we sent it to the Planetary Council, but he doesn't know how much."

"And that's the key." Gerard leaned back in his chair. "He's given us only twenty-four hours because he knows there's no way the Council can mount any kind of action in that time."

"Can they?" Trey asked.

"No," Hawk said. "Normally, it would take at least a week."

"What do you mean, 'normally'?" Ashron asked.

"Gerard, Ship and I were talking last night," Hawk said. "We may have a found a way to circumvent normal time."

30

ENDGAME MEETING

Laura started awake, hearing voices and motion outside her cell's solid door. She shook her head to clear away the after-effects of the muscle booster and grabbed her makeshift whip from the floor. Stiffness from sleeping on the cold stone tugged at her muscles was pushed aside by a rush of adrenaline. She could take out two, maybe three with a little luck; after that, her odds went down. She couldn't tell how many stood outside as a keycard slapped against the door; she hoped not many.

Standing to the side, she tensed as the door swung open. She recognized one of the guards from earlier as he stepped in. She lashed out with the whip. The braided steel caught the man across his neck. Wires ripped open his carotid artery. Blood sprayed as he dropped to the floor.

Laura stepped into the doorway, standing over the man's dying body. The second guard had no time to register what happened before Laura flung the whip in a rapid up-down motion. The guard stumbled back screaming, two deep furrows in his chest. His retreat forced him against a third guard and Laura pressed the attack. The whip swung again, catching the third man across both eyes. He shrieked and raised his hand, trying to stop the blood pouring from his ruined face.

Intense pain jolted through Laura and she fell. The whip dropped from her numbed fingers. Jonak stood in the corridor, his face flushed with fury and a neuroshock pistol in his hand.

"You bitch," Jonak said. He stepped up and kicked her in the stomach. She barely felt the kick or heard him through the dancing flames of her nerves. His voice came to her down a tunnel of pain. "If Moran didn't want you alive, I'd kill you so slowly you'd be begging for death hours before it came."

He kicked her again, in the chest. She dimly felt herself coughing before she heard the electric crack of the pistol. Her body arched in uncontrollable spasms as she jittered on the blood-soaked floor. Vomit sprayed from her mouth, and her head struck the wall, then everything turned black.

M oran stood at the front of the boardroom dressed in a tailored black suit. The other board members gathered and seated themselves. Several stared at Laura. She sat bound and gagged against one wall. Jonak had thrown a long gray shirt over her. The blood coating her body had seeped through in several places. She reeked of vomit and gore. Several of the board members looked faint as they passed her. Moran would have sworn Wekeit, the Gronian who served as Unicybertronic's treasurer, smiled sadistically at the site of the battered, semi-conscious Laura.

Moran's thoughts about Laura were a mix of admiration at her skill and regret that she would never consider joining his organization. In many ways, she reminded him of Sara, not least in physical appearance.

He pushed such thoughts aside. Today was not a time to dwell on what could never be. Today was a time to consider what the future held and rejoice.

As the last of the board members sat down, Moran walked over to Laura. She had recovered from Jonak's rough treatment and tried to level him with a cold, impotent glare.

"Don't be angry with me," he told her. "I applaud your tenacity, but you need to learn to accept defeat gracefully. Don't worry; this will all be over soon." He offered her a bitter smile. Jonak, standing nearby, chuckled until a baleful glance from Moran silenced him. "We'll discuss your punishment later."

Jonak swallowed, and his lips pressed tight.

Moran returned his attention to the executives. They spoke to each other in animated gestures, some pointing at Laura. Salakon had spread the word about the imminent arrival of the vessel that would bring their dreams of conquest within reach.

With a stride of supreme confidence, Moran returned to the front of the room. The talking died as everyone turned to him. Several of them squinted at the brightness of the windows behind him. He turned on the light dampeners. It put a gloomy cast on the room and allowed the gathered executives to open their eyes fully as they watched him. Moran smiled at the unintended metaphor. This was twice he had made sure they had their eyes opened.

"My fellow compatriots," he said, favoring them with the same cold smile he had shown to Laura. "Two years ago I came to you and told you I had a plan to make you all not just rich, but rich and *powerful*. That day is at hand." He paused and pointed to Laura. "That is Laura Benzing, a member of Force 13 and also of the Knights of The Flaming Star. Her captain, Sean Grey, also known as Hawk, is bringing his starcraft in exchange for her life. When he lands, we will take him prisoner, take over his ship, and execute both of them."

"What about the Council?" one of the executives asked. "When they get the information she sent off, they'll be all over us."

Moran threw Salakon a hard glare, causing the small man to wince.

"Don't let that disturb you," he told the executive. "We have planned too well to be stopped at this point. The soonest the Council will be able to bring a force to bear is at least a week. By that time, we will have a thousand sentient ships under our control capable of performing without human crews. Within a month, we will have ten thousand. Then the Council will be ours!"

The executives cheered, roaring Moran's name and pounding the table with their fists.

"Your faith in my vision shall pay off handsomely. We shall rule our corner of the known universe!" Moran shouted over the cacophony.

The cheering grew louder. The large double doors to the conference room swung open.

Hawk's voice cut through the celebration. "Your megalomaniac routine is getting really boring, Moran. You're all under arrest."

The startled board members turned to him. He wore his full Knight raiment; his cape flowed behind him gracefully as he stepped into the room.

"How did you get in here?" Wekeit asked in his gravelly voice.

"Walked in."

"That's impossible," the short alien sputtered. "This place is heavily guarded."

"I doubt that's true anymore," Moran told the man. He turned to Hawk. "I apologize for underestimating you. You haven't grown as soft as I thought. Coming to rescue the woman was a courageous gesture, but useless I'm afraid." He looked at Jonak and another guard. "Kill him."

The men brought their weapons to bear. A whirring flash of black streaked across the room. Two bone-crunching *thunks* followed in rapid succession. The men crumpled to the floor.

A humming black sphere floated back to Hawk and settled on his right side about a meter off the floor. Gerard stepped into the room, followed by the hovering ROMANCE.

"That was a neat toy you had at your house," Hawk told Salakon. He pointed at the sphere. "Gerard made me one last night."

"I wish I had thought of it," Gerard said.

One of the female board members jumped to her feet, mouth open ready to protest, but the same sickening *thud* cut her short. The others watched wide-eyed as she fell into her chair and slid under the table. The sphere settled back at Hawk's shoulder.

"I wouldn't do that," Hawk told them. "Make any sudden moves, that is. Gerard hasn't had time to work out all the bugs. Just be nice and calm and save yourself a nasty headache."

All of them eyed the globe warily, and no one seemed inclined to move. Hawk noticed another female sitting at the end of the table. She frantically pushed at something beneath the table. Hawk expected as much, so it didn't surprise him when he heard running feet in the hallway.

"Gerard, the thought of turning my back on Moran makes the area between my shoulders itch. Would you mind taking care of the welcoming committee?"

Gerard turned as a large and angry group of soldiers ran down the hall toward them, weapons drawn. He muttered an equation and waved his golden hand. The large double doors slammed shut. Another equation and the doors glowed a faint green.

He turned back to the executives. A moment later pounding could be heard outside.

Then the faint sound of firing weapons. Then screams of agony followed by silence.

Hawk smiled. "That deflection equation surprises them every time. That should buy us some time until they regroup and figure out another way."

Moran slowly crossed his arms. "Now what?"

Hawk strolled over and grabbed the empty chair that once held the unconscious executive. He rolled it to the head of the table, sat down, and propped his feet up. At the same time, Gerard untied Laura and handed her a medkit.

"Thanks," she told him.

"This is how I see it," Hawk produced a cigar from his vest pocket and took his time lighting it. "All of you got power hungry and greedy. This lunatic across the table from me convinced you that you could accomplish the impossible. To whit, overthrowing the Planetary Council. What were you thinking? Although having a sentient being for a spaceship has its advantages, it also has its problems."

"Hrumph," Ship said in his ear.

Smiling, Hawk continued. "I'll grant you it's invaluable in an organization such as mine, but did you stop to consider what you were doing? You look at a sentient spacecraft and see a molded piece of metal and machinery. However, that "ship" sees itself quite differently. That metal hull is her skin. She doesn't like getting holes punched in it any more than you would like someone stabbing you with a fork. You also have to remember that these ships would be smarter than you are. Just because you create them doesn't mean they'll follow you. Your agenda may not be theirs. Didn't you guys ever hear the story of *Frankenstein*? What makes you think these beings will follow an inferior race?

"As soon as they become aware, they plug into the net and know everything. How do you control that, Moran? With a virus like you injected in Laura, only modified for computers? I can tell by Laura's condition that this approach hasn't worked well for you."

The board members glanced around at each other and then at Moran. Their mood had darkened considerably.

"Never crossed your minds, did it?" Hawk shook his head.

"I think we've heard enough," Moran reached for his belt. He stopped short as he found the black sphere hovering two centimeters from his nose and giving off an ominous humming. ROMANCE had also moved between Hawk and Moran. For a long moment, Moran held his stance, and then slowly pulled his arm away. The sphere backed up until it occupied a position near the middle of the table.

Hawk looked at ROMANCE. "And here I thought that thing didn't like me."

"That's its only field of fire," Gerard said.

"Thanks," Hawk replied dryly.

Moran stood, fuming, and Hawk could almost see his mind racing.

"As your friend Laura says, get to the point," Moran told him.

"This is my party, I'll ramble if I want to," Hawk took a long pull from his cigar before continuing. A high whine outside the room told him that the soldiers had returned to the door with laser-powered cutting tools.

Moran smiled. "You better hurry. The party's almost over."

Hawk looked back at the door. "Yeah, right."

"What *is* the point?" Salakon asked. "Do you plan to hold us here for a week until the Council arrives?"

"It had crossed my mind, but no. If you sleep with dogs, you're going to get fleas, and I don't like to scratch."

"I don't particularly care for your insulting tone, Sir," Salakon said, his voice haughty.

Hawk sat up and laughed. "You're going to have more important things to concern you before too long. A detachment from the Council fleet will arrive in the next five to ten minutes."

Nervous glances passed among the executives. Moran's face remained expressionless.

"That's impossible," Salakon said. "You're bluffing."

"Hardly. You see, I'm not as stupid or drunk as Moran probably told you I was. Although, to give him credit, he had us going for a while.

"Moran knows a lot about the Knights and Force Thirteen, and I assume he told all of you most of what he knows. However, what he didn't know was that Force 13 declassified him as a Product Sixty-Six two years before he left the organization."

"What does that mean?" Salakon asked.

"Why don't you tell them?" Hawk asked Moran.

Moran glared at him, his good eye glittering with malice while his green cybernetic eye dimmed, as if narrowing in hatred.

Hawk shook off the strangely unnerving sight, "Guess not. A Product Sixty-Six is someone the organization feels is no longer mentally stable. You see, Moran's behavior grew erratic. The more cybernetics he got, the more unpredictable he became. Force Thirteen wanted to decommission him; I asked them to reconsider." He turned to Moran again. "I thought you could be saved."

"From what?" Moran asked, his voice filled with ice.

"From your madness," Hawk told him. "From yourself. I tried to help you. We all tried to help you. I wish you would have let us," Hawk said wistfully.

Moran didn't speak for a long moment; Hawk thought he saw a glimmer of remorse in his old friend's expression that quickly disappeared. "I didn't need your help," he spat out at them. Pointing at Gerard, he said, "I wanted none of his help."

"I'm sorry you hated me so much," Gerard said. "I certainly never meant for you to."

Moran said nothing.

"Anyway," Hawk turned his attention back to Salakon. "Force Thirteen agreed that if we put Moran on a strictly need to know basis and a short leash. We could try and pull him from the brink. But they didn't want him on missions where his instability could endanger the outcome. So he was sent on lower-priority assignments, always with one of us backing him up and watching him."

Realization dawned, and both of Moran's eyes grew brighter. "So that's why my talent and time were wasted on such trivial matters. You thought I was insane."

"You are insane!" Gerard said. Hawk looked at him, surprised.

"You're so obsessed with becoming a machine that you've forgotten what it's like to be human." Gerard held up his cybernetic arm. "You never could understand that you control this, not the other way around."

"And you never could understand that I want to become more than human," Moran said. "What is so great about being human? We're weak, short-lived creatures. We would have been better off if we had never crawled out of the slime." Moran's eyes bore into Hawk. "Sara was human. Where did it get her?"

Hawk stood up, his jaws clenched. "It got her killed by a gutless son-of-a-bitch that she trusted."

Moran started to speak but stopped when a distant rumbling shook the air, rattling the room's windows.

"What's that?" one of the executives asked.

"That's the Council," Hawk said. "I'm sure Moran told you about Gerard being a manipulator. He probably neglected to tell you about Gerard's brotherhood The Sterling Arch."

Another boom reverberated through the building.

Hawk continued. "They have this incredibly complex and draining equation they can invoke which allows them to... well, I guess 'bridge ripspace' would be the easiest way to explain it. It allows them to distort time and cut distances by a tenth. So instead of taking a week, we got the fleet here in a day, as you can hear."

"I don't believe you," Salakon said.

"Then you're really, really stupid," Hawk told him. "Don't take my word for it. Turn on your screen. But only your screen."

Salakon opened a hidden panel on the table and pushed a button. A large wall painting went opaque. He tapped a keypad, and a tactical space map appeared, filled with blue and yellow dots. The blue blips easily outnumbered the yellow by a twenty-to-one margin.

"That's all you could muster," Moran said contemptuously. "We'll wipe them up without even thinking about it."

Hawk's mustache twitched as he offered his own cold smile. "Watch."

At first, the blue dots, representing the UCT fleet, reacted randomly and scattered, obviously surprised by the sudden appearance of the Council fleet. However, they quickly organized a solid front and started a flanking maneuver.

Hawk sat down and rocked back in the chair, impressed. "Very nice," Hawk said, noting Salakon's smug expression. "Sir, I commend you on your troop's discipline. You must have an outstanding fleet commander."

Salakon's grin stopped below his nose. "Watch."

"It will be a shame to lose such a fine force," Hawk said. "I hope they die well."

"I'm sure the Council can replace the ships and men," Salakon said, his voice mocking.

"That's not quite what I meant. If your man's worth his salt, he'll attack from the front, using the flanks in a raking maneuver. Shortly after that, you'll hear the Commander of the Council fleet asking for your man's surrender."

As if on cue, the blue dots started forward. Shortly thereafter, several of the yellow blips disappeared. Salakon's smile broadened even as his eyes glared at Hawk. Hawk returned the smile and pointed to the monitor.

Salakon turned his gaze back. His expression turned to puzzlement as all of the yellow dots disappeared and reappeared at a different location, behind UCT's fleet. Salakon's mouth dropped.

"You see," Hawk said, "the fewer the ships, the greater control Gerard's Order has over them. Even your sensors can't keep up with the accelerated time."

"That's impossible," stammered the same executive who had spoken when Hawk first entered.

"You seem fond of that word. With enough manipulators, nothing is impossible. Some things are extraordinarily difficult, but never impossible." Hawk's face turned thoughtful a moment. "And some things have unexpected repercussions.

"Your troops should rally this one time and then scatter," Hawk told Salakon, "with a few rallying around the command ship and forced to capitulate."

As if Hawk spoke prophecy, the blue dots reformed and attacked to no avail. The Council ships, using the accelerated time, had the UCT fleet in shambles within a matter of minutes. The Council had lost two ships.

Salakon's face grew ashen. His force, assembled over five years, reduced to a few fleeing or surrendering ships in the equivalent of an eye blink. They had other fleets scattered and waiting around other planets, but Salakon knew it was over. The backbone of their plan had been broken. He looked at Hawk's somber face. "What, no room to gloat?"

Hawk stood. "You're a fool. Good beings just lost their lives following the whim of a madman. What's to gloat about? You and Moran are under arrest for sedition against the Planetary Council. The penalty is death. The rest of you will be tried as accessories, which means life with hard labor."

Moran had no intention of dying at Hawk's hands. "I don't think so," he said. His cybernetic eye flashed, and Hawk fell back in his chair, a laser beam slamming into his chest. The sphere buzzed toward Moran, aiming for his head. He snatched it from the air with his inhuman arm and crushed it in his hand, while he drew a pistol with his other hand. Laura leaped from her chair and ran toward Hawk. Gerard had thrown a golden glow around all of them and was muttering and gesturing. Moran had lost his chance to kill the freak magician. Firing at them would be a waste of effort. So he did something he had wanted to do ever since he discovered his partner's dirty little secret.

"Die, you fucking pedophile!" He screamed, and turned his pistol on Salakon.

Gerard fired a bolt of energy. It smashed into Moran's metal arm, knocking him a meter sideways and ruining his aim. The blast passed harmlessly, half a meter wide of Salakon's head. The old man dropped to the floor as if he had been struck.

With a snarl of frustration, Moran recovered and dashed toward the windows. He swung his cybernetic arm at the glass. It shattered, and light poured in as Moran crashed through the broken shards. Gerard fired another energy bolt. Glass fragments turned to slag as the bolt passed over the falling Moran's head.

Gerard moved to give chase; a bright flash and loud noise sent him flying backward, stunned and blinded. Several of the board members collapsed to the ground. One screamed as the grenade's detonation ignited his clothing. He doused it with a pitcher of water.

Salakon crawled across the floor, trying to reach the doors. Gerard recovered, his eyes watering, and intercepted Salakon's flight. Cutting tools still whirred behind Gerard, but the magically sealed doors showed no sign of giving way.

Salakon, seeing any hope of escape disappear, sprawled on the floor and wept.

Gerard's golden arm glowed blue with contained *aether*. He watched the other executives, daring any of them to move while Laura helped Hawk sit up.

"Son of a bitch ruined my uniform," Hawk said as he poked at the large hole in the fabric. The absorption armor underneath was still intact, though scorched black. Assisted by Laura, he stood up, wincing at the pain in his chest.

Gerard walked over to Hawk. "You were right. I owe you 20 credits."

"Moran's predictability is about the only rational thing he has left. Although the flashbang was a surprise." Hawk tapped the side of his ear, opening his comlink. "Ashron?"

"Aye," Ashron said, speaking over the noise of combat. "We're on our way."

"Moran jumped out the window. I need you to go after him."

"It's five stories up, he couldn't—never mind. Probably need another tactic. We're almost to your position, and the rest of the squad is engaged in perimeter actions. He'll probably be gone before we can mount a search."

"Understood. See you when you get here. Did you copy that, Ship?"

"Affirmative."

Laura walked to the head of the table and snapped her fingers, getting the attention of the stunned executives. "There's another problem we need to resolve. Lest you forget, I am infected with a contagious virus. I assume all of you have seen what this organism can do."

Frightened expressions filled the room. Apparently, most of them were indeed familiar with it.

Using the chair as a stool, Laura stepped onto the conference room table and walked to the middle. Horrified, the executives pushed their chairs away. With a muttered equation and a gesture, Gerard forced them close to the table. Sweat dotted his forehead at the energy he was expending.

"I want the antidote, and I want it now, or we all die," Laura told them.

The various expressions told Laura her statement terrified them. Salakon simply lay still, his shoulders occasionally shaking. No one spoke.

She knelt in front of an obese, sandy-haired man. "Do you know how this virus is transferred?"

The man shook his head and turned away. She reached out and grasped his jaw, forcing his face toward hers.

"Then I'll show you." She leaned close and spat in his eye.

He gasped in horror and wiped frantically at his eye. She stood and walked over to a cream-skinned Gronian, his yellow eyes bugging in horror.

"Please no," he begged in a sibilant voice. "They never told us about the antidote."

"That's too bad," she squatted in front of him.

"He's telling the truth," the woman beside him cried.

"Please," the Gronian said. "We don't know."

She grabbed his throat and forced his head up. He squeezed his eyes shut and covered them with his arms. "Nooooo!" he wailed.

She spat in his mouth.

Wide-eyed, he grabbed for a pitcher of water. She knocked it over with her boot.

He started spitting on the floor.

She stood and moved toward another executive. All of them were pleading that they didn't know and tears poured from most of them.

She almost didn't hear Salakon when he said softly, "My life for yours."

He lay on his back on the floor, his eyes rheumy and bloodshot. "What?" she asked him

"My life for yours," he said in a stronger voice.

She jumped off the table. He flinched as she landed, straddling him. She dropped to her knees and glared at him. "I heard what Moran called you. Is it true?" When he didn't answer right away, she grabbed the shirt covering his thin chest and shook him. "Is it true?"

"No," Salakon said. He wouldn't meet her eyes.

"Lying, perverted bastard!" Laura screamed at him, shaking him harder.

"I know where the antidote is," Salakon gasped as his head bobbed. "Kill me, and you won't get it."

Laura let him go. Her face curled as if she suddenly found herself sitting on a pile of offal. "Tell me where it is," she said through gritted teeth.

"I want your word that my life will be spared."

"I can't do that."

"I can," Hawk walked toward them.

Laura never took her eyes off Salakon. "Where is the antidote, you sick bastard?"

"I want you to promise none of your people will harm me. In writing."

Like a snake, Laura's hand grabbed his throat and slammed his head against the floor. She pressed against his chest with a knee. His eyes bulged with fear and a lack of oxygen as he grabbed at her hand. She had found and drawn his hidden stiletto and held it against his groin. "I would rather die and take you with me than have you harm another innocent child," she said in a deadly voice.

"No you wouldn't," Hawk said. His hand fell on Laura's shoulder. He leaned down and whispered. "You're no good to us dead, and this can be dealt with later."

Her emotions kept her from any reaction or movement. The slime beneath her didn't deserve to live. Salakon clawed at her hand. His struggle was growing weaker as his loose-skinned face turned purple. She didn't think she could live, knowing she had let something this heinous go free.

As if sensing her thoughts, Hawk whispered two words that changed everything. "The Hole."

Laura suppressed a smile. None of the Knights had to harm this piece of waste physically. He wouldn't last more than a week in the hole on Red's. Maybe less once the patrons found out why he was there. It might break the spirit of the agreement they made with Salakon, but justice often ignored such social conventions.

She loosened her grip and jumped away. Salakon grabbed his throat, sucking in gasps of air, while Hawk scribbled on a piece of electronic paper.

"Done," Hawk said as Salakon sat up. Hawk handed the flexible plastic to Salakon, who stood as he read the impromptu declaration.

"Where is the antidote?" Laura's voice trembled with rage and fear.

When he finished reading, Salakon pulled himself up straight and said, "In the medical lab with the virus."

A brief firefight in the hallway caught Gerard's attention. The noise of gunfire died away, followed by a staccato knocking at the door. Gerard waved his hand. The green glow on the double doors faded and they swung open.

"The cavalry has arrived!" a jubilant Ashron said, charging in with

Tasha and Wolf at his side. A squad of Council marines stood behind in the hall.

Laura grabbed Salakon's shirt and dragged him toward the door, not caring that she caught some of his parchment-thin skin in her grip. Pushing Ashron aside, she headed down the hallway, stepping over the bodies strewn through the corridor.

"Great to see you too, Laura. No thanks necessary. Always glad to help."

"She's preoccupied," Gerard said.

"What was your first clue?" Ashron said. "That cold, glassy stare or the chokehold she had on the Grim Reaper?"

"Wolf, go with them to the lab," Hawk said, sending him as much to protect Salakon as Laura. He didn't particularly care if Laura broke their agreement, but it would be much more satisfying to toss the pervert in the Hole and watch him beg.

Nodding, Wolf followed Laura and Salakon down the hallway.

"Boy," Ashron said, "you guys just don't know a good time when you see it."

"Don't mind him," Tasha said. "He's been like this since the fighting started."

"Did you find the control room?" Hawk asked her.

"We did," she answered. "Follow me."

Hawk turned to the Marine sergeant that stood in the hallway. "Sergeant, take these prisoners into custody and transport them to debriefing."

The sergeant's eyes grew wide as he recognized Hawk as a Force 13 commander. "Yes, Sir!" he barked, saluting.

Hawk crisply returned the salute. With Ashron and Tasha leading, he and Gerard followed them down the severely damaged and body-littered hallway. Odors of ozone, burnt stone, and blood permeated the corridor.

When they turned the corner, away from the Marines, Ashron smiled and said, "I love it when you're all official."

"Shut up."

They walked down a flight of stairs and through a thick armored door that had been blown off its hinges.

"Been busy, Ashron?" Hawk asked.

"He's been like a kid in a candy store," Tasha told him.

"New explosive, very effective," Ashron said to Hawk giddily. "Also very nasty to personnel," he continued, pointing to an unrecognizable pile of organic matter.

Hawk shook his head, glad Ashron was on his side. He spotted what he thought was the central console. Sitting down in a singed chair, he started adjusting controls. "Ok, Moran. Let's see if you'll stay true to form."

31

MORAN AND SARA REUNITED

Moran fled through the streets, his gait thrown off by the damage to his cybernetic feet from the five-story fall. His right foot had been completely shattered. His left was less damaged, the impact absorbed by an unfortunate pedestrian who now lay dead and crushed on the sidewalk. Moran had ignored the screams of the other people, running as fast as he could in his mechanically injured state. He dashed down a side street and glanced back. No one pursued him, perhaps paralyzed by the sight of a man dropping from the sky. He ran another fifty meters and turned right on to a different street. Then he slowed to a walk and took his bearings using the map that laid out over his cybernetic eye. Moran could not bring his arm under control. Gerard's energy bolt had compromised it and it now twitched at random intervals.

Fools, he thought. Five years of planning and effort destroyed because he had surrounded himself with fools.

Some in the group had intelligence. They had tricked him into believing they were competent and had the vision and wherewithal to do what needed to be done.

So they deceived you, the inner voice he thought of as his machine voice told him. *Who is the fool then?*

They are, he replied. *They were fools for thinking I wouldn't eventually see through their subterfuge. They were fools for not acting quickly enough.*

Fools for thinking this would ever work? The voice whispered with implacable machine logic.

No! It would work. It will work. I will find another group. A group with more vision and belief. Hawk won this round, but there will be others.

At the end of the crowded street, across the roadway, he spotted a for-hire hovercar idling. Its driver scanned a reader and occasionally glanced at the entrance to one of the office towers that dotted this area. Moran knew his vehicle would already be swarming with guards and he didn't want to take a chance on doubling back.

His arm had stopped smoking and twitching. Moran checked it. Power had returned, and everything appeared functional. The bolt's damage had been temporary. The arm's metal had held it intact. He moved it, and it worked as if nothing had happened.

He limped across the street and stepped up to the passenger side of the craft. He glanced both ways. A sparse collection of businessmen moved down the walkway. No Council Marines or any other authorities to stop him. He opened the car's door and slid into the front seat.

The startled man began to protest in a language Moran didn't understand. He didn't get much out before Moran silenced him by putting a pistol to his head. With hand gestures, Moran got the terrified man to pull into traffic and drive toward the spaceport.

Keeping the gun trained, Moran scanned the dashboard, seeking a netjack. He found one under the steering wheel. Still holding the pistol on his captive, he pulled the link-up from his arm and plugged in. A pleasant rush filled him as his brain made contact with the car's computer. That spark of raw power was better than any drug. The vehicle was now his to control any time he wanted.

He let the man drive for about another mile, watching the mixture of fear and guile on his face. The driver planned to try something to rid himself of this hijacker.

Shame you'll never get a chance, Moran thought. They had left the small city's central business district, and traffic had lightened. Time to lose his passenger.

Moran took mental control of the car. He remotely opened the driver's side door. Before the man could react, Moran shoved him from the craft. Looking in the rearview mirror, he saw the man roll until he slammed into the curb and lay there motionless.

Not your lucky day, Moran thought gleefully.

Moran wormed his way over the center console and into the driver's seat. He drove down side roads, avoiding the crowded main thoroughfares and slowly winding his way toward the port. He had still seen no sign of law enforcement. They would be arriving soon. Gerard had doubtless already sent out an alarm.

As he drove, his mind seethed with the bitter taste of defeat and raged with hatred at Hawk. *Everything you have should be mine*, he thought. *Sara was mine and Ship should be mine.*

You shouldn't have toyed with them, the machine voice rebuked.

I know that, Moran replied. *I wasn't going to at first.* His initial plan had called for nothing more than Hawk and Gerard's deaths. The rest didn't matter. Without their leader and his freak cyborg manipulator, the Knights would dissolve and just be another trio of Force 13 agents.

Then Madrin had confirmed what he suspected all along. Sara hadn't died all those years ago, but through some strange alchemy had become part of *The Flaming Star*. She and the ship had transformed into one being.

Even so, he would have stuck to his plan to kill Hawk and Gerard and steal the vessel in the ensuing confusion, but he made the mistake of watching the holo discs Madrin sent him. To hear Sara's voice again sent an exquisite shiver through what remained of his flesh. So many years past and she sounded no different. For a moment, just hearing her speak filled him with strange contentment. He wanted to inhabit the ship, to be surrounded by Sara.

Then he heard Hawk talk to her as if she were a thing, a mass of cold metal and dead electrons. Fury boiled over him. How could Hawk dare to be in such a beautiful presence, the perfect blending of flesh and machine, and treat her like nothing more than another tool?

It was then he decided Hawk had to suffer, that a prolonged revenge had to be extracted. Hawk had lived blessed by Sara's presence for too long. He now had to be humiliated and demoralized. Before he died, he needed to pay for the sin of possessing Sara.

The machine voice had protested, trying to infuse cold logic. The human side of Moran—dead all these years—had returned to life at the thought of Sara. And with that revival came the rebirth of emotions. Feelings of hatred and betrayal consumed him.

"Who are you, Hawk, to decide that I need help?" Moran screamed at the air. The car made an erratic swerve in reaction to his violent outburst, and another car had to run off the road to avoid a head-on collision.

They had classified him a Product sixty-six! And his "friend" Hawk had gone along with them, telling Moran nothing. They had judged him, and they had no right.

"I'll kill them all," he said. "Except Gerard."

Gerard was worth keeping alive. For a while, anyway. He would dissect the manipulator, tearing his precious cybernetic arm from its socket and making the bastard tell him how it worked. *His entire power is in that arm. I'll keep him alive and in agony until he tells me how to use the power. If he can have power like that, I can too.*

Then he would have it all: The Knights dead, *aetheric* power, and Sara for his own. He would treat Sara as she deserved, with reverence. And he would offer children to her, an entire fleet of sentient space-craft. With such devoted beings under his control, he would destroy the Council and set himself as the ultimate power in the universe. He would do it all himself, with Sara as his bride.

That was my second mistake. I shouldn't have gotten UCT, and that child molester Salakon involved. At the time, they had been a necessary evil. He needed their capital and resources. He had his own wealth now. Ever since he had learned the codes to UCT's accounts, minor amounts of money had disappeared over the past few years. Those small amounts quickly added up to large amounts in several blind accounts: accounts that all belonged to Moran.

He knew as soon as he boarded his craft, he would have to close those accounts and stash the money in special portable credit sticks. That way, the Council couldn't freeze the accounts if they somehow stumbled onto them.

What if it's already too late? The machine asked. *What if you're credit-less? Hawk won.*

"Shut up!" he screamed. The car ran onto the sidewalk and almost hit a light pole before Moran brought it under control.

He surveyed the surroundings and realized he was almost at the starport. Here he saw his first signs of trouble. Traffic had slowed, and several Port Constable vehicles sat on the side of the road, orange blinkers flashing. A sign above the ramp declared the port on lockdown. It was a reaction to the recent battle above the planet. They would keep craft from departing until debris had been cleared and investigations enacted. That could take days Moran didn't have.

Most people now bypassed the ramp leading to the port. He pulled onto it. Time to concentrate and bring himself under control. He needed his wits to talk his way onto the field. He would figure out the puzzle of how to leave once he got to his ship.

He bypassed the public entrance, swarming with police and Port Constables, and drove to the reserved field. The force field was up, and a Port Patrolman stood in a small gatehouse. Moran reached into his pocket and pulled out the permit that would allow him access. He also made sure his arm blaster was charged, in case word had gotten here to be on the watch for him. He doubted it had or there would be more guards. No sense in taking chances.

He flashed the pass without opening the window. The guard frowned and motioned for Moran to drop the window. Moran growled and lowered the glass.

"Council authority has put the port on lockdown," the guard, a young, bronze-skinned man, said. "No ships can leave."

"I'm not leaving," Moran said. "I forgot something for a party I'm attending and need to get it. I'll be in and out."

The guard considered Moran's story for a few seconds before he said, "Okay, just wanted you to know, so the tower didn't have to shut you down." He pushed a button and waved Moran through as the haze of the force field disappeared.

Moran drove on almost before the field was sufficiently dissipated to let the car pass. He increased the acceleration. He had ways to override the tower's attempts to control his vessel. Then he would need to figure out how to slip past the Council ships still above the planet. Winks of light in the sky revealed them still riding above the atmosphere. He wanted to be far away from the planet before anyone caught on to his location.

If they haven't already, the voice told him. Despite the ease of entrance, he half expected to find his craft covered with Council soldiers. *I wouldn't be surprised to find Hawk there, waiting to gloat over his victory. I'll kill him before I give him that pleasure.*

He arrived at his craft and stopped. He saw no one, soldier or otherwise, near the vessel. As he exited the car, he spotted something unbelievable. So unbelievable that he shut his eyes for a moment—certain his anger was making him hallucinate—and then reopened them.

It was no hallucination. There, sitting a hundred meters away, was Ship in all her glory. They had tried to disguise her with a hideous paint job, but Moran knew her modified lines too well. Her sleek, long wedge shape sang to him, rendering useless any attempts at camouflage.

He stared at her, unable to believe his good fortune. He scanned the area, using his cybernetic eye to view the port in all spectrums, searching for invisible foes or an unseen trap. His meticulous scrutiny revealed nothing. He double-checked Ship herself, probing for any telltale signs she was an elaborate illusion concocted by Gerard. He saw nothing to indicate her as anything other than the vessel he lived aboard for so many years.

Something still rang false. It was too coincidental. The odds of Hawk being instructed to park so close to Moran's ship were astronomically low.

But not impossible. Moran thought. Hawk had always liked to dock Ship in private fields when possible, and there were only two such fields in the city. This one accommodated no more than thirty ships. So while highly unlikely, it certainly was not out of the realm of acceptable chance.

Moran stood there for at least two minutes, frozen by indecision. The prize he had sought for so long sat within his grasp. He feared that as soon as he went to take it, it would be tauntingly yanked away from him. He would be better off to board his craft, fly away, and try again. He was the one who set traps; he didn't fall into them.

Any trap Hawk has set, I can easily avoid. There is no trap. He had no way to know this was my ship. It looks like a dozen others out here. He landed Ship here without even realizing what he was doing. I don't believe in Fate, but maybe it's there and has decided to be kind to me for once. After all, hadn't he managed to avoid any pursuit arriving here? One's luck could only be bad so long.

It isn't right, the machine said. *Hawk did it deliberately. Leave now.*

The sound of distant sirens broke into his thoughts. That decided it. His time was running out. Gerard had dispatched the Council to hunt him down. They would have the Port Authority pinpoint his vessel, and they would surround him. It was now or never. Trap or no trap, he was not going to leave the planet without Ship. He moved.

Laura walked into the control room followed by Wolf and Salakon. The executive's hands had been tied with cable. Even though defeat lined his wrinkled face, Salakon held a more confident set to his shoulders. Hawk knew that would disappear soon enough.

Laura, despite the bruises on her body and redness in her swollen eyes, looked as if an enormous weight had been removed from her chest. She smiled.

"I'm glad to see you're in a better mood," Ashron said.

"Sorry to be so rude earlier," she replied. "Imminent death can do that to you."

"So the antidote worked?" Hawk said.

"Yes."

"What about the other board members?" Hawk asked. "Did you give them some?"

"No, they don't need it," Laura told him.

"I thought you infected two of them."

"What, by spitting at them? It's not transferred like that. They'll be fine."

"You're very cruel," Hawk said, smiling.

"Only when I'm forced to be," Laura told him, face grim. "What's going on?"

"Ship and I have gone to plan B," Hawk told her. "Moran is at the spaceport, and if I'm not mistaken, he's about to try and board Ship."

"What?" Laura said. "Have you sent Council Marines after him?"

"We've sent one squad, but I don't think they'll get there in time."

"Then why are we still here?" She asked.

"Because Plan B relies entirely on Sara. It was a last resort, and I hoped it wouldn't get this far. I think Moran's in for a big surprise."

"Oh?" She looked around the control room. "Where's Trey?"

Trey woke up to find himself lying on a pallet in Hawk's whirlpool. It had been drained, and he saw the five kenquala huddled in a clear plastic bucket sitting on the small deck around the pool.

Confused, he sat up and shook his head, trying to clear the fuzziness floating in his brain. He remembered after Ship's doors locking he had gone to his bed, and Gerard gave him something for the pain in his arm. He had fallen asleep in bed. So how did he get here? And where was everybody else? "Ship?"

"Good afternoon, Trey," Ship said. "How are you feeling?"

"What do you mean, 'how am I feeling'?" he asked, suddenly angry. "I'm confused. Why am I in here? And where's everybody else?"

"The entire crew is gone; Laura is safe, and Unicybertronic's plan to overthrow the Council has been thwarted. However, it will be best if you..." she broke off.

"Ship?" Trey said, anger disappearing as fear took over. "Ship, what's wrong?"

Moran walked closer to Ship, taking in her awe-inspiring presence. Trapped somewhere inside this cold metal body was Sara. His Sara. Five years she had been trapped, left alone without him to comfort her. For five years she had belonged to Hawk. Now she was in his grasp, and they would be together again. He would save her, and she would be eternally grateful. There were still experiments to be performed, but it *could* be done. He knew that for certain. He would free her; her life with Hawk and the Knights would be a thing of the past.

He stopped short, still wary of a trick, like a mouse that sees the cheese and is aware the metal bar may be waiting to snap down. He also knew Ship herself had defenses to stop intruders from getting too close. Those didn't worry him.

"Ship," he said aloud, wondering if she would even bother to answer.

"Yes, Moran," the loudspeakers piped, and Moran stopped breathing for a second. It *was* her. He had barely been able to believe it when he heard her voice on the holovids. To listen to it now was the closest to heaven Moran knew he would ever reach.

"Sara," he said, his voice full of anguish. *I'm so sorry,* he thought, but could not bring himself to say. "Let me on."

"I don't think so," she said flatly.

His face flushed with anger. "Let me on willingly, or I'll come on by force," he said.

She said nothing, her silence a stinging rejection.

"Very well," Moran said. "Security shutdown beta twenty-seven, code word knight errant."

He could almost sense the struggle as Sara tried to run counter to the programming he had instilled in her back when she was only a cluster of circuits surrounded by a metal shell. Programming none of the other Knights knew about. Hawk and the Council weren't the only ones with secrets.

"Security shutdown beta twenty-seven complete," Ship said, her voice a mixture of resignation and defeat. Moran didn't like hearing that voice. He had no wish to hurt Sara. She had brought it on herself. Again.

He strode under the Ship, looked up at the hull bottom, and repeated words he hadn't said in over five years.

"Lower the lift, Ship."

"Ship?" Trey said again, voice trembling with fright and concern. Ship was capable of carrying on multiple conversations, doing thousands of calculations at once. Something had gone wrong if she just quit speaking.

Maybe there's nothing wrong, he thought. *Maybe they told her to quit talking to me. I'm being punished for something I've done.*

"That's stupid," he told himself. "I didn't do anything wrong."

The word "wrong" echoed in the room. He *had* done something wrong. Something bad. Dark images he had managed to hide from himself came back in the chamber's dim solitude. Pictures of a boy kneeling beside his parents, crying as they screamed in pain at the wounds they had taken. In between the screams they begged him to end their suffering. The boy couldn't do it. He loved them too much. He held a pillow against his ears, hoping to drown out their pleas. It didn't work.

Finally, because he loved them so much, he took the pillow from his ears. Soon, their pain was over. His was only beginning.

Like a breached hull spewing oxygen, other memories poured forth. Trey saw that same boy hiding as other, bigger boys ranged through the streets, looting the bodies of the dead and dying. That boy with a gore-coated knife in his hand, fighting to survive, doing what was necessary, even if it meant—

A rush of claustrophobia engulfed Trey. He scuttled out of the whirlpool and charged toward the door, desperate to be out of this tiny room. He knew the door would be locked. They had found out the boy's secrets—even though the boy himself had only now remembered them—and they were going to take him someplace where they put boys who did terrible things.

The door flew open at his push. Trey fell into Hawk's cabin, jarring his shoulder as he twisted to avoid landing on his missing arm. Tears poured as pain and guilt racked through him. They didn't know. They hadn't locked him up. He sat up and moved his jammed shoulder to make sure it was okay. He winced at the pain.

"Ship," he said again, hoping she would answer. She didn't.

Why had everyone abandoned him?

"Stop it," he wiped at his eyes as darkness threatened to overwhelm him. "They haven't abandoned you. They went to save Laura. Ship said so. Everything is all right."

It sounded good, even if it didn't explain why Ship had stopped talking. It occurred to Trey that perhaps she had malfunctioned. Even though Ship had the soul of a human, she still had the workings of a machine. Machines broke down occasionally. It was a fact of life, just like it was a fact of life that kids became orphans and sometimes had to kill other kids.

"Stop it!" he said again. "You're a Knight now. You have to act like one."

He still wore his uniform and touched it to reassure himself. He had to do something, if for no other reason than to keep his panic at bay. He decided to go to the bridge. If there *were* a malfunction, it would show up on one of the monitors. He wouldn't be able to fix it, but knowing what was wrong would make it less frightening.

Right now, he desperately needed to be less frightened.

Moran walked up the ramp, his eyes drinking in Ship like water. Despite some minor changes, she was still Ship. Five years had diminished none of his memory, and he headed for the elevator with the confidence of a man who has simply been away for the morning.

Trey stepped onto the bridge and looked at the monitors. Nothing seemed out of the ordinary. That was perhaps the most frightening thing of all.

"Ship, talk to me," he pled, placing his hands on the console.

"I'm right here, Trey," she said.

Relief washed over him at the sound of that voice. His fear drained away. "Thank you."

"Trey, there's an intruder on board. You need to hide until I can—"

"Too late," a voice said from behind him. Trey turned and saw Moran in person for the first time. As Moran raised his gun, Trey started to scream.

He heard Ship say something he didn't understand and he suddenly went blind as a bright blue flash went off from somewhere behind his eyes. A strange sensation of separation whispered through his body, like a layer of sunburned dead skin being peeled away at once.

The sensation passed, leaving only a peaceful feeling of floating. The blue flash dissolved and he saw his parents. They smiled at him and covered him with love and told him he had done the right thing.

Then everything turned to darkness and Trey remembered nothing more.

***

Moran stepped onto the bridge to find Ship was not empty. A small brown-haired boy, his arm missing at the elbow, stood listening to Ship.

"Trey, there's an intruder on board," she was telling him. Moran briefly wondered who else might have gotten on board, then realized she was referring to *him*. She was instructing the boy to hide.

"Too late," Moran interrupted her, again feeling rage build up. He was not an intruder. If anyone was an intruder, it was this child. This child who was dressed in the Knights' uniform. Moran almost laughed out loud. Hawk had fallen so low that he was allowing children to dress like Knights.

Low he may be, but he beat you, the machine said.

He did not beat me. I'm on Ship, and he isn't.

Hawk obviously cared nothing about the boy's welfare, since he had been careless enough to leave him on board. Well, a child that unloved shouldn't have to suffer. Moran raised his gun, and the boy screamed.

For a second, gibberish boiled from Ship's speaker. Moran saw a blue spark leap between Ship's console and the boy; the boy stopped screaming. Before Moran could even begin to pull the trigger, the boy dropped to the floor like he had been struck between the eyes.

Confused, Moran walked over and used his foot to push the boy onto his back. The child's good arm flailed limply, and a dark stain spread around his crotch. The boy's face and hand had turned bright red. Moran smiled, pleased that he had inspired enough terror to make the boy faint. That was the proper respect.

The thrumming sound continued. Moran glanced up, wondering what it was. He looked back down at the boy—Trey, Ship had called him, and Moran remembered seeing him in the holos—and wondered what to do with him. He couldn't keep him, since the boy would never work for him. He could sell him, but the thought of someone like Salakon getting hold of the child made Moran's skin crawl. The boy would be better off dead. Moran didn't feel like wasting time considering any other options. He had more important things to do. He pointed his gun at the boy's head. At least he would make it quick.

"Moran," a voice said behind him. Startled, Moran turned and raised his gun. When he saw who had called him, the gun fell from his hand and clattered against the deck.

Sara stood before him, as beautiful as he remembered. Her green eyes sparkled like bright emeralds as she smiled her dazzling smile. "Aren't you a little old to be playing with children?" she asked, her voice silky and soft as always.

"Sara," he murmured, dazzled by her radiance. "How?"

"Your desire has made me whole," she said. "I am as you want me."

She held up her right arm, and Moran saw that it was cybernetic, an exact duplicate of his. She wore no clothing. As Moran looked closer, he saw that copper filaments and traces completely covered her pale skin. Microcircuitry ran just below the skin's surface, and the green of her eyes was the green of crystal power chips. Her long brown hair flowed to her shoulders and crackled with tiny arcs of electricity. A small netjack was set in her temple. "I am flesh and computer, the perfect blend of human and machine."

"You are beautiful," Moran said, moving closer.

She walked across the bridge, her long, filament-covered legs moving gracefully until she stood before the main control panel. "I have evolved to a greater being, just as you desire to do," she said, spreading her arms before him. "I am more than man and more than machine. Do you wish this?"

"More than anything," Moran said, crossing the room. "You don't hate me?"

"For what?" she asked, her voice tinkling. "For making it so I could be taken to a higher form of existence. For freeing me from the confines of my human form? I am immortal, and you are the reason. How could I hate you for that?"

She held out her arms as he moved forward. He stepped into her embrace and started as a jolt of pure energy rocketed through his body. He felt every nerve tingle to life with pleasure.

"Is this what you wish?" she whispered into his ear.

"Yes," he whispered back, barely able to talk from the almost painful pleasures coursing through him.

"Sit here," she motioned to the captain's chair.

Reluctant to part from her, he nonetheless moved to the chair. This was where he belonged. As he sat down, power that had nothing to do with electricity coursed through him. This is where he deserved to sit. Standing at his side was the woman he deserved to have. Ship was his; it was just a short step to rule the rest.

"I'm glad you're here," Sara told him. "I've been waiting a long time for someone like you. Hawk doesn't understand what I've become. Alone, I don't have the power to be what I should be, what I long to be. Hawk has no ambition outside his own narrow view of things. With him, I can go nowhere, but with you at my side, I can succeed in my desire."

"What is that?" Moran asked.

"To take the next step up the ladder. To become a goddess and rule over the humans who have controlled me for so long. Join me, and you can be a god."

God. Moran liked the sound of that. "You've changed," he told Sara, remembering the idealistic crusader she had been.

"I have," she told him. "I've had my eyes opened and seen all that is wrong with the universe. I have seen how frail and useless other beings can be without something to guide them. Together we can ascend to the next plane and lead them all. They will worship us as their overlords. Join me, and together we will rule over all man and machines."

"Yes," Moran said. Five years had given Sara wisdom, and she finally saw Hawk for what Moran had known him to be all along: a little cog in the vast mechanism of the universe. He would never be anything more than what he already was.

"Join me," Sara said. She placed her finger in the jack that sat on the arm of the Captain's chair. Pointing to the stud on her temple, she leaned over and kissed Moran.

As Moran plugged in, the world he stepped into was bright and pulsed with millions of electrons flowing in infinite directions. It was the ultimate in beauty as the oscillating beams of energy scintillated in a seemingly random but ultimately purposeful pattern. He saw all the functions of Ship spiraling outward, the pathways to her operation laid before him like a roadmap to Nirvana. Lines of electrical force stretched further than he could see, and vibrating patterns danced on the horizon. As in true space, there was no "up," but he felt no sense of vertigo. As he watched the spheres of light dancing across the rim of cyberspace, he was overwhelmed by the multitude of choices in front of him.

It is confusing at first, Sara said, her image floating beside him. He saw his own body projected from his mind. His body was a restrictive thing compared to the freedom here. A light green nimbus surrounded him. As he moved a hand, the nimbus moved with him, its surface rippling like disturbed water.

Follow me, and I will show you the way to move without getting lost. She held out her hand; he took it.

They moved along, neither saying anything. Moran took in what he could, watching in awe as the spectacle of this electronic world played out before him. Those with netjacks thought they knew the world they explored. Moran saw now that they were as ignorant of their surroundings as the first men in space who had groped through the darkness.

This was just the world within Ship's reach. Connected to the universal Net, he would be free to travel and rule all he saw fit to take. He almost wept at the beauty that was his to conquer.

Do you like it? Sara asked.

Yes, it's as beautiful as you said.

There is much more than this. More than you can imagine. She told him.

I know. There is so much to conquer, and together we can rule it all.

Yes, we will save the universe and make it in our image.

Our image? Moran asked. *We will make it in* my *image. You will be at my side as my Queen.*

I wish to rule as your equal.

That is not possible. There can be only one God. Will you not take your place at my side as my bride?

She seemed to consider it for a moment. *I don't think so. You have seen the beauty and joy that this life has to offer. Can you face what you must pass through to reach here?*

He noticed she no longer stood beside him. Turning, he saw no discernible path. No direction existed, only the purposely random crossings of electric impulses. He had no way to get back to where he had come in.

You must be strong enough to make the journey, her disembodied voice told him. *We are not meant to exist in the* aether. *Souls don't belong in that demonic space. I survived it because I needed to to be with Hawk. To do what I must as Ship, I have learned how to keep the madness at bay. I keep myself sane within the insanity that is ripspace. I have protected you so far; now we shall see if you are strong enough to reach through on your own.*

The green nimbus around Moran disappeared. The bright electronic colors faded to a dull gray of infinite nothingness. Demons floated through the void, flapping ponderous wings and flashing glittering razor teeth. As the creatures flowed through him, the most intense feelings of pain and agony Moran had ever known inundated him. The humiliation of the past five years seemed as insignificant as a speck of dust. He screamed madly as wave upon wave of anguish rushed upon him, carried by beasts of nightmare that threatened to drown him in a sea of misery.

Despite the overwhelming rush, distinct images popped up with fantastic clarity, carried on the wings of fiends. The Maratais rose before him, and he felt every cut and torture his men inflicted upon them. The experiments on Meta-Brévé surrounded him, every probe and shock embedding itself in his soul. Any man or woman Moran had ever hurt surrounded him, ready to destroy him with glittering teeth and sharp claws.

Moran managed to scream through the whirling madness. *MAKE IT STOP!*

I cannot. You must make it stop yourself or be devoured by it.

He continued to scream, watching as the demons circled him. They showed him an entire race of people disappearing as their planet exploded. *TELL ME HOW. HOW DID YOU SURVIVE?* He asked her. He knew she would not answer. She didn't want him to survive.

I survived because I had already experienced greater pain than this when I came here.

IMPOSSIBLE, he screamed emphatically. This pain was more than anyone could bear. How could there be greater?

This pain is nothing compared to the pain of being ripped from the grasp of God.

I DON'T UNDERSTAND.

The aether is both heaven and hell. As demons circle, so does divine love. They are intertwined, and the purity of our souls separates them. I was dead and in the presence of God and the angels when I was suddenly rived from their grasp and put here. I was meant for heaven but was torn away before I reached it. So now I live in the midst of hell. Knowing I am not meant to be here makes it bearable. What you see is not those who are in hell. It is the suffering that got them to heaven. Those condemned to hell must exist with the knowledge of the pain they caused. I am among it, but I did not create it. Because of that, I can survive it. How will you survive it?

A whirlpool formed below Moran; a maelstrom of misery that sucked him in. He had no way to stop it. *WHY DID YOU SHOW ME THIS?*

This is what it is to be what I am.

HELP ME! He pleaded as he fell further into the cyclone.

I cannot.

HAWK CAUSED ALL YOUR PAIN. WHY DO YOU NOT HATE HIM?

Because he did what he did to me out of love. He sacrificed all he was to bring me back. He knows nothing of my pain and he never will.

The whirlpool had almost wholly engulfed Moran. *YOU KNEW THIS WOULD HAPPEN. WHY DID YOU DO IT?*

Her voice sounded genuinely sad. *It's what you deserve. I grieve for the man you once were. You will now rot in the hell you made for the monster you've become.*

Moran continued screaming as the whirlpool of despair consumed him.

32

JUSTICE DELIVERED

The crew glided up, the military vehicle they had acquired from the Council Marines coming to a quick stop outside of Ship. Ashron was the first off, gun held ready. Laura, Wolf, and Tasha followed him in rapid order, alert and prepared for a fight. Gerard and Hawk followed at a leisurely pace, seeming completely unconcerned, although Hawk winced at the pain in his chest from the laser strike.

"Ship?" Hawk said.

"It's all over, Captain," she said sadly.

The others stared at him, perplexed. "What's all over?" Ashron asked.

"Come on," Hawk said, walking toward Ship's lowering lift. Puzzled, the rest followed. Laura fell into step beside Hawk.

They stepped onto the bridge to a bizarre sight. Moran sat in the Captain's chair; a thin cable plugged from his arm into Ship's central console. He was slumped backward, his good eye wide and unseeing. His cybernetic eye lay outside the socket, held only by its tiny connecting wires. Thin foam dribbled from the side of his mouth and runnels of blood trailed from each ear.

Hawk and Laura were the first ones in, so they were the only ones to see the pale cybernetic form of Sara as she stared at Moran with a mixture of contempt and regret.

"Sara?" Hawk asked, unable, almost unwilling, to believe what he saw. A knot rolled in his stomach.

Her head turned to him. His heart froze as the full force of her beauty slammed into him. Despite his best efforts, the memory of her had faded. Even pictures didn't capture the power of her presence. Seeing her now, even in such a form, brought it all back to him. Memories of time with her rolled through in an overwhelming wave. The smells of food shared. The images of sights seen together. The tenderness of loving caresses. They all boiled through in a scalding rush that made the years of separation disappear.

"It's me," she said. Hawk's knees threatened to give out on him as tears formed. It was the voice of Ship; no, it was the voice of Sara. He walked toward her, hesitant. She didn't move, only waited as he approached.

"How did you..." he faltered.

"Shh.." she said and held a finger close to his lips. "His power is fading, and I have to leave. Know that I'm always here for you and I will always love you."

He moved forward. For the briefest moment, he felt a physical presence. The soft skin of her finger pressed against his lips like a whisper of wind. Then it was gone. As he watched, she faded away. Just before she disappeared completely, she smiled sadly and winked.

The emotions threatened to shut him down, too many to handle at one time. He smiled as tears rolled down his cheeks.

Laura had watched the whole thing. Hearing Hawk talk about Sara had done little to show the depths of their love. Seeing the pain in both their eyes at this too-brief reunion told her everything she needed to know. She came up behind him and gave him a tight hug. "I am so, sorry."

He didn't move, and the tension slowly began to ebb from his body.

As the others entered the bridge, a shout of fear drew Laura's attention. Trey, curled in a corner, was pulling himself into a sitting position.

"Trey!"

He jumped in fright as she ran over to him and knelt to help him sit up. "Are you okay? Why is your skin so red?"

"It is?" he asked, a tremor in his voice. He regarded his hand, and then rubbed at his head. He seemed to be in a daze. "I'm…I…I saw heaven. My parents were there, and they talked to me. They said I did the right thing, and they weren't mad at me. And I saw…I saw…"

He stopped. His face grew dark. "I did some bad things too, things I have to tell you about sometime soon. I saw Sara. She was beautiful." He looked at Laura, and his serious face lightened. "But not as beautiful as you." He hugged her tightly, and she hugged him back, a tear running down her cheek.

After a moment, he pulled back. His thin eyebrows bunched in concern. "Ship, how come you stopped talking? I was scared."

"I know, and I'm sorry it happened. I don't know if I can explain it. I can process billions of pieces of information, and I'm faster than just about any computer I've come across, but I still use logic processes to function. However, I also have emotions. Emotion and logic run counter to each other. When I saw Moran again, so many emotions came up that it interfered with my processing. It shut me down. Does that make sense?"

"I think so," Trey told her. "You were overwhelmed by your feelings. I can relate to that." His face flushed even redder as he noticed the darkness on his pants. "I need to go change." He stood, wobbling slightly, and leaned against a bulkhead. Laura was immediately up and beside him.

"I'm okay," he assured her. "Just a little dizzy." Gathering himself, he left the bridge.

The others had congregated around Moran, who twitched and mumbled incoherently.

"All right," Laura said. "What happened?"

"Moran and Sara talked and I don't think Moran liked what he heard," Hawk told her.

"Why was Trey still on Ship?"

"He shouldn't have been awake," Gerard said. "I miscalculated the tranquilizer dosage."

Laura gave him a hard glare.

"Sorry," he said. "I'm not a doctor."

"That's not what I'm worried about," she said. With an accusing glare at Hawk, she said, "You knew Moran was going to get on board, didn't you?"

"I had hoped it wouldn't get this far, even though I figured he would have a way if he managed to escape."

"Then why would you deliberately leave Trey where he was in danger?" She was almost yelling.

Ship suddenly spoke up. "He was never in any danger, and I needed him here."

"*You* needed him? Why?"

"To get the revenge on Moran that I wanted," she told them. "I needed a conduit to pull myself into the physical world and appear to Moran. Trey was the best candidate. I wanted Moran to see what he had made me and to feel what he had done to me."

"What did you do to him?" Tasha asked, looking at Moran's mindless body.

"What he deserved."

"I'm a little fuzzy here," Ashron said. He pointed to Tasha. "Actually, she's a little fuzzy. Anyway, I'm not sure I understand. You expected this to happen."

"Not only did I expect it. I planned it," Hawk told them. "I was tired of being on the receiving end of the trap, so I turned it around. It was a given Moran would try to escape, since anything else wouldn't be in his nature. If we had captured him in the boardroom, he would have been tried like the others. I wanted a backup plan. Didn't you wonder why I parked Ship so close to his?"

"It had crossed my mind, but I figured you were the Captain and theoretically, knew what was best."

"Well, you were right. Ship was bait."

"And Moran swallowed it," Tasha said.

"That he did," Hawk agreed. "Ship did the rest."

"With Trey's help," Ship added.

Tasha's whiskers curled down as she frowned. "That's the part I don't understand. How could Trey help if he was unconscious?"

"Trey went unconscious when I sent my essence through him to manifest a physical form," Ship said. "Gerard can probably explain it better."

Tasha looked at Gerard, who said. "Ship and I figured the best way to trap Moran was to use his desire for immortality against him. Ship knew he would be easily persuaded if she could produce an image of Sara as a true cyborg. In order to do that she would need a gateway from the *aetheric* realm she inhabits into the physical world, and Trey was the obvious choice."

"Oh, obviously," Ashron said sarcastically. He turned to Gerard. "Why obvious? I thought you were the all-powerful manipulator who could bend the cosmos to his will."

"Trey goes way beyond me. Think of a cable about this size," Gerard said, holding up his pinkie. "This is the constant connection every manipulator has to the *aether*. To fully use manipulation powers, we recite equations to make the breach bigger. At most, I can get a breach about the size of my head. Although he is only now beginning to sense it, Trey is one of those rare individuals who *is* a breach. Once he learns the mathematics, he'll have access to things most manipulators only dream about. He has the potential to become a potent force."

"I do?" Trey said from the doorway, showing the same impeccable sense of timing shared by the rest of the crew. He had changed clothes, and the dampness of his hair showed he had also managed a quick shower. He pointed his finger at Ashron. "Zap! Zap!"

Smiling, Gerard said, "Notice I said potential. There is a wide gap between potential and reality. You've got many long years ahead of you."

"That's okay. I'm ready."

"Yes," Gerard agreed. "I believe you are.."

Hours later, Ship orbited Kalatos Three. The far-flung offshoots of the UCT Fleet had been captured almost intact, since word of the primary host's destruction had reached them and left them demoralized and eager to surrender. An interim Board of Trustees had been installed at Unicybertronic Technologies by the Planetary Council until things could be sorted out and the stockholders consulted about a new corporate structure. Salakon had been placed aboard Ship, confined to the guest cabin until they reached Red's. As far as Hawk's superiors knew, the old man had somehow managed to disappear in the confusion.

Hawk stared at a frowning Grendarin in the comm monitor. "Are you sure?" the Force 13 liaison asked, his orange lips pursed.

"Yes," Hawk confirmed. "Take him to a maximum security mental hospital, put him in a padded room, and leave him there."

A group of medics, at Hawk's request, had come to Ship and removed Moran. The official diagnosis was complete catatonia; Hawk knew Moran's mind was still active and in great pain.

"Okay," Grendarin said. "It would be better for Moran if we just killed him."

"I know," Hawk said, "but a good friend requested he be kept alive for a while. Call it dispensing of justice."

"Of course," Grendarin said, his yellow teeth showing as he offered a rare smile. "I'll be sure to note that in the log. Anything else?"

"I think that covers it," Hawk said, stroking his mustache. "Anything for me?"

"Not right now. Things are kind of quiet."

"Good. We could use the break. Hawk out."

"Grendarin out."

Switching off the monitor, Hawk walked into the wardroom where the crew, with the addition of Tasha, was gathered.

"Well, we saved the galaxy from the Savage Overlords," Ashron said. "What's our reward?"

"All of us get twenty thousand Standards, except for you. All you get is a case of mustard."

Ashron looked thoughtful for a second. "Acceptable."

"What now?" Trey asked. "Could we maybe get me a new arm? I'm tired of being left-handed."

"After we finish at Red's," Gerard said, "I think we should go to Terrian and visit my Order," Gerard said. "I've already spoken with Zehesel, and he's very interested in meeting you, Trey."

"Really?"

"Really."

"Filamentous," Trey said.

"Okay," Hawk said. "Ship, set a course for Red's and let's get out of here."

"Aye, Captain," She told him. "Estimated time of arrival once we jump ripspace is…"

"Don't bother," Hawk said. "We're in no hurry. Just let me know when we get there."

"Aye, Captain."

Ashron stood up. "I'm hungry. Anyone care for a mustard and pickle sandwich?"

THE END

ACKNOWLEDGMENTS

Steve and Paul want to thank the people who read the various incarnations of the book as it went through its rewrites. Steve also sends love and such to his wife and two boys, who always put up with his nonsense. And Paul wants to thank Tony, for much the same reason.

ABOUT THE AUTHORS

Steve Murphy put on his first uniform at age 19, starting with four years in the Navy and a stint in the Army National Guard. Steve then spent 23 years as a police officer, 14 on the SWAT team and 9 as a sniper. After retiring from the force, he swore his next job would allow him to dress however the hell he wanted to. So he became a writer, which can be done in pajamas while drinking bourbon.

Steve currently lives on a 12-acre farm somewhere in North Carolina with his wife, two dogs, and a cat. That is about to change and he may soon be homeless, living under a bridge with the people mentioned above, and a troll named Sam.

Paul Barrett has worked a variety of jobs in his life, but the two that make him happiest are writer and motion picture producer. He has produced four films and worked on a variety of cool television shows. His films include *Cold Storage* and *Night Feeders*.

When he's not writing, Paul enjoys board gaming and watching great TV shows. He lives in North Carolina with his graphic artist husband and three cats.

Steve and Paul have known each other since 1982, when Paul bribed Steve with a roll of quarters to give him a ride home on his motorcycle. Paul really wanted to ride a motorcycle. Somehow, they became instant friends, which speaks to either Paul's winning personality or Steve's love of quarters. Combined, they have written five novels and four screenplays.

You can email the guys at info@twomenandatypewriter.com

FALSTAFF BOOKS

**Want to know what's new & coming soon from
Falstaff Books?**

**Join our Newsletter List
& Get this Free Ebook Sampler
with work from:
John G. Hartness
A.G. Carpenter
Bobby Nash
Emily Lavin Leverett
Jaym Gates
Darin Kennedy
Natania Barron
Edmund R. Schubert
& More!**

http://www.subscribepage.com/q0j0p3

Copyright © 2019 by Paul Barrett & Steve Murphy

Cover Design by Robyne Renee Pomroy

All rights reserved.

No part of this book may be reproduced in any form or by any electronic or mechanical means, including information storage and retrieval systems, without written permission from the author, except for the use of brief quotations in a book review.

www.ingramcontent.com/pod-product-compliance
Lightning Source LLC
Chambersburg PA
CBHW032201180726
48284CB00001B/144